LIPSTICK
VOODOO

LIPSTICK VOODOO

Kristi Charish

A KINCAID STRANGE NOVEL

VINTAGE CANADA

VINTAGE CANADA EDITION, 2019

Published by Vintage Canada, a division of Penguin Random House Canada Limited, in 2019. Distributed in Canada and the United States of America by Penguin Random House Canada Limited, Toronto.

Vintage Canada with colophon is a registered trademark.

www.penguinrandomhouse.ca

Library and Archives Canada Cataloguing in Publication

Charish, Kristi, author
Lipstick voodoo : a Kincaid Strange novel / Kristi Charish.

Issued in print and electronic formats.

ISBN 978-0-345-81590-3
eBook ISBN 978-0-345-81591-0

I. Title.

PS8605.H3686L57 2019   C813'.6   C2018-900997-7
                                               C2018-900998-5

Text and cover design by Five Seventeen

Cover images: (alley) © Tao Wu / EyeEm, (woman) © Vladimir Serov, both Getty Images; (powder) © RedGreen / Shutterstock.com

Printed and bound in Canada

2 4 6 8 9 7 5 3 1

Penguin
Random House
VINTAGE CANADA

For everyone I know who's ever thought
'If I had to do it all over again . . .'

CHAPTER 1

LIPSTICK SEANCE

I tapped my foot on grass crunchy with frost, let out my breath and watched it condense into white fog around my face. This mid-October cold was not a good sign for my perpetually chilled state. I'd planned on spending my Thursday night wrapped in a blanket in front of the TV, not standing in a graveyard beside a marble tombstone easily worth about four months' rent. The soil in front of it was freshly turned, and the grass surrounding the gravesite sparkled under the overhead sodium lamps. Though, I had to admit, the layer of frost made the graveyard look a lot prettier than it had any right to be—except for all the mud around the recently dug-up grave, that is, and the current company.

I let out another breath and watched the air condense. *Concentrate on the job, Kincaid.* "Look, Mr. Graeme—" I started again.

"Ah—now what did I say?" The eighty-five-year-old man standing in front of me frowned and wagged his finger. He was dressed in a suit that probably also cost a few months' rent.

"I always get pretty girls like you to call me Michael," he said. He smiled, or tried to—only the left side of his mouth turned up and a week's worth of desiccation in the grave meant his lips stretched into a thin grimace. "And where'd you get such pretty, curly black hair like that? You Irish?" He leaned in and added in a whisper, "Or part black maybe? I know that's a lot more common nowadays."

I shot a glance over my shoulder at my client for the evening, Cody Banks, a young lawyer who'd contacted me two days ago with an urgent job. He'd offered more money than I usually demanded for expedited will cases, and I needed the cash, so it had been impossible to say no. He gave me a fake smile, but his eyes communicated something very different: *Get the job done.*

That was my first mistake: taking this job. I turned back to Mr. Graeme and squeezed my arms, wishing to god I'd worn something warmer than my leather jacket—my second mistake.

"Okay, let's try this again, *Mr. Graeme.* You aren't alive anymore." There, I'd said it. Again. Here's hoping this time it stuck. Zombies usually remember how they died, why the hell this one was being so stubborn about admitting it . . .

Michael Graeme, a.k.a. tonight's zombie of the hour, furrowed his brow . . . which contorted unevenly due to the paralysis from the stroke that had killed him.

"You know what I think?" the late Mr. Graeme said. "I think this is all a hoax. Jonathan's idea of a bad joke." He raised his arm and jabbed a pale finger in the direction of the sixty-year-old woman dressed in a tasteful black suit and veil standing to the left of my pentagram. "Bertha, are you and your brother behind this?" he shouted.

The recently widowed Mrs. Graeme clutched at Cody's jacket and launched into a fresh round of sobs—though considering her serene state before I performed Mr. Graeme's raising, I had trouble believing the grief was genuine.

Cody cleared his throat—loudly.

I sighed. "Wait right here, Mr. Graeme," I said, though it wasn't like he had a choice. I'd raised him and set the limits so he couldn't step outside my summoning ring, regardless of whether or not he believed he was dead.

With effort Cody detached himself from the widow and headed for my pentagram. I met him at the edge, sage smoke and gold Otherside billowing between us—though I was the only one of us who could see the Otherside. All Cody would see was smoke.

As soon as his back was turned on his clients, he dropped the smile. "You said this would be fast," he hissed.

Cody was a lawyer and, in my experience, they were to be treated as carefully as you would the devil himself. "Normally, yes, but he is refusing to acknowledge the fact that he is dead."

"I thought all zombies knew they were dead."

"That doesn't mean they don't try to lie to themselves."

"How the hell can he lie to himself? I mean, it's obvious he's a zombie, look at him."

I clenched my fists, trying not to lose my temper. Damn it, I wished I'd pushed harder for cash up front. I hate being desperate for work. "I don't see why it's so surprising. People do it to themselves all the time."

Cody held up his hand. "Look, I don't care how you do it. Just get him to sign the paperwork."

I watched Cody stalk back to his clients, shook my head and turned my attention back to the deceased Mr. Graeme. He was staring at the small collection of lawyers and family gathered ten feet away, the left side of his face frowning in concern, creating a wholly unpleasant effect.

How were the people gathered outside the pentagram handling tonight's entertainment? Well, it depended on who you were watching. Mrs. Graeme—the deceased's wife—her two sons and their wives were weeping and clinging to each other. Cody was comforting them and sneaking acid looks at me. The tall, thirty-something redhead keeping her distance from them—Samantha Diamond, professional entertainer, was how she'd introduced herself—was shaken up but otherwise composed, and huddled with her own lawyer. And why shouldn't she be composed? Mr. Graeme had left her all his liquid cash.

Man, what I wouldn't give to be anywhere else but here. . . .

I checked my phone. A quarter to twelve. I was running out of time to get the papers signed by midnight. Time to employ more direct measures. I pulled my compact mirror out of my pocket and held it up to Mr. Graeme.

"Michael, you are most certainly dead. You died one week ago of a massive stroke." I'd read the full examiner's report before agreeing to the raising to make certain there'd been no other mitigating factors. Before raising a zombie—even a four-line like Mr. Graeme—you need to do some fancy footwork with Otherside lines to repair the damage. Otherwise, when I activated the temporary zombie bindings, Mr. Graeme would only have stood, looked at the crowd surrounding his grave and collapsed from a stroke all over again.

I'd used some new bindings—better artery reinforcement in the head but took more Otherside and didn't last as long. Still, I'd thought it would leave me plenty of time to get this damned will sorted out.

I glanced back at Cody, who had his arm around Mrs. Graeme and was still staring daggers at me. I sighed and turned back to the late Mr. Graeme, who was examining his face in my compact, probing the paralyzed side with shrivelled fingers.

"Your doctors have been warning you about your blood pressure for the last thirty years." I took back my compact and retrieved a folder from my backpack: his medical files—the pared-down version, mind you, with the important details. Namely, his doctor's bitching about Graeme's refusal to take his blood pressure medication.

Graeme squinted at the folder and I held out his glasses, which I'd had tucked in my jacket pocket. According to his wife, he needed them to see just about anything.

He sniffed at the air—a common reaction for any zombie on account of the subconscious parts of their brain picking up familiar scents. Probably his wife, or the girlfriend, or even faint traces of his old life.

He hesitated for a moment then snatched the glasses from my fingers, placing them on his face and motioning for me to fork over the folder.

"Knock yourself out." I crossed my arms and watched as he flipped through the pages. For a slim man, his blood pressure had been obscenely high. It was a miracle he'd made it to eighty, let alone eighty-five. . . .

He snorted and looked up, jabbing at the last page. "Says here I'm dead," he said. "Can't be dead, I'm standing here talking to you."

Bingo. I opened my mouth to explain, but I was interrupted by a tug at the sleeve of my jacket and turned to find Cody at my shoulder. "You gave him the autopsy report? Are you nuts?"

"Trust me, it moves things along. And you're supposed to stay the hell outside of my pentagram."

Cody ignored me. "If by moving things along you mean making the zombie angry—didn't you see the New Mexico case?"

This time I couldn't stop myself from rolling my eyes. The marshals had shot down the White Picket Fence Killer, a.k.a. Martin Dane, two weeks ago. He'd targeted families in California living behind—you guessed it—white picket fences. He stabbed and strangled the sleeping family and after everyone save one was dead, he dressed their corpses in 1950s clothes. The survivor, usually a girl, was taken hostage. Martin would kill her after he had chosen the next family and leave her body in the new hostage's home, a sick and twisted game of "musical corpses." With over a dozen murders in three years, he'd terrified suburban Americans chasing the middle-class dream. Luckily for suburbia, he'd been identified courtesy of a hidden nanny camera and shot by the police at a New Mexico gas station. Unfortunately, his last kidnap victim, a ten-year-old girl, hadn't been with him. She was presumed to be alive . . . which is why they had tried to raise him.

"Okay, first off, any serial-killer zombie is going to be angry." I smiled at the memory of how spectacularly Dane had acted once the raiser told him he was dead. Liam Sinclair, celebrity practitioner and TV host, liked to get the recently deceased to acknowledge their shortcomings in life and commit to self-improvement in the afterlife. This approach might give closure to the families of expired drug addicts and be spectacular for ratings, but it really wasn't the tack you wanted to take with a serial killer.

Serial killers kill people for sport. They are the definition of unrepentant. Scratch that—their life's regret is that they can't kill people anymore. Raising Dane gave him one last chance to commit murder, and Liam happened to be standing right in front of him with the TV cameras rolling. What the hell other outcome would you expect? The only surprising part was that Liam had survived.

Now, convincing the serial killer he's still alive and that cooperating and telling you where his last victim is will get him off death row, and therefore secure another chance someday to kill someone? That took finesse beyond the capability of a half-rate pseudo-celebrity zombie raiser.

Aaron, a Seattle detective who worked afterlife cases—and my ex-boyfriend—had been right about one thing: I'd been insulted that Liam, a practitioner with no criminal experience, had been asked to raise Dane and not me. Why hire a professional with a track record when you could hire a camera-friendly, D-list celebrity with a syndicated TV show?

Not that I was going to bother telling Cody any of that. Instead, I said, "Do you want this will settled in the next fifteen minutes or not?" If we didn't get the will revoked soon, no one got paid, including me . . . well, except Graeme's mistress.

Cody didn't nod, but his eyes shifted back to Graeme's widow. I took that as an affirmative.

"Then stick to the sleazeball lawyering and leave me to wrangle the zombie." I pulled my sleeve free and turned back to Mr. Graeme, and shivered against a fresh gust of cold wind. The sooner this will was signed, the sooner I could get back to my apartment and take a hot shower . . . and deal with my own personal zombie predicament.

Still holding his medical folder, Graeme had started examining his surroundings: the gravestones, falling leaves, and the freshly dug-up grave and coffin where he'd been buried until a few minutes ago. He was looking a hell of a lot less confident about the whole alive thing.

"I'm really dead?" he said to me, pointing at the tombstone.

I nodded. "You bet you are, Graeme." I held out my hand. Now was as good a time as any to make introductions. He took it, albeit reluctantly.

"I'm Kincaid Strange, voodoo practitioner." I inhaled deeply. There's never an easy way to broach this one. "I raised you as a zombie this evening so we could address some business you left unsettled before you died."

It's hard to know how much you should tell a four-line zombie about their temporary state of being. Personally, lying to the dead is a level of seedy I'm not comfortable with—unless it's a serial killer. Totally comfortable lying to those. My recently deceased instructor and mentor, Maximillian Odu, wouldn't stoop that low either. The fact is, most dead people are grateful to get the truth. And, let's face it, deep down they know they're dead.

Graeme threw the medical report into the dirt. "Well, shit, damn doctor was right. You've got no idea, young lady, how much that pisses me off."

Cody cleared his throat, drawing Graeme's attention, and I shot Cody a dirty look. I'd made it clear at the beginning that the peanut gallery, lawyers included, had to keep quiet. Four-line zombies like Graeme are easily distracted. I spoke loudly to regain his attention.

"So, the discrepancies in your will—"

He gave a dry snort and turned his attention back to me. "Discrepancies? I left everything in order with my lawyers."

"Yeah, about that . . ." I fished another folder out of my backpack, one Cody had given me earlier with the copy of the will and the complaints from Graeme's family. By law, the licensed zombie practitioner—i.e., me—is the only one allowed to explain legal issues to the zombie in question.

I pulled out the sheet sitting on top of the will and handed it to Graeme. "Apparently it says here," I added, pointing to one of the bullet points, "that you left all your liquid assets to your—friend—Samantha Diamond."

"I did," Graeme said, and motioned me to hand over the file. He managed to pull out his will and flipped to the page that named Samantha as his beneficiary. He tapped it with the more dexterous of his hands and then pointed at his mistress. "That's her over there. No discrepancy at all." He raised his voice. "Samantha, did they rope you into this too? Aww, I'm sorry you had to come out in the cold."

To her credit, Samantha only waved and blew kisses. Unlike Cody, she knew how to follow the no-talking instructions. . . .

Cody cleared his throat. Again.

"Yeah, so that's the problem. Your family"—I gestured to the Graeme clan—"have filed a complaint against Samantha claiming she manipulated you into giving her all your money."

"Oh, of all the—" Graeme mumbled a few choice words under his breath, pushed his glasses back up his nose and craned his neck until his eyes found the widow Graeme. "Samantha didn't have to convince me to do anything. Let me guess, my harpy of a wife hired you?" Graeme said, so everyone outside the pentagram could hear.

The widow Graeme gave an audible gasp and covered her mouth, gripping Cody's arm.

Oh, fantastic. Here we go . . . Lawyers, mistresses, family spats, who gets the goldfish: when you raise a zombie for financial reasons, things are guaranteed to get ugly.

"How much did she offer you if you could claw back some of my money, hunh?" Graeme shouted, though the volume and tone made it plain his disgust was directed at his wife, not me.

"She didn't offer me anything," I said, keeping my voice calm. That was true. There was a three-thousand-dollar bonus on top of my fee if I could get Graeme to agree to sign over five million in cash for the family, but technically that had come from a desperate Cody, not Bertha Graeme.

Graeme wasn't finished. He jabbed his finger at his widow. "You had to go and get a zombie raiser, didn't you, Bertha? Weren't happy with the houses and company, no, you want all my money too."

"You left that whore our bank accounts!" Bertha yelled back.

And here we went, ignoring my zombie-raising rules. It was one simple rule, folks: don't talk to the zombie. . . .

"*My* bank accounts, not that you knew the difference—and she earned it," Graeme shouted back around me. "And you lot are a far stretch from destitute. Sell something, Bertha." He switched his focus to his sons. "Or better yet, sell one of their houses, I paid for them. Might actually make them get off their asses and work for once."

Cody was at the edge of my pentagram again. I faced him, leaving Mr. Graeme to entertain himself.

"I thought you said you controlled the zombie?" he whispered.

"I *am* controlling him. He's pissed off at his wife, which I'm guessing from the will and the shouting was a general theme in their marriage."

"Well, make him stop yelling at her!"

"I can't *make* the dead be nice." If anything, the dead usually want to tell people exactly what they thought of them while they were alive. Like afterlife therapy. To me, it felt like punishment for agreeing to a lipstick seance.

Lipstick seance: a term coined by voodoo practitioners of the early twenty-first century that refers to a seance where no one really wants to hear what the ghost/zombie has to say. Lawyers, family, mistresses—they want papers signed, locations revealed. Well, maybe the family dog is happy to hear the zombie out. Dogs are always pleased to see their owners walking around again. . . .

A lipstick seance is necessary for social graces, legalities, et cetera, but no one actually has any illusions as to why they're there: to make everything look nice and proper before they completely fuck over the wishes of the deceased. Like a cheap coat of dollar lipstick—to give the illusion of respecting formalities, and keep things pretty, like.

"You won't even let a man die in peace—" Mr. Graeme shouted.

"Forty years of my life!" Bertha shouted back.

I closed my eyes. Once, just once, why couldn't someone hire me to say goodbye to their loved ones? Why do the people with enough money to shell out for a raising always want to fight about the money?

I ignored Cody and turned back to the zombie. "Mr. Graeme, I'm going to level with you—"

He peered at me. "Look, if we're going to do this sordid business, practitioner, you might as well call me Michael."

I exhaled slowly. "All right, Michael. Look, I'm sorry I had to raise you as a zombie so your family could yell about not getting enough money, but this is what I do for a living and I need to pay my rent—"

He stopped me with a sad shake of his head. "I've danced these kinds of legal shenanigans before, just never figured on being dragged out of my grave to the tune of one. What's it going to cost to make all this," he said, waving a hand at the assembled people, "go away?"

I swallowed. This was the part I hated. "Five million," I said.

He snorted. "That's all this is about? I'd have thought they'd be going after all of it."

I inclined my head. "You did leave them all the property."

"Probably need the cash to pay off the worthless offspring's gambling debts. Kid never did know which pony to back." He shook his head again, and held out his hand for a pen. I gave him one, along with the addendum to the will, then turned around so he could use my back to sign. As I felt the weight of the pen, I reflected that there was something profoundly sad about the fact that Mr. Graeme—Michael—had capitulated to his family's demands without more of a fight, as if he hadn't really been surprised. . . . I shelved the thought to revisit after I had a double whisky sour in front of me.

I picked up bits of a hushed conversation between Cody and Mrs. Graeme.

"Unfortunately, with the time press, she was the best practitioner available," Cody said.

I frowned. Ingrate. The words *she's new* and *inexperienced* drifted over. I was one of the most experienced practitioners on the Pacific Coast, and I'd explained to Cody when he called what problems might come up, including a belligerent corpse. It said a lot about Cody as a lawyer that his go-to strategy for managing client expectations was to blame everyone around him. I considered putting Graeme back right there and then, but I needed the money. . . . Instead, I resolved to scratch Cody Banks from my client list.

Mr. Graeme finished with his signatures. I turned around and he handed me the pen and addendum. "Trouble with the lawyer?" he asked.

"You have no idea," I said, shaking my head as I checked the paperwork.

"Lawyers," he said. "Not good for anything. So how did that despicable specimen find you? Curiosity," he added when I arched an eyebrow. "You're not the legal type—no offence meant." He nodded at Cody. "In fact, take it as a compliment. You don't have the layer of sleaze dripping off you like they tend to."

"Michael, you sure you want to do this? I mean, you don't have to—"

Graeme leaned in. "The fact is, I didn't want any of them getting my money, including Sam, though she's the only one who ever worked a day in her life. But after I'm dead, what am I supposed to do with it?" He looked up and raised his voice again. "Fact is, Bertha, they'd be better off having to work for their dinner. That's on you, spoiling them both rotten."

I kept silent and nodded. I mean, what did someone say to that? Though I sure as hell could relate. Sometimes you just drew a bum deck of family cards in the life lottery.

"Just give them the papers, and put me back in the ground so I can finally get some peace and quiet." He stepped into his coffin and sat down, a more weary expression on his face than when I'd first raised him. Then again, maybe it was just the glasses. I figured he could keep them.

I inclined my chin at Cody and tapped the Otherside, ready to unravel Mr. Graeme's bindings.

Graeme glanced up at me. "Is there anything to look forward to? Beyond the Otherside, I mean?"

I shook my head. "Honestly, Mr. Graeme? If I had the answer to that, I'd be doing something a hell of a lot better with my life."

"Yeah, I suppose you would." He lay down in the coffin and I tapped the barrier, spooling Otherside out and forming a globe of it inside my head. The gold threads of his four animating lines flared at the surge of Otherside in the air around us, and I grabbed hold of the line near his heart. The fastest way to un-animate a zombie is to pull on the heartstring. No pun intended.

"Word of advice?" Mr. Graeme said.

I waited before unravelling his lines.

"Just make sure you get that lawyer to pay you up front. I was in business for over seventy years. I know a cheap bastard when I see one."

"Don't I know it. Time to put you back, Mr. Graeme. Don't worry, this won't hurt a bit." I pulled the gold threads of Otherside that were animating him and waited a few seconds for the action to take effect. Graeme widened his eyes and breathed one last automatic breath before the last Otherside thread dissolved into nothingness and he became still.

"So long, Mr. Graeme. I'm sorry life dealt you a family almost as bad as mine." Though he'd certainly been a voluntary participant in their collective misery, I still felt bad for him. I closed the coffin, made sure the locks were set and waved at the groundskeeper, who'd kept a very safe distance from our proceedings, well out of earshot. He'd rebury the coffin after we were gone.

I drew in my own breath and let go of the Otherside still in my head. The nausea was almost absent this time. As much as I hated to hand it to Gideon, the violent and hair's-breadth-shy-of-psychotic sorcerer I'd encountered on my most recent and disastrous Otherside job, he'd made good on his promise to mitigate my need to tap the barrier in return for my services as a practitioner. Good thing, too, since the price had gone up . . .

Cody crossed my pentagram as the Graeme family, Samantha and the other lawyer headed for the parking lot. Now to face my other lousy deal, this one with the lawyer who'd already proved himself an opportunist. Heads or tails which one was worse. I walked towards him with the will tucked under my arm.

"Lawyer," I said to him the same way I might say *thief* or *man who pushes old women down tall flights of stairs*. For all I knew, he might.

He held out his hand for the folder. I gave it to him and watched as he flipped through it, examining the signatures. I cleared my throat. "My fee," I said, when he finally looked up. "I'd like it. Now."

Cody gave a short laugh as he closed the folder and tucked it under his arm. "You expect me to pay you, for that?"

I crossed my arms. "Yeah, I do. Or I'll lodge a complaint with the bar." Or whatever the hell organization you complain about lawyer misconduct to . . . It had never gone that far, and I'd dealt with sleazier bottom feeders than Cody.

He chuckled again. "You dress like a high school grunge star reject who doesn't realize the nineties were done two decades ago, and the Seattle PD cancelled your contract, probably because you couldn't do the job." Cody leaned in, giving me more of a whiff of his cheap cologne than I cared to inhale. "Who do you think people are going to believe?"

I closed my eyes for half a beat. My natural inclination was to tell Cody to fuck right the hell off. But I'd watched Max handle rabid legal sharks like Cody over the years and had sworn to take a couple of pages out of his book from now on.

I leaned right into Cody until he had to take a step back. "I expect you to pay me because I did my job and I'm the best practitioner on the Pacific Coast, including Hawaii, Canada and Alaska." I pointed towards the now-closed coffin and open grave. "And if you think anyone else on the west coast could have gotten that zombie raised as quickly or as competently as I just did, you're deluding yourself."

Cody gave me his false smile. "Here's the thing, Strange. What you've said could easily be true, but I've won enough cases to know that the outside package is what matters. Not the talent." He sneered and looked me over. "And your package says the only person anyone is going to give two bits of credibility to is me."

I stepped back and nodded. Max had also taught me that there's no point getting upset with someone who's decided facts are not relevant. "Have yourself a nice night, Cody," I said, and turned towards the graveyard entrance and my bike.

Cody laughed. "That's it?" He called out, "Wow, I expected the infamous Kincaid Strange to put up more of a fight."

I smiled to myself and kept walking. "That's it. You weren't happy with my services and feel that I didn't raise Mr. Graeme in accordance with your licence. You won't be paying me, so the conversation is over." I reached my bike. "But that also means I'm not signing the licence release to confirm Mr. Graeme changed the will." One, two, three . . .

I heard Cody rustling through the paperwork. Will revision was obviously a new game for him, otherwise he'd have been more concerned about me signing off on the licence before I handed him the folder. Without my signature as a registered prac-titioner in Washington . . . Like I said, this wasn't my first lipstick seance rodeo.

Cody came to the same conclusion, and I heard his feet hitting the pavement behind me. I ignored him as I put my helmet on and flicked the ignition on my Honda Hawk, forcing Cody to run in front of my bike.

"You screwed me over," he shouted over my revving engine.

I held my hand up to my ear. "Sorry, what was that?"

Cody swore and reached into his jacket to pull out an envelope. He held it up and waved it in front of me. "You made your point. I'll pay you."

Music to my ears.

I turned the ignition off and removed my helmet. I then took the proffered envelope from Cody and pulled out the cash, counting it carefully while he stood there fuming. Fifteen hundred. Short the three thousand extra I was supposed to get for netting the family five million. "Bonus?" I said.

Cody cursed as he pulled out another envelope. I counted the three thousand and pocketed it before pulling out my own release form, handing it to Cody along with a pen. An enthusiastic law student and huge Nathan Cade fan at the University of Washington's free legal clinic had recommended I get all my lawyer clients to sign one saying I had performed the raising to their specifications. He'd even helped me draft it.

After making sure the signature and dates were accurate, I gestured for Cody to hand over the licence release. I signed it as fast as I could and handed it back. Money inside my jacket, I slid my helmet back on and lifted the kickstand.

Cody stood there watching me with something akin to fury. He shook his head. "You have got to be the worst voodoo practitioner in Washington state."

Before I hit the ignition, I flipped up the mask on my helmet. "No. I'm the only voodoo practitioner in Washington state."

He started to storm off towards his clients and the parking lot. "Hey, Cody?" I shouted.

He glanced at me over his shoulder.

"Lose my number."

I didn't wait for an answer. I hit the ignition and took off down the road, leaving Cody standing in the graveyard. I needed to get away from the rot. Cody was about to learn real fast what happens when you burn bridges with one of the only people qualified to do legal zombie raisings in the next three states. At least as far as will contests are concerned.

Served me right for agreeing to a lipstick seance.

I shot one last look at Michael Graeme's grave before heading home to deal with the colossal undead elephant waiting for me in the apartment. One Nathan Cade.

CHAPTER 2

CAN'T TAKE NO FOR AN ANSWER

I jiggled the key in my front-door lock three times before it opened. Aaron had threatened to fix it more times than I could count, and at this point I was holding out on principle. Though, considering how cold my hands were, I just might be ready to give in . . .

Finally. The door opened and I pushed myself and my bike inside. The heat was on—a luxury I'd afforded myself since finishing a job for Lee last month. I'd been trying my best to push memories of that experience out of my mind, and between willpower and nightly doses of whisky I'd been relatively successful. Three people had died, and those were the ones I knew personally. No amount of money had been worth that loss, which is why I was sticking to legal work from now on—or trying to.

Speaking of legalities . . . "Nate?" I called out. I couldn't smell the sickly sweet formaldehyde that followed him everywhere now, but I checked the spare bedroom anyway. Maybe I was becoming desensitized to the odour after a week of exposure.

Besides the MP3 player and a couple of comic books, there was no sign of him. The cargo jacket and shoes he'd been using were both gone from the stand by the door.

Nate must still be out dealing with Lee. I'd walked him to the underground city gates early in the evening and let him in myself, mostly so Lee could get a look at him but also thinking that an excursion would do wonders for his dismal mood. I'd tried keeping him under lock and key in my apartment, but after one week of being in each other's hair . . . Still, I wasn't sure sending Nate out in his current condition had been a wise move.

Two weeks. Two weeks since Nate stole Cameron's body right from under the psychotic sorcerer ghost's nose.

During the zombie and practitioner murders in Seattle, I'd made a blind deal with Gideon, a powerful sorcerer's ghost. Stupid, but I'd been desperate—not only to find Cameron's killer and figure out what the hell Max had been up to with Cameron's strange zombie bindings, but because of the sheer volume of Otherside I'd been using. I hadn't realized the fiascos with Cameron, Max and Gideon had been intertwined—not until it was too late, anyway. Which is why I hadn't held up my end of the bargain with Gideon to deliver Max's payment for services rendered. Namely, handing over Cameron's body.

I couldn't do that to him. Cameron hadn't remembered signing away his body when he was a living artist desperate to preserve his legacy. Once his bindings had been cut and Cameron's spirit was gone, I'd tried to burn the body, which had pissed Gideon off. And then, somehow, some way, in an alignment of the stars designed to completely fuck me, Nate had managed to get himself tangled in the remnants of Cameron's rapidly deteriorating zombie bindings.

Or that's about as much as I could figure from looking at them. Cameron's bindings had been an unstable mess—a complicated, intricate arrangement, but a mess nonetheless.

Given another chance to go back and change things? I still wouldn't have given Gideon what he wanted. Like I said, handing over Cameron's empty body for the sorcerer to use had just felt wrong.

But at the moment, that was a moot point. We—meaning I—were no closer to finding a way to get Nate the hell out of Cameron's body then we had been a week ago. Which meant as soon as Gideon found out about Nate's epic fuck-up, I figured we'd both be dead, or seriously incapacitated. Gideon was only a fraction shy of being a poltergeist, at least as far as temperament went. He was already well past any other ghost I'd ever met on the power scale, and paired with his mercurial nature . . .

Luckily, Gideon was still pissed off enough about me trying to burn Cameron's body that beyond writing a *You owe me* message on my bathroom mirror immediately after the incident, he'd stayed out of sight. I had no illusions about how much longer the cold shoulder would last. As soon as Gideon figured he could speak to me without killing me, he'd come collecting. I was amazed I'd got this much time.

I headed into the kitchen and set the kettle to boil, holding my hands over the top waiting for it to steam. When I screw up, I screw up spectacularly: in debt to a potentially homicidal sorcerer's ghost and with my own reckless, kleptomaniac rock star zombie to baby-sit. Maybe I'd get lucky and Gideon wouldn't show up until I got Nate out of Cameron's body.

Steam billowed out of the kettle. I poured myself a tea and added a shot of whisky, then grabbed half a BLT sandwich from the fridge. Now that I had cash again, I'd gone out and stocked up on groceries. That reminded me: I took the forty-five hundred out of my jacket and put it in the jar over the fridge. I'd tuck it under the loose floorboard beneath my bed after I warmed up. I hovered over the mug so the steam warmed my face, then wrapped my hands around the cup and breathed in. The Otherside sight Gideon had sold me had significantly lightened my Otherside hangovers, just not the bone-penetrating chill that came with using it. Now if there were only something I could do about Seattle's unique brand of October cold that didn't involve running up my heating bill. I was mulling over whether to take a shower before bed when I heard the door jostle as someone tried the lock.

Holding my mug in one hand, I opened the door to one sheepish-looking Nathan Cade.

"Hey, K. How's your night been?"

"Lousy." I stepped out of the way to let him in. He closed and locked the door behind him before leaning up against it.

Nate had managed to find sweatpants, a dark grey sweatshirt with a hood, a blue plaid flannel shirt, an old beat-up cargo jacket also with a hood, and a black toque. He'd pulled the toque down over his forehead and both hoods were pulled up and over the hat. They were the only clean things of Aaron's left in the apartment. The previous clothes Cameron had been wearing were either burned or so smoke damaged there had been no point trying to clean them.

"Nate, if you were aiming for grunge star, you passed it a while ago and went straight to bouquet de three day bender."

"Okay, one: you won't let me shower or comb my hair. For good reason," he added, holding up both hands in defence before I could launch into another lecture. "But that really limits my fashion options here." He held up the sleeve of his coat. "And I like to think I've managed new grunge hipster. Not everyone in the twenty-first century shares your passion for wasting precious water and electricity taking hot showers."

I snorted. I noticed his vintage red Converse runners, the same ones he'd preferred as a ghost. They certainly hadn't been amongst Aaron's things. . . .

I didn't like the way he was standing with his back against the door, as if worried someone might try to break in. "Nate, what the hell?"

Nate pushed off from the door, as if just realizing he looked suspicious. "Oh, just ran into some people a few blocks over. Wanted to know where I got my runners. Pretty sure I lost them down the—"

I stopped him with a shake of my head. "Nate, I sent you into the underground city to talk to Lee, not to stroll around downtown Seattle! If anyone finds out you're a zombie—"

"It's fine. No one knows. I stayed in the shadows just like you said and used the alleys. The only people who saw me figured if I smelled homeless, and looked homeless . . ." He shrugged.

I took a sip of my tea. "Well?"

Nate gave me a blank stare.

"How did things go with Lee?" I was no closer to figuring out how to untangle Nate from Cameron's body, but Lee Ling Xhao, the underground city's foremost and one of their oldest zombies, their veritable queen, might have some insight. At the very least, she was our best shot.

"Ah, yeah. About that—"

I frowned at him. "Yeah. That. The reason I dropped you off at the underground city. To see if Lee knows how to get you the hell out of Cameron's body," I said, letting a note of warning bleed into my voice.

"Okay, so something might have come up."

I almost dropped my tea. "Nate. This isn't a game."

"And you're better at talking to Lee about this kind of stuff than I am."

"What the hell did you think the note was for?" I shook my head. This was irresponsible even for him. Maybe the unconventional bindings were disrupting his thought processes. . . . "And I wouldn't have sent you if Lee was returning my phone calls. Un-fucking-believable." I headed back into my kitchen. A second shot of whisky was starting to look like a good idea.

It is *possible*, in *theory*, for the wrong ghost to get caught in a zombie's bindings when a practitioner first raises them. It's one of the reasons I make a pentagram and use sage smoke, to keep undesirable ghosts out. But in this case it shouldn't have been possible. For one, Cameron's bindings had been jerry-rigged in a highly unusual way, but more importantly, I'd dismantled them *and* watched whatever was left of Cameron disappear back to the Otherside. Trust me, I remembered—it had hurt. I wasn't used to things hurting.

Nate wasn't bound to the body like a zombie should be. Looser than a four-line zombie but stronger than a ghost possession. It shouldn't be permanent. . . . I just had no idea how to get him out.

It would help if he could share a few details, like what he'd been doing in Randall's burning cellar, whether he had touched a particular Otherside thread, or what he'd been damn well thinking. Unfortunately, Nate was being Nate. He didn't remember anything, except that he'd seen smoke and gone in to check what had happened. . . .

He followed me into the kitchen. "Look, I'm sorry, all right. I'm serious. Something came up."

I set my mug down on the counter and whirled around. "One thing, Nate. I asked you to do *one* thing. This is serious. You're a ticking expiry date." I'd been banking on Lee's insights, but she hadn't spoken a word to me since Gideon dropped me off in the underground city half dead from smoke inhalation.

"Okay, what happened with the raising that's made you so touchy? It was a lawyer with a licence. It doesn't get more clear-cut."

Deflecting. Again. "Unless they try to screw you over."

Nate waited. "Well?" he finally said.

I ignored him and topped up my tea.

"Look, you tell me what happened, I'll tell you why I didn't make it to Lee."

Oh, what the hell. At least I could find out what he'd been up to instead of delivering my message. I gave him the short version of my altercation with Cody after I'd finished the raising, including the grunge reject comment, because it still stung. My bike leathers were *not* grungy.

Nate didn't exactly jump to my defence. "You know, that probably wouldn't have happened if you'd worn a suit and dressed like a lawyer type."

"The flannel is warm and I'm qualified enough I shouldn't have to worry about the way I dress. Isn't that how it worked for you? You used to wear ripped jeans and plaid shirts—Actually, you never wore the plaid shirt, you only ever tied it around your waist."

"Um, yeah. About that. I was a rock star—"

"And I'm a voodoo practitioner."

"And they're lawyers. You think I showed up in flannel shirts and ripped jeans to sign multi-million-dollar contracts? No, I wore a suit like everyone else, so I wouldn't give them a reason to screw me over."

That made me pause. Nate had a practical side. . . . "You seriously wore a suit?"

Nate hedged his answer. "Suit jacket over a clean T-shirt, non-ripped jeans and nice shoes—but it's the west coast, and the shoes and jacket were fucking expensive."

I had a hard time picturing Nate in anything respectable, especially smelling like he did now, of formaldehyde and rank sweat, and wearing Cameron's body. "The lawyer should be happy I answered his call," I muttered. I took another sip of tea and breathed in the steam. "All right. Your turn, twinkletoes."

"Yeah. Okay, I totally meant to go, but I had a really, really good reason to get sidetracked. I'll even go tomorrow—promise."

"Out with it."

Nate winced. "Okay, you're not going to be happy—"

"Jesus Christ! You were stalking Mindy again, weren't you?"

"K, you don't understand, we have a connection that transcends death!"

Back in 1997, a year before Nate had died, when he'd been at the peak of his short-lived fame, he'd had a girlfriend. Mindy. Who'd been famous in her own right as a sort of, well, professional grunge rock girlfriend? She'd even tried her hand at being a rock star after appearing in magazines with Nate and the other grunge star cohorts. I guess some music exec figured, why not? It hadn't lasted. Mindy found her calling and a talent for peddling the inky glamour of the nineties on her radio show, *Glitter Hole*, and more recently in YouTube videos. She also made a killing selling Nate's memorabilia, which didn't sit well with me. I'd called in to *Glitter Hole* once to say as much. They'd blacklisted my number. Indefinitely.

Okay, Nate's ongoing obsession was partially my fault. I hadn't come down on him hard enough when he'd been stalking Mindy's mirrors because it's not unusual for ghosts to fixate on their pasts. It hadn't seemed serious—I mean, she didn't have any set mirrors like a practitioner would, Nate had said as much. He couldn't catch more than a very foggy glimpse of her, let alone talk to her.

"She cares so much she's never once sought me out for a seance, not in the entire year you've been doing gigs at the university."

"She might not know—" Nate tried.

"Bullshit. Everyone knows you're a ghost. Your shows have had close to a million hits on YouTube and you think no one's ever called in to *Glitter Hole* about it? Nate, she screens the calls. She's never once come looking for you."

"Okay, but she was never into voodoo."

I shook my head. "I'm going to say this once, because for all intents and purposes right now you're not a ghost, and this time your stupid obsession might just land me in jail: she doesn't care. She never did!"

Nate stared at me.

I sighed. "Maybe she cared for the couple days after you drowned, but considering how fast Mindo shacked up with your drummer . . ." I let that thought sink in.

Nate was silent for a full minute. "That was brutal, K. Even for you."

"Consider it a good thing. Most people spend decades not letting go. She moved on with her life. Move on with your afterlife."

I expected Nate to argue, but he just stood there looking defeated. I was doing him a favour and saving myself from trouble. So why the hell did I feel so bad?

Nate took off his jacket and hung it on the coat rack, then removed his shoes. He took the toque off last and I noted his hair still wasn't falling out. It would. It was a sheer miracle Nate looked as good as he did—or maybe it was a testament to Cameron's genetics. At least his skin hadn't taken on too yellow of a sheen yet. I gave it another week.

He slumped onto the couch and I refilled the kettle and turned on the stove again for my hot water bottle.

"Cole."

I glanced over my shoulder where Nate had sunk to the couch. His head back, eyes closed.

When I didn't say anything, he added, "My drummer's name. He was my friend. It was Cole."

The pit in my gut widened. "And he's never bothered looking you up either."

Nate didn't have anything to say to that.

I sat down at my laptop while the kettle warmed and logged into eBay, hoping maybe I'd sold a few more books. Zombies are expensive and Nate was quickly eating up my savings in food. Cameron's body had already been a few barrels short of a tank as far as the bindings were concerned, and Nate needed to fuel up regularly on fresh brains in order to stay upright.

Hunh. *Rudimentary Bindings* had a couple of bids. If I got a hundred bucks I'd be happy. . . .

"Don't you help zombies reconnect with their loved ones?"

I glared at Nate over my shoulder. "You aren't in any shape to reconnect with anyone. You are squatting in a barely functional stolen body trying to stalk your ex-girlfriend."

"Note, you did say *functional*—"

I swore and swivelled my desk chair around. "It's temporary, Nate! If I can't get you out of there, it's game over for your afterlife! Helping you understand that is the best thing I can do for you, unless you want to move into the underground? I can smell the formaldehyde from here."

"Which is all the more reason why I should see Mindy now."

"You've been dead fifteen years."

"Our love was forever!"

I gave Nate an incredulous look. He realized how idiotic he sounded and ran his hand through his hair. "Okay, maybe not forever."

I turned back to my computer screen, shaking my head. None of my other books had reached the minimum bid yet. "You're dead, Nate."

I could smell him as he came up behind my chair. "Yet I have a body. I'd argue that in the grand scheme of things I'm in a better position than I've been in a long time."

"Being a formaldehyde dump is not exactly putting you ahead of the game—if I can't get you untangled from that body. . . ." I shook my head. "You've already burned a good five years off your afterlife, maybe a decade. There's no precedent in the books for this."

Nate darted around me and grabbed the copy of *Rudimentary Bindings* destined for a lucky eBay bidder.

I swore. "Give that back."

"Help me see Mindy and you can have it back," he said, backing up towards my kitchen table. "Just so I can make sure she's all right."

"Nate, if you had any grasp of how much you've screwed over Gideon and what he's going to do to us—" I snatched at the book, but with Cameron's height and reach, Nate kept it away easily.

"But I don't, because I don't care!"

I chased after him, but he darted around the kitchen table to keep me at bay. Damn his long arms . . .

"And as far as Gideon goes, there's one thing I'm sure as hell certain about."

I pulled two chairs into the kitchen doorway so I could corral the son of a bitch into the tiny room. "What's that?"

"He'll blame you over me. Because if there is one thing on this planet I'm famous for, it's being *completely fucking incompetent!*"

"You're famous for a handful of songs and getting drunk before falling off your yacht." Damn it, he was standing by the kitchen sink full of dirty water and dishes, dangling my book over it. I winced as steam from the now-boiling kettle drifted towards the pages.

"I couldn't be left alone to tie my shoes without the very likely chance I'd get high. There's no way I'd have the wherewithal to occupy a freebie zombie. I can't help myself, K. Hell, I couldn't help myself when I was alive, and you expect me to as a ghost?"

I started to climb over the table but stopped when Nate lowered the book a few inches.

I clenched my teeth. Nate wouldn't drop it. He was desperate and obsessing—Zombie/Ghost Psychology 101. Now that he had a body, he was convinced he could fix everything—past mistakes, things left unsaid. I met his eyes, a watery pale green from more than two weeks of death and a week's worth of formaldehyde. "Nate. You can't fix it."

He looked at me. The bravado evaporated and he handed the book back. "Okay, what about one visit?"

I steered him towards the mirror in the spare bedroom. Gideon had always used the bathroom mirror for his random appearances, and Nate wearing Cameron's body like a cheap suit was the last thing I needed him seeing.

"Take a good look at yourself," I said, and waited until he faced his reflection. Oily mess of fading red hair, waxy skin, watery eyes.

"You really know how to put a damper on a guy's hopes and dreams, don't you, K?"

I retrieved his toque from the stand and handed it to him. "That's me. Paranormal buzzkill."

Nate groaned. "Are you sure we can't move the PlayStation in here?"

"No, Nate. If I have my way, you are back to being a ghost as soon as possible. Now stay here for the time being." I walked away, leaving him in the room and well out of Gideon's sight.

Before I could shut the door behind me, he said, "Look, I know you're doing your best to help me. What can I say—I screwed up."

"Then try to remember why and how—and don't think for one second I believe you when you said it just 'happened.'"

Nate's usual carefree expression closed up. "Sorry, K," he said, and pursed his lips. "I can't explain it." And with that, he softly shut the door.

I stood there, staring at the door, fuming. I couldn't shake the feeling Nate was hiding something, but if there was one thing Nate was good at besides saving his own skin . . .

And then again, maybe Nate was telling the truth. What if it was a case of getting too close to Cameron's highly volatile and unstable zombie bindings at the wrong time? A simple case of bad luck, or stupidity he didn't want to cop to?

Whatever was going on with Nate, he didn't want to talk about it, and I couldn't *make* him do anything. No one could.

I fixed the locks on the outside of his door into place. The zombie bindings might be acting stable, but they were warped and twisted-looking to my practitioner's eye, and he ran the risk of going feral. Nate or not, I would err on the side of caution.

Maybe the ghost binding texts at the university library archives would help. I'd see if I could pick them up tomorrow.

My phone buzzed in my pocket and I pulled it out, half-expecting a call from Cody to bitch about getting stuck paying me. Aaron's name flashed across my screen. Shit. I shoved it back in my pocket, rushed into my bedroom and looked out the window for his unmarked sedan. No way in hell was I letting Aaron in. But neither the car nor Aaron were in the alley out back.

I looked at my phone again. It was a text. Thank god.

Aaron and I were talking again. We'd even hung out a few times, after the fiasco with Randall and before Nate showed up wearing Cameron's corpse. I hadn't let him come over since Nate had taken up residence in my spare room, which had made things between us . . . strained, to say the least. That and the fact that two of the only people I'd liked and trusted had ended up dead. One of them, Randall, I couldn't think about without seeing smoke. . . . I needed more time to decompress before I could consider the next step with Aaron.

I shook the thoughts out of my head and opened his text. I'd eventually get over it. I hoped.

Give me a shout tomorrow morning. It's not definite but I might have work for you with the PD.

That got my attention. In fact I read it twice to make sure it wasn't a 1:00 a.m. vision tricking me.

How? I messaged back. The Seattle PD had put a new policy in place almost four months back banning the use of paranormal consultants—namely, me. Captain Marks thought all zombie raisers

were charlatans. He had a point: a lot of self-described voodoo practitioners are hawking snake oil. But Marks blamed the recent surge
in paranormal activity—ghosts, poltergeists, you name it—for lend-
ing undeserved legitimacy to real practitioners like me, which was
a dangerous stance to take. And that got my nerves on edge . . .

Call me tomorrow and I'll tell you.

You just want me to call you.

Get some sleep.

I stared at the phone and placed it on my nightstand. Things
were better between me and Aaron than they had been in the three
months since we'd broken up. We weren't sleeping together—I'd
had the brains not to let that happen again. I wasn't ready to have
a healthy relationship with anyone after everything that had happened and my guilt over Cameron's and Max's deaths. But we were
communicating better than we had for months. Go figure.

But even though we were checking in with each other and getting along, it felt as if something was missing . . . the rush I used to
get whenever he called, whenever I saw him at my door or in the
alley outside my bedroom window. There'd been a reminiscent
spark between us a couple of weeks ago but with everything going
on I'd had no time to reflect on my feelings.

I put the phone down on my nightstand and contemplated showering. With my luck, Gideon would be waiting to yell at me. . . .

Screw it.

I filled my hot water bottle and poured another cup of tea before
stripping out of my jeans and T-shirt, and after throwing on a flannel shirt left lying on my chair, I crawled under my duvet. Any
messages Gideon might have left on my bathroom mirror could
wait until tomorrow.

CHAPTER 3

DEAD MEN AND DEAD ENDS

It wasn't an alarm or my phone ringing that woke me up; it was the sunlight seeping through my bedroom curtain and flickering over my eyes. That was a less familiar sensation. I stretched in bed and pulled the duvet over my face. It had been ages since I'd woken up without a prompt. I was guessing it had something to do with the fact that I didn't need to use near as much Otherside as I had even two weeks ago, courtesy of Gideon and his bindings. I turned over and buried my face back in my pillow—just because the sun had the indecency to be up didn't mean I needed to be—when I picked up the distinct scent of bacon.

Shit. I threw the duvet off and slid a pair of track pants on. Nate might be fine with a set of PlayStation controllers, but no way in hell did I trust him with a gas stove. And just how the hell had he got out of the locked room?

"Nate?" I threw my door open to see what the hell he'd done to my kitchen and stopped. Nate was standing by the stove, carefully holding a frying pan over the flame. He turned to look at me with a tentative smile.

Nothing on fire, nothing broken. The kitchen window was even open and the smell of formaldehyde was more or less gone.

Nate held out the pan to me. "Peace offering?"

I edged towards the crispy, smoky bacon. There was also a spread of eggs, sunny side up, toast with butter and a carafe of coffee on the kitchen table. My stomach rumbled, taking a side in my internal debate between scolding Nate for escaping my zombie-proof room and sitting down to breakfast. . . .

"How did you get out?"

"Peace offering?" he said again, gesturing with the frying pan towards the food.

I grabbed one of the plates, helped myself to the eggs and toast and a generous cup of black coffee, and put it all on the table. I then went to check the spare-bedroom door while Nate finished with the bacon.

There wasn't any outward damage to the door or the lock—the doorknob and hinges hadn't been dismantled, and I was pretty sure Nate no longer had the dexterity for that anyway. So how did he get out?

I glanced over at him while he loaded the bacon onto my plate. "You crawled out the window?"

"And deal with the front door? Guess again—and your food is getting cold."

Even though my stomach protested, I checked inside the room and found a strip of wire, thinner than a coat hanger, lying on the desk. The end had been bent into a hook. I took it and tested it against the closed door. It slid through. With enough fiddling I could see Nate releasing the extra locks, including the chain. "Still doesn't explain how you got the deadbolt," I said, holding up the wire. It was thin enough to unhitch my extra locks, but the deadbolt turnkey was heavy.

"Well-placed piece of tape. The deadbolt has a spring release. You only thought you closed it."

I tested it and, sure enough, when I held the deadbolt in place with my finger, the turnkey still turned. I sat down at the table shaking my head. "Nate, what if you had gone feral in the middle of the night?"

"Then there'd have been no way I could have worked that wire. Feral zombies at most only turn handles." He sat down across from me.

Still shaking my head, I dug into my breakfast and savoured each sip of the coffee. Nate had gone all out—there were even sliced tomatoes. I took a piece of toast, bacon and tomato and made a half sandwich. Nate knew my weakness for BLTs. "And for all this spread, you expect no nevermind from me?"

"I was doing you a favour. I bet you didn't realize that door was so vulnerable."

I bit into my sandwich. I hated to admit it, but Nate had a point. "I'm changing that deadbolt model and adding a second one higher up," I said. He couldn't rig two of them at once, could he?

"I'm sorry for being a jerk last night and bailing on Lee. I shouldn't have done that and followed Mindy."

I gave him a stony stare as I ate. I'd believe Nate was giving up on his obsession with Mindy when I saw it. In the meantime I was enjoying the reprieve, and my breakfast.

"I'll even do the dishes," he added.

I snorted. Like I said, I'd believe it when I saw it. A few minutes of silence passed before Nate cleared his throat.

"So . . . what's been happening? Besides the lawyer asshole last night," Nate asked.

"Figuring out how to get you out of there." I finished my sandwich and Nate stared at me as if I'd said the new Demon Walker game was delayed. Scratch that, he'd be losing his shit if that game got delayed. Yet here we were talking about the rest of his rapidly dwindling afterlife as if it was a bothersome inconvenience. "Nate, I don't think you realize just how incredibly fucked you are if we can't figure this out."

"I'm more stable than Cameron was, you said yourself—"

"I said you don't have the sensitivity to Otherside that Cameron did." Or he didn't seem to. Whether it was the combination of Nate being a ghost or just the warping of Cameron's original bindings, Nate was stable when I pulled a globe—though he shouldn't be. I'd tested it ad nauseam.

Still, better safe than sorry. I closed my eyes and pulled back up my Otherside sight. It was visible any time I wanted thanks to my devil's deal with Gideon; I just had to focus on seeing it, otherwise it stayed in the background, kind of like white noise. The real benefit was that I didn't need to tap the barrier and pool Otherside into a globe every time I needed to see it. That's what had been taking such a toll on my body for the last few months.

I opened my eyes and looked at Nate. The tangled, uneven, warped mess of Otherside bindings flared a bright gold.

The problem with the bindings tying Nate to Cameron's old body was twofold. When I bind a ghost temporarily to their old body, as I had with Graeme last night, I leave an easy out, like the ends of a shoelace slipknot. Something I can grab on to and pull quickly so everything else unravels and the ghost is released, hopefully without too much burnout so they can spend the rest of their time on the Otherside doing whatever the hell it is ghosts like to do.

A permanent five-line zombie like Lee is a different matter. Her ghost had been inextricably bound to her body by her brother over a hundred years ago. The bindings between her ghost—or spirit, if you prefer—and her body were as unbreakable as they get. Zombies don't last forever, but they can go a few hundred years if the bindings are conservative in the way they burn Otherside, like Lee's were. It was one of the reasons I figured five-line zombies were illegal now. The conservative powers that be didn't like the idea of anyone lasting longer than their "god-given" lifespan—especially the undead. A well-crafted five-line zombie like Lee can function for 300-odd years, extending the average 150 years a ghost lasts, but once the Otherside is gone, that's it. There is no ghost left.

But a zombie's long life isn't a given. Any reanimation burns the spirit as fuel, and shoddy or amateurish work drains any zombie's ghost that much faster. When everything is used up, the bindings unravel and the corpse either drops or turns to dust.

Nate's bindings were burning more Otherside than I was comfortable with. As far as I could tell, Nate was bound to Cameron's body in a tangled mess of five-line and four-line bindings. He wasn't permanently stuck, but ensnarled just enough that I couldn't release him like I had Graeme last night.

My best guess was that Nate wasn't really a zombie—not in the sense that Cameron had been or Lee was, or even Graeme had been, albeit temporarily, last night. I suspected Nate was possessing Cameron's corpse the way a ghost can possess a pay phone . . . except there is no record of a ghost ever doing that with a body. In rare circumstances, poltergeists, the really strong, vindictive ones, can possess a body of the very ill or recently deceased. But they only ever manage to animate them for an hour or so at most, and it doesn't happen often.

Optimistically, I didn't give Nate much more than a month in there, if his body lasted that long—which I wasn't counting on, even with the formaldehyde. Worse, every time I'd tried to extract him, the bindings only seemed to tangle themselves up more, as if I was just adding to the knot holding Nate's ghost in place and burning his Otherside up in the process.

If I didn't get him out soon, there'd be no Nate left—and he either didn't care or didn't grasp the trouble he'd got himself into. . . .

There was a line off to the side, looped around Nate's ghost but fainter than the other heavier tangles, and wavering, reminding me of a guitar string. I hadn't noticed it before—or it hadn't been there. If I pulled it, it might release a few of the others and cause a cascade. One side effect of the warped mess was that Nate's bindings were more resistant to Otherside now than they had been, like a giant ball of knotted string. Meaning a little probing shouldn't do any harm.

I ran through my head the last time I'd tapped the barrier: besides last night, I'd only used Otherside one other time this week. I should be fine. . . . Cold Otherside seeped into my skull, chilling my face to the bone. There was a wave of nausea as I pooled it into a globe, but nowhere near as bad as it had been in the past. No chills or sweats.

Nate wrinkled his nose. "You're doing it again, aren't you?"

"Just sit still," I said, clenching my teeth as I reached out carefully with a stream of Otherside and tried to tease the wavering line out. For a moment it flickered and gave way. Before I could get a really good grip, it recoiled, snapping back like a rubber band. I swore and leaned back in my chair, defeated.

"Okay, this time that stung," Nate said, rubbing his eyes.

I brushed a black curl out of my face. Only a half-rate practitioner goes out of their way to explain something they don't understand. I'm experienced enough to know when I'm out of my depth. Again. Just like with Cameron. And this time there was no Max to help me out. "We need to talk to Lee." I narrowed my eyes. "Nate, if there is anything else you remember about getting tangled up in Cameron's body, anything, even the smallest detail . . ."

He tried to run his hand through his hair, but it got tangled in Cameron's longer, oily locks. "Nothing, K," he said, though he avoided eye contact with me.

I shook my head and went to the freezer to retrieve a Thermos of brains and place it on the counter. It was a mixture of cow and human brains with a strong dose of formaldehyde thrown in. Formaldehyde "fixes" tissue, preserving the proteins that make up skin and organs. It is exceptionally good at stopping the more aggressive decomposition that had already begun to plague Cameron before he'd, well, not died—abandoned? Unfortunately, formaldehyde has some nasty side effects. Namely, it yellows the skin and adds a dusky-grey sheen to everything else—eyes, hair, lips. A few more doses and Nate's body would be more stable, but it also wouldn't pass for human. Not unless he confined himself to darkly lit corners.

"I'm going to see Aaron—apparently he has a job for me. With luck I'll only be a few hours," I told him.

"Got it, K," Nate said, taking the first of the dishes to the sink. "Want me on cellphone duty?"

I shot him another look as I headed into the bathroom to take a much-needed shower. "What I want is for you to stay in this apartment and be ready to go see Lee when I get back." Lee was going to talk to me and evaluate Nate if I had to drag him into her place myself and prop him up on the creosote-soaked bar. "And stay away from the bathroom. I have no idea how often Gideon checks that mirror."

"Will do, K. I promise. No screw-ups this time."

A too-short steam-filled shower later, I threw on jeans, a fresh T-shirt, and my leather jacket before grabbing my Honda Hawk and helmet. I always kept the bike in my apartment, as I didn't trust my neighbours and the garage downstairs. Besides, the freight elevator in the converted warehouse made it easy to bring up, so why not? I locked the door behind me, loudly, emphasizing my point to Nate to stay inside. I shook my head as I headed down the hall to the elevator. Nate wasn't completely oblivious to the severity of the situation—he wasn't as dense or selfish as he let on—but for whatever reason he was playing dumb. Now, whether that was for his benefit or mine . . .

I shelved that one. Worrying about what the hell was going on in Nate's head was going to get me nowhere. Sometimes I wondered if even Nate knew what the hell was going on in his head.

I texted Aaron on the elevator ride down to see where he wanted to meet. Time to find out exactly what kind of work he'd scared up for me.

"You're still sore about the serial murder case," Aaron said as he led me to the cold case file room, a broom closet in the bowels of the police station. He was dressed casually in a red rain jacket—there was a chill in the basement—and jeans. I wondered if the informality was to put me at ease.

"They didn't even call me."

He glanced at me over his shoulder. "Did you apply?"

"No."

"Then how would they have known you were interested?"

"By looking for the most qualified candidate?"

He made a disparaging noise. "It doesn't work that way, Kincaid."

I couldn't believe it. I'd been here five minutes and already Aaron was criticizing me. "That's how they found Liam," I said, not bothering to keep the bitterness out of my voice.

"You mean Liam Sinclair? Doesn't count, he's on TV."

"And look where that got them. Jesus, between you and Nathan."

"Why?" When I didn't answer, Aaron looked up from the back door he'd stopped in front of. "What did Nathan have to say about it?"

"Nothing . . . exactly, just insinuated I carry some of the responsibility in my presentation, or lack thereof." Aaron frowned at me and I added, "Never mind. What did you want me to look at?"

Instead of answering, he opened the door. I craned my neck to gaze at the familiar rows of cardboard boxes stacked in twos and crammed onto metal shelves that went all the way up to the ceiling of the narrow room. So many unsolved crimes marking the ends of people's lives packed into these small boxes. . . . I knew them well. This was how I'd mostly been working for the Seattle PD—seeing which of the dead in here I could track down on the Otherside—looking to them for clues to solve their own cold cases.

But I hadn't been in this room. It was an offshoot, the place where they sent the cold cases deemed hopeless, or worse—a deserved fate. The ones that no one wanted to work on, because no one cared. Like *The Island of Lost Toys*, a Christmas special I remembered from back when I was a kid . . .

I glanced over at Aaron, who was standing by the door doing his best not to crowd me.

"Not exactly what you were expecting?" he asked when our eyes met.

I shrugged. "At least it's not a crime scene."

"No, I wouldn't do that to you—not so soon after . . ." He trailed off. We had an unspoken rule not to talk about Max, or Randall, or Cameron. Weird from someone who handled corpses, ghosts and zombies on a regular basis. I'll be the first to admit it made me feel like a bit of a wimp, and I forced myself to shake the feeling off.

Who the hell was I to be uptight about the dead? Even when it was people I knew . . .

"Not that I don't like cold cases, Aaron, but you want to explain how you got shackled with one of these?" I said, gesturing at the dusty boxes.

He inclined his head. "I'm on thin ice with Marks for the murdered practitioners. He's got me combing these."

"You solved the murders."

"You actually get credit for solving the murders, not that it matters who did. It was a supernatural case that made the news. It very publicly and spectacularly sidelined the captain's plans to completely shut down the city's paranormal divisions. Some of the politicians and captains from other precincts are now complaining that it's unrealistic, what with poltergeist season coming up." He sighed and shook his head. "Never mind the department politics. Let's just say I stumbled onto something in here I want your opinion on."

I crossed my arms and leaned against the metal rack. "You need me to wrangle a ghost to look into a cold case?"

"In a manner of speaking." He grabbed a box, one that had had the dust brushed off it recently, and carried it into the slightly larger archives room.

I followed, relieved to be out of the claustrophobic closet. Summoning murder victims was decidedly in the paranormal wheelhouse. "Somehow I doubt the captain lifted the moratorium on my consulting contract."

"No, he didn't, but I need some information from Nathan." He placed the box on a table and began to unpack the files.

I narrowed my eyes. "Aaron, Nathan is a ghost. By definition, that's paranormal."

Aaron grunted in acknowledgement as he removed a series of files from the box. It was then I noticed a second one on the table. Another old cold case from the yellowed cardboard that had also had the dust recently brushed off it. One that had been examined recently. My curiosity was piqued.

"Not exactly, but we'll get to that one in a minute." He handed me one of the manila folders. "Before this man died, he was a semi-successful Seattle musician on the grunge scene during the mid-nineties."

Damien Fell was typed in the folder margin. I looked back up at Aaron and shook my head. "It doesn't ring a bell."

"It wouldn't. He was a member of Cadmium Coffee, a grunge band that made some headway in the bar scene and got some radio play—nothing that made them any money, but that was more due to circumstances of bad luck." He tapped the file, prompting me to open it.

I cut my eyes at Aaron, wondering what angle he was running. Might as well kill the cat. I flipped the cream-coloured folder open to the first page.

The life of Damien Fell made for light reading. No juvenile record, but no exceptional academic performance to speak of either. He'd finished high school in 1991 and entered a music programme at a university in Utah. A couple of years later he'd up and left his programme and moved to Seattle for the grunge scene.

There were clippings of four or five magazine articles spanning 1993 to late 1995. Reviews of shows mostly, and mention of a few songs off a demo album that had garnered radio play. Hard to do for an indie band back before YouTube and the Internet. One thing all the reviewers agreed on was that Cadmium Coffee had no shortage of talent, and that it was only a matter of time before they were signed to a big label. Finally, I pulled out a typed list of all the venues Cadmium Coffee had played over their short-lived career. It was a long list, and I recalled Nate mentioning a few of them. They had been popular spots for new bands in the nineties.

Another grunge band that had everything going for it but never made it. Not unique, if it wasn't for the fact that they'd been critically acclaimed, and had some commercial success to boot. I thought I remembered one of their songs—might even have it buried in my old CD collection, relegated to the one-hit-wonder pile. . . .

I glanced up at Aaron, who was watching me go through the folder. "So what happened?"

Aaron leaned over, close enough I picked up the scent of his amber-tinged cologne, and sorted through the pieces until he found what he was looking for—not a magazine article but a newspaper clipping. "December 5, 1995, Damien Fell was found dead of a heroin overdose."

I skimmed the article. There had been a rash of deaths between October and December 1995 from a batch of heroin that was more pure than it had any right to be. Eventually the dealers caught on—it's a big problem if your income source starts dropping dead in large numbers—and began diluting the heroin. But it became clear from the death toll that it had been a large batch and the distribution had been extensive. There had been one hundred deaths from drug overdoses in three months, a record, and those were just the ones that were reported. Damien had the honour of being the most newsworthy of the bunch.

"No offence, Aaron, but a musician in the mid-nineties dying of a heroin overdose isn't exactly an anomaly. How did you get roped in?"

"His family contacted me."

I shot him a sideways glance. "After twenty years? What on earth prompted that?"

"Never mind. I want to get your feeling for the case first."

I frowned as I read through the coroner's report. Aaron's insistence on getting a cold read off me was irritating. I understood his reasoning—he didn't want a bias influencing my opinion—but it also left me not knowing what I was looking for. It wasn't the first and it wouldn't be the last time. "They classified it as accidental overdose. Why is it even here? It shouldn't be a cold case," I said.

Aaron smiled. "Unusual circumstances."

"Such as?"

"Keep reading."

I did as he suggested. Much of the report was run-of-the-mill, except for an odd note near the end. "His body was found in a pool of water, his clothes soaked through," I said to Aaron. "Any idea why?"

He smiled. "Not a clue."

"Suspicious, but by no means a smoking gun. He could have spilled it, or stepped out of the shower before he collapsed to the kitchen floor. Overdosing while wet doesn't equal foul play."

Aaron made a face. "That's not all, and initially I had the same reaction. His family contacted me a couple weeks ago asking me to reopen the case. His mother is terminally ill, and . . ." He trailed off and sighed at the incredulous look I gave him. "Call it intuition or a gut feeling—or maybe she caught me at a vulnerable moment."

That surprised me. Aaron was sympathetic, but he wasn't one to let it cloud his judgment on a case. Then again, maybe even Aaron couldn't turn a blind eye to a dying parent's request.

As if reading my mind, he added, "I don't have a lot to lose professionally, looking into it, do I?" He nodded at the file. "His mother was adamant he couldn't have overdosed. They also claimed he'd never done drugs. It's all in there."

I shook my head but flipped the pages. Sure enough, there were testimonies from his family. "They do that—lie to themselves." They lie harder than the addicts, in my experience.

"Except in this case, Damien was Mormon. Devout."

I glanced back up.

"Practising. When they searched his apartment and the studio, they found no alcohol, painkillers—not even tea or coffee."

All right, I'd give it to Aaron that it was odd, but people with addictions were good at hiding them. Even from themselves . . . An uncomfortable shiver ran down my spine as I thought about my own brush with, well, not addiction in the conventional sense, but something that verged on it. Thinking of Otherside brought Gideon to mind, and I shoved that unpleasant thought aside for later. The point was, there were always consequences.

"Up-and-coming musician who refused to touch caffeine overdoses on heroin? Don't tell me you aren't intrigued. This is right up your alley, Kincaid. Suspicious death, no overt signs of foul play," Aaron continued.

If I could find him he'd be an easy ghost to call and question. Accidental or not, non-traumatic deaths didn't carry the same level of baggage as violent murders and suicides, which Aaron knew.

"The circumstances are curious, I'll give you that, but there's nothing here to suggest foul play—no motive, no enemies, no debts, dumped girlfriends, ex-bandmates. Everyone liked the guy."

Aaron's mouth twitched up at the corner. I recognized that tic.

"You do have a motive?" The tic turned into a smile. "Spit it out, Aaron."

He pulled the lid off the second box on the desk. He removed a series of newspaper clippings from a folder and spread them out on the table. I took a closer look and went cold. It was Nathan's box—his body had never been found, so there was still a cold case on him, though it was no mystery how he'd died. "What does Nate have to do with this?"

"The heroin that killed Damien? It's a match to the one in here, the one that was found amongst Nathan's things. I double-checked them yesterday. That's why I called you."

"Not that unheard of. Probably had the same dealer."

"Three years later? Nathan died in 1998." He retrieved two articles—one from Nate's pile and the second from Damien's folder. The latter was promoting a 1996 New Year's show at the Cage, the venue where record producers would have seen Cadmium Coffee for the first time. Damien Fell died weeks before that show and the band hadn't been able to find another singer in time. I looked at the article from Nate's pile, which was from two weeks later, a write-up showing who would be replacing Cadmium: Dead Men. It was the show where Nate and his band had got their big break. They'd only been asked to perform because most other bands had already been booked.

"It's a coincidence," I said.

"It's called motive."

I stared at Aaron, incredulous. "You think Nate killed another musician for a gig?" I didn't know whether to be furious or laugh.

There was no way. Nate was a lot of things—more than a few of them uncomplimentary—but he was not a murderer. I'd stake my reputation on that.

"I'm not accusing anyone," Aaron said, holding up his hands. "What I'm saying is that Nathan and other people in his band stood to benefit from Damien's incredibly timely death."

I took a deep breath. "It's a lot of straws. If Damien was murdered to take him out of the competition, then why hold on to a lethal batch of heroin?" I asked Aaron.

"I never said it was Nathan. I said the same batch of lethal heroin that killed Damien was found amongst his things. Accidents happen. Nathan could have found it, or maybe Damien was killed for a different reason. What if the same person who had gotten rid of Damien decided Nathan had outlived his usefulness? Or wanted to implicate him?"

"Now who has the overactive imagination?"

Aaron shook his head. "Once a person makes their first kill, the second is always easier—especially if they don't get caught."

Like a dog that bites for the first time and learns that biting isn't a half-bad problem-solver.

"Okay, so someone possibly hoarded a bad batch of heroin for nefarious purposes. It's twenty years later, Nate drowned—"

"We don't know that. We never found the body, so there was never an autopsy."

"No, we have Nate's ghost and witnesses who say that's what happened. But still, you're looking for what? Someone who might have passed around lethal doses of heroin in 1995?"

"Will you help or not?"

I did not want to get involved in this right now, but if Aaron really wanted to chase this lead with Nate's old band, he'd want to talk to Nate . . . which would be worse. Nate was a zombie—a highly illegal zombie. It didn't matter how sympathetic Aaron was to the paranormal community, he wouldn't, *couldn't*, work around Nate. Agreeing to help Aaron now was easier than having him kick down my door looking for my delinquent ghost of a roommate. "Yes, god help me, I'll help you. I'll ask Nate about this and see if I can scare up Damien's ghost, but I think you're bored and looking for a zebra to explain the hoofprints in Central Park." But then again, Nate had proven on more than one occasion he could be observant and insightful. Maybe he would remember something useful.

"Which is why I need your help. Find out from Nathan if he knew Damien and if anyone held a grudge. Also if he remembers the heroin and where he got it from."

"If I contact a ghost as part of a case, it won't be admissible evidence."

"I'm not hiring a paranormal investigator," Aaron said, smiling. "I'm hiring the biggest Nathan Cade expert in Seattle."

I sighed. "Even for you, that's pushing it." A murder mystery from over twenty years ago around grunge rock. If the right people found out in the media . . . "So this is part of your great plan to get back at the captain? Be more trouble in cold cases than you were solving real crimes?"

"Works for you."

"Have I ever mentioned that my personal brand of bullshit usually gets me in trouble? As in *fired*?"

Aaron put both his hands on the desk and leaned towards me. "What if I told you I don't care anymore?" There was an uncharacteristic intensity in his eyes.

I looked at him. Really looked at him. "Aaron, I know you feel that way now. I sympathize. I know what it's like to be screwed over—"

"I'm sick and tired of it."

"But it will pass. You're a good detective, and you, unlike me, are capable of acting professionally."

"Are you trying to tell me this is a phase?"

I shrugged my shoulders. Not exactly, but if the shoe fit . . .

Aaron looked perturbed. "You're the one who's been telling me for the past three months to stick up for what I think is right. I didn't expect you of all people to tell me to back down."

No kidding. "Look, Aaron, you're right, I have said that, but—" What? I'd been upset? I didn't believe that anymore? I'd moved on? That one unsettled me; it also rang true. "I think you've spent too much time and energy salvaging your career to throw it away over a setback."

His frown deepened. "Now you're sounding like me."

I realized Aaron had never taken a hit from the policy change before, not really. *I'd* taken the hit while he watched. Part of me wanted to say that he was being a hypocrite. I didn't, though.

I've always been one to avoid polite confrontation. I wait until things get ugly. Years of ingrained experience and bad examples.

I nodded at the pile of files. "Get me copies of those if you can." If there had been a murder—and I wasn't all that certain there had been—I'd want to contact Damien myself and see whether he'd really been the teetotaller everyone claimed. I'd hand it to Aaron that the heroin and the pool of water were unusual, but there might be a very simple, straightforward explanation to both. If you find a hoofprint in Central Park, look for a horse, not a zebra.

"Kincaid?"

I glanced back at Aaron. "Don't worry. I'll ask Nate and see if I can scare up Damien."

"No—I mean, yes—please ask Nate for anything he knows." Aaron looked awkward for a moment. "I wanted to see if you were free Saturday night."

"Ah—maybe. Why?"

"I wondered if you wanted to see a movie." He shifted his feet. "Maybe grab dinner?"

If I didn't know better, I'd say Aaron was nervous asking me out—which was strange for a whole cache of reasons.

For a week following the shit show in Randall's bar, I'd been in a bad way. Aaron had been over a few times and I'd appreciated the company and someone to watch movie reruns with. But I hadn't called or talked to him since Nate had shown up.

"Maybe next week? I'm still trying to get things back on track." I wasn't lying, but it felt like I was leaving something out.

Aaron nodded. He walked me upstairs and out back to where I'd parked my bike and waited until I was about to start the engine.

"I meant what I said—about trying to do better. And see you this Saturday."

Three months ago I would have given a lot to hear that. Now? I nodded to Aaron before sliding on my helmet and turning on my bike. There was something seriously wrong with me.

I needed to gather my thoughts about Aaron's case and Nate, so I grabbed a coffee near Pike Place and sat at a wire garden table outside. It was cold, but the sun was out for once. In Seattle you take what sunny days you can get, especially in October. I sipped my coffee and worried about what to do if Aaron wanted an interview with Nate, considering Nate couldn't even talk on the phone right now . . . not with his voice, at any rate.

I shoved the strange circumstances surrounding Damien's death to the back of my mind. It was circumstantial. Nate had got drunk and high and fallen off the back of his yacht, he'd said so himself. Aaron was grasping for something to do now that the captain had effectively iced him.

Whether or not his suspicions were justified, I still needed to get to the library and then drag Nate to the underground city. I checked my phone: 11:00. Plenty of time to do both.

I yelped as something heated up in my pocket. I reached in to feel my compact mirror—the one I'd stashed in there to keep in contact with Nate when he was still a ghost. I yanked it out and flipped it open, to see a message scrawling across the glass.

Time for us to talk, little practitioner.

"Shit," I said. There was a loud shush behind me. I swore again before covering my mouth and glancing over my shoulder. A woman with two kids shot me a dirty look and I mouthed sorry. Damn it, Kincaid, clean up your language.

I turned my attention back to the message from Gideon and sat there for a moment, paralyzed. He knew, he had to know. I steadied my shaking finger enough to scrawl back, *About what—and when?*

About our arrangement, what else? And now would be appropriate.
Shit. *Right now?*
Yes, right now.

I looked around. Not the ideal spot to talk business with a temperamental ghost. "All right, just not here. I'm in the middle of a coffee shop," I whispered into the mirror.

There was a pause. *You have twenty minutes to get home. I'll meet you at your set mirror. Do not be late.*

The message erased itself and the heat dissipated from my compact. I downed what was left of the coffee even though it burned my throat, and headed for my bike. I needed to get home and hide Nate before Gideon showed up—or two of us would be dead.

CHAPTER 4

NO REST FOR THE WICKED

Come on, pick up, pick up . . . I bal-
anced my cell between my ear and shoulder as I manoeuvred my
bike through the back door of my building, an old warehouse by
the docks that had been converted into apartments for artists in
the 1960s. I guided my bike around the various art installations
in the lobby's makeshift gallery.

It wasn't until I was in the elevator that Nate picked up.

"Hey, K," Nate said.

"Took you long enough," I said, closing the gate behind me and
pushing the third-floor button a few more times than I needed to.

"Nice to hear from you too."

"No time. Seriously, Nate, I need you to hide. Gideon is coming."

There were several broken expletives from his end as the signal
faded out. "I'm locking myself in the spare bedroom."

"Too close— Nate? Damn it." I swore as the connection cut
completely and shoved my phone back in my pocket. Gideon might
be a ghost, but he was the powerful ghost of a sorcerer. I had no

intention of playing Russian roulette with his ability to sense Nate's warped bindings.

The elevator door opened to my floor and I rushed to my door. I may have set a record for getting the damn lock open while negotiating the bike.

Nate jumped up from the kitchen table as I flung open the door.

"I thought I told you to hide?" I whispered, leaning my bike against the wall. I flinched as it gouged the paint.

"You said not to hide in the spare. Besides, I don't feel anything—Hey!" he said as I shoved past him and took stock of my apartment.

"You're not a ghost anymore, Nate." A ghost might feel a shift in Otherside a few rooms away, but a zombie wouldn't. Besides, Gideon was a sorcerer, and we didn't know exactly what he was capable of.

The spare bedroom was too close to the bathroom. I could set a couple of sticks of sage smoke going in there with Nate, which would help cover up the Otherside from his bindings, but what if Gideon caught the scent of that? My bedroom was better, but still too close. Outside the apartment would be best, but I couldn't stick him in the hall—someone might see him and ask questions.

"Come on." I dragged Nate into my bedroom and unlocked the bolts on the window.

"K, I'll freeze out there!"

I snatched a wool blanket from the end of my bed and threw it at Nate before running back towards the entrance and grabbing his coat, hat and Converse shoes. I tossed them all onto the fire escape platform. "You'll be a lot worse than frozen if Gideon picks up on your bindings and decides to investigate."

Nate swore but obliged, shuffling himself out my window and tripping over the thick sill—a remnant from the original warehouse.

I held out my hand. "And fork over your phone."

"I need that."

"So you can stalk your ex?"

He swore again as he forked it over. I didn't trust Nate right now not to call Mindy. I suspected he'd already done it a few times, and a quick look at the call history confirmed this. All just a few seconds—enough to let her pick up and say hello a few times . . . "One complaint is all Aaron needs."

"Fine. I'm on my best behaviour—promise, K," he said, crossing his heart.

"Now stay there," I said, once he was crouched on the metal grate, the blanket wrapped over his shoulders.

"For just how the fuck long do you expect me to sit here?"

"As long as it takes to get rid of Gideon." I shut the window and pulled the curtains closed. I felt a little guilty shutting Nate outside but smothered it. It was a problem of his own damn making.

I headed back into the kitchen-living room and turned around, looking to see if there was anything I'd missed. I spotted a bottle of formaldehyde along with a cooler on the counter. I swore and shoved them both under the sink. I'd have to yell at Nate about that later. . . .

There was a change in the air, like an electric charge, and the inside of my nose felt chilled.

I focused on seeing Otherside, and found a loose trail of it leading from me towards the bathroom.

Gideon. His version of beckoning, I imagined.

I took a deep breath and willed my heart rate to return to normal. No sense getting worked up now. This was my screw-up to own up to and fix.

Well, that, and the fact that ghosts can smell fear . . .

The bathroom door was closed—I'd been leaving it that way for obvious reasons. Tentatively, I touched the door handle and gasped as a shock of ice shot up my arm.

Gideon was just trying to unnerve me. I shouldn't be surprised. One thing I knew from our brief acquaintance was that he loved his entrances. I wrapped my sleeve around my hand before grabbing the handle a second time.

As soon as I cracked the door open, the scent of cold ozone hit me—or that was the closest description I'd come up with for the Otherside that followed Gideon everywhere. I scanned the small bathroom, but besides the scent and the trail of Otherside leading to the mirror, there was no sign of him.

"There's no point lurking there," came Gideon's voice from inside the bathroom. I recognized the slight accent, one I couldn't quite place but suspected was from somewhere in Europe—one of the cold, northern parts.

"I already told you—I'm not going to kill you," he said.

Yeah, and that left an awful lot of ground to cover . . . Still, standing in the doorway was pointless and probably pissing him off. I stepped inside.

I caught a glimpse of his face in the bathroom mirror, then it disappeared. Less than a second passed before a white fog coalesced before me as Gideon, evil sorcerer's ghost extraordinaire, materialized—as much as a ghost can materialize.

I don't know if it was my imagination or Gideon's effect, but I could have sworn the temperature in the room dropped a few degrees. I'd met him only a few short weeks ago after encountering Cameron, who had been part of a deal between Gideon and my old mentor, Max. A trade, if you will. Gideon offered help for Cameron's struggle with addiction and his painting in exchange for—well . . . his body, eventually. Needless to say Cameron's murder had complicated the deal—and triggered Gideon's search for his payment: Cameron's empty body.

I'd taken issue with the deal—mostly due to the fact that Cameron, in zombie form, couldn't remember striking it.

I tend to keep to myself and not pass judgment on others. Easiest way to stay out of trouble is to stay out of the way of people—and ghosts—who are more powerful than you. Or, failing that, make an effort to stay on their good side.

But after everything that had happened—Max, Cameron, Randall . . .

I just couldn't let it go. Why is it my moral compass has to rear its ugly head when it has the greatest potential to wound me?

And so here we were: Gideon, still angry about the body I'd stolen from him, the one he thought I'd left to burn in Randall's basement—the same one Nate now inhabited; and me, now in the uncomfortable position of being in debt to a powerful sorcerer. A sorcerer's ghost, I corrected myself. Still powerful, and I was pretty certain more homicidal than the live version . . .

I recognized his clothes, the same ones he'd been wearing when I first saw him, lurking in a set mirror stowed in my building lobby. He wore leather pants and a leather jacket that would have looked more appropriate on an actor in a Renaissance play than a ghost. Though the colours were probably supposed to be black or dark brown, they were dulled with a grey cast that Otherside seems to paint over all ghosts. Even his close-cropped blond hair and pale skin had a grey cast. Regardless of how corporeal he could make himself look, the ghost-grey sheen was always present.

Except for right now. His normally ghost-grey eyes were a glittering black. They were Gideon's most striking feature, and a tell that he was angry. I felt my resolve not to show fear waver as he stared. Steady, Kincaid, steady.

I counted three breaths as we stood there, neither of us saying or doing anything except watching the other, while the temperature dropped another few icy degrees and I reconsidered the whole running-to-another-city idea.

Scrap that. Gideon would eventually find me wherever I ran.

"We need to come to an agreement," he finally said, breaking the tension.

"About?"

He sneered. "About how you plan to pay me back for stealing Cameron's body."

That took me aback. I wasn't sure if I should be happy that Gideon was willing to negotiate or terrified. I checked behind me to see if the door had closed or if an animated electrical appliance cord had appeared. Gideon had twice tried to strangle me—once with a string of patio lights, the other with a hairdryer cord.

"What exactly did you have in mind?" I said, keeping my voice as even and measured as I could.

Gideon *tsk*ed. "I already told you, I have no intention of killing you. Otherwise, you'd have seen me much sooner than now."

And that there was the other significant detail I couldn't quite get my head around. Why the hell hadn't Gideon just let me burn in Randall's cellar? Why bother saving me? I'd be lying if I said that question hadn't kept me up at night these past few weeks.

Gideon lowered his head. It wasn't a comforting gesture—more like a predator stalking prey. "My proposal is very simple, Kincaid. Due to recent events, I find myself in need of an assistant."

I rolled the wording over in my head and licked my dry lips. "I already agreed to run errands for you." That was how I'd paid for the ability to see Otherside without tapping the barrier. . . .

He *tsk*ed again. "I'm well aware you already agreed to run errands for me, something you have yet to deliver on. This would be in addition to my errands. I'm afraid that ever since that fiasco with Max, I require an assistant for my other works."

His other works. Trading things, with both the living and the dead—specifically, finding something you couldn't live without and figuring out a way to offer it to you. The proverbial devil's deal. It made me feel sick and slimy all over. After all, he'd figured out what to offer me.

"What would it involve? Being your assistant, that is," I asked, ill at ease at the idea of wading further into Gideon's particular brand of quicksand.

He shrugged. "Lots of things. Delivering messages, acquiring supplies are a given. Anything and everything I need you to do that my current form makes difficult."

Not an answer—an evasion. "So that would be it? Running messages and fetching you supplies?"

"Of course not. I will also require your help setting the foundations for my spells. That's what sorcerer's assistants do, or so I've been led to believe these last few centuries."

Sorcery. He wanted my help with sorcery. I tried to swallow, but my mouth had gone dry.

I'm an accomplished practitioner. I channel Otherside from

across the barrier and use it to animate the dead or set mirrors so I can talk to ghosts. Otherside is from the place where the dead go, where ghosts live; using it to bring them across and animate them isn't outside the natural order of things. It's not without its risks, as I'd recently learned, but it tends not to make things blow up. As far as I'd been able to glean from Lee and from Gideon himself, sorcery also uses Otherside, but where practitioners use it within the bounds of the afterlife, sorcery is the manipulation of Otherside to alter the order of the natural world. A sorcerer warps Otherside until it does whatever the sorcerer damn well wants.

"I'm not a sorcerer," I said.

Gideon's lip twitched. "Sorceress. And clearly. That is why I'm proposing an apprenticeship."

No way. If there was one thing I'd learned from my bodily decline over these last few months, it was that I did not need to use more Otherside. "Gideon, there's got to be something else—" I started.

He made an impatient noise. "Oh, will you stop panicking. You wouldn't be practising real sorcery—not to start, anyway. I'll give you that you're a talented practitioner, but no one is that talented and I'm not stupid. The basis of most sorcery spells involves simple Otherside bindings as groundwork. The manipulation comes later, and requires a trained sorcerer."

Okay, better. But still—putting myself in a position where I'd be seeing Gideon—what? Day in, day out? Not exactly an appealing option . . .

As if sensing my reluctance, Gideon added, "I've thought long and hard on this these last two weeks, Kincaid. You have nothing else of value I want, and your debt to me is substantial." He lowered his head again. "And expensive. Trust me, you can't afford it. I already looked."

The prospect of working with—no, *for*—Gideon was making my head spin, and something bothered me about the proposal. "I've already gone back on my word once. I didn't deliver you Cameron. What makes you so sure I'll hold up my end of the deal this time?"

Gideon gave me a slow smile. "Simple. Because you know me well enough to never do that again."

"Why, because you'll kill me?"

There was that glittering, predatory stare again. "No. You value your own life very little, I've decided—but those around you? The ones you call friends? The zombie who runs the underground city; the detective you hold dear and his partner; your ghost." He leaned in until his face was only inches from mine, close enough that I could feel the chill from his corporeal form. "Do not think I can't find them at a moment's notice."

I thought about what would happen if I didn't agree to his proposal and Gideon took it upon himself to track down Nate. It was the rock and a hard place I'd been worried about. Or the bear in the tree with the cougar waiting below might be a more appropriate analogy. "How long?"

Gideon inclined his head.

"This is to clear my debt to you for scuttling your body, correct? How long until it's paid off?"

He pursed his ghost-grey lips before saying, "Six months. To start."

I sucked in my breath. "To *start*?"

"And that doesn't include the errands you've agreed to run for me in exchange for the Otherside sight you've been making so much use of these past few weeks. Don't think I hadn't noticed. And with regards to the term, not everyone takes to sorcery. Though I suspect you can, *provided* you apply yourself, which—mark my words—is an *absolute* requirement of this deal. Consider the six months a trial period."

I closed my eyes. Six months. To start. I had to pay off my debt, and I knew Gideon kept his word. He might not be nice about it, but he always delivered on his bargains. Which meant if he promised to hunt me down and exact revenge, he'd do it.

Why the hell did morals and ethics have to be so expensive—or why were mine?

"What about after the trial period?"

"If I find you do not suit my purposes, then our lessons end. You'll spend the next five years performing only the most basic Otherside workings."

"*Fuck me*, five years!" I covered my mouth as soon as it was out.

Gideon's eyes flashed from their normal ghost-grey blue to black. "I'm being generous," he said carefully.

I pushed on. "And if I do suit your purposes?"

He smiled, and his eyes shifted back to a ghost-grey blue. "Then you will serve as my apprentice for the next year and a half, in *my* definition of the word. Mandatory lessons and Otherside bindings at whichever hour I require."

There was a real incentive to work at the sorcery thrown in there, I'd give him that: I'd be out of my deal in two years. "And after that?"

"We re-evaluate. I'll decide if it is worthwhile to continue instructing you and you can decide whether you want to continue. We can determine terms then."

I racked my brain for other reasons to reject Gideon's proposal. It would help if the son of a bitch weren't so good at making his deals seem reasonable. "What about sorcery being dangerous?" I asked.

"You'll be working under my instruction, and none of my apprentices have even managed to blow themselves up—you would be the very first." There was that smile again.

Two years . . . I took another deep breath to calm my nerves. This wasn't making a new deal; this was settling the terms of my debt, terms that didn't involve Gideon killing me and everyone I cared about. So why did part of me feel as though I was making a huge mistake? Lee's warning about not trusting or making deals with Gideon rose in my mind.

"I'll work for you, under your terms, *but* I have some ground rules."

Gideon arched a ghost-grey eyebrow. "And they are?"

Here's hoping I'd manage to cover all the bases . . . "First, I'm not killing anyone for you or delivering any body parts."

Gideon made a derisive noise. "I wouldn't rule out the body parts."

"I'm serious, Gideon."

There were those glittering black eyes again. "And so am I. You've already ruined my arrangements once. Might I add that you've already benefited from our deal?"

Not fair. I'd been desperate. "Offering people something they can't possibly refuse—"

"Is fantastic business. Everything has a price, Kincaid. You're deluding yourself if you think otherwise. Might I remind you other people's choices are not yours to make?"

I closed my eyes. He was right. I'd had no control over Cameron's deal with Gideon. The agreement had been witnessed by Max and signed by Cameron while he'd been of sound mind.

"It's the taking advantage of people's weaknesses that I can't stomach. It's like pushing a drug."

Gideon's expression lightened and a slight smile played at his mouth. "I'm good, but I'm not that good. My spells and bindings are hardly a drug."

Unbelievable. Still . . . I crossed my arms and glared at Gideon. I wasn't budging on the not-killing-people clause.

Gideon rolled his eyes. "I'm in a generous mood. Fine, your term is acceptable, minus body parts. I don't need you to kill anyone for me. I'm perfectly capable of doing that on my own. What else? I can tell from the way you're fidgeting you have more clauses."

I gave myself a moment to figure out the wording. . . . "I won't do anything that goes against my ethics."

Gideon snorted. "Such as? Clearly, breaking agreements isn't one of them."

I ignored the barb and started counting off the ones that really worried me. "Enslaving people, creating weapons or diseases that could wipe out whole populations, torturing cats—those kinds of things."

"No. I'm neither inclined nor willing to ask every client what they want a spell for. I will agree to not involve you directly in client interactions you might find distasteful, but once I give you a task, I expect it to be completed."

Shit. Well, I'd been aiming high with that one.

Now for my final condition: this was the make-or-break clause. "No more using my friends to coerce me into doing something I don't want to."

· "Quid pro quo. You uphold your end of the bargain and I won't have to. If you don't?" He shrugged. "I can agree not to hold them over your head for minor infractions of our agreement, but the overall threat remains." The temperature in the room dropped again, and I couldn't resist rubbing my frozen arms. "If you go back on your word and break this agreement, mark my words, I *will* kill everyone you've ever cared about. And I've made sure there's something special in store for those that are already dead."

"I agree," I said, before Gideon could offer me any more visuals. Two years as an assistant. I'd imagined much worse.

Gideon's face was unreadable as he watched me. He held out his hand and gestured for me to take it.

I hesitated.

"It won't hurt—much—but considering your previous transgressions in our dealings, I require more than just your word. I'm sure you understand."

I couldn't stop my hand from shaking as I reached out. His hand wasn't solid, but the Otherside had condensed to give it an icy cold weight. Gideon said something I didn't catch, and gold threads of Otherside began to weave their way around my wrist. I gasped as they stung my skin with burning cold. I tried to pull back, but Gideon's grip was viselike.

"What is this?" I asked, unable to keep the quaver out of my voice.

"Sorcery," Gideon said. "And it's essentially the terms of our agreement being set. A six-month trial period of you working as my apprentice, after which we will decide on another four and a half years as a practitioner or a year and a half as my full apprentice. For that six months you *will* apply yourself to the tasks I give you, at whatever hour and time I request. A grace period of one hour will be applied when my need of you conflicts with your own work this side of the barrier. None of my tasks will require you to kill anyone and I will attempt to consider your particular ethical sensitivities. I will also not seek to harm or threaten your friends.

"However, if you willfully breach this contract," Gideon continued, "I will take my vengeance out on everyone you ever cared about, including the dead." His eyes flashed more gold than black for a moment and he squeezed my hand tighter. "Agreed?"

"Agreed," I whispered.

And just like that, with one word, the Otherside bindings stopped their undulating movement around my wrists and settled on my skin. It was like watching a horror movie in slow motion, except I was the victim.

"Son of a bitch!" I shouted out as they seared into my skin. Like hell it didn't hurt much. I tried to pull away, but Gideon wouldn't let go, not until the last gold thread had burrowed itself into my wrist.

When he did release me, I took a step back and looked at my arm. I could see the bindings glowing just under the surface of my skin. They weren't like zombie or ghost bindings, or even the ones around my eyes granting me Otherside sight, which all hover on the surface. These ones branded my flesh.

"Son of a fucking bitch!" Sorcery, my ass. I grabbed my wrist and put pressure on it. It still burned. "What the hell was that?" I said, shooting Gideon a vicious look.

"The pain will fade. And it does something unpleasant if you attempt to break your word or our deal." He leaned across my small bathroom sink, glaring at me. "And don't ever do that again."

"Do what?"

"Break away from a casting. They all hurt when they're cast, but it fades. You'll have to learn to live with it. Understood?"

I glared at Gideon, not able or inclined to hide my anger. "You could have warned me a little more accurately," I said.

"You might have said no. Easier to ask forgiveness."

I snorted at the idea of Gideon asking for forgiveness for anything. I yanked my sleeve down so I wouldn't have to look at the brand. "Is that it?"

"For the moment. We'll start tomorrow. Five p.m., here. Don't be late."

And without so much as a goodbye, Gideon started to fade.

Something occurred to me as he dissolved into Otherside smoke, and I blurted it out before my filter kicked in. "Was that what Max was doing for you?"

Gideon paused, his face resolidifying enough to glare at me.

"Before he died, I mean. Was he your apprentice, or assistant?" It was hard to imagine Max in a subordinate role. "Is that why he was dealing with you, to learn sorcery?"

Gideon's lip curled and his eyes went black again. "None of your business. And never ask me that question again."

With that, he dissolved into gold Otherside smoke and siphoned back through the mirror. The temperature immediately warmed up a few degrees.

I shuddered and turned to leave, but before I could close the door behind me I caught a message scrolling across the mirror.

Tomorrow. 5 p.m. sharp. Be ready to work with Otherside.

"Yeah, yeah. I got it. Five p.m. and don't be late," I said, knowing full well Gideon could probably still hear me. Shaking my head, I left the bathroom, closing the door carefully and making sure the catch took.

Despite the fact that I was now indentured to Gideon, the meeting had gone better than I'd expected. At least he hadn't tried to kill me or thrown things around the room like a poltergeist—and, most importantly, he hadn't discovered Nate.

Two years. I could handle two years. Or that's what I was going to keep telling myself until the trial period of running errands and setting up bindings for Gideon was up.

I took a deep breath as I opened the door to my bedroom. Now all I had to do was make sure I got Nate out of Cameron's body before Gideon found out about that little transgression. . . .

I headed to the window and threw the curtains open. Nate was huddling on the metal stairway, clutching the blanket around him and glaring at me. I opened the window and gestured for him to come back inside.

"I take it Gideon isn't going to kill us yet?" Nate said, more appropriately serious about our current predicament than he had been in the last week. I have to admit, I was surprised that the first thing out of his mouth wasn't a complaint. Maybe I should lock him out in the cold more often.

I shook my head. "Not yet, but we're really on a timeline now." And with that I gave him the short, edited version of the new agreement.

"Jeez, K—you have to work for him? For two years? I'm sorry, if I'd known—"

I stopped him with a shake of my head. "It's got nothing to do with you this time, Nate. This has everything to do with me screwing over Gideon for Cameron's body—your body now, I guess," I corrected myself, and headed back into the kitchen.

Nate was uncharacteristically quiet as he followed me. I stopped him as he started to take his hat and jacket off, grabbing my own from the stand, having decided to postpone my trip to the library. "Leave them on, we're heading into the city."

"Now? I thought we'd wait until dark," he said, hat in hand.

There was the Nate that I knew and roomed with. . . . I think I preferred self-absorbed Nate to thoughtful Nate because I was more used to him and therefore equipped to deal with him. "Now," I said, and grabbed a couple of wrapped and addressed books that I'd sold on eBay and shoved them into my backpack. I could mail them on the way. "I meant it when I said Gideon changes things," I told Nate.

As an afterthought and because my computer was still open, I checked my eBay store to see if any of my other books had bites. None did, but the listing still had a few days to go.

Instead of continuing to argue, Nate peered over my shoulder. "Why are you still selling your books? You aren't broke anymore after—you know . . ."

Nate meant the ten thousand dollars Lee Ling had paid me for my last case, the one we didn't discuss. "Because I need a slush fund for the winter, not a reference library. Especially if you stay a zombie much longer and we can't book any Halloween seances. Those brains you need to function are draining my savings." Even with the formaldehyde, they were expensive—three to five hundred dollars a cooler expensive.

"Well, technically I could still do a seance—"

"No."

"Spoilsport."

Nate's pissy mood was gone now, and I wasn't complaining. I grabbed my bike and tossed him my spare helmet. "Here, put this on."

"I'm not going to fall off."

I shook my head. "I'm worried about people seeing you—and smelling you."

"That hurts, Kincaid." But he took the helmet and wedged it on over his hat.

I slid my own jacket on and grabbed the Hawk, mentally crossing my fingers that Lee could help Nate. Preferably before Gideon's next scheduled visit.

I opened the door and pushed my bike towards the elevator. "Come on, twinkletoes. Time to go see Lee. For real this time."

I didn't care if Lee wasn't taking my calls—I was going to make her talk to me if I had to camp out at her bar, Damaged Goods, for the next two days.

Here's hoping that wouldn't be necessary, and that once she did talk, she could shed some light on how to free Nate.

CHAPTER 5

YOU GET WHAT YOU PAY FOR ...

"Why is everyone looking at me, K?" Nate whispered.

I sighed and grabbed Nate by the arm. "Because they don't need to see your damn bindings to know there's something seriously wrong." I steered him to the side of the wooden boardwalk—the version of First Street that runs through the underground city proper. I wanted him out of the way of foot traffic, particularly the ghoul variety that would smell him if they got too close. Ghouls, unlike zombies, eat rotting meat.

"Are you kidding? How?"

How. I shook my head. "Nate, three of your anchoring symbols are flickering, for Christ's sake." Well, what I could make of the binding symbols . . . the ones that weren't a tangled mess. "I'm amazed you aren't keeling over."

Nate glanced down. "I feel okay."

I gave him a pointed look.

"Okay, not great, but I don't feel like I'm about to fall apart or anything."

"Cross your fingers that holds up." Even if I didn't have Otherside sight, I'd have known Nate's bindings were off just by his appearance. The waxy skin, greasy hair and funny smell could be written off as poor health and hygiene, but his knees had stiffened and his gait now had an awkward drag.

I watched the nearby ghouls to see which ones were eyeing Nate. They'd picked up his odour almost as soon as we'd stepped off the underground city's stairwell, the brick spiral that winds its way down from the tunnels above to the main boardwalk. It couldn't be helped, I suppose, since the ghoul market tends to hover around the staircase. Even though we'd veered to the other side of the street, a few were still sniffing in our direction. I picked up my pace and guided Nate down a more secluded and less busy side street. It'd take us a little longer to reach Lee's, but I'd much rather explain our predicament to her in private than from the wrong side of a ghoul mob.

I decided to switch topics to get Nate's mind off the ghouls. "Hey, Aaron was asking me about a cold case he's looking into. Damien Fell."

Nate's sharp look caught me off guard.

"You knew him?"

He shrugged and mumbled a half-assed affirmative.

For someone who usually jumped at the chance to regale me with stories from his grunge days, he was uncharacteristically tight-lipped. "Aaron seemed to think you guys were rivals."

"I mean, sure, I knew the guy—saw him occasionally—but we weren't friendly. He was a Mormon or something. Didn't drink, wouldn't even touch coffee, almost never partied. We didn't have much in common, well, except . . ." He trailed off.

I nudged us towards an alley, away from a group of zombies hanging out ahead of us. "Except what?" Silence as Nate trudged ahead of me, dragging his feet along the boardwalk.

I stopped him and forced him to face me. "Nate, it's important. Aaron's looking into Damien as a *cold case*."

Nate frowned. "He thinks Damien was *murdered*? That's—" He shook his head.

"You said it. He didn't party or drink. How often does someone like that overdose?" I added, "And Aaron wants to talk to you about him."

"Me? K, seriously, I barely knew the guy."

"I hate to say it, but Aaron's not wrong. You guys got your big break because the lead singer of Cadmium Coffee died and you lucked into their spot. I'm not saying that makes you guilty of murder"—I rushed to finish as Nate started to argue—"but it is motive. Now, what did you have in common?"

Nate glanced at me and sighed. "Okay, but you're going to take this the wrong way."

I inclined my head and waited for him to continue.

"Mindy and Damien were hooking up. It wasn't like she was cheating on me—Mindy left for other reasons, and we were on the outs when I found out. She was pretty shaken up by his death."

"And you started dating again?" Shit, that was two motives.

But Nate shook his head. "Nah. She went through a couple other guys before we got back together. Saw her around, but"—he shrugged—"it was a bad breakup, okay?"

"What about someone else in your band? Not that they did something intentionally," I clarified as Nate glared at me. "Just that they might know something. Accidents happen." That would explain why they might have hidden the heroin once they realized it was bad—or, worse, if they thought someone was watching them, tried to hide it on Nate. *Who what, Kincaid? Just happened to stumble across it three years later?* I stopped my mind racing ahead. I wasn't quite ready to jump to the conclusion that someone had tried to kill Nate. Not yet . . .

Nate nodded slowly. "I don't know. Mindy knew him. Cole used to hang out with them a lot too. I think that's how Mindy met Damien."

"Cole? Your drummer?" Nate and his drummer hadn't exactly got along. Cole had also been involved with Mindy while Nate had been seeing her. Oh, the wonders of nineties-era relationships. And the fact that they were now married . . .

"Could Cole have had a gripe with Damien over Mindy?"

"Naw. Back then they were friends. Cole used to threaten that if we didn't get off our asses and book some decent gigs, he was going to jump ship to Cadmium Coffee. It was never a real threat, just a way for him to blow off steam. I think he was pretty choked up when Damien died, but we weren't exactly talking. Cole and I were always fighting over songs by then."

"Not upset enough to skip the concert," I said before thinking. "Sorry, Nate. That was insensitive."

"Maybe that's why Cole was so upset." After a moment he added, "Cole wouldn't have done anything to Damien, but he might know where he would have gotten the drugs from. Mindy might know too."

Yeah. I'd come to that conclusion as well. Nate was playing it cool, but considering how much he wanted to see Mindy . . . "I'll see if I can get in touch with Damien first. See if he remembers anything useful." Why depend on the living's testimony when the dead have absolutely nothing to lose? "If I don't get anything from him, I'll contact Cole or Mindy."

I expected Nate to jump at the chance to talk to Mindy, if not Cole. But he didn't. "Look, can we change the subject? The afterlife isn't my favourite topic right now," he said, and turned his back to me so I couldn't see his face.

"Nate, you've been dead almost twenty years."

"Yeah, but I'm about to become more dead—or worse-off dead." He shook his head. "Either way, it's depressing."

Nate walked ahead of me and I let my interrogation go. It wasn't the smoking gun Aaron had hoped it would be. It sounded more like Nate, the Dead Men and every other grunge band in Seattle at the time being true to form. . . .

Besides, I thought as we exited the alley and I spotted the red saloon doors across the street with the wooden sign hanging overhead that read *Damaged Goods*, we'd reached Lee's bar. I'd worry about Aaron's case later. For the moment, I had bigger issues to deal with.

I slipped in front of Nate, pushed the red saloon doors open and met a curtain of bamboo beads painted white with red flowers on them. Sure enough, as soon as we were past the curtain, I spotted the white lanterns in all shapes and sizes hung around the room, each one decorated with delicate red blossoms. It brought to mind the set from a Chinese western, which now that I thought of it was a pretty damn accurate description of Lee's place.

Nate stopped short just past the beaded curtains.

A table of ghouls started sniffing the air and glanced up from their drinks . . . confirming my suspicion that the formaldehyde wasn't doing its job. They were still picking up on the decay.

I searched the bar for Lee, but she was nowhere to be found. Instead, her partner of sorts, Mork, was manning the well and engaged in a shouting match with a pair of zombies, probably over the amount of formaldehyde in their drinks. Well, that's what you got when you didn't want to pay for top shelf.

As much as I needed a whisky sour, I relished the idea of dealing with Mork right now about as much as wrangling a poltergeist. And I was pretty sure I couldn't banish Mork. I grabbed Nate by the sleeve of his jacket and pulled him towards a dark corner booth, thinking we could stay inconspicuous and wait for Lee to appear. She couldn't be far. . . .

I slid into the booth across from him.

"You know, K, if you really want to ask Mindy about Damien and Aaron's case, I'm more than happy to talk to her for you—"

"A minute ago you didn't want anything to do with her."

"Yeah, well. You know, as a favour to Aaron."

"Why is it you're so set on talking to her this time?"

"I'm not—" he tried, his pale knuckles turning paler as he gripped the table. "It's important, all right?"

"Nate, if you want me to help you talk to Mindy, then you need to tell me why it's so damn important."

Nate's serious expression shifted into something resembling anger. I was startled. He could be belligerent, occasionally insulting, visibly annoyed, but he was always genial. He never really got angry. I'd just always figured it wasn't worth the effort for him— until now, apparently.

"Does this have anything to do with what Aaron's looking into?"

"No, of course not." He tried to run his hand through his hair, forgetting he had the hat and hood on. He dropped his hands back to the table. "K, why do you always need an explanation? Can't it just be important to me?"

"*No.*" Nate glowered at me and I added, "You're asking me to risk incarceration—for the rest of my life. If you want me to help, you need to tell me *why*—"

"Oh, you have *got* to be kidding me," a male voice, just shy of nasal, said beside our table.

I winced. I'd been so wrapped up in Nate's bullshit that I hadn't noticed the shadowy figure approaching, and now looming over us. Without cringing—too much—I glanced up at Mork, Lee's tenuous business partner at Damaged Goods and the purveyor of all things brains. My working theory was that he was a morgue assistant.

Mork's real name was Michael, and he was human. However, his appearance and mannerisms were so odd I'd nicknamed him after the alien on TV I remembered from reruns when I was a kid. The nickname had caught on. Mork hadn't changed his shag haircut since the late nineties, but what set him apart from the rest of his high school grunge cohort was his uncanny knack for taking nineties Seattle stereotypes to the point of absurdity. Tonight was no different, as he stood before me in his leather duster trench coat, a western-style red flannel shirt and a pair of yellow Doc Martens. To top it all off, he'd added a white cowboy hat. Mork had really taken the Chinese western theme and run with it. . . . He often brought to mind an old Stephen King novel—the one about the gunslinger.

Mork bared his bleached white teeth at me in something resembling a smile. Another thing about him I found unnerving: he managed to make good teeth cringeworthy.

"Mork," I said, doing my best not to invite further conversation.

He pointed a gloved finger at Nate. "Lee said you got rid of that zombie," he said.

One thing I had to give Mork, he was damn good at making an innocuous statement sound like an accusation. But this time the implicit accusation actually had merit, unlike all the other times he'd levelled them at me . . .

How best to de-escalate this situation before anyone else looked this way and caught a whiff of Nate?

"Oh, will you lay off, you sadistic creep," Nate said before I could stop him. "K, let's find Lee, Mork gives me the creeps— Ow!" he yelped as I kicked him under the table.

Mork stood there staring at Nate, his mouth hanging open. Then his face contorted into an unappealing mix of disbelief and anger as he turned his attention back to me. "Oh, for the love of— Do *not* tell me that's Nathan Cade in there."

"Ooookkkkaa—" I started.

Mork placed both his hands on the thick wood table and leaned in to get a closer look. "How did you get him in there?" he demanded.

Now it was my turn to be indignant—and do some damage control. Mork was deplorable, but he was the only reliable source of human brains in Seattle, maybe Washington state. I couldn't afford to torch that bridge. "Easy, I didn't. As far as I can tell, it was a complete accident. I'm trying to figure that detail out, so if you would be so kind as to go get Lee—"

"Kincaid, feel free to take this the wrong way, but I don't want anything to do with your current shit show," Mork said, and once again pointed at Nate. "And *that* is a shit show."

"That's why I didn't ask you, Mork. Now just tell me where Lee is—"

He shook his head and started to walk away.

I glared at Nate. "I thought I told you to keep a low profile?"

"It's *Mork*."

"It took him less than a minute to figure out you weren't Cameron. What if he tells someone and it gets back to Gideon?"

Nate frowned at me. "I repeat. It's Mork. No one listens to Mork."

I swore. "Stay," I told Nate, and scrambled out of the booth. If I was fast, maybe I could catch Mork before he disappeared into the back cooler or somewhere else I wouldn't be able to yell at him.

"Mork, all I want is to talk to Lee."

He didn't respond as he walked behind the bar. He did, however, open the cooler door and shout something in Chinese.

I don't recognize many words in Chinese, but the ones I do aren't complimentary, and there were definitely a few of those mixed in there. . . .

"Kincaid Strange." Lee's low, throaty voice carried through the bar. Too rough a texture to be feminine, but refined with a touch of a British accent. The kind I'd imagine hearing in a 1920s speakeasy. And tonight she did not sound happy.

I threw one last glare at Nate, still huddled in the booth, and turned to face Lee as she stepped out of the cooler.

Lee usually wore her hair up, but tonight it was tied in a long braid that hung down her back. She was dressed in a dark grey Chinese-style silk dress covered in red, pink and white flowers. An off-white apron was draped over the front and she held a blender containing a grey, frothy mixture out to the side. Lee usually wore colours that flattered and contrasted her pale skin and dark hair, but the dark grey was an odd choice. Where she often dressed to draw attention away from the scars that ran across her face like cracks in porcelain, the colour of this dress made the grey rivulets stand out. It did bring out her pale green-blue eyes, however, ones that had been bought and paid for. Dearly.

"What are you doing in my bar with him?" Lee said as she handed the blender to Mark and strode over.

"It's not what it looks like—" I started.

She stopped in front of me and crossed her arms, staring me down. "When things are not what they seem, they almost always end up being much worse. Bad luck has been following you around like a stray kitten lately, Kincaid. You know how I feel about bad luck."

Yeah, I certainly did. Bad luck had been the story of Lee's life. . . .

Lee Ling Xhao had died during the summer of 1889, the year the great fire destroyed most of Seattle courtesy of a dry summer, a city built on wooden stilts, and a carpentry shop full of turpentine.

Lee didn't die in the fire, though. She had been murdered three weeks before the carpenter ever had the bright idea of downing a bottle of whisky and striking a match.

At the tender age of fifteen, Lee had had a flourishing career as a high-end courtesan in Shanghai. Known for her gold-coloured eyes, a coveted symbol of freedom from worldly cares, she expected to have a long and illustrious career . . . until her twin brother, Lou, was exposed as a practitioner of the dark arts. Perfectly acceptable in China at the time, but not so much so with her predominantly foreign and very Christian clientele. The two fled to the west coast, once again setting up shop, Lou selling his talents and Lee selling hers.

To hear her tell it, Lee had quite the distinguished clientele, all of whom she and her brother planned to extort and blackmail into comfortable retirement. Until the wife of one of Lee's more ardent customers got wise to where her husband's money was going.

Stories of Whitechapel's infamous Jack the Ripper murders had reached the Northwest by then, and had inspired Seattle's own copycat, a ghoul as I had recently discovered, who'd preyed on crib girls, the indentured Chinese prostitutes who were kept by the Seattle docks. Which is where the merchant's wife, Isabella, got her inspiration.

Drugged with chloroform in a dark alley, her single scream muffled by the evening crowds, the very last thing Lee saw was the paring knife as Isabella sliced into her beautiful porcelain face. Lee's brother did his best to stitch her up before raising her as a zombie, but the grey china cracks running over her beautiful face were daily reminders of her violent death.

I asked her once why she hadn't replaced her stolen eyes with another golden pair.

"I like green," she'd said. "It is a good reminder that I am not free from worldly cares. And Isabella had such beautiful green ones."

So yeah, Lee had a tempestuous relationship with luck. . . .

"Lee, wait, let me explain—"

Without a word, she gracefully manoeuvred around me as she

headed for Nate. I swore and followed before she could lay into him in front of the entire bar.

She didn't, though. Instead, she stopped just short of the booth where Nate was watching us in fear—his usual reaction to Lee's often intimidating presence. She crossed her arms and regarded him shrewdly.

Her face didn't soften exactly, but it did lose its hard edge, and her scars seemed to still their angry dance, though that may have been a trick of the light. She uncrossed her arms and nodded towards her office. "Bring him into my office, Kincaid. We need to talk."

"And what about when I do this, Nathan?" Lee said, probing the gash that I'd inflicted on Cameron's torso weeks earlier, which had never healed despite massive doses of formaldehyde.

"Ow! Yes, that hurts too. Just like the last time you pinched me."

"*Nate*," I warned.

Lee stood and wiped her hands with a rag she'd brought into her office along with a bowl of boiled water. I couldn't help wincing at the less than ideal sanitation measures, but doubted exposure to a fungus or bacteria would make much of a difference to Nate now.

"And you say your symptoms have not changed since you took over Cameron's body?" Lee asked. It was strange hearing her question Nate from such a detached place. I hadn't been able to do it.

Nate wavered. "It's not getting better. I mean, I smell, and my skin is starting to yellow, and I think my hair is starting to fall out, though I haven't showered in a while, so—"

Lee nodded absently. "Put your shirt back on, Nathan, and go find Mork in the cooler. I've told him to re-dress the wound with a stronger formaldehyde mix, and give you a mixture of embalming fluid that should allow you to shower, so as not to draw any more attention to yourself than necessary," she said, and nodded towards her office door.

Nate looked as if he might argue—Mork had that effect on him—but he wasn't inclined to push Lee. Not when she used a stern tone.

He pulled down his shirt and grabbed his jacket. "First I get prodded by the queen of the zombies, now the reject from the Dark Tower is going to douse me with formaldehyde. . . ." He may have added something else, but it was muffled through the closing door. "K, find me by the pinball machine after."

"Think that's a good idea?" I called after him. Zombies have an unhealthy penchant for pinball machines and jukeboxes, something to do with the bright lights, the chimes. I wasn't optimistic that Nate would be able to tear himself away, considering his impulse control issues.

Nate held his hand and wiggled his fingers. "I have hands for the first time in twenty years. I figure it's about time I tasted the zombie vices, see how the other dead live."

I watched Nate from the doorway to make sure he headed into the cooler.

Mork's impatient voice carried into the hall. "Strip, grunge boy. Oh, come on, it's nothing I haven't seen before."

Nate was going to love that. I turned back to face Lee.

"You're surprisingly contemplative considering recent events," I said.

Lee took a seat at her desk and gestured for me to do the same. "First tell me what has transpired with the sorcerer's ghost, Gideon Lawrence, then we will discuss Nathan Cade. Gideon has come to collect by now, yes?"

Which she would have known if she'd returned my calls. I'd get to that later, along with what she really thought about Nate's predicament. Lee liked things to progress in a particular fashion. Time wasn't exactly in short supply for the dead. I inclined my head. "In a manner of speaking." Lee motioned for me to continue, so I added, "I'm to be his assistant—I think Max's replacement. Apparently, sorcery requires some basic practitioning."

"For how long?"

"Six months."

She let out a short huff of air and arched her perfectly shaped eyebrows. "That's all?"

"For starters," I admitted. "Then we renegotiate. Five years as his personal messenger if I suck or he thinks I'm personally trying to fuck up, two years as an apprentice if I'm any good."

Lee sat back, nodding to herself as she stared at her neat desk. "A little harsh, but fair, all things considered. He has certainly given you a strong incentive to accommodate his request. Knowledge of sorcery could be very valuable to you, regardless of whether you choose to pursue it."

"I could sure have used your opinion on that a few hours ago. Or a couple days ago. When you refused to return all my calls? And what happened to your warnings that Gideon is dangerous and should be avoided at all costs?"

Lee glanced up and frowned. "You've already ignored that advice spectacularly, so repeating it does you no good. Your only option is to make the best of a bad situation. And as for the phone calls? As I believe Mork said, I want to be drawn into as little of your bullshit as possible."

"You're right, I owe you a huge apology—"

Lee raised a hand. "I do not want nor need your apology." She glanced down at her desk again. "In all honesty, I do not know what Nate is. Your theory of Nathan being partially bound and partially animated at the same time I believe is accurate," she said carefully. "Though I would argue it is less animation, more a binding of his spirit. He is not a zombie, but he is also no longer a ghost. The closest thing . . ." She trailed off for a moment before her eyes narrowed and she looked back up at me. "I'm sorry, Kincaid, I do not have answers for you this time," she said, and stood up.

"That's it? No, Lee, you were about to tell me something—"

"It was inconsequential," she said, with a note of warning in her voice.

"Lee, I have nothing to go on right now. If I didn't know any better, I'd say he managed to possess that body, but that's impossible, even for a poltergeist."

"Did Nathan tell you anything else about how this transpired? Anything at all?"

"No. He says he saw the smoke and I hadn't come out yet, so he went in to check up on me. That's the last thing he claims to remember."

Lee made a derisive noise. She'd asked Nate questions along the same lines and had no more luck than I had dragging answers out of him.

There were too many variables: the bindings that Max had animated Cameron with; whatever Gideon had done to him; me throwing a ton of Otherside at him; the fire; and then add a ghost. I had no idea how they might have interacted with each other, and that was factoring in the things I *knew* I didn't know. What I didn't know I didn't know was another problem. Even after Lee's examination, I still didn't buy that Nate was being completely straight with me. . . .

"Half of the problem is I don't know if Nate is telling the truth or is afraid of me finding out what he's not telling us—"

"Or whether there is something else that frightens him," Lee finished off.

And that was the kicker. Nathan was a lot of uncomplimentary things, but he was my friend. He'd gone out of his way to try to help me, at significant personal cost. Ghosts don't have an infinite amount of energy to waste, and Nate had done just that—leading the police on a wild goose chase so I could get away and trying to save me from a serial-killer ghoul.

I think it hurt a little that he didn't trust me to do the same. . . .

In a change of heart or a moment of pity, Lee said, "Nathan Cade is stuck in a limbo of sorts, between this world and the next, linked with Otherside and burning it brightly. The closest thing I've ever seen to that kind of undead possession was a wraith. But Nathan is most definitely not a wraith, so I do not see the point in discussing it."

I headed Lee off as she swept gracefully around her desk towards the office door, stopping short of touching her. I'm not that brave, and I also have too much respect for Lee . . . but I wasn't above grovelling right now for whatever I could get. "Wait a minute. Possession of a body like that shouldn't be possible. Not for two weeks. A strong poltergeist can only handle a possession for a couple hours, maybe a day if they get lucky, but not weeks."

She inclined her head. "You are once again correct. What Nathan has done should not be possible." Lee motioned for me to move, which I did, and she exited her office to head back to the bar. I followed and grabbed a seat, hoping she'd elaborate.

On top of that, I desperately wanted a drink—no, I deserved a drink after the day I'd had. A couple. I braced myself against the bar, happy that the creosote had worn into the wood and Lee had wiped the rest away. Lee soaked the giant beam that made up the bar with the tacky preservative every now and then to keep the dampness that plagued everything in the underground city at bay. I still hadn't got the stains out of my jacket from my last visit.

I waited until Lee had passed me a whisky sour—the best in Seattle, topside or underground—before prompting again. "So how come, in all the binding texts, all the paranormal accounts, all the papers, I've never seen any mention of wraiths or even of regular ghosts like Nate possessing bodies? And there is no way this is the first time a ghost has tried to steal a body." Ghosts aren't exactly an altruistic bunch. If they thought for one minute they could scam a body lying around . . .

Lee sighed as she began lining up freshly washed glasses along the bar.

"Well, if you won't tell me that, do you at least believe Nate when he says he has no idea how he ended up there?"

Lee's not one to give much away, but I could see the muscles around her eyes twitch. "He is not being entirely untruthful," she said, choosing her words deliberately. "I do not believe he realizes how the bindings work, nor how exactly he came to inhabit Cameron's body."

"But?"

"Though I feel this is more an accident of opportunity than a calculated deception, he is most certainly hiding something," she said, and retrieved a blender full of brains from an ice bath sitting in the well.

Fantastic. I swore. "His trying to avoid blame is going to kill him—again. Lee, those things are no more stable than they were when Cameron was in there. Less so. You know what will happen as well as I do if I don't get Nate the hell out of that body. He's got a couple weeks before he burns out, at most."

Lee made a soft hissing noise and turned her back on me as she filled the glasses, decorated them with red umbrellas and loaded them one by one onto a tray.

No time to start heeding warnings now . . . "Come on, Lee, you owe me."

She placed the blender on the counter behind her and, with more grace and speed than I could have managed, pivoted, reached across the bar and grabbed me by the collar of my jacket. "Kincaid, listen well, because I will only say this once. I cannot help Nathan because I do not know how," she said, her teeth clenched.

"Lee, you just said you've seen Nate's kind of possession before. You can't expect me to believe—"

"Knowing *about* a type of possession is not the same as knowing how it has happened or how to fix it!"

"Bullshit," I said. Wow, Lee had a stronger grip than I'd banked on. "You know everything to do with the paranormal. Nothing goes on in the underground city without your say-so—"

She let go of my jacket and pushed me back into my seat. "I am familiar with practitioner work. *Not* a sorcerer's."

I rubbed my neck. Not bruised, but I wondered if Lee realized her own strength. "What do you mean, a sorcerer's bindings? You mean Gideon might have had a hand in this?" Gideon was the one who'd set up the deal with Max for Cameron's body in the first place. . . . Who was to say he hadn't had a hand in the actual bindings? Or in what had snared Nate? I knew practitioning and how to unravel zombie bindings, but I didn't know a thing about sorcery except that people who practised it, or their ghosts at least, were real assholes. Granted, I only had one example. I'd thought I'd watched all of Gideon's bindings burn off Cameron, but what if I'd been wrong? Maybe all I'd done was prime them for the next hapless ghost who came by.

"I am saying that from your own admission and with what Nathan claims to remember, the fact that Cameron had been one of Gideon's experiments is an outstanding detail. I'm not saying that is the cause, but it would be very foolish to discount it just because you wish to avoid Gideon." Lee took a moment to line up another series of glasses on the bar. "The first and only time I ever saw an undead creature caught in between was with my brother, Lou. In China."

"I would think a wraith in 1880s Shanghai would earn at least a footnote in one of my textbooks."

Lee inclined her head. "I agree. But we did not see it in Shanghai— we saw it in the farming town where we lived and worked in rice fields, well outside any city."

That surprised me. I guess I'd always assumed that Lee and her brother, Lou, had grown up in a city; she'd always struck me as cultured, not as a peasant.

As if reading my thoughts, Lee said, "We can't always judge someone's origins from the outcome.

"Lou was the one who had an interest in books and, more than any of us, wanted out of our life of drudgery and indentured servitude. It led him to frequently visit the local witch, a woman whose talents lay in the grey area between practitioning and sorcery. An old hermit, she had lived on the outskirts of town as long as anyone could remember, in a rundown hovel. Lou's interests earned him our mother and father's anger and our siblings' ridicule. He endured many beatings at my father's hands for visiting the witch."

"Wasn't practitioning well respected in China?" That's what I had always believed; what with the culturally ingrained respect for the dead and one's ancestors, practitioning had flourished in China and Japan over the past fifteen hundred years. Most of the real breakthroughs in modern bindings had occurred in Asia on account of the religious backlash in western Europe that had only abated in the last hundred years.

Lee finished settling the drinks onto the tray and excused herself to take them to a table. When she returned, she continued. "Our village was very superstitious, and did fear angering the dead over most things, as did most rural villagers. But do not mistake fear for respect. Though my father would never in a million years have confronted the old village witch, if he hadn't needed the extra hands in the fields so badly and my mother hadn't stopped having children, I suspect he would have disowned Lou for pursuing his apprenticeship."

She began pouring another set of drinks, this time layering the grey mixture with a colourful concoction of pink, green and blue liquids—embalming fluids, from the scent of formaldehyde. The colour scheme reminded me of a bad T-shirt I'd brought back from a California vacation as a kid.

"But superstition and fear only go so far," Lee continued. "You have to remember that we grew up in China during a time of great upheaval and discord. The Taiping civil war and the Second Opium War happened barely a decade before we were born. Because of concessions made during the Opium Wars, missionaries were expanding their presence in rural China. The uneducated working class were vulnerable, and fell under the foreigners' influence."

I frowned. "I don't get it. I mean, wouldn't villagers have wanted to protect Chinese culture and drive out the white devil ghosts?"

Lee pursed her lips. "You are oversimplifying. Between the Opium Wars was the Taiping civil war—by all accounts one of the most brutal in human history. To many, the missionaries' arrival was an invasion of sorts, but it also introduced attractive ideas to an already very dissatisfied working class."

I reached back in my brain to my history classes. "The Han working class versus the Manchu ruling class?"

"More or less correct. Historians focus on the ethnic sides of the Taiping civil war because those are simple labels. It is true that the working Han middle class was very unhappy with what they perceived as the corrupt Manchu, but that wasn't the whole problem. There is always corruption in the ruling class. Even in your United States today."

"Except the US is a democracy where we vote on our leaders. They aren't elected by their family members."

Lee made a derisive noise. "Never mind that two families, the Bushes and Clintons, have appeared in all of your elections since 1988 and split the presidency between themselves for twenty years, and the orange man has instated his offspring in positions of power. No, there is certainly no corruption or nepotism occurring in the choosing of your candidates."

I did the math in my head. Damn it, she was right. . . .

"Even in a democracy such as yours, where the supposedly hard-working peasant can become the leader of your nation, a select group of families and special interest groups are the ones who share the true power. It was an identical situation during the time of the revolution, except that the Han figured out they were 'being screwed,' as you are so fond of saying, in large part due to the missionaries."

Touché. "Okay, the Han were being screwed and decided they should overthrow and replace the corrupt Manchus, hold power long enough to become corrupt themselves, teach the Manchus a well-deserved lesson, switch roles and repeat the cycle. I still don't see how that resulted in eschewed traditions or a wraith."

"You are forgetting the most important factor in the Opium Wars and the Taiping Rebellion: the West." Lee finished loading the grey-rainbow concoctions onto a tray and headed over to the waiting zombies, leaving me to think over the complexities of the nineteenth-century political climate in China and what the hell it had to do with wraiths.

Lee returned with a tray full of empty glasses, which she deposited one by one in the sink. "Imagine, Kincaid, that you are a peasant living on a state-owned rice farm in 1860s China. You have no love of your ruling class, whom you perceive as not only corrupt but also weak. They've lost not one but two wars with the white devils, and as a peasant, you are expected to make up the taels of silver the idiots in power have lost. Though you do not fully understand this relationship, you nonetheless are paying for their mistakes in sweat and blood. You feel powerless and resentful. You crudely grasp that it is the Manchus' fault and that they are weak and the Westerners are powerful. Then come the Western missionaries with their Christian god, which must be more powerful than your Chinese gods, because look how they have defeated yours."

"They blamed the gods?"

"Among other things. But I think it was more our traditions of worshipping our Chinese gods and paying our respects to our dead, who should have protected us from the white god. Remember the governing rule and wisdom of peasants the world over throughout history: side with the more powerful god and army."

"So peasants started siding with the Christians?"

Lee nodded. "The leader of the Taiping Rebellion proclaimed that he was Jesus's brother until he was assassinated. For fifteen years the Rebellion held off the government's armies. The disdain for their own gods and customs became well cemented; the continuation of a weak and corrupt regime was viewed with suspicion and mistrust. *That* is the climate we grew up in."

"Fascinating. The wraith?"

"Patience is a virtue, Kincaid."

I narrowed my eyes at her. "I'm sorry, did you not get a good look at Nate?"

Lee frowned and her scars seemed to dance across her face, a trick of the lamplight and shadows. "The Taiping Rebellion might have been defeated, but the dissension was sown too deep. There were small armies and rebel forces that moved through the regions, some who upheld Chinese traditions, such as those who would be behind the Boxer Rebellion, and others yet who followed the Christians. Half fought groups of bandits and thieves, something peasants can understand and grasp, and the other half *were* the bandits and thieves.

"One day, one such group was spotted on the outskirts of the farm where we lived and worked. Lou caught sight of them on his way back from the old witch and was able to warn me and our other siblings. We were not stupid—we hid, not in the house or barns, but in the rice paddies, breathing through reeds where no one would think to look. Others were not so smart, and therefore not as lucky."

I flinched at Lee's particular brand of pragmatism. Granted, her formative years had been spent in a brutal place and an unforgiving time, and this wasn't the first time she'd laid the blame partially on the victims. I guess I'll never understand what it was like to watch a gang of bandits ride through town raping and pillaging. . . .

"One such unlucky girl, the highly valued daughter of a merchant, did not hide wisely. Viewed as a representative of the wealthy, corrupt class—though she was not—she was taken by the bandits, used until her body expired, then discarded by the road like trash. She had been promised to the local governor, a small, powerless official who'd barely managed to hold on to his land and needed the marriage to secure income. Both families desperately sought vengeance, more due to the loss of economic opportunity than for any thought of the girl. They enlisted the help of one of the rebel bands they knew to be sympathetic, but they were not successful. Some said it was a witch who protected the bandits, though it's more likely they were simply very good at hiding or paid the other band off with enough silver to make them 'forget.' The rumours of a witch were easier to grasp and gained momentum. The town needed little encouragement to confront a witch they already resented and feared, and to a degree my brother, who was her assistant by then. The townspeople accused her of hiding the bandits out of spite, and cited as proof the fact that I and my siblings had escaped their attack unscathed, never mind that we were simply more clever in choosing our hiding places than a girl who was terrified of dirtying the hem of her dress."

There she went with the victim blaming again. I reminded myself never to come to Lee when I was in need of sympathy. . . .

"As you know, practitioners don't have much in their arsenal besides the anger of the dead and the odd zombie. The villagers wanted vengeance, but the governor and merchant, the girl's father, did not want to incur the wrath of their ancestors. They were not uneducated men, and knew the witch had little or nothing to do with the bandits. But they felt they needed to appease the villagers, who had had their daughters abused and children taken. They wanted a scapegoat."

"Is this where they strapped her to a stake and did as the Christians did?" Gideon claimed to have been burned at the stake. . . .

Lee shook her head. "They gave her a choice: get the spirits to exact revenge on the bandits, or be given to the villagers."

Angry masses show up at your door claiming you're responsible for the fire-and-brimstone circumstances that have befallen them, and it's your job to make things right? Substitute perky news show hosts for enraged villagers and you had a similar modern version of a witch hunt. If I had to listen one more time to Candy Calhoun on the CC *News Hour* speculate on the depressive nature and dishonesty of those who sought out or trucked with the dead . . . "I take it she didn't take kindly to being threatened?"

Dark shadows flickered across Lee's face as someone swung open the saloon doors, sending the lanterns dancing. "She was very angry. Lou stayed with her in her home on the outskirts of town for two days, and when I saw him, there were dark circles beneath his eyes, and a perpetual sheen of sweat on his face that he claimed was from talking to the spirits."

Or channelling more Otherside than was prudent or wise. I'd learned that lesson the hard way. . . .

"The witch came into town in the middle of the third day. She appeared a fearsome, unkempt creature, unused to crowds. She waited until the entire town had gathered in the square, silent and wary. When she finally spoke, she said the task had been completed, and that once the sun had set and the stars shone in the sky, they would have their vengeance." Lee's eyes narrowed as she watched me. "I was not a timid girl, yet her words and her manner of speaking frightened me.

"Promised a spectacle, the villagers congregated again in the town square at dusk. I think by now some realized they did not truly want vengeance delivered, but they were so set on their course that none were willing to voice their concerns."

"Cognitive dissonance," I offered. Like when you know your boyfriend is bad for you but you can't bring yourself to kick him out. "The adult version of the emperor's new clothes. So what happened?"

"The witch sat and waited like the rest of us, with Lou at her side. As soon as the sun set, so did the ice, covering everything around the square, chilling our hands and feet though it was late summer. The villagers stared at each other, and I exchanged glances with my siblings and watched Lou, but he kept his eyes lowered. It was then we heard the howl, as if a beast had been skewered by a hundred arrows and was bellowing its death throes. All of us jumped a little out of fright and huddled in closer. Some of the villagers broke away and ran for their homes, and others cried out for the witch to explain herself. What monster had she and my brother wrought? She only smiled and continued to sit silently.

"The wraith materialized in the darkness. I'd seen ghosts a few times in my life, but even then I knew that this one was different. It was a cross between a ghost and the animated dead, substantial, but not corporeal like I am. It was the merchant's daughter, the girl who had been murdered, but she did not look recently deceased, even though she had died no more than two weeks past. She was a husk of herself, more so than the oldest ghoul, a deep, dark grey cast to her skin and hair, as if she'd been painted with a thick veil of Otherside. If not for the tattered dress she wore, the same one, I realized, she'd been so afraid to dirty in the dust and mud, I would not have recognized her.

"Even at fifteen I was no coward, but at the sight of her, floating off the ground, neither a ghost nor a zombie, but something in between . . ." Lee shook her head. "Two of my sisters and I tried to run, and would have succeeded if Lou had not appeared behind us.

"'There are some things in this world you never run from, for they will chase you down and hunt you,' he said. We stood perfectly still beside Lou as the wraith moved through the crowd, while others ran. Some of them were heard from again, others were not.

"It was then the old woman finally spoke to it. 'Find those who killed you and feed on their hearts, and may you enact vengeance on bandits who violate young women such as yourself and those who question the intentions of a witch.' The wraith gave a long-drawn-out howl and disappeared in a gust of ice and snow, leaving us all bewildered and shaken."

"Did she kill the bandits?"

Lee frowned at me.

"What? Come on, I had to ask. That's what everyone wanted, didn't they?"

"Yes. A few days later a report came that an entire bandit camp was found frozen along with all their horses. The villagers were appeased, and cowed by the show of power, despite those who were never heard from again. Some even left offerings to the witch for giving them a powerful spirit that could actually protect them."

"Why do I think there is a *but* coming?" I asked.

Lee smiled. "A few days later a rebel group who had camped close to our village disappeared. Then more villagers began to go missing. Girls whom the merchant's daughter had quarrelled with over insignificant, trifling things began turning up dead, their faces frozen in expressions of agony. After that, her family began to die off.

"When the merchant was found frozen in his bed, his entire room covered in frost, Lou came to us. He arrived before sunrise, more frightened than I had ever seen him. He told my father to leave, and if he would not, at least send us away, out of the wraith's reach. When he refused, clinging to denial like most of the remaining villagers, my brother told me to pack my things and warned our other brothers and sisters to leave if they valued their lives. I don't know if any of them heeded him. We left just after sunrise. Frost coated the dirt road and rice paddies, as if the wraith was watching us, waiting.

"I didn't return to my village. Lou barely spoke for days, and it was a month before he practised the dark arts again, though he never told me what had happened. I think he saw the witch perform something with Otherside that scared him until the day he died. He never called it sorcery, but I believe that is what created the wraith that haunted our village. Regardless, he never spoke of it again."

Despite the urgency of Nate's situation, my curiosity was piqued. "What happened to the witch, and the village?" I asked.

"I do not know. I like to think my siblings were not fools, and left before the wraith preyed on them. But I did hear a story years later of an ancient woman in an abandoned town who still followed the old ways. When asked why the town had been deserted, she answered that the people had all forgotten that the living must solve their own problems—the dead are only meant to offer occasional guidance." Lee leaned in, a frown touching her face. "And do you know what the point of that story was, Kincaid?"

"With regards to Nate and how to get him out of Cameron's body? Not a damn clue." I shook my head. "He's nothing like the wraith the witch in your town came up with. He might be in the same family, but—"

Lee slapped her hands on the bar, her lips curling over her teeth. "The point was that you should stop pestering the dead and wasting their time coming up with ways to solve your problems! Especially after we say no. You will not like the answers the dead come up with."

I leaned back on my bar stool. Goddamnit . . . "Lee, come on, there has to be more to it than that."

But Lee was already walking away. "If you continue to pester me, Kincaid, I will make certain the next story wastes even more of your time—time you do not have. I have now given you all that I know."

I opened my mouth to fire back, but just then Nate emerged from the back cooler where Lee had sent him to be patched up by Mork.

"You okay, Nate?"

He shuddered. "Besides spending half an hour with Mork?" He pulled a roll of quarters out of his jacket pocket and tossed them in the air, almost fumbling the catch on the way down. "I'll, ah, be at the pinball machine," he said, giving Lee a wary look as she studied him from behind the bar.

The pinball machine was enclosed by a set of photo-booth curtains at the end of the bar, and I watched Nate duck inside, his bright red Converse sneakers visible below. I turned back to my whisky sour. Probably not the best idea to down it on an empty stomach, but I tossed it back anyway.

Lee watched me with her blue-green eyes, the scars on her face once again seeming to ripple under the lamplight. "May I offer a suggestion?" she asked.

I shook my head. "Please don't tell me to ask Gideon, Lee. Right now that's my last resort. . . ."

She frowned. "You've gotten yourself into enough trouble with the sorcerer. My suggestion was to speak to Michael."

It took me a second to figure out who she meant. "*Mork?*" I said.

"I realize you and he do not get along, but Mork, as you insist on calling him, is knowledgeable in some of the more arcane types of undead. He may have come across texts that talk about things similar to Nathan. He might be able to direct you where to look."

Mork or Gideon . . . "Lee, you don't happen to know any other sorcerers, do you?"

"*Kincaid.*"

"Seriously, Lee. Living or dead, just not Gideon . . ."

But Lee had already busied herself filling more glasses behind the bar. I could smell the formaldehyde drifting back. "I suggest you go and find Mork," was all she said.

Unwilling to push Lee any more than I had—I didn't think it'd be good for my health—I stood up and ducked around the bar. The cooler door was open a crack, enough so the cold air escaped in drifts of white fog, bringing to mind Lee's wraith.

I pushed the metal door open.

Mork was facing away from me, standing in front of a butcher block of some sort. I tried to avoid looking at the frozen slab he had on the cutting board.

I cleared my throat.

He turned around, cleaver in hand, a leather apron draped over his trench coat. He narrowed his eyes at me.

"Mork," I started, "you don't like me, I don't like you—"

"Save it, Kincaid. Lee already called in a favour."

"What about not wanting anything to do with my bullshit?" I should have held my tongue, but I blamed it on the whisky sour.

"I don't, but it's a far sight better than being on Lee's bad side." He put down his cleaver and I relaxed. "Look, I don't know exactly what your scaredy ghost is right now. I took a look at him and he's not really a zombie or a ghost."

"That helps me not at all."

He sneered and picked up the cleaver again. "I can tell you where to start looking. All of the extensive stuff I've read on wraiths came out of eastern European bestiaries. They're thorough, and go beyond the Otherside stuff when it comes to descriptions. They list all sorts of little-known undead and undead constructs. There are a few of them floating around. I'll drop one off here tomorrow. No guarantees you'll find anything."

"What's the catch?" I asked.

He gave me an unfriendly smile. "Like I said, Lee called in a favour. She's the one you should be thanking, not me."

He turned back to the block of frozen . . . I didn't want to know. . . .

"As for your degenerating grunge ghost, he'll be all right for now. I gave him my number—he knows the drill."

Figuring I was dismissed, I turned to go.

"Oh, and Kincaid?" Mork called out.

I glanced back at him.

"Seriously, whatever bullshit your scaredy ghost and you are involved in—"

"He's not involved in any bullshit. This whole thing was an accident."

Mork snickered.

I frowned. "What?"

"I find that hard to believe," he said, still laughing as the cleaver came down.

I was feeling uneasy, and for once it wasn't about Mork. "And why is that?" I asked.

"Because he asked me to pass on the message not to worry, that he had some business to attend to and would see you back home," Mork said, and raised his arm again.

"That's not possible. He's playing pinball . . ." I trailed off. I'd seen Nate *start* to play pinball.

Of course Mork had taken his sweet time passing along the message. I swore and made for the door while Mork laughed behind me. "Come get your book tomorrow, Kincaid. Provided your scaredy ghost doesn't land you in jail."

I swerved around a group of zombies and hightailed it for the pinball machine. Relief hit me. There was a pair of red Converse shoes sticking out from under the curtain.

"Nate, come on, time to go—" I threw the curtain back and stopped. It wasn't Nate standing in front of me, but a completely different zombie.

Son of a— He'd switched shoes. . . .

I shouted a quick goodbye to Lee as I ran out the front door of the saloon onto the boardwalk and searched the crowd for Nate. No sign of him. He had a head start on me.

I continued into the street, electric sodium lights casting shadows off the crowds of zombies and ghouls as I searched for Nate. He wasn't exactly easy to miss. I mean, he'd hijacked Cameron's six-foot-four frame.

I ran a hand through my hair. Where the hell would Nate go?

The answer hit me and I turned and headed for the staircase at a run. Mindy's. Maybe if I was lucky I could head him off.

Who was I kidding?

I picked up my pace and hoped Aaron wasn't on the job when the screaming zombie calls came in. . . . He wouldn't just suspect it was me, like the rest of the force. He'd *know*.

CHAPTER 6

DEAD MEN AND THE TALE OF MINDY MAY PINE

I found Mindy's place without too much difficulty—I knew where it was on account of Nate's Internet stalking. I parked my bike outside a row of shops an alley over from her building and scanned the nearby trash cans and alley doorways first, and also checked a few of the fire escapes. Nate could be damn creative when it came to hiding—especially when there was a good chance he'd be yelled at when discovered.

There!

Hunched over and squeezed behind a Dumpster at the end of an alley within sight of Mindy's door was the back of Nate's jacket.

I swore under my breath. At least he'd had the sense to keep his hood up.

Luckily, his zombie hearing wasn't great and I was able to sneak up behind him without him noticing. I tapped him on the shoulder.

I won't lie, I felt a surge of smug amusement when he jumped.

"K, son of a bitch, you scared the hell out of me— Hey!" he hissed, and raised his hands to block me as I smacked him on the shoulder. Not too hard, just enough to get the point across. "Hey, knock it off! You realize you could actually knock something off?"

"And you'd deserve it, you ungrateful—" I stopped and shook my head. "I might have known. Tell me, Nate, did you plan on bailing as soon as we reached Lee's, or was that a moment of inspired creativity on your part?" I did my best to keep my voice low, but it was a struggle.

Nate gave me a sheepish shrug. "Honestly? A little of column A, a little column B— Ow!"

He shielded his face as I smacked him on the shoulder again.

"Okay, I probably deserved that, but let me explain."

Oh, this was going to be good. I crossed my arms and waited.

Nate drew in a breath he didn't need on account of him being a zombie and said, "Okay. I'm worried Mindy is in trouble."

I stared at him.

Nate gave me a pleading look. "Seriously. I'm worried about her, all right? I can't get it out of my mind that something is going to happen, and I just want to talk to her and see if she's okay. She was never able to hide it when she was worried about something. *Please, K.*"

I sighed. His concern translated to paranoia, and I wasn't buying it.

"Look, I just need to see how she reacts in person—to anyone, anything. Less than a minute is all I need, I won't even tell her it's me."

"Seriously, Nate? You can't talk to her! You're a zombie—a really decrepit one. You're lucky someone around here hasn't smelled Mork's formaldehyde bath yet."

I stopped myself from rolling my eyes as Nate sniffed at his jacket.

"Smell receptors started dying off two weeks ago and you're not growing them back," I told him. "You shouldn't be in public, let alone stalking Mindy."

"I'm not stalking her, I'm concerned. There's a difference."

Yeah, and the difference was splitting really thin hairs . . . I shook my head at him. "Nate, what has gotten into you? Even in your most obsessive moments, you've never acted like this before." I was starting to wonder if all the formaldehyde was doing something to his brain. This wasn't reckless—it was just plain stupid, and stupid was one thing Nate was not.

"If you want me to help you, Nate, you need to give me more to go on."

Nate clenched his jaw and tried to run his hand through his hair. "Okay, I'll tell you, but you have to promise to help me."

I glared at him. "If this has *anything* to do with her being married to Cole—"

He shook his head. "You know how you were asking me about Aaron's cold case? Damien Fell's overdose?"

"The one you didn't know anything about?"

He ignored my comment. "Look, I remember the deaths. It was pretty shocking, hard not to take notice. One day everything was fine, the next people we hung out with were dropping dead. It was a bad couple months. And then Damien. I never saw that coming, no one did."

"I'm waiting for what that has to do with Mindy."

"Promise you won't tell Aaron?"

I gave him a noncommittal shrug. It depended on what Nate told me—he knew that.

Nate swore. "All right, but I'm trusting you with this." He took another breath he didn't need and said, "Mindy was there when it happened."

My mouth dropped open. "*Nate!*" I yelled, before mentally chastising myself for raising my voice. I checked to make sure I hadn't caught the attention of passersby. Luckily, no one was looking in our direction. Funny that—in Seattle, people don't care much what goes on in back alleyways. I imagine that's par for the course in most big cities.

"K, you said you'd hear me out."

"She's a witness," I said, this time keeping my voice lowered to a hiss. "One who lied." I remembered from the files Aaron had shown me that Mindy had been the one to find Damien and call the police, but there'd been nothing about her being there. Christ, they'd written it off as an accidental overdose. . . . "Nate, she was probably the last person to see him alive!"

"She didn't have anything to do with it. She passed out on his couch after a show, and the next morning . . . it happened."

The possibilities raced through my mind. "How do you know she's not lying? You're biased—"

"I know how you think, K," Nate said, his voice taking on a warning tone. "You don't know her like I do. She wasn't involved—couldn't have been. You didn't see her afterwards. She was a *mess*."

Yeah, and in my jaded mind that only raised the likelihood she was involved a few more notches. But I stopped myself from voicing that concern. Nate didn't look like he could take it, and I knew from experience that Nate was loyal to a fault. When he managed to rise above his own selfish interests . . .

Nate kept watching me, his eyes earnest. He really didn't believe Mindy might have done something to Damien, and I had nothing to challenge him with.

I gestured for him to continue.

"Mindy came to me and Cole afterwards and told us she'd stepped out of the living room for five minutes, and when she came back, he was lying on the kitchen floor, needle in his arm, already dead. I think she saw something else that spooked her—like I said, she was a mess—but whatever it was, she never said."

Now that caught my interest. Not that I think a ghost is behind every problem, but a poltergeist? A teetotaller in the grunge scene—Damien might have been too tempting to resist. He had died right smack in the middle of poltergeist season. . . . "Did she say anything about the pool of water he was found in?"

"No. She just sat in the corner with the TV on for days, didn't want to talk about it." Nate shook his head. "We just thought it was shock over finding Damien dead. I mean, if it had been me, I would have been pretty shaken up. But now? I think she saw something."

Even the skeptical part of my brain had to admit the idea was interesting, and it piqued my curiosity . . . but then, Nate knew how to push my buttons. "You still haven't told me what this has to do with you wanting to talk to Mindy *now*."

"Because before you brought up Aaron looking into Damien's death, I heard some stuff on the Otherside."

I frowned at him. "What *stuff*?"

"You know how ghosts are, they'll gossip about anything if they think it'll get them called to some practitioner's mirror. But there were a lot of questions being asked about Damien, trying to find him." He squared his shoulders, and after a moment added, "And me."

My frown deepened. "You?"

"Or some of my songs. A handful I never recorded, *private* ones," he added, bringing that line of questioning to a halt. "All the chatter asking about Damien's whereabouts was also looking for my songs."

I connected the dots. Mindy had not only been the last person to see Damien alive, she was also the curator of all things Nate, and the likely guardian of his unrecorded songs.

Nathan knew how my brain worked. "Come on, K," he said. "It's too much coincidence. Aaron reopens a twenty-year-old case and starts asking you questions about Damien a couple weeks after I start hearing his name on the Otherside and find out that people are asking about my hidden songs? No one's supposed to know they exist!"

Nate also knew I didn't believe in coincidences. "But why not go to you? It's no secret you're a ghost."

He shook his head. "As far as I can tell, no one's been able to find Damien, or get him to answer a seance call. Probably assume I won't talk either."

There are only two reasons a ghost won't pipe up when called out by a practitioner: either they really don't want to talk or they aren't a ghost. I knew where I was willing to put my money as far as Damien was concerned. Ghosts are often people who died young and/or violently; so a twenty-something guy who abstained from all things vice murdered by a staged overdose? It screamed ghost. Which meant it was more likely Damien didn't want to answer questions, and if the person doing the asking was serious enough, they'd have to employ a ghost binder. I shivered. Ghost binding is . . . distasteful in most practitioners' books. When a ghost stubbornly refuses to speak, they can be bound and forced to do whatever the practitioner wants—whether it is answering questions or god knows what else. It almost never goes well for the ghost; they tend to fade into absent-minded shells as soon as they are bound. Not a lot of practitioners or voodoo priests are willing to bind a ghost—not without a really damn good reason, like a poltergeist pushing small children under moving buses. But soothsayers? It is their wheelhouse. I'd met a few—they were an unsavoury crowd.

If someone wanted to speak with Damien—or Nate, for that matter—badly enough to round up a soothsayer, that would be disastrous. For all of us.

Still . . . "Nate, you recorded dozens of songs. What's the big deal with these? And why now? They've been sitting in a drawer for twenty years. That's plenty of time for someone to chase after them—or for you to go collect."

Nate clenched his hands by his waist. "These are different. And like I said, no one was looking for them until a few weeks ago, and now someone's looking for Damien—"

"Someone? Who?"

"My old band, shady producer, bored Silicon Valley super-fan gazillionaire—take your pick, K, the possibilities are endless."

True enough, but still, this had gone far beyond what I'd consider a reasonable response from Nate. "Are the songs bad? You didn't exactly shy away from making an idiot of yourself."

"I did not—"

I started counting off the incidents I could remember on my hand. "Sex tape, nude photos, saying idiotic things on national television and radio while drunk or high—"

"K! They're mine!"

I stopped, surprised at the outburst. As I've always said, ghosts are not the most altruistic bunch. I wonder if the self-sacrificing even become ghosts. Maybe that is one of the underlying qualities you need to end up on the Otherside: a selfish refusal to let go of your most beloved things. But Nate had never before coveted his possessions that had ended up with Mindy.

He bit his lip and appeared to calm down. "I didn't mean to yell, but they're important to me. They're personal, they can't get out." He looked up and met my eyes with Cameron's green ones. "Mindy doesn't realize what they are, otherwise she probably would have sold them already. I hid them amongst my things before I died. But if whoever is chasing them wants them bad enough . . . And considering how scared she was when Damien died . . ."

Shit. I frowned at him and dragged him farther into the alleyway before a pedestrian gave us a second glance. "You think someone's using whatever it is Mindy knows about Damien's death to blackmail the songs out of her?"

"K, I don't think she realizes what she's sitting on. You need to find them—and help her."

Nate knew how to make a point. Regardless of what I believed about his ulterior motives, there was enough coincidence wrapped up in the situation that his concern—however selfish at its core—might be warranted.

It was also totally outside my territory as a practitioner. "Blackmail and extortion are exactly the kind of thing Aaron deals with."

"No!" Nate looked down at his bare feet before giving me a sheepish look. "I wanted to see her again, too, okay? And besides, she's a lousy liar in person, to me at least. If she lies, I'll see it. Aaron won't."

I sighed. As much as I loathed the idea of giving in to Nate, if he was right and Mindy had seen something the night Damien died, then it made sense to talk to her.

And speak of the devil.

I spotted Mindy heading for her apartment. She was wearing a white jacket, heels, and carrying an oversized purse and a paper bag from the kind of shop I can't afford to walk into. Her hair was dyed blond and styled in an elegant bob. I had to admit the clothes threw me off—they were classy, expensive. A far cry from the things she wore in promo shots for *Glitter Hole* . . .

Then again, Nate had died almost twenty years ago. There wasn't any reason to think that, just because Mindy had lived through the grunge age and was still making a living off it, she wouldn't have changed over the years.

Nate saw her too. He held his hands up, pleading. "I *promise*. If you help me with this, I will do *everything* you say."

I watched her walk towards her building, then I glanced back at Nate. All I had to do was find out about Nate's songs . . . and feel out whether she was being blackmailed. In the grand scheme of things it was within reason—it just required a few well-placed questions.

"No more chasing after Mindy? The next time I say stay put in my apartment, you'll stay?"

"Cross my heart," Nate said, and even went through the motions.

Well, that was one thing at least. The dead have a bitch of a time breaking their word—and Nate had never broken an actual promise to me. He just went the hell out of his way to avoid making them.

I made up my mind and tied my frizzy black hair into something resembling a neat ponytail. "Where were the songs hidden?"

"Untitled, crappy, red-paper-cover notebook. She's probably forgotten it in the bottom of a box."

I sighed. I couldn't believe I was about to do this. "Stay here," I told him, and shoved him farther behind the Dumpster.

"Whoa, wait a minute—"

"You wanted my help, Nate. This is the only way you're going to get it. Besides, it's almost dusk on a weeknight. The only thing you'll get is pepper-sprayed." And that was the best-case scenario. More likely she'd think he was homeless or start screaming zombie.

I broke into a jog to intercept Mindy before she could enter the building, leaving Nate in his hiding spot. When I reached her, she'd put her shopping bag down and was fiddling with her keys; luckily, the building didn't have a concierge. "Excuse me, Mindy?" I said.

Key in lock, she turned towards me. She narrowed her eyes and frowned. "Do I know you?" she said, still holding the key.

Yeah, I have that effect on people. Though be damned if I can explain why—I'm five foot nothing and small, pretty much the least physically threatening person you could meet. I have a theory that it has to do with my Otherside association; like cats, some people pick up on it and naturally shy away from it. A normal and understandable reaction.

I smiled as professionally as I could, wiped my hand on my jeans and extended it. I wasn't sure how much formaldehyde scent might be on me, or what else I'd picked up in the underground. "Not directly. Ah, my name is Kincaid Strange."

She took my outstretched hand with some hesitation, but she shook it, still frowning until recognition flickered over her features.

"You're the voodoo chick. The one who hangs out with . . ." She trailed off, an uncomfortable look crossing her face.

So she knew about Nate's afterlife, and still hadn't tried to get in touch with him. Sometimes it's easy to lie to yourself. Other times it's much easier to lie to everyone else. This was the latter.

Gut instinct, don't fail me now . . . "Yeah—I'm, ah, not here about that. I'm, ah, here about, well, *Glitter Hole*."

Her brows knit with curiosity, so I rushed on.

"You're the expert on all things Seattle grunge. I was actually just hoping you had a couple minutes to talk about Damien Fell. He was a singer in Cadmium Coffee twenty years ago—did you know him?"

She nodded. She still wasn't friendly, but the frown had disappeared.

I went with a white lie. If Nate was right and her knowledge of Damien's death plus her unknowing possession of the songs put her in someone's crosshairs . . . I needed to find out. "I'm working with the police. They're looking at a bunch of cold cases again, and Damien's death is one of them. They've got me contacting people who knew him, and, well"—I shrugged—"you are the local expert on that time-scene." She opened her mouth and I plunged ahead before she could respond. "I was hoping you might be able to offer some insights about Damien that would help me contact him. Maybe there's a piece of memorabilia I could borrow, or buy." I hoped Aaron had a budget for that sort of thing. . . .

Mindy watched me. Up close I could see lines on her face, carefully hidden under makeup. If she'd had work done, it was very good; she was forty, but she hadn't made the mistake of trying to look twenty. I could see why Nate was still in love with her, twenty years later. She was beautiful—no, *striking* was a better description. And she knew it.

If Mindy was involved, I'd just given her a very good reason to invite me in. If she knew something about Damien's death that wasn't on the record, that might have put her in danger . . . well, here I was, maybe with information, and a connection to the police. If she turned me away, I could take what Nate had revealed about Damien and the songs to Aaron. But I didn't think she would—especially if what Nate suspected was true, that someone was holding details of Damien's death over her head. She couldn't afford to turn me away. Mindy hadn't struck me as stupid. Mercenary, yes, but like Nate she wasn't stupid. Under the circumstances, if there was a hint of threat, even an innocent person would want to know what I knew.

Mindy looked away from me and paused, then opened the door, gesturing for me to come in. "Come on. I don't have much from Cadmium Coffee, but we can talk upstairs."

Aaron would be proud—or he'd be pissed I'd mentioned a police investigation. As Gideon had said, easier to ask forgiveness.

I obliged, following her into a wide hallway, and glanced around. The building was reminiscent of my warehouse—an industrial place converted into heritage apartments, though more elegant and better maintained, and closer to the downtown core. If the owner of the warehouse I lived in ever took it upon himself to clean the place up and sell it, this might be what it ended up looking like. "Nice place," I offered.

Mindy shrugged, but gave me another assessing glance over her shoulder as she headed for the stairs. I kept my face neutral and blank.

"It was Nathan's," she said.

"Oh . . ." I shoved my hands in my pockets. Though she'd said it with the inflection of the still-grieving girlfriend of a grunge legend, a persona Mindy had perfected, it reminded me of a really old ghost, or a four-line zombie. All the components are there, there's just something missing—a spark, or maybe the will to keep going. I kept my big mouth shut as I followed her up the wooden stairs. I wasn't here to ask about Nate. . . .

Mindy climbed silently until we reached a door on the fourth floor facing the harbour side. "I use the stairs instead of the elevator. For the exercise," she said, then opened her front door and waved me in.

If the building had been renovated in the spirit of the original, then Mindy's place was the modern outlier. It had been given a major overhaul, and recently.

Despite Mindy's reputation as a radio personality grunge queen associated with flannel, thrift clothing and shabby-chic surroundings, her home was minimalist and classy. No sign of Nate or Dead Men anywhere—no framed posters or any decor remotely to do with grunge.

"Not what you expected?" Mindy said, a slight smile playing on her lips.

I shook my head and stopped looking around. "Ah, no. It's really nice." Some tasteful modern art, but otherwise the living area was spare, devoid of clutter.

"You've said that twice now. *Nice*." She dropped her bags and headed for the kitchen. "In my experience, when people say *nice* they mean anything but. Want something to drink?"

"Ah, no, thanks."

"You don't mind if I do, then?" She didn't wait for me to answer, only reached overhead into a cupboard and pulled out a bottle of vodka. She proceeded to fill a glass with ice and pour herself a generous drink. Clearly not a rookie at imbibing hard liquor. I filed that away for later. . . . "Yeah, it's never what people expect from me." She levelled her gaze at me over the glass. "I keep history to *Glitter Hole*, social media and promo," she said, taking a long sip. "It's not healthy to live in the past."

She gestured to the bar stools on the other side of the counter.

I started to unzip my jacket then stopped, suddenly conscious of the shirt I had on underneath—a Dead Men concert T.

I rezipped my jacket before taking a seat on the chrome and white leather bar stool. Why make things more awkward than they already were?

"So, what is it you want to know about Cadmium Coffee?" Mindy took a sip of her drink and shook her head as she swallowed back the bite. "Christ, haven't thought of them in a *long* time."

I kept my face and voice as neutral as possible, going for polite indifference at the very least. Just here doing a little research as the only practitioner in town . . . nothing to do with Nathan . . . "Just what you might remember—about Damien—and the people he hung around." I shrugged. "I haven't tried a seance yet, but I may not be able to reach his ghost. I find doing research beforehand helps—and in Cadmium Coffee's case, since they never really—"

"Made it big?" Mindy offered. She looked up from her drink. "Not everyone becomes a ghost, do they?"

"Ah—no, they don't," I replied. "There's no real rule—but as far as I can tell, about 75 percent of people end up ghosts when they die. Or that's my calling success rate. Though they don't all last as long as . . ." I'd been about to say *Nate*. "As some," I said instead.

Mindy nodded and swirled her glass of vodka and ice. "And why is that, Kincaid Strange?"

Her interest surprised me. I grinned to try to lighten the mood. "No one knows."

"Guess," she said, the corners of her mouth turning up in a smile. "Curiosity."

There was a game we were playing I didn't think I liked or understood. I shifted uncomfortably on the bar stool. "I don't like guessing. People have a habit of turning it into gospel later on."

Mindy let out a small laugh. "Speculate, then. I won't hold you to it. Promise."

With the exception of Sarah, Aaron's partner and a talented detective in her own right, and Lee, I didn't get along with a lot of women. My therapist—for the whole anger management thing—had a theory I didn't have many female friends because of my own troubled relationship with my mother. My mother certainly had enough female friends, and a lot of good they did her. They weren't the ones helping her out of the hospital or around the house after "domestic incidents," as they were called in the police reports. Hear no evil, see no evil. I have my own theory: Women like my mother spend most of their lives trying to make nice, mend the bridge, keep the peace, not rock the boat—real feminine-like. The reason I butted heads with most women? There is only so much I'm able to feed into the circle of bullshit. I think it is disruptive—not for Sarah and Lee, I figure they're more like me in that regard, but for the ones who rely on group validation. Those kinds of friendships require an awful lot of bullshit, and people don't like other people pointing out their bullshit. Especially when that person ends up being me.

That's not to say I don't have my own giant can of bullshit. Most of the people I associate with are dead, for Christ's sake; I'm not one to act superior. But figuring out a way to pretend nothing is wrong . . . that's a whole new level of self-deception. And a great way to get yourself thrown down a flight of stairs. Just like my mother had been by my father, the fall she never woke up from.

Mindy was waiting, sipping from her glass. I could see how she'd had Nate wrapped around her finger. She wasn't just a pretty face; she had an edge—women who live and look like this usually don't pour themselves a glass of vodka like a pro—and she knew how to use that edge to her advantage. A quiet, invisible tool to fuck the minds of her opponents.

I was feeling uncharacteristically out of my league, and decided my best bet was to stick to the direct approach. "I give you my professional opinion on ghosts and you tell me everything I want to know about Damien?"

Her smile widened. "Deal."

I took a deep breath and thought about how best to phrase it for a layperson. "As far as I can tell, there are no rules as to who ends up a ghost. Anyone and everyone can become one, or be raised as a zombie for that matter."

"But?"

"But, in my and a lot of other practitioners' opinion, it's the people who have unfinished business that become ghosts."

"Not the people who need to learn from their mistakes?" Mindy asked.

I wondered if she meant Nate. "Only the ones who think they should have learned from their mistakes. Again, unfinished business. But it's their own issue, not anyone else's."

Mindy laughed softly. "That does make an awful lot of sense, doesn't it? Also makes me wonder why people don't try harder not to make mistakes."

Before I could think twice, I said, "It's not the mistakes part people need to worry about. It's the regretting-it part."

That got another laugh out of her, except this one sounded more sad than amused. She held up her glass. "I can drink to that." She finished off the vodka and poured herself another. "So what is it you want to know about Cadmium Coffee, Kincaid Strange?"

I took a deep breath. "For one, whether Damien was using." Mindy raised her eyebrows, so I added, "Like I said, I'm helping someone go through cold case files. His family seemed to think he abstained from drug use completely. His mother—she's not doing well and asked the Seattle PD to open the case again." And Aaron was there to listen.

She nodded. "I remember his parents. Only met them once— before Damien died, not after." She lowered her head. "No, Damien wasn't using. Anything. Wouldn't even touch coffee, let alone alcohol." She held up the glass and took another sip to make the point.

"What do you think he was doing with the heroin?"

"Honestly?"

I nodded.

Mindy shot back what was left of her vodka and slammed the glass on the bar, licking her heavily glossed lips. "I think someone killed him," she said.

"Why?" I remembered Mindy hadn't reported being present at the time of death, only finding the body, so I added, "I mean, who would have wanted him dead back in '95? Did you ever tell anyone what you suspected?"

She snorted. "Because anyone back then wanted to know what a supposed junkie's girlfriend thought?"

"Damien wasn't a junkie."

Mindy shook her head. "Things have changed, but they haven't changed that much. Practitioners do legal cases, right? Will contestments and such?" She smirked at me. "I suppose all those suits like calling you in, showing you off in front of their well-heeled clients? No offence, but you don't look like the professional consultant type. I know better than to make snap judgments, but most people . . ." She let the thought hang. "It was worse back then. Garage band musicians dressed like us meant junkie. Case closed." The smirk faded and she paused to pour herself another drink. "Now as to who did it?" She glanced up and fixed me with her eyes—hazel, set off by copper eye makeup applied with a light hand. "You should really be asking your friend Nate about that."

"Nate didn't kill anyone," I said, and mentally chided myself for jumping to his defence so quickly.

She laughed and shook her head. "I'm not suggesting he did, but your defence of him is real cute. Jesus, I must have sounded like that at some time or other. No, Nate was egotistical and he always wanted to be the star, but it'd never occur to him to kill anyone. I meant you should ask him about the rest of his flannel-clad troupe. You know how they got their big break?" She smiled to herself. "Of course you do, otherwise I don't think you'd be here."

I nodded. "The gig at the Cage."

"That helped, but it was only part of it. There were the songs."

My palms felt clammy as I did my best to hold a neutral expression. "What songs?" I asked.

"The ones Nate co-wrote with a 'ghost writer' right after Damien died. They were different, new, better. Those were what really put Dead Men on the map." She walked over to a desk hidden behind a corner alcove in her kitchen. "Nate always had a certain style, but it lacked what you might call a commercial polish and appeal. After Damien died, Nate's music changed." She pulled out a binder from a drawer, the numbers 93–96 written in what looked like whiteout on the cover, and began flipping through. "Ah, here—this one." She stopped on one of the album pages where a collection of old newspaper clippings had been pasted, tapping on the page. "This review really made the connection for me. I quote: 'It's as if Dead Men took a lesson from Cadmium Coffee's late Damien Fell in songwriting. There's a depth and musicality now that melds with Cade's rough edges, creating something unique and altogether special.'" She pulled out the article, came back to the bar and handed it to me.

I looked down at the yellowed clipping and back up at her. "You think whoever killed Damien did it over a handful of songs?"

She inclined her head. "Maybe. Or maybe Damien wasn't the songwriter everyone thought he was. Maybe whoever was helping Damien got tired of not getting credit. Or maybe there is no connection. All I'm saying is, it's a big coincidence."

It sounded as though she shared our suspicion about coincidences. And then there was the fact that Mindy had witnessed Damien's death, according to Nate . . . For all I knew, she could be trying to deflect attention from herself.

"He talks about him, you know. Nate," she said.

I glanced up from the article.

"Cole. Cole's been talking about him more lately," Mindy said.

I'll bet he has, especially since Nate's first seance performance ended up on YouTube about a year ago. When Nate had first agreed to work with me around then, the phone calls from the living members of Dead Men had rolled in. But not a word from Cole.

"Cole will be back soon. He won't want to talk to you."

She opened up a pack of cigarettes and held them out, as if daring me to stay. I shook my head. She took one for herself and lit it up anyway.

She didn't ask if it bothered me. Well, it was her place. Another personality quirk I filed away—I had to admit I admired it. Not apologizing for yourself. Something I tried not to do. Maybe we had something in common beyond Nate.

"Nate and Cole go a long way back," Mindy said, taking a drag off her cigarette. "They went to high school together, if I remember—they started Dead Men. I figure they must have been friends to start a band, but by the time I met them they argued more often than not. Cole also knew Damien." A smile played at Mindy's lips as she took another slow drag. "Cole was thinking of leaving Dead Men for Cadmium over Nate's inability to take criticism—or that's how Cole puts it. It never came to blows, but it was going that way."

She disappeared into another room and after a moment came back out holding a T-shirt. "Like I said, I don't have much of Damien's—We weren't seeing each other for long, before . . ." She trailed off and held it out over the counter. "If it'll help you find him in a seance or whatever it is you do, you can have it. Tell him I say hi."

I nodded and took the T-shirt. The image on it was from an old cartoon show, *Scooby-Doo.*

"And Kincaid?"

I glanced up. There was a harder look on Mindy's face than had been there a moment before. One that highlighted the lines and emphasized her age.

"Next time, call," Mindy said. "I'm sure Nathan has my number somewhere."

I cringed. I bet she knew exactly who called her and never spoke before hanging up. She wasn't stupid.

And neither was I. If we were broaching Nate, my guess was it was about time for me to leave. I stood up to go, *Scooby-Doo* T-shirt in hand.

I had just about made it to the door, but one thing still bugged me, and I had to ask. . . .

Damn it. "Mindy?"

"I didn't ask because I don't want to know," she said, smoke from her cigarette billowing out of her nose and mouth. Her eyes were down on the counter—or her drink. "Some things are better left in the past, and no offence to your friend Nathan, but I've had to see his shit every day of my life for the last twenty years. He's about the last thing I want to talk about. At least I can leave something of his in the past."

It wasn't the reaction I was expecting. I could understand it, the impulse to let things be, but still, it was sad and strange.

I reached for the door—but I'd promised Nate. "Nate did want me to ask you one thing. He wants to know about a notebook of his—red paper cover, worn. That was it."

The smile on Mindy's face dropped. She stabbed her cigarette out violently in the near-empty vodka glass. "I fucking knew it." She glanced up at me, the veil of friendliness replaced with something more feral. "You tell him it's none of his goddamned business."

I nodded and reached for the door. I might not know many women well, but I know these kinds of mood swings. The best way to deal with them is to back away, fast.

"And tell him if he calls me one more time and hangs up the phone, I'll hire a binder to get rid of him!" she screamed.

She threw the glass and I heard it shatter against the door above my head as I ducked.

The lock turned behind me and I stepped out of the way as the door swung open.

Cole Brighton, drummer from Dead Men Tell No Tails, stuck his head in and looked around before coming inside.

Like Mindy, Cole had aged but managed to retain his youthful good looks. His expression of bewilderment quickly shifted to irritation as he took in the scene.

"I see you're in a great fucking mood," he said to Mindy. "And who the hell are you?" he spat at me.

"Music reporter," Mindy said, a little too fast, but Cole either didn't notice or didn't care.

He gave me a once-over while I faced him in my beat-up leather jacket with my arms crossed.

"Another reporter asking about Nathan Cade's triumphant return on YouTube?" He swore and pushed past me, heading for the kitchen, where he got his own glass tumbler out. "And you let her past the front door? You're really slipping, Mins."

Mindy didn't say anything, but her rage seemed to have subsided. She reminded me of a house cat waiting for a toy or a treat—or to be swatted away.

I cleared my throat. "Uh, yeah. I was just asking Mindy about some of Nate's old songs—the stories behind the big hits, inspiration."

He snorted. "You had me fooled for a second. Thought you might actually be a music reporter. Who hired you? Private or one of the record execs?"

"If the record execs wanted to ask about Nathan's songs, wouldn't they just call one of you?"

"Seriously, does it look like I'm on the record companies' good side? Look at me. I'm a forty-year-old drummer who's lucky if I can get a gig with a band I wouldn't be caught dead with ten years ago." He frowned at me. "I thought I recognized you. You're the practitioner, aren't you?"

I nodded. No point lying when the jig is up.

"What does he want?" When I didn't answer, he added, "Nate. What does he want with Mindy?"

I shrugged. "He's looking for an old notebook. It's his. The dead tend to obsess over things like that."

He nodded and looked at his tumbler, though he didn't touch it. "Trying to take his stuff with him. That doesn't sound like the dead, that just sounds like Nate."

He glanced at Mindy, who'd been silent the whole time. Then, as if her inaction made his decision, he stood up and headed for the door, opening it for me. "Come on, I'll walk you out."

It wasn't a suggestion. I followed, and waited in the hall while Cole closed and locked the door behind him.

"Saw the concert a couple weeks back. Nate was good. Amazing what he can do when he's not falling off the stage. Looks the same— except maybe the hair. How did you get him to do it?" He sounded uninterested, but I caught the note of accusation.

I shook my head. "Nate decides the shows. We have a no-binding agreement."

Cole nodded. "I'll bet he never once asked you to find any of us?"

Stick to the truth, Kincaid. "He talks about you guys often."

"Not what I asked."

"No."

Cole headed down the stairs ahead of me. "I don't know where Nate's stuff is. Mindy might've hawked the notebook on eBay years ago." I didn't miss the contempt in his voice. "Mindy wouldn't get that riled up over an old notebook," he said when he reached the bottom steps. He stood in front of the door, blocking my way.

"I was asking some questions about Damien Fell."

Cole let out a whistle. "Now that is a name I haven't heard in"— he let out another whistle—"forever. Damien wasn't a star, not like Nate. Why were you asking about him?"

I hadn't wanted my white lie about the Seattle PD to go past Mindy, but Cole had been around at the same time—and a member of Nate's band.

"I work with the Seattle PD sometimes. Damien's file was recently reopened."

Cole raised his eyebrows. "He overdosed."

"Maybe, maybe not," I said. I held up the T-shirt. "I just wanted to see if Mindy remembered anything about his death. And if she had anything of Damien's."

He frowned. "Why would you want something of Damien's?"

"The dead respond better to their stuff."

"Wow, the dead really do try and take their shit with them," he said with a derisive laugh.

"What about you? Do you remember anything? Mindy said you and Damien were friends."

Cole smiled at me, but it didn't reach his eyes. He shook his head. "Naw. It was twenty years ago. Barely remember the guy."

He stepped past me and headed up the stairs. Apparently our conversation was over. I grabbed the door handle, suddenly eager to get out of the building.

"Hey, Strange?"

I glanced over at Cole, who'd stopped at the first landing.

"Mindy tossed a bunch of Nate's things into storage a while back. Might be the notebook he's looking for is in there."

Interesting . . . she hadn't mentioned that.

"I'll ask when she's in a better mood. You know Nate and I were best friends since ninth grade?"

Nate hadn't told me that. I didn't say anything, but it must have shown on my face, because Cole added, "Figured he wouldn't bring that up. I read once that the dead hold grudges. Nate was bad to begin with, hate to see what he's like now." He started walking back up the stairs. "You know, Nate always said if he died he didn't want to have his shit hawked to the highest bidder. He said it a bunch of times."

"And you don't think Mindy—your wife—respected those wishes?"

Cole smiled. "You go look at eBay and tell me."

I headed straight for the alley on the opposite side of the building, where I knew Nate would be waiting. I was reeling from the dysfunctional relationship that was Mindy and Cole. They'd practically implicated each other—without knowing what they were implicating each other in.

Nate was watching for me and stepped from behind the Dumpster as soon as I was near. "Hey, K—"

I didn't answer, but grabbed him by the arm and started walking towards my bike.

"K, what happened?"

I shook my head and kept walking. "I don't know what she was like when you were seeing her, Nate, but she is *not* the same person anymore."

He grabbed my shoulders and turned me around. "I know—I just—I know, okay?" Despite the fact that his borrowed body was not at its best, his face still creased with worry. "Tell me what she said about the notebook."

"That, and I quote, it was none of your goddamned business."

Nate didn't seem fazed as he searched my face with Cameron's green eyes—a wholly unsettling experience. "That was it?"

"No. She threw her vodka glass at me. And then Cole stepped in."

"I thought she'd say—something else," he said, and let go of my arm.

I don't know what I'd expected, but not for Nate to look . . . dejected. I sighed. "She doesn't look like she's in trouble. At all. And she gave me some leads on Damien." I held up the T-shirt.

That got Nate's attention. "You're going to contact Damien?"

I nodded. Of course I was going to contact Damien. "It's the only chance I have of getting a straight answer out of anyone. She said he wasn't a junkie either, but, like you, couldn't come up with a concrete enemy. All roads lead to him." And Nate and all his surviving bandmates . . . I frowned. "How come you never mentioned you had a co-writer? And how come it's not mentioned on any of your albums?"

He balked. "How did you know that? Did Mindy tell you? Damn it. They wanted to be anonymous. Just— Look, it's not important."

"If it's not important, why are you acting this way? Nate, I'm not an idiot. You're leaving something out."

"I'm sorry, K, what else do you want me to say? I'm sorry I sent you in to see her, sorry I wanted—" He tried to run his hand through his hair and let it fall to his side, frustrated. "I don't know what I wanted."

I knew I should probably yell at Nate, or at the very least make him tell me what the hell he was leaving out. But I couldn't. He looked defeated enough. I let out a sigh.

"Come on. We're going home. I need to try and summon Damien, and you owe me a huge favour. You're going to tell me everything you know about Cole Brighton."

✳

By the time we got home, Nate was in a mood and locked himself back in the spare bedroom as soon as we entered the apartment. I left him to ruminate on Mindy; it's not every day you get your heart ripped out by someone whose entire living is made off you.

On the one hand, it seemed like a lousy thing for her to do, pushing the dead aside. On the other hand, I'm not sure there is a right way to grieve. If half the people who called me could just let go of their deceased family members . . . And there I went being a hypocrite again. If I started counselling people not to contact the dead, I'd cut my business in half.

I headed into the kitchen and turned on the kettle before checking the time: 8 p.m. It was early, but I'd tapped the barrier today and I'd probably need to a few more times over the next few days if I had any hope of channelling Damien. I needed as much sleep as I could get.

As I waited for the water to boil, I did my best to push thoughts of Mindy and Nate to the back of my head. Our conversation kept coming back to me, though—the strange way Mindy had tied herself to the memory of Nate but resented the fact that her lifestyle and persona depended on him. I wondered if Nate realized that, or if he'd even understand it.

And the strange, antagonistic dynamic with her husband, Cole.

I guess we all have our price. If I'd learned anything from my dealings with Gideon so far, that was it. All you have to do is figure out what someone is willing to sell themselves for.

I poured the water into my pot of jasmine tea—another splurge since Lee's payment and Nate's gig at the university had both boosted my funds. While I waited for it to steep, my stomach growled, so I rifled through the fridge. Lettuce, tomato, bread, bacon, mayonnaise . . . Lucky for me, Nate had stocked the fridge after stopping at the grocery store on one of his outings, knowing my love of BLTs. He wasn't always selfish—just when he got to obsessing about Mindy.

I stuck the bread in the toaster, loaded the bacon into the frying pan, and began cutting up the lettuce and tomato to keep myself from thinking about Aaron's case and how my meeting with Mindy fit into things. It didn't work. By the time the sandwich was ready, I'd made a list in my head—a new list, I might add—of everyone who could have benefited from Damien dying. Of note were the members of Nate's band, but I didn't discount the idea that Damien might have had help writing his songs. What if it had been someone from Dead Men? Hell, what if he'd been working with Nate? The reviewer had said there were similarities. . . . What if it was more than imitation? But Nate would have told me that—wouldn't he? I filed that one away until I decided how trustworthy Mindy's account of events was.

Which meant I still couldn't scratch Nate from my list.

I turned my attention to the other elephant in the room.

I opened my laptop and typed "wraiths" in the search engine. I perused the results while I ate my BLT and warmed my hands around the tea.

The first hits were what I expected: references to video game monsters and role-playing game characters and, below that, links to myths and legends of the dark arts. It was more story and speculation than historical material. Certainly not any reputable practitioner texts or research I recognized, but I wasn't looking for facts; I was looking for patterns—hints of what constituted a wraith, and more about the "limbo" state Lee had said Nate was in.

As I chewed and clicked through the pages, something jumped out at me—a characteristic Lee had mentioned as well in her recounting of the wraith that haunted her village: the cold. The details were never the same, but all the stories noted that a deathly cold followed the wraiths and plagued their victims. Even the video game monsters and RPG characters agreed on that point.

It rang true. I mean, if a wraith's power came from the Otherside, it stood to reason that there'd be cold. But why was it so deadly? Gideon's visits were always accompanied by drops in temperature, and tapping the barrier never failed to chill me—but freezing to death wasn't a real risk.

I polished off my sandwich and finished my jasmine tea then closed the laptop. Tomorrow I'd consult Mork's books for any explanation of what might have happened to Nate. And I'd also take a look to see if there was anything on why the wraiths froze things. I was willing to bet the extreme affinity for cold had something to do with the limbo state.

I headed into the bathroom to shower and warm up before turning in for the night.

Wraiths, zombies, ghosts and twenty-year-old murders. It was almost enough to make me want to crawl back to Vancouver. At least there weren't any poltergeists to worry about. Yet.

I was brushing my teeth and concentrating on a rusted part of the sink when the cold hit me. Shit. I spit out my toothpaste and looked up into the mirror. It had begun to fog over and a message was scrawling itself across the glass.

Remember. Five o'clock tomorrow. Don't be late.

I snorted. "Like I could forget," I said. "And this is my bathroom. A little privacy?"

But there was no response. The fog faded and all that was left was my ghost grey–tinged reflection. I caught the flicker of Otherside as it dissipated—not like bindings from a zombie or a set mirror, but like the mechanical and constantly moving Otherside bindings that seemed to follow Gideon everywhere. Why wasn't I surprised Gideon had figured out a way to send Otherside e-mail? Just what I needed.

I shook my head and decided against showering just in case Gideon made a surprise appearance, a follow-up to the creepy message. I washed my face and left the bathroom, closing the door behind me. I'd have a talk with Gideon tomorrow about mirror etiquette. . . .

I checked the locks on Nate's door before locking my own behind me. I didn't think there was really a risk of Nate going feral in the middle of the night and trying to hunt me down, but with a zombie as unstable as he was . . . I crawled into bed and pulled the duvet up to my neck to warm up, in lieu of the shower.

I wanted to close my eyes and fall asleep, but couldn't switch off yet. Eyes half-lidded, I grabbed my phone from where I'd plugged it in on the bedside table and checked my messages.

I'd sold another book on eBay, and flagged the message as a reminder to mail it off tomorrow. There were a few more concert inquiries about Nate, and I flagged them too. Another inquiry about a seance for will purposes from a lawyer I knew and could tolerate, and I typed a quick reply. I swore as I deleted an e-mail from Cody without opening it.

And finally, at the top of the list was an e-mail from Aaron labelled simply "Cadmium Coffee." There was a file attached, so I opened it. A brief rundown of the case with the scanned articles I'd requested.

I started to draft a reply.

Spoke to Nate. He doesn't remember much about Damien, but he confirmed he wasn't an addict. He also said both his old bandmate Cole and his ex-girlfriend Mindy were close to him around the time he died. In my opinion you should really take a closer look at Mindy. Call me tomorrow and I'll fill you in. I'd thought about including Cole in my assessment, but besides his antagonistic relationship with his wife, I didn't have a reason to. Yet.

I read the e-mail twice before sending it. I didn't want to imply I had anything concrete on Mindy, but I did want to stick the worm of an idea in Aaron's head. He had more resources than I did and my motives weren't altruistic. I wouldn't mind knowing what there was to know about Mindy Pine—if not for Nate's sake, then to satisfy my own curiosity.

I tossed my cell on the nightstand and pulled the covers over my head.

As I drifted off to sleep, I thought of Mindy and how, despite her carefully manicured appearance, it seemed as if she was unravelling underneath. Maybe that was just part of the enigmatic appeal that had driven so many rockers like Nate crazy. Or maybe the years had left scars on her—deeper and uglier ones than can be concealed.

CHAPTER 7

FROZEN GHOSTS

It wasn't my alarm that woke me up. It had already failed to do that, earning my phone a spot under two pillows. My ringer, on the other hand, was louder and more irritating.

It took me a second to root around for it under the pillows, but I managed to answer by the fourth ring.

Eight-fifteen. I rubbed my eyes. Oh, it was so not going to be a good morning. . . .

"Aaron, feel free to take this the wrong way, but you are nowhere near good-looking enough to call me before 9 a.m. on a Saturday." And we were doing so well with the e-mail . . . Why was it that Aaron had a knack for calling ridiculously early?

Because he was a morning person. Annoyingly so.

"It's an emergency," he said.

I wiped more of the sleep out of my eyes. "No 'Good morning, Kincaid, how are you? Sorry for calling before 9 a.m.'?"

"Kincaid—"

I cut him off. "We agreed no phone calls this early." I'd pushed half my comforter off then rethought the whole idea of getting up. I could deal with Aaron just as well in bed as out of bed.

Okay, not what I meant. Never mind.

"Unless it was an emergency, which this is," he said.

I closed my eyes. Yeah, that sounded like something Aaron would get me to agree to while I was fully awake.

I sat up. "How about you tell me what's happened."

"It would be better if we could talk in person."

Aaron always thought it was better to talk in person. It was easier to get me to agree to things in person. Damn it . . . I threw my legs over the side of the bed.

"You only ever want to talk in person when you think I might say no."

"Kincaid, at the risk of being an asshole, I need you to get out of bed *now* and come look at something."

Aaron had a couple of modes. He wasn't above mild manipulation to get me to help him, but his tone was too serious for that. "Now you really have me worried."

"We've had some repetitions in methodology of that cold case I showed you," he said. After a brief pause he added, "There's been a new victim."

I swore. A new homicide—and for whatever reason, Aaron didn't want to mention over the phone that it was paranormal. "I take it you're at the office?"

He didn't answer my question, instead saying, "And it might be a good idea to bring Nate along."

I balanced the phone under my chin and started to pull on my jeans. Yeah, that wasn't happening. "Look, Aaron, Nate is still recovering from the—well—everything that's gone on the last couple weeks." Actually surprisingly true. "He's in a mood and I don't think he's going to be useful to anyone. Besides, like I said in my e-mail, I grilled him and he doesn't remember much." Still shockingly close to the truth. Lying was coming more and more easily to me, and it didn't feel good.

"Why don't I swing by and pick you up. Does fifteen work?"

I sighed and scanned the floor for a T-shirt. "Fifteen it is, Aaron. Just call me when you get here so I can come down and meet you." I didn't think he'd smell the formaldehyde coming off Nate from the door, but even the slightest whiff would pique his curiosity. Regardless, I wouldn't risk it.

"Just be ready to go. You're going to need to see this to believe it." He hung up.

Aaron would be surprised at what didn't surprise me. . . .

I found a clean 1980s *Voltron* cartoon T-shirt I'd forgotten about sticking out of my dresser drawer and a flannel shirt to toss overtop, smelling it first to make sure it was still wearable. I'd have to do laundry soon. . . . *Voltron* meant I was getting to the absolute bottom of my pile.

Cleanish clothing in hand, I unlocked my door and made a beeline for the shower. I stuck my head through the door with caution. No chill in the air, no notes scrawled on the bathroom mirror. Phew. I breathed in and accessed my Otherside sight, scanning the washroom for any sign of Gideon. There was none. Just to be on the safe side, I grabbed a dark towel and hung it over the mirror before disrobing.

After an all too brief turn under the hot water, I dressed and headed for the spare room. "Nate?" I called.

There was a bang on the inside of the spare-bedroom door.

I frowned. "That's not an answer, Nate. A feral zombie can still bang on a door."

"Yeah, totally feral in here, K. You should totally let me out so I can go on a zombie rampage."

I swore and unlocked the door. Nate was leaning on the inside of the door frame, glaring at me. He'd taken the hat off and his hair hung in greasy, limp strands. I didn't know if it was the sleep or the new embalming fluid Mork had treated him with, but the chemical smell almost knocked me over. I breathed out and held my T-shirt over my nose. Not that that did me a lot of good. "In the shower," I told him, and ran ahead to the bathroom to make sure there was still no sign of Gideon.

"Be fast about it," I said to Nate. "Mork said the embalming fluid would allow you to clean yourself, but I don't want to test the extent of it—and besides that . . ." I stopped myself from mentioning Gideon. I'm not a superstitious practitioner by a long shot, but even I had misgivings about speaking the sorcerer ghost's name out loud. Speak the devil's name and he will come. . . .

"Just hurry it up," I said, and shoved Nate inside before closing the door. I waited to hear the sound of water running before I turned on the coffee maker. I brushed my teeth in the kitchen sink and grabbed my laptop from the kitchen table. Ten minutes until Aaron arrived.

There was an e-mail from Lee stating simply that Mork's books were available for me at the bar.

Hopefully, whatever Aaron wanted me to look at wouldn't take too long and I could swing by the underground city before my lesson with Gideon. I'd have to figure out what to do with Nate while Gideon was here. If the shower dulled the smell, I could send him to a coffee shop instead of making him sit out on the fire escape again.

I filled my travel mug with fresh coffee before getting back to my unread messages. Mostly spam, but there was an inquiry about the condition of one of my textbooks. I sent off a quick reply, saying it was the definition of *used*. All the pages were there and readable, along with a handful of carefully curated coffee stains. . . .

I had just pressed Send when I heard the bathroom door click open.

I glanced over my shoulder. Nate was dressed in clean sweatpants and a flannel shirt. His red hair was damp and still thinning but less greasy, almost healthy-looking. Even his skin didn't seem as waxy.

I checked the time. Eight minutes left. I wanted to be downstairs in five. "Glad to see you listened to me about the shower times. How's the skin?"

"Prune-like, but I still have all my fingers." He shoved his hands in his pockets before I could look.

"Just remember you promised to do what I said. Which means staying inside."

I was half-waiting for Nate to argue as I logged off the computer.

"I owe you an apology for yesterday," he said, after a moment had passed.

I paused, fingers suspended over the keyboard. "Do you want to make it up to me?" I asked.

He nodded.

"Then stay here." I held out my now-empty travel mug. Nate took it and started to fill it while I closed my laptop and gathered the things I'd need. I wasn't sure exactly what to expect, so I packed a bit of everything: china marker, sage, a couple of mirrors . . .

"I think Aaron's taking me to a crime scene. Something to do with the cold case."

"Damien?" Nate said, handing me back the refilled mug.

I nodded and took a sip. Four minutes before I wanted to be downstairs.

Nate nodded. "Won't leave the apartment. It's me and the PlayStation."

I relaxed and threw my jacket on. Nate was a lot of things, but he'd never broken an outright promise. Just bent them.

"K?"

I looked back at him as I was buckling up my brand new motorcycle boots. A necessary splurge because the heel had snapped off my last pair.

"Can I help? Maybe if I look stuff up online—about Damien, that is. Who might have wanted him dead . . ."

"That's not a bad idea," I said. I couldn't trust him to examine Mindy's role with any objectivity, but maybe he could find something else. He had the time. Speaking of time . . . I checked my phone. No text from Aaron and two minutes left. "The files Aaron sent are in my e-mail folder. Take note of anything you find or think is important—and no answering the door, and careful going into the bathroom." Not that he needed to use it often, but zombies still have waste to get rid of—albeit much less frequently than the living.

"On it, K."

"We'll take a look at Mork's reference books tonight." I took a deep breath as I examined the contents of my bag, then glanced up at Nate. This was the tricky part. . . . "But if I still don't have a clue how to get you out of Cameron's body by tomorrow, we're going to Gideon."

I'd gambled on Lee's help to get Nate out of Cameron's body, but she hadn't come through and now Mork's books were my last resort. If that didn't work . . .

Nate's face fell. "K? Are you nuts? Gideon will kill us."

I shoved the book I needed to mail, along with a padded envelope, into my bag before tossing it over my shoulder. I shot Nate a wry look.

He rolled his eyes. "You know what I mean. It's a figure of speech."

I opened the door and stepped outside. "It'll be a lot worse if we wait any longer to tell him. I don't know about you, but I already don't relish the idea of explaining a week of hiding you from him. I'd rather not make it two—especially now that I'm going to be seeing him on a regular basis. We'll comb through Mork's books tonight after Gideon leaves. Promise," I said.

"Fine," Nate said after a moment, but he sounded anything but.

Well, he'd promised to follow my lead. Make your bed and lie in it . . .

I held up my mug of coffee in a wave before closing the door and locking it behind me. Time to see what kind of paranormal disaster Aaron had cooked up for me.

*

I stubbed the toe of my boot into the floor of the Rex. Full wood grain—well worn from decades of people's boots. Considering the wear on the place and the area of town we were in, it might have been a century old. A floor with grooves worn from a hundred years' worth of drunk, shuffling feet. The things you notice at a crime scene . . .

I glanced up at the bright lights suspended from the high, raf-tered ceiling. Well-lit loft spaces were rare these days—or maybe I was used to dank dive bars, where there was just enough light to stop you from crashing into things but not enough to illuminate any unpleasant details.

There was something awfully familiar about this place. I crossed my arms to try to warm myself up. My coffee was long gone and despite this place having a healthy respect for modern lighting, they didn't believe in modern heating.

Still, something about the rafters and the pane window facing the street . . . "Didn't this use to be a music venue?" I asked, glanc-ing back at Aaron, who was giving me space as he always did when I first stepped into a crime scene.

He nodded, keeping a neutral face. "Cadmium Coffee and Dead Men used to play here, along with a slew of other grunge bands back in the nineties."

That's where I remembered the place from. A few of Nate's old band photos had been taken here. "The Cage?" I asked.

"Hasn't been called that in over ten years. Was bought out by a restaurant group in 2005 and renovated. They went back to the original name, the Rex, after the historic Rex Hotel from the late 1800s, early 1900s."

I nodded absently as I took in more of my surroundings. Lots of businesses on the northwest coast had been gutted in the early 2000s to appeal to a changing demographic, one with money and a taste for west coast charm. The Rex was a classic example: the decor was shabby chic—mainly items that carried a high price tag for looking worn and beat up. The chalk-painted, mismatched tables and chairs, red curtains, and black-and-white photos from Seattle's log-ging heyday set in birchwood frames gave the place the veneer of an old bar, but it lacked the darker, grittier soul of the time period it imitated.

I'm sure it turned a good business with the locals and tourists, but it only made me sad. I'd take Lee's over this place any day, or Catamaran's, the charred and condemned sports bar by the docks that Randall had owned . . . where I would have died if not for Gideon's intervention.

I rubbed my arms once again, willing them to warm up. "Well, you've got me here, which means you think it's paranormal, though I'm not seeing anything," I said, turning to Aaron.

"Nothing?" he asked.

I could have sworn there was a flash of surprise, but with Aaron it was often hard to tell; he hid his emotions well on the job. I shook my head. I'd taken a look with my Otherside sight when we'd walked in. "There's nothing to do with the Otherside in here, Aaron. Not even a trace."

"If there was, say, last night, could it have disappeared already?"

I felt the corner of my mouth twitch up—more from irritation than amusement. "Impossible to answer without knowing what kind of Otherside you're looking for." As he frowned, I added, "If you're thinking a ghost or a poltergeist passed through, sure. The trace of Otherside they leave behind is minuscule at best and disperses back across the barrier almost instantaneously, as if it had never been here. But bindings? If someone bound Otherside here, it could linger for years—or the practitioner could have dispersed it themselves."

"How long can bindings last on the ground?"

I thought about the wards that had been tied to Marjorie's coffee shop to block out prying Otherside eyes and prevent any stray practitioners from discovering she was a zombie. The same wards I'd discovered while investigating her murder, as a favour to Lee. "The longest I've seen had been in place for decades."

"And how far can their effects stretch? The bindings, that is."

Again, not that wards are my area of expertise . . . "An entire room like this, I suppose, if we're talking about a ward for a shop or a house. Max's house was warded against ghosts pestering him, and Marjorie had the window in her coffee shop warded." I gestured around us. "But there's no Otherside anywhere in this room."

Aaron walked past me towards a set of stairs leading to the basement. "Come on," he said, taking the first step. "I'll let you be the judge of that."

I followed. I wasn't sure what angle Aaron was running, but if there was a paranormal element in here, I was a—

Damn.

I let out a low whistle as we reached the bottom of the stairs. I'd assumed the new owners of the Rex had retired the place as a music venue entirely, but they had moved it downstairs. And at the moment, it was completely covered in frost—no, wait, frost wasn't right. It was ice fractured into a thick, crystalline white powder that covered everything in sight.

"Holy shit," I said. My warm breath fogged before me and the air that replaced it stung my throat and lungs.

It coated the stage, band equipment, furniture, even crawled up the walls. I traced the pattern of ice with my eyes and realized it had formed a tight ring around the room. And in the centre of it all, ten feet away from where I stood, was a body—a man's, on his side and facing away from the stairs, his arms stretched out as if he'd tried to fend something off and been frozen in motion. There was a ring of yellow tape around the room.

I felt warm breath at my ear and jumped.

"What about this, Kincaid? See any Otherside in here?" Aaron said.

I shot him a dirty look, letting him know what I thought about him sneaking up on me. "You could have skipped the upstairs show, you know."

He shrugged, but didn't crack a smile. "Figured it was worthwhile to get a baseline. Also, I was curious whether it had crept to the upstairs floor considering how it's climbed the walls. Still think there's no Otherside involved?"

I turned back to the body. "I reserve my right to not give you an opinion just yet."

"Wouldn't have it any other way." He handed me paper slippers from inside his jacket and stepped back, true to his practice of letting me absorb the scene undisturbed.

I put on the slippers before I stepped off the stairs and crossed the crime scene tape, grateful for the barrier against whatever might be mixed into the ice, and edged towards the body. Once again I pulled up my Otherside sight so that it was hovering just behind my eyes, ready for me to use as I approached the cordoned-off area. The ice crunched under my boots with each step; the air became crisper and colder as I reached the corpse. It didn't escape my notice that besides Aaron, there were no other police or forensics present. I arched an eyebrow at him.

"Just the two—I mean, three—of us?"

"I called in a few favours," he said.

"You have that many favours left?" After the fiasco with Randall and Cameron, I'd assumed Aaron had used up all his goodwill. That's what happens when you solve a murder case no one wants acknowledged.

"No, but Sarah does. They were about to move the body and she arranged a delay so we could get you in. Forensics has already been here. And let me tell you, it took some doing to get them down the stairs."

I snorted. Probably thought it was a poltergeist, and the scene did have a certain . . . extremism about it that poltergeists are fond of.

I glanced back at Aaron to get his okay before crossing the tape, and he nodded for me to continue.

I crouched down to get a better look at the body—careful, mind you, not to let my knees touch the ground. As I said, I had no idea what was mixed in with that ice. The victim was mid-forties, carrying a little extra weight around his midsection, but nothing out of the ordinary that would suggest a natural cause of death.

I glanced back at Aaron, who was standing by the stairs just outside the frozen area. "Who was he?" I asked.

"Jacob Buchanan, forty-eight. Single, no kids. Worked as the bar manager and was in charge of the music venue, booking bands, making sure the equipment got set up. He was a roadie through the nineties but got into arranging live bands when he settled down here. Still liked to be involved in the music scene."

I held up my hands. Aaron tossed me a pair of latex gloves, which

I put on. Gently, I touched one of Jacob's outstretched hands. It was frozen solid.

"How long has he been frozen?"

"He was like that when we got here. A line cook arrived at 4 a.m. to start breakfast and noticed the door to the basement was open, came down here and found him."

Five hours ago . . .

I tried to move the hand to see if the frost had permeated the tissue, and yanked my own hand back as an unnatural chill shot up my arm. I pulled off the glove and rubbed my fingers until the cold left them. If that frost wasn't paranormal, I'd eat an entire bag of sage. . . .

I moved around the body until I could see Jacob's face, and recoiled, almost falling backwards. I'm used to seeing dead bodies in various stages of decomposition. Not much gets my nerves going, but Jacob's face was contorted in terror, as if he'd been scared, not frozen, to death.

I let out a breath I'd been holding and watched it condense into a white fog.

Time to see what the Otherside was doing here . . .

I closed my eyes and waited for my Otherside sight to slide back into place. Normally, I dropped it as soon as I could. It could get disorienting if I accidentally wandered around with it, and on top of that, I didn't want to rely on it like a crutch. Every time I used it, Gideon came to mind, and I didn't need any more reminders of him than I already had.

I felt it click in, a bit like having sand in my eyes. I opened my eyes and took a good look around.

I let out a low whistle.

Everything was covered in gold Otherside dust. Not symbols or threads, but a fine dust. The ice on the floor and especially Jacob's body was coated in a thick, glittering layer of it, almost like a crust.

I frowned as my breath stirred the air in front of me, and reached out my hand. The Otherside dust swirled around it, before settling back on my fingers and jacket. It wasn't just clinging to the ice—it was suspended in the air.

I shivered and reflexively tried to brush the gold dust off on my jeans. It left behind a glittery smear.

I shoved my own discomfort down and searched for the anchors or lines that had to be binding the Otherside here. But no matter how hard I concentrated, I couldn't see them.

But then how the hell was the gold dust being kept here? And why hadn't it filtered back? Otherside—energy, essence or whatever you want to call it—comes from the afterlife. Max always said it was the fuel ghosts run off of, and when the ghosts travel back across the barrier, the Otherside is supposed to follow.

Otherside is used this side of the barrier to animate a zombie or draw wards—against the dead, the living, perceived evils, even unwanted attention. But you have to do a lot of tricky binding work to keep it in place. Like water through a drain, Otherside tends to flow back across the barrier; it doesn't belong here with the living, it's what powers the dead. The living can bring it over, but it takes a stubborn streak and an even stronger stomach to bind it into threads and anchor it to this world with symbols.

And when the symbols are scratched out or destroyed, then the Otherside filters right back across the barrier, all on its own.

Except here it hadn't.

There were no symbols that I could see anywhere, not even on or around Jacob's body, where the Otherside was most concentrated.

It occurred to me that there is one way to get Otherside to do what it isn't supposed to do, to warp it into something new. Sorcery . . .

I took another look at the gold dust dispersed around the room and suspended in the air. If this was sorcery, I was seriously out of my league.

I glanced over at Aaron again. "When was he last seen alive?"

"At 1 a.m. The bartender saw him before he left. We got the call at 4 a.m., when the cook arrived."

Hunh. Three hours unaccounted for. I wondered how long it took to freeze a person solid like this.

I gave Jacob's corpse one last look before heading back to Aaron.

"Paranormal?" he asked.

It crossed my mind to lie about the disturbing nature of the strange gold dust, but I quickly decided against it. I had no idea what the paranormal implications were, so I had no idea which details to downplay. I related what I'd seen.

Aaron listened attentively, taking notes. "I'm thinking a poltergeist?" he said when I was finished.

I considered it. "A little early for poltergeists." There'd be a few showing up later this month for Halloween—they always did—but it isn't until November and during the holidays that they really come out in full force. . . .

"I've never seen a poltergeist do this," I said, choosing my words carefully. "The brutality and terror is right, but it seems a little more planned out than they go for—though I've seen them come up with premeditated attacks."

"Have you ever seen one freeze a person like this?"

Again, I hedged my answer. "Any ghost is going to drop the ambient temperature a few degrees when they step in the room. It's in their nature." I gestured to Jacob's body. "This effect is unusual, but it wouldn't be the first time a ghost had learned a new trick."

Aaron frowned at me. "I thought ghosts couldn't learn?"

"They can't learn from their mistakes—I never said anything about new tricks and bad habits." Ghosts are fantastic at picking those up.

It occurred to me that there was another undead that could have done this. This scene was eerily reminiscent of the wraith story Lee had spun me and the limited information I'd found about them online. Not that I was going to tell Aaron that—not yet anyway. He'd already had an almost-encounter with undead that shouldn't exist when Randall tried to turn me into a Jinn. Another new species of undead appearing within a month would rattle even him. I wouldn't bring up the wraith so soon—not without proof. And it just seemed too coincidental. Chances were I was connecting dots where none existed.

I nodded back at the body. "Aaron, mind if I try a little experiment?"

He pulled out his phone and checked it before nodding an affirmative. "Sarah says keep it quick."

I drew in a breath, closed my eyes and, reaching out until I found a familiar cold, tapped the barrier. For once I welcomed the chill that flooded my head. It was a relief after the icy cold that accompanied the strange Otherside dust. On top of that, there wasn't nearly as much nausea as usual. I'd held back on pulling a globe lately, and though the nausea was still there, it was nowhere near as disorienting.

I waited until I'd pooled enough of it for what I wanted to do, and opened my eyes.

The dust was still there, but this time, instead of just looking at it, I could do something. I sent a pulse of Otherside out towards the dust.

As I expected, it caused a ripple to travel through the dust like a stone dropped in a pond, but otherwise there was no reaction. It simply returned to its suspended state, as if I hadn't just stirred it up.

Hmm. Odd. If it wasn't anchored in this world by symbols, then it should have scattered everywhere, at the very least—preferably back across the barrier.

I had another idea. I turned back to Aaron, and flinched at the sight of his ghost-grey body before realizing I still had my Otherside sight and globe up. I shook my head. I was so used to looking at ghosts and zombies lately with the Otherside sight that Gideon had gifted me that I found it unnerving to see someone without a few bindings attached to them. I was becoming more adept at dealing with the dead than the living. I gestured towards my bag that I'd left by the stairs, hoping Aaron hadn't noticed my reaction.

He handed it to me and I pulled out my mirror along with a china marker. The pulse of Otherside I'd sent through the dust hadn't been completely ineffectual. Let's see what funnelling the dust back to the Otherside did.

I drew the symbols necessary to make an open mirror on the reflective surface and flooded them with Otherside. I glanced back at the gold dust. No change—so far, so good . . .

I added the symbols that would turn my mirror into a portal of sorts, a trick I used to exorcise poltergeists, but it worked just as well for siphoning errant Otherside back across the barrier. I flooded the symbols with Otherside again and watched as the bindings glowed gold and the mirror turned a ghost grey. As the funnel kicked in, I felt it draw on my globe; I turned it towards the dust. Let's see what happened.

The gold dust stirred, as I'd expected it to, but instead of siphoning into the mirror, it settled again, just as it had with the pulse.

Maybe something was anchoring it here besides symbols. . . . I sent another pulse of Otherside out towards the dust. More stirred this time, but it didn't go anywhere near the mirror. The siphon wasn't working. It was Otherside dust, but it wasn't acting like Otherside—it was warped. And I had no idea how to get rid of it . . .

As the dust returned to its suspended state and the cold settled back on my skin, a disturbing possibility occurred to me. Lee had mentioned she thought the wraiths had been a product of sorcery. What if someone was trying to make a wraith—or, even more terrifying, what if there was a wraith loose and this was its work?

I smothered a wave of panic—there was no point scaring myself over pure speculation. If it killed like a poltergeist, was mean like a poltergeist and elicited the same spine-chilling fear a poltergeist did, chances were it was a poltergeist. As Aaron said, despite the anomalies, a poltergeist fit. I couldn't make an assumption about Otherside that was behaving awry based on Lee's story alone.

I noticed Aaron was frowning at me. "Something wrong, Kincaid?"

I did my best to shift my expression back to neutral. "Sorry, Aaron—I haven't pulled a globe in a while, just dealing with the nausea." Now, how to explain my findings . . . Cautious, not reckless, that was my new motto. "If it's a poltergeist, it's using a trick I haven't seen before," I said carefully. "It's—changed the Otherside so it's not behaving properly. To be honest, I'm not sure how to get rid of the cold. Not without doing some more reading."

"Is it dangerous?" Aaron asked, looking more concerned than he had a moment ago.

I shook my head. "I don't think so, but don't rule it out. I suspect it might fade, but I have no idea how long that will take." Something occurred to me as I exited the heavily frozen area around the body. "You're removing the body, right?"

Aaron nodded. "Coroner's assistants just got here, they're waiting upstairs for the okay."

I nodded, more to myself than him. "Let's see what that does." Maybe removing Jacob would disperse the Otherside . . . "And tell the coroner to monitor the body for thawing." I wanted to know how long it took to unfreeze. And hopefully, I could get a look at Jacob's corpse and the basement afterwards to see if the dust dissipated. Maybe the basement itself was the anchor and once the body was removed, it would go away on its own.

I glanced at Aaron. "You said you think this has something to do with your cold case, didn't you?" I said.

"You read the case. What does the practitioner think?" he said, his face carefully neutral.

"Deductive reasoning, not practitioning. Grunge rocker dies mysteriously in an old grunge venue?" I followed my intuition: the timing, Aaron starting to look into Damien's death . . . "Jacob used to be a roadie for Cadmium Coffee, didn't he?" I saw Aaron's eye twitch. "Son of a bitch, I'm right."

There was something else, though, there had to be. I was the one who jumped on coincidences like this, not Aaron. He always needed more.

He was about to say something when we heard steps on the stairs, along with the unmistakable sound of Sarah's booming voice projecting into the basement.

"Coroner," she called.

Aaron gave me a final, questioning look. I shook my head. I was done. If there was anything else worth gleaning here, it was well beyond my capabilities.

Aaron motioned for me to stay where I was as he met the coroner's assistants at the bottom of the steps. Even though I was standing off to the side, it was clear they were terrified of the ice, but between

Aaron in front and Sarah behind, there wasn't any retreat for them.

After Aaron's assurances, they capitulated and headed for the body. I caught their accusing glances directed my way and glared right back. Great. Anything even smells of paranormal . . .

"Hey, why not blame the body on me too while you're at it?" I said, raising my voice. Aaron took me by the arm and steered me back up the stairs while Sarah stayed with the assistants.

I let him, but before we were out of sight I took one last look at the scene over my shoulder. The assistants had the body on a stretcher, probably wanting to get it out of the ice before bagging it. The Otherside clung to the corpse, even as it left the ring of ice.

I turned and followed Aaron up the stairs. I'd return once I knew more. I just hoped that would be sooner rather than later.

A weight lifted off my chest as we reached the upper bar and the scent of cold and Otherside was replaced by beer and pine cleaner.

"So you going to tell me why else you think this murder is linked to your cold case?" I asked Aaron. I jerked my head back towards the basement. "On the phone you said there were similar methodologies. No offence, but that didn't look like a faked heroin overdose to me."

I waited. Aaron inclined his chin but didn't offer anything up. I rolled my eyes and jabbed him in the arm. Typical Aaron, he couldn't resist goading me.

Finally he relented. "There was a detail in Damien's file that still bothers me. Something that was glossed over in '95. They found Damien soaked through and lying in a shallow pool of water on his kitchen floor."

I nodded. I'd read the same thing and also noted it was odd, but no one at the time had deemed it worthy of investigation. There were plenty of reasonable explanations. He could have fallen with a glass of water in his hand or Mindy might have thrown it on him in an attempt to rouse him.

"Doesn't mean Damien was frozen—and you didn't say anything about a heroin overdose downstairs."

But this information did give me options. I now had two ghosts to try to raise, Damien and Jacob. Chances were I'd get one of them. Depending on how stable their ghosts were, I could ask them if there was any link in their deaths. I had no idea what freezing did to a dead person's mind . . . or to other parts of his body.

But I wasn't going to raise Jacob just yet. I prefer to wait a few days after someone dies. Let them adjust to the afterlife and such.

"Hmmm?" I said, as I realized Aaron was still speaking.

"I said you might as well come see."

"See what?"

"What happens when they thaw him out."

I shook my head and followed Aaron, wondering what other paranormal surprises he might have in store for me today.

If it wasn't for the disaster of a clusterfuck the rest of my life had become, I'd probably be close to calling this fun.

CHAPTER 8

DEATH AND TAXES

In my experience, the proverb about the two certainties of life holds true. You're going to die and you're going to have to pay taxes, sometimes even after you're dead.

And what amazes me is that people's taxes were funding the work of Dr. Heathcliff Blanc. Not that he didn't know what he was doing. I hated to admit it, but he was the best coroner I'd ever worked with, and that included some of the researchers who liaised with the Vancouver police.

But let there be no mistake. He was nuts.

I covered my nose and mouth with the sleeve of my jacket in an attempt to block out the lingering morgue fragrance. An exercise in futility. Morgues all have an antiseptic smell that just barely covers the scent of dead bodies, but there is no way to completely conceal the odour. I work with dead bodies and Otherside for a living, so I have about as strong a stomach as you can get. I could also handle the headache-inducing fluorescent lights down here. That didn't mean I enjoyed it.

Aaron had offered to take me out for a late breakfast after we'd finished with the crime scene, while we waited for Jacob's autopsy. I was starting to regret the massive plate of food I'd ordered. It had been on Aaron's dime, so I'd gone all out on the bacon and hash browns. The conversation had gone better than I'd expected as well—easy, friendly, comfortable. Normal. Until I probed about the potential contract with the SPD and Aaron's hint from yesterday, that in exchange for my co-operation Captain Marks was willing to renew my consulting contract . . . Aaron had clammed up and the conversation had turned decidedly stilted.

The food and the smell of the morgue alone wouldn't have got my stomach roiling, but Dr. Blanc, who had an unsettling fascination with the undead, had decided to display some special items when Aaron mentioned he was bringing me by.

I wondered what people would think if they knew their tax dollars went to pay for his particular specimens and . . . unconventional preserving materials.

I frowned at the jar. I was guessing the thing inside it was a ghoul's hand but couldn't be certain. The colour was wrong, a pale green-yellow, but that could be due to age, whatever preservative Dr. Blanc had decided to stick it in and where it had been beforehand.

The real question was, where the hell had he got a ghoul's hand?

I realized Dr. Blanc was watching me and tried my best to appear unfazed. I was looking at a detached ghoul's hand, after all, and whatever preservative he'd used in his . . . samples . . . had seeped into the air to mix with the antiseptic and underlying dead people smell.

I snuck a look at Aaron, who was holding up surprisingly well. I'd tried to catch his professional demeanour slip, but so far it hadn't happened. Then again, he was used to seeing dead bodies, if not undead ones. . . .

Dr. Blanc followed my gaze. "Oh, I assure you he wasn't using that anymore when I found it."

Oddly, that didn't assuage my concern. "When you found the ghoul or the arm?" I asked, despite the look Aaron shot me. If the latter, what had he done with the rest of him? I shook the thought aside. I was better off leaving the goings-on of the underground city to Lee. If she wasn't concerned about missing ghoul parts . . .

Dr. Blanc stared at me. "I could show you some other undead specimens. One incredibly well-preserved example of reanimation from the Victorian era—"

"No, no, that really won't be necessary," I said, shaking my head.

My response seemed to surprise him. He watched us, slightly hunched over, hands in his pockets and elbows out at an angle. I still couldn't get over how gangly he was; it just added to the overall morbid effect.

"Well then, how about I fetch Mr. Buchanan for you?" Dr. Blanc said, and made a beeline for the body storage area.

As soon as he left, Aaron dropped his composure. "Stop making snide comments about his samples," he hissed. "We're here to see Jacob's frozen body autopsied."

I wondered how that would progress—would he thaw it? Use a chainsaw?

"Dr. Blanc only agreed to do this immediately because I said you were coming."

I narrowed my eyes at Aaron. I was painfully aware that Dr. Blanc had originally accepted the job in Seattle because he was under the impression he'd be working with a practitioner. Me. Specifically. Hence some of my apprehension. I'm not a fan of being the centre of attention.

"You embarrassed him," Aaron continued.

I glanced over my shoulder to make sure Dr. Blanc wasn't in the doorway. "That ghoul was probably still using that arm when it was removed." I wondered if there was a black market trade in undead body parts, and how much collectors like Dr. Blanc fuelled it. Yeah, I was not going to play the enthusiastic practitioner—no matter what Aaron wanted out of me. . . .

"Look, just play along so that we can get out of here," he whispered.

"I don't like seeing the dead get used," I whispered back. Or me for that matter . . .

Aaron rolled his eyes at me. "Do I need to pull up your latest Nathan Cade YouTube performance? It has almost a million hits now, or so I'm told."

"Very different situation, and also not exactly my choice." I jerked my head in the direction of the morgue proper. "He makes me uncomfortable, all right?"

"Dr. Blanc is one of the best paranormal coroners in the United States. We need him."

"No, *you* need him," I said, stabbing a finger into Aaron's chest. "I don't work for the Seattle PD, and since a consultation contract isn't about to cross my desk . . ."

Aaron opened his mouth to argue but stopped when he saw the expression on my face. He played the straitlaced good guy well, but he could be—and was—as manipulative as Nate when he decided the situation called for it. The reasons behind our three-month blowout were coming back loud and clear. . . . I felt my nails dig into the soft skin of my palms as I clenched my fists. "The entire reason I'm helping you is because you said you could rope my co-operation into real work."

For the second time since breakfast Aaron actually looked uncomfortable. "I said I might be able to—"

"You don't barter with *might*, Aaron. Even Nate knows that. God, I'm comparing you to Nate now."

"I'm working on it, all right?"

"That's the kind of iffy language people use when they're about to balk on my bill."

"Before or after you threaten them with a poltergeist?" Aaron said. "And before you deny it, the lawyer complained."

Cody. Of course he'd gone to the police. Before I could level another accusation at Aaron, Dr. Blanc cleared his throat behind us.

I unclenched my fists and turned to see him standing awkwardly in the doorway behind a metal gurney holding a body draped with a white sheet.

"Perhaps we should look at the body, yes?" he said after a moment.

I took a step away from Aaron and cleared my own throat. "Yeah, that sounds just fine."

Dr. Blanc began to speak as he rolled the gurney into the observation room. "One Mr. Buchanan, forty-eight years old, was in moderate health with no history of heart trouble or other pre-existing conditions." Dr. Blanc stopped the gurney in the centre of the theatre. "In fact, there is no natural cause of death beyond the obvious."

With a smooth movement Dr. Blanc removed the sheet covering the body. Jacob's face was still contorted with fear and his arm held out before him as if fending off some invisible assailant. Exactly as he had been in the basement of the Rex—still frozen solid.

I frowned. I figured he would have begun to thaw by now. Not completely, but a bit . . .

Dr. Blanc gestured for me to help him move the body onto the examination table, and I obliged after pulling on gloves. I had more experience dealing with actual dead bodies than Aaron. It's one thing to examine victims at a crime scene, a totally different matter to handle them.

The first thing that struck me as I gripped the ankle of his boots was that the body of Jacob Buchanan was most definitely still frozen. Solid. The air around him even had a cold scent to it, as if the body itself was somehow generating the cold. I tried not to stare at his terrified face. Between the ice and the rigor mortis, there'd be no way to change the expression now. I stifled a shudder. Something else occurred to me as I avoided his face: he was still clothed. Not usual procedure.

I glanced up at Dr. Blanc across the table, where he had started examining the head.

Meeting my eyes, Dr. Blanc said, "I attempted to remove Mr. Buchanan's clothes when he was admitted. However, the fabrics are still frozen to his body. I can't take any of them off without risking damage to the skin, which is why I haven't started my examination yet."

"It'd compromise potential evidence—wounds to his body," Aaron clarified for me.

I shot Aaron a look. Yeah, I'd got that part. It hadn't been that long since I'd been on an investigation. "How frozen is he still?" I asked Dr. Blanc. He gave me a baffled expression, so I added, "I mean, it feels like he's frozen on the outside—is it all the way through?"

"Ah, yes—solid, all the way through. When I realized he wasn't thawing, I performed an ultrasound. I assure you, he is very frozen. In a way that suggests he was frozen from the outside in."

Hunh. Interesting. "Correct me if I'm wrong, but as I understand it, freezing something all the way through like that is quite a feat. Isn't it supposed to take hours?"

Dr. Blanc gave me a grim smile. "That would be correct, Ms. Strange. The term you are looking for is *flash freezing*, which I have concluded is how Mr. Buchanan came to be in this state from the minimal organ and tissue fracturing."

"What does it take to flash-freeze someone?" Aaron asked.

"Something very cold. Conventionally, liquid nitrogen or dry ice are required to flash-freeze." He nodded at Jacob. "For a person this size, I would say that he would have to have been immersed in liquid nitrogen to be frozen all the way through."

I glanced at Aaron. I didn't remember any signs of liquid nitrogen at the bar, though I supposed he could have been frozen elsewhere and moved to the Rex Hotel basement. But again, that was in line with looking for zebras. Didn't mean it wasn't a possibility, just unlikely.

I checked the time as Dr. Blanc examined Jacob's body. We'd been at the scene at 9 a.m. at the latest, Jacob had been found at 4 a.m., and now it was half past 11. . . .

"Shouldn't he be thawing by now?" I asked.

Dr. Blanc peered up at me from the body again. "Very astute, Ms. Strange. He should be, or at the very least the outside tissue should have begun to thaw out." To prove his point, Dr. Blanc tapped Jacob's still-frozen arm. It sounded like tapping a hard surface—not a thawing piece of meat. "I'm not ashamed to admit I'm quite perplexed," Dr. Blanc continued. "My professional opinion is that the frozen state is unnatural. And I haven't been able to find anything on frozen bodies by paranormal means, despite my contacts in the research community." He seemed to perk up. "I have to say, I'm rather excited. I might be able to publish a paper on this."

"Just don't let any poltergeists get wind of it," I told him. "They might take your interest in odd paranormal deaths as a challenge."

It may have been a trick of the harsh fluorescents, but Dr. Blanc's face actually seemed to go white. I felt a little guilty for alarming him, but only for a minute. It was a valid concern.

I caught Aaron raising an eyebrow at me from where he was standing on the other side of the examination table, beside Dr. Blanc. Time to check the Otherside.

I drew in a breath and shut my eyes, reaching mentally for the gold threads of Otherside that were now permanently etched on the backs of my eyelids. Letting out my breath, I waited for the cold Otherside sight to slip into place over my eyes. Sand settled under my eyelids and I felt a chill like an air conditioner blasting on high in front of my face. I opened my eyes and focused on the body.

Just like back at the Rex, there was a thin layer of gold dust covering Jacob—his skin, clothes, shoes, even the metal table. It hadn't dissipated or faded at all. Funny Otherside or not, it shouldn't have this kind of staying power.

I searched again, but I still couldn't see any bindings, and certainly no concentration or bundling of Otherside that I'd expect to see if there was an anchoring symbol hiding somewhere. . . .

I hated to admit it, but I was stumped. I'd expected to see the gold Otherside dust gone or at the very least lessened once he was moved, but that hadn't happened. If I had to put money on it, I'd say it was as present as when I'd first seen it at the Rex.

I glanced up at Dr. Blanc. "Can I move his jacket and shirt?" I asked.

He nodded, then he raised his phone and announced the time and who was present. Great, a recording. I wasn't thrilled about being on camera. I shot Aaron a glance.

"Unusual circumstances, Kincaid," he said.

Well, I needed to get a better look at Jacob and the only way that was going to happen was if I started fiddling with the body. I figured Aaron's presence meant he would take the flak. It wasn't like I was contracted to the Seattle PD anymore. Just an innocent bystander.

I tied my hair back before pulling on the fresh pair of latex gloves Dr. Blanc passed to me. I leaned over the body, shot the phone a quick look and angled my face away from it. "Okay, Dr. Blanc, the first thing I'm going to do is check under Jacob's jacket." I chewed my lips. How to word the why and what I was looking for . . . "Basically, I'm checking for Otherside anomalies." Well, it was accurate, if vague. There were already enough Otherside anomalies on Jacob and at the Rex to fill a book—and that was before we got to the freezing part. I glanced up to see if he'd accept that as an explanation and got the nod to go ahead.

I reached out and carefully touched the corner of Jacob's jacket. Crispy and cold to the touch, though since it was fabric, it was moderately mobile.

I opened the jacket and watched the Otherside dust shifting like sand under water. Underneath was a Dead Men's T-shirt from the nineties. Appropriate or bad taste, I wasn't certain which to call it.

I focused on the Otherside dust, watching to see if it trickled towards a particular point, or followed any pattern that would reveal a hidden line or anchor. But the only pattern it seemed to follow was the pull of gravity as it slipped away from Jacob's jacket and shirt, caught on the rest of his clothing or body, and took its time settling on the metal table and floor.

The slow way it fell, though—that piqued my interest. I abandoned the body and crouched on the concrete floor, keeping my eyes on the Otherside particles as they continued to roll off the metal gurney. I held out my hand and a few grains of the dust clung to my skin, imparting an immediate chill. I sniffed my gloved hand. It smelled cold, and was tinged with the burnt scent that Otherside sometimes carries.

I straightened up and watched the rest of the dust drift around me. If I didn't know better, I'd say that it wasn't really Otherside, only a close facsimile—one that chilled to the bone and didn't have an affinity for the afterlife anymore.

I turned to face Dr. Blanc and Aaron again. They both watched me with keen interest. I had nothing to give them. I'd swum out of my depth a couple of hours ago. "Otherside doesn't behave like this, or it's not supposed to," I said. Or not that I'd heard of. As far as the paranormal world was concerned, what I'd never heard of could fill a very large bucket. . . .

I went back to checking Jacob's body. I examined the frozen sleeves of his flannel shirt, with effort moving the stiff fabric to get a peek under his wrists, looking for some clue, a distinct symbol, a trace of a concrete Otherside thread. But all I found was the dust, even under his fingernails.

I managed to tease a corner of Jacob's frozen T-shirt away from his skin and gave Dr. Blanc a questioning glance.

He motioned for me to stop and with efficiency if not grace, managed to reach over and take the corner of the shirt from my hands.

"Our paranormal expert has requested we look at the skin, yes?" Dr. Blanc asked me.

I frowned. Of course I wanted to look under his shirt. Why else—

Ah. He nodded emphatically to the phone mounted on the overhead examination light and aimed down. I sighed and said, "Yes," for the recorder.

Because of the strange frozen nature of Jacob's clothing, we eventually settled on stainless steel tongs, a pair each, with Dr. Blanc and me on either side. On the count of three and with effort, we both peeled the corners of his shirt from his body, exposing a stomach now more blue than white. The Otherside dust did pretty well exactly as it had before, shifting and falling to the table and floor.

The fabric cracked, exposing even more of Jacob's pale torso and sending another shudder of Otherside dust to the floor.

My hunch was right. "It's permeated everything," I said. When Dr. Blanc and Aaron glanced at me, I added, "The Otherside powder."

I gestured to the body and floor. "If I had to guess, I'd say that some-one had altered it. I've never seen anything like it."

"Is that even possible?" Aaron asked.

I shrugged. "Anything is possible. Just because I haven't heard or seen it before doesn't mean it can't be done." I withheld my suspicion that it was an act of sorcery warping the Otherside to its will. For one, it would require an explanation from Gideon—whom I really didn't think Aaron needed to know about yet, if ever.

"Can you describe it, the powder?" Dr. Blanc asked, sounding intrigued.

I shot a look at Aaron. He nodded at me to continue, so I told Dr. Blanc, "You can't see it with your bare eyes, but the body is covered in an Otherside—dust." I settled on that word. It really was the most apt description. "The crime scene was covered in the dust too, as if someone had sprayed him and the surrounding area with it." I strongly suspected it permeated his flesh, but we couldn't tell without cutting a sample. . . .

"Were there bindings—ones that you recognized?" he asked, sounding more excited than concerned.

I shook my head. "No bindings—or anything I remotely recog-nized as practitioning." I paused. "The closest analogy I can give you is that it behaves and looks like an Otherside version of sand or dust, but nothing seems to be holding it here. It isn't bound into threads or symbols. It doesn't even react to Otherside anymore—not like it should, anyways. . . ." I gestured at the body. "It's still clinging to his clothing. It moves and falls off if you disturb it enough but quickly settles again."

"Could you collect it? Like in a jar?" Dr. Blanc asked.

Good question . . . "It might be contained for a moment, but it'd just as quickly move through the glass. It's still Otherside, as far as I can tell, it's just—misbehaving."

The more I thought about it, *stagnant* seemed like a better description than *warped*. I ran my hand across the metal examina-tion table, collecting the dust on my fingertips. As expected, it was icy cold. I held up my hand and reached towards the men, waiting

for them to extend their arms before touching them. I touched
Dr. Blanc first. He jumped back at the chill. I did the same to Aaron,
though to his credit he was ready for it.

"And that's only a little," I said. "It chills substantially more than
normal." I wiped my hand on my jeans and touched Aaron again.
"See? Already gone."

Dr. Blanc examined my hand. "What I wouldn't give right now
to be able to see Otherside," he said.

"Trust me, it's not all it's cracked up to be. And you need one
hell of a strong stomach, though I suppose if you work in here . . ."
I let the thought trail off.

"What will happen to it—here and at the crime scene?" Aaron
asked.

No clue. "I think it will disperse." I held up my hand. A little of
the dust was left on the tips of my fingers, but not enough to chill
them. "I don't think it goes anywhere."

"Disperse—back to the Otherside, then, no?" Dr. Blanc asked.

I shrugged. "I'm not sure it can anymore. It doesn't react to
Otherside anymore, if it ever did. Sorry, Dr. Blanc, but like I said,
the professional in the room is at a loss."

"Could it be dangerous?"

Yeah, I was wondering that myself. "Best guess?"

Aaron nodded.

"I *think* all it does is chill whatever it comes into contact with—
like dry ice or liquid nitrogen, as Dr. Blanc suggested. But is that all
it can do?" I shuddered at the possibilities. Carcinogen? Psychosis
inducing? "Your guess is as good as mine."

Aaron swore and pulled out his phone. Dr. Blanc was also looking
decidedly less comfortable and intrigued than he had a moment ago.

Aaron said hello to whoever picked up on the other end. I thought
I heard him mutter the words *paranormal* and *quarantine*.

"Aaron, what are you doing?" I hissed.

He mumbled a few words I didn't catch before covering the mic.
"I'm having the Rex Hotel cordoned off as a potential biohazard.
Dr. Blanc, I suggest you do the same for this morgue."

Biohazard? I swore. "Aaron, I've never once heard of Otherside being treated as a biohazard—"

"Yet by your own admission you don't know what this dust does, and it's not behaving like Otherside. I believe *warped* is the term you used?"

It did have an ominous ring when someone else said it. Aaron returned to his call and I looked apologetically at Dr. Blanc. "I'm not sure what to suggest, besides being careful with the body and keeping it locked in a cooler." I shrugged. "And even then I'm pretty sure the Otherside—or whatever it is—will still seep through."

"You might want to get out the Geiger counter, Dr. Blanc," Aaron suggested, having ended his call. "Just to be safe, and to document you've tried ruling out deleterious effects. Even though that's unlikely, if it's dispersing."

Dr. Blanc nodded. "I could bring in some test subjects as well, of the rodent variety, and see if they show any more extreme reactions." He looked thoughtful. "I'm not ready to panic yet. We'll see if we can rule out the possibility that it's emitting anything more dangerous than the cold, shall we? In the meantime, I'll put Mr. Buchanan back in the cooler."

"I'll have Aaron update you as soon as I find out more," I offered. "You'll do the same? No matter how insignificant any changes might seem?"

Dr. Blanc gave me a grave nod. "I'll keep you updated on any and all changes to Mr. Buchanan, however insignificant. And if I find anything more sinister in the preternatural cold."

Dr. Blanc might not be my favourite person to share personal space with, but I'd be lying if I said I didn't admire his dedication to caring for the dead, whatever form they arrived in. Not many people did—care, that is.

Aaron nodded to me. I turned to follow him out of the morgue but stopped as Dr. Blanc gently grasped at my elbow.

I frowned as I turned to face him.

"In the meantime, Ms. Strange, might I suggest the showers?"

My frown turned to confusion until I saw what he was gesturing at: a single showerhead in the corner of the morgue theatre with a drain fixed underneath.

Ah, yeah, I was not walking out of here soaking wet. I glanced back up at him. "Not that I don't appreciate it, but I'll be okay until I get home." He looked as if he might protest, so I rushed to add, "If you find it does anything besides make things real cold, I'll perform whatever decontamination or quarantine you want."

That seemed to appease him and he stepped out of my way. I rushed from the morgue as quickly as politeness allowed. Aaron was waiting for me in the hallway.

"Couldn't wait for me? Not the way to treat your paranormal liaison," I said, shaking my head.

Aaron smiled and fell in step beside me. "My loyalties only go so far."

I snorted, though I was grateful for the light banter. "And apparently a chemical shower is that limit."

The closer we got to the parking lot, the more certain I became that I'd have to broach the subject of the mystery dust with Gideon. The question was, how to phrase it so it didn't sound as though I was asking him for a favour . . .

"Hmmm?" We were halfway across the parking lot before I realized that Aaron was talking to me.

"I said that I'm thinking of having the entire building cordoned off."

"If it hasn't spread yet, I don't think it will, Aaron. Besides, no one else who's been at the Rex has reported any symptoms, have they?"

"No, there's that. I'll still be happier when you and Dr. Blanc can confirm that besides being cold, it's harmless."

I inclined my head. Couldn't argue with that.

"Still think my theory about a poltergeist is off?" he asked when we reached the car.

"Aaron, the more of Jacob's murder I see, the more convinced I am that it isn't a poltergeist."

He opened the car door for me. I paused. I could see Aaron delving into one of his pensive moods. Not the best time to be around him. "No offence, Aaron, but I don't think the two of us being silent together is going to help any."

I expected him to disagree, but he didn't. He only sighed and closed the car door. I could get used to this acquiescent version of Aaron.

I nodded a goodbye, but before I could turn to go, he reached out and grabbed my arm, just like he used to do.

I tensed. Not because he'd stopped me—it was that I didn't feel anything inside. The usual electric attraction that spiked through me at his touch—the quickening pulse, the flutters of anticipation, the warmth in my belly—was missing.

What had changed? And what the hell was wrong with me?

Either because of my lack of reaction or in spite of it, Aaron let go of my arm and said, "I'll try to work on Marks." He paused. "Whatever work comes, it won't be quite in the same capacity as before, but you'd be with the SPD again."

There was a reluctance in Aaron's disclaimer that bothered me. I shoved the misgivings down. This was Aaron. He could play his cards close because he didn't have a deceptive bone in his body. Well, not unless you were a suspect he believed was guilty—then he could be as deceptive as all hell.

"Are you sure you don't want a ride? Promise I'll be better company than the silent thinker."

I forced a smile. "I've got some errands to run. A book to mail off, people to see." I held up my bag, where I'd placed the text I'd sold before leaving. "Better if I go on foot," I said. A few weeks ago I would have jumped at the chance to ride home with him. . . .

Whatever I felt or didn't feel right now, I was nostalgic for the days when things were better, *normal*. Before every second day was a fight with Aaron, when I wasn't dealing with crazy ghosts and paranormal anomalies, and when my sole income wasn't a choice between dealing with seedy lawyers like Cody or pimping Nate out at frat parties.

I wanted to get back to what I'd been doing before everything fell apart: raising ghosts and zombies to find murderers. Simple, safe . . . Okay, maybe not safe, but at least familiar. That was what I needed—to get back to a familiar way of life, despite all the death and destruction of the last few weeks.

Maybe once normalcy resumed, I'd go back to feeling the same way I used to around Aaron.

"You'll keep me posted?" he said.

I met his eyes and nodded. I wasn't completely dead inside—just numb.

Keep it together, Kincaid. It's the chaos. You need time to put Randall, Max and Cameron behind you. Once you do, you'll be back to your old self.

Or that's what I needed to keep telling myself . . .

Aaron reached out again but then thought better of it. He frowned and said, "You mentioned Mindy before, in your message. Why should I look into her?"

With Jacob's murder, I'd almost forgotten about Mindy. "Well, I ran into her by accident," I rushed to say. Not a lie—it *had* been an accident when I'd let Nate out of my sight . . . "I think it's worth arranging a chat with her is all, over your cold case." I gave him a slight smile. "I'm good, but I don't quite have your talent for dealing with the living."

His frown only deepened. "Did Nate say something?"

Nate said a lot of things . . . frequently . . . and of dubious meaning . . . but I wasn't ready to betray Nate's trust like that. Not yet, anyway. I hedged what I said next. "Let's just say she's a little more mercenary than I think anyone ever gave her credit for. I get the impression she knows more about Damien's death than she let on." I shook my head and avoided looking at Aaron directly. "But like I said, I don't have your talent for interrogation."

"I don't interrogate—"

"Okay. You have ways of making people talk about things they probably don't want to."

His mouth quirked. It wasn't amusement, but he did move out of the way. "I'm not nearly as manipulative as you're making me out to be."

"No, but the power is there. Lurking underneath the mild-mannered detective facade. Just consider it this way," I said, before the conversation could veer into a discussion about whether Aaron was manipulative or not—yes, he was. However unintentional. "For a woman who's made a career off being the grieving girlfriend of Nate, she's not particularly interested in seeing him. Ever. At all. If you talk to her, it's best not to bring him up." As an afterthought I added, "And I may have let her believe I was still a police liaison . . . and there because of you. It'll probably come up."

He snorted. "Why am I not surprised. And it doesn't mean she's guilty. Not everyone wants to—or should—live in the past. You say that all the time."

"Yup." I turned to leave but only got a few steps before spinning on my boot heels, hands in my jacket pockets. "But I'm a voodoo practitioner. Which raises the question, why is she so militant about it?"

"You're saying it's all a show?"

"I'm saying . . ." She—what? Has an agenda? A penchant for vodka? A volatile nature? She struck me as damaged and greedy, but did that make her an accomplice somehow in Damien's death? No. I was certain she was hiding something, though. To Aaron I said, "You're the detective—you go figure it out."

"Say hi to Lee Ling for me," Aaron called after me.

"No such thing, Aaron," I said, making another turn. "And make damn sure you call me as soon as you find anything interesting on Cole or Mindy."

"Likewise, Kincaid."

I gave him a last wave over my shoulder as I turned the corner. It figured that the only times we were easy with each other came when we were dealing with a paranormal case.

I stared down at the sidewalk as I made my way back to Pioneer Square. I needed time to reflect. I also needed to get the books from Mork. With any luck, even if there wasn't any information that shed light on Nate's predicament, there'd be something about that Otherside dust.

And maybe Lee would be disposed to answer some of my questions . . . without the lesson this time. Or maybe she'd just threaten to throw me in a pit with feral zombies. With Lee, you never really could tell what you were in for, even more so since recent events.

I sighed, earning a few glances from passersby. Aaron, Lee, Nate—all my relationships, it seemed, had been warped and twisted by my encounter with my psychotic teacher—much like the sorcery Gideon peddled.

I couldn't help feeling there was a strong correlation between the two.

CHAPTER 9

GREAT EXPECTATIONS

I took another sip of my whisky sour. I'd checked the bar for fresh creosote this time before propping my elbows up. Normally I'm not a day drinker, and it's unusual for me to drink two days in a row, but after the morning's trip to the crime scene and the coroner's office I'd decided to make an exception. I'd been making a few of those lately. At least I wasn't constantly nursing an Otherside hangover. . . .

I'd managed to drop my book off at the post office before heading into the underground city. I had to make the trip in person in order to get a tracking number. Pro tip: never sell anything on eBay without a tracking number. I swear there are people out there who *look* for no tracking number when they get packages just so they can claim it never arrived and save a buck.

It takes a certain type of asshole.

I'd been screwed on my *Curses of Louisiana* text. If I ever lowered myself to siccing poltergeists on folks for petty vengeance, that would be the straw that broke the proverbial camel's back. . . .

Note, we're talking petty transgressions. No one said anything about serious vengeance.

If I ever got Nate out of Cameron's body, maybe I'd send him to give Johnny2000 a good old-fashioned haunt. If he was buying—make that stealing—practitioners' texts on eBay, what were the chances Johnny had a set mirror lying around?

I felt Lee brush behind me as she bussed another tray full of empty glasses and discarded umbrellas back behind the bar. After I'd relayed the morning's events, she'd gone silent and meditative. I perked up as she rounded the bar.

"You have answered your own question. If it is behaving like dust, it cannot be Otherside," she said as she set the tray down and began loading the glasses into the dishwasher. A new addition. Mork's work, I was guessing. As the one bar employee still on the side of the living—at least as far as I could tell—he'd been spearheading upgrades such as the dehumidifiers and fans that brought the place up to something resembling code. The dishwasher was a smart move; it would sterilize the glassware better than handwashing ever could. The wrong bacteria wreak havoc on a zombie who isn't taking a daily dose of formaldehyde. While admiring the new appliance, I noted Lee piled the glasses in carelessly, making them clink together.

"You're going to break them," I told her.

She didn't look up, only snorted and continued to load the glasses.

"And I never said I thought it was dust. I said I told them it looked like dust because they can't see Otherside to begin with. It was Otherside, Lee, just . . ." I gestured with my glass, trying to come up with a better description for someone who knew what Otherside actually looks like. ". . . in between—and cold, like a chemical deep-freeze." Lee gave me an odd look, so I added, "Imagine if Otherside was a bottle of talc powder."

Lee's eyebrows knit in irritation, something that took effort considering the muscles in her face were mostly paralyzed. "That is impossible. Otherside bindings are non-corporeal."

I grimaced. Lee was not one for metaphors. "I realize that, and I'm getting to it. Just imagine that you could grind them up and what you got at the end was a fine powder."

I stopped and waited for Lee to attend to a patron who'd approached the bar. She poured a shot of whisky and filled a mug with a frothy beer-and-brains mixture. Then she gracefully deposited the whisky into the beer-brains before passing it to him. Hunh. The underground city's very own version of a boilermaker.

"Now," I said when she faced me again, "imagine that the talc powder only half behaves like Otherside. You can see it and it's still non-corporeal. It slides through just about anything eventually, *but* it won't fade back to the Otherside. At all. It just . . . stagnates."

The corners of Lee's mouth turned down and her red-lacquered fingernails tapped the bar as she looked down. "I have no experience with such a thing."

Which meant that she knew something. "I never said you did."

"*But* I have heard of such things." Her fingers drummed to a stop and she glanced up, fixing me with her green eyes. "Sorcery can have such an effect on Otherside."

"Because it can warp it?"

Lee inclined her head.

Shit. "Fantastic. A sorcerer is my most likely culprit, leaving a total of one suspect." Gideon wasn't above a little glorified violence, but I was drawing blanks as to what the hell an old roadie could have done to piss him off.

"No, Kincaid," Lee corrected me. "I said sorcery was the most likely cause—not that it was a sorcerer behind the murder. Remember the wraith?"

I nodded. "Built by sorcery." Considering the ice and frozen body, Lee's story had been at the front of my thoughts. It explained the murder and the cold but not the omnipresent dust. "Wait a minute. You mean sorcery can create something that can warp Otherside all on its own?" Spectacular. Just how many sorcerer's constructs were out there?

Lee inclined her head again before turning the dishwasher on with an aggressive flick of her wrist. I was starting to wonder if the goal was to break the machine, or maybe she just resented the modernization and this was the only way she had to vent. Either way, I wasn't about to question her treatment of the appliances.

"Whether it's a wraith or another construct, a sorcerer has to be behind it." And there was only one in town that I knew of. Or a ghost of one.

But Lee clicked her tongue. "You are thinking like a practitioner, not a sorcerer. Sorcerers manipulate Otherside. Unlike a zombie or a bound ghost, a sorcerer's construct is not necessarily bound to its creator's will." Lee stressed the last few words as Mork appeared in the hall, having crawled out of whatever pit he lived in. He snorted as he made his way into the cooler, his butcher's apron still on, and spat something at Lee in Chinese. Lee replied with an equally vehement-sounding string of words.

I wasn't sure I wanted to know. "Fight?"

The corner of Lee's lip quirked up. "A difference of opinions at the moment."

I was guessing it was about the dishwasher. "Sorcerer or sorcerer's construct, the part that concerns me is that it doesn't fade back to the Otherside like it's supposed to. It lingers, doesn't even react to an open mirror. It reacts to gravity when it shouldn't." I took a too-big sip of my whisky sour and bit back the sting. "And it freezes anything it touches. Do you think it's dangerous?"

Lee pursed her lips. "It is possible, but I doubt it," she said after a moment. "Otherside doesn't last forever. By its nature it prefers to be across the barrier, or wherever else it calls home in its altered state. Just because you do not know the way does not mean it has not already found it."

I huffed, "You make it sound sentient."

Lee gave me a wry look. "Hardly. Most likely some factor you are unaware of will dispel it, either actively or passively."

Not helpful. But Lee had said something interesting. "You said 'wherever else.' What else is there besides here or the Otherside?"

"A figure of speech. I simply meant it's likely trapped between this world and the next."

In an unstable limbo, like the wraith and Nate. If that wasn't ominous . . . I made light of it, though. "Funny, I always thought that in-between place was the underground city." I finished off my drink and slid the glass to Lee. She grabbed it, her green eyes fixed on me.

I checked the time: 4 p.m. I had to leave now if I wanted to get home in time to hide Nate before Gideon arrived. I collected my books—well, Mork's books, the ones he'd left on the bar for me—and put them in the bag of supplies I'd bought from Lee. Sage, rosemary and another herb I hadn't heard of before, which Lee had tossed in—ironwort, I think—and a small bag that looked like ash, along with a slip of paper with instructions for burning. "You sure this will work?" I asked.

"No—not if Gideon is truly looking for a paranormal entity. But otherwise it should help obscure any redundant Otherside that may be escaping Nate and prevent it from garnering his interest."

Better than I could do, by a long shot. Gideon wouldn't be looking for Nate—he thought the body had been destroyed. I just needed to cover Nate's tracks while Gideon was over, to hide him from the sorcerer, paranormally speaking.

I slung the bag over my shoulder and started to pay Lee for the drink and supplies. I held on to the money as she reached for it. "The Otherside. That's where he took me, isn't it?"

She gave me a blank stare, but I caught a flicker in her eyes.

"When Gideon dragged me out of the fire at Randall's. Somehow, some way, he pulled me through the Otherside, didn't he?" The first few days after the fire and Randall's betrayal, I'd wondered how Gideon had saved me and brought me to the underground city. It should have been impossible.

Lee must have perceived my desperation to know, because she nodded once.

She could be cagey, but she didn't lie. I let the money go and she took it and slipped it into the folds of her dress. She held my gaze.

"A word of advice, Kincaid. Do not hide Nathan from Gideon for much longer. You are a talented practitioner and the sorcerer's ghost is clearly in need of one, but no one is that valuable. Gideon is not known for having a mild temper."

I could have told her that, but I only nodded. Foolish was the person who ignored Lee's warnings.

Her lips parted as if she was about to say something else, but then she was distracted by another patron shouting for her from across the bar and the sound of a glass breaking inside the dishwasher.

I gestured towards it. "I did tell you," I said.

Lee slowly closed her eyes and I could have sworn I saw her draw in a breath. She glided away, as if she'd never issued the warning.

I stifled my own shivers as I moved towards the swinging doors with my loaded backpack and bag of goods both slung over my shoulder. If the past few weeks were any indication, I should really start heeding Lee's warnings.

Her words weighed heavily on my mind as I left Damaged Goods, back to the land of the supposed living. Sometimes I really wondered about that too—whether people topside were spending their lives any better than the undead spent their afterlives.

By the time I reached the stairs, only two things were on my mind: what Gideon had in store for my lesson, and what he'd do when he eventually found out about Nate.

It took me four tries to jimmy the lock on my apartment door this time. Maybe Aaron was on to something about me needing to get it fixed. Though I'd be damned if I was going to admit it to him.

When it finally clicked, I nudged the door open and stuck my head around. "Nate?" I said in a loud whisper.

There was the noise of dishes being dropped into the sink and I heard a curse before Nate came shuffling out of the kitchen, dragging his sock feet across the beaten-up hardwood floor.

"You're going to get splinters," I said.

"Cutting it close," he said.

I glanced over at the clock above my kitchen desk. "I've got fifteen minutes." He was right, though, I had cut it close. I dropped my backpack and bag of supplies by the door and frowned as I got a better look at the socks Nate was wearing. "Aren't those mine?"

"They're soft and don't scratch the skin off my feet."

I shook my head as I dropped my jacket on the coat rack. "Cameron's feet. And don't tell me the skin is starting to peel off."

"Fine. I won't."

I smothered a sigh. It wasn't Nate's fault. Feet are tricky. Everyone's are covered with calluses, and they are the first thing to separate from a decomposing body that is still walking, especially once you introduce formaldehyde. Has to do with the skin already being rough and flaky . . .

I grabbed Aaron's remaining pair of old flannel pants and a terry bathrobe and tossed them at Nate. "Save the bellyaching and put these on. If your feet are getting fragile, everywhere else will be following. . . . Now," I added when he hesitated.

"Yeah, yeah. Before Gideon gets here. Save the speech."

I checked the time: 4:49. The walk back from the underground city had taken longer than I'd thought. I rummaged through the bag of supplies Lee had given me while Nate stepped back into the bedroom, presumably to change. Here's hoping she'd sold me more than snake oil. I headed into the kitchen and pulled five bowls out of the cupboard—one for each corner and the door, as Lee had advised on the slip of paper she'd included with the herbs, which I read on the walk back. I put one-quarter of each packet into each bowl before adding the ash and crushing them together with the mortar.

Nate stuck his head out of the bedroom and sniffed the air, then came out wearing the robe and flannels. He picked up the empty bag that the ash had been in. "What is this?" he said, crinkling his nose. "Smells funny."

"Didn't ask, and now that your zombie olfactory system finds it interesting, I really don't want to know. Now, if you don't mind?"

I ushered Nate outside the makeshift pentagram I'd created with the bowls.

When he was well and truly on the sidelines, I tapped the barrier like I normally did and pulled a globe, just as Lee had instructed. With the exception of the last twenty-four hours, I'd been good about not pulling consecutive globes. I held my breath as I did it. When it rains, it pours, right? I braced for the cold that filtered through my head and the wave of nausea that followed.

When I had stabilized my globe, I opened my eyes to the world bathed in telltale grey. Here went everything. I struck the match and lit the mixture in each of the bowls, one right after the other, watching the brief flicker of Otherside released by the sage and other dried herbs and the unidentified ashy powder that had interested Nate's zombie nose. Finally, when each bowl was burning, I flooded them with Otherside.

Sage, rosemary, pine needles and the like all have an affinity for the Otherside. They toe a strange place between the living and the dead. Something to do with the fact that they never quite lose their colour when they're dried out. Smoke helps channel Otherside, so burning the herbs acts as a catalyst. I'd found through trial and error that sage and rosemary work best, though I had a theory that peat moss might work in a pinch. One day I'd get around to testing it.

I cringed, suddenly remembering that Gideon said he'd been burned at the stake. The macabre part of my brain wondered if he'd tried to cast a spell when it was happening. The fire and smoke from the wood and whatever else a medieval lynch mob piled on would have drawn the Otherside into the flames, making it harder to manipulate.

A flare from one of the bowls brought my attention back to the here and now. The Otherside had catalyzed the flames, keeping the herbs burning bright.

I shook my head. I wouldn't be the first practitioner who'd been drawn into a trance of Otherside flames. One thing was certain, Lee's herbs had made the wall of smoke and Otherside stronger than I was used to. Good thing the fire alarm had spent the last year stowed safely under the sink.

Carefully, not wanting to disturb the bowls' burning contents, I placed each one in a corner of the spare bedroom. Nate stepped inside and I put the fifth bowl on the floor just inside the doorway.

"Won't he smell it—or see it?" Nate said, looking around.

I was opening my mouth to reply when the shot of Otherside hit me. Not like an uncontrolled wave, but a cold, sharp claw tapping my shoulder, summoning me.

"The mix should pull the Otherside in, and Gideon's dead— ghosts can't smell, remember?" I said through clenched teeth. I'd need to have a word with Gideon about appropriate and inappropriate ways to get my attention. "In here until I come get you," I said, and closed the door. I think Nate mumbled, "Don't have to tell me twice," but I was concentrating on fighting the pull of the Otherside as I wiped what remained of the ash and herbs off my hands. I shoved my bag and supplies into my bedroom before closing the door.

I gave my apartment a once-over before turning towards the bathroom. I brought up my Otherside sight and saw a thin, reinforced line leading from me all the way into the bathroom. Well, it's not as though we'd set up a meeting spot. . . . I caught a glimpse of Otherside from the brand on my wrist. I grabbed a long-sleeved flannel from my couch and threw it on over my T-shirt, not wanting to be reminded of the brand or give Gideon the satisfaction of seeing it. In my experience, people brand their victims because they want a visible sign of submission; I figured ghosts were likely the same.

I strode over and placed my hand on the door handle. It was cold to the touch. I took a deep breath and opened the door.

The bathroom was thick with Otherside. Symbols and lines hung in the air, connected in weaving patterns, bathing the small room with the pungent scent of burnt ozone.

I held my finger under my nose to stop myself from sneezing and focused until my eyes cleared. When they did, I made out a figure, leaning against my chipped bathroom sink with his arms crossed across his translucent chest.

Gideon.

I opened my mouth to say something about the smell and onslaught of Otherside—to think I'd been worried about him sensing the sage wall hiding Nate—but I stopped as I took in his clothes.

Gone were the eighteenth-century jacket and pants, and in their place were modern clothes—or the grey-cast semblance of them. Jeans, a plain white T-shirt and leather jacket, all set off by the symbols and threads of Otherside that clung to him like translucent gold tattoos. It was generic but surprisingly well put together. And here I thought ghosts couldn't adopt a new style . . .

I must have stared at him a little too long, because he quirked his mouth in an unfriendly half smile and said, "Being a sorcerer's ghost comes with some perks, one of which is sartorial flexibility."

I filed that one away for later. Unlike Nate and every other ghost I'd met, Gideon wasn't tied to the appearance he'd had when he'd been living.

Gideon didn't move from his spot by the sink. "You're almost late," he said.

"It's called being exactly on time." I held up my phone. It was 5 p.m. on the dot.

I could have sworn his nostrils flared. "Don't cut it so close next time," he said, then his ghost pushed off the sink and slid around me and into my apartment, not touching me exactly, but chilling me on his way by. I held my hand over my nose again as the strong scent of Otherside overpowered me. Gideon had really outdone himself this time.

I shook my head and followed. "Hello to you too, Gideon. How have the last twenty-four hours been for you?" I said it under my breath, not really sure if I wanted Gideon to overhear or if I just needed to get it out of my system. Likely the latter. Asshole ghost . . .

Gideon glanced over his shoulder, his ghost-grey eyes shifting to an angry black. Panic coursed through me as I saw the line of his mouth tighten. Definitely do not want to piss off the sorcerer's ghost . . . I considered the fact that Gideon wasn't yelling or attacking me with animated electrical cords to be a real bonus at the moment.

I froze and held my breath as Gideon paused in the living area. He began to turn in a slow circle, his feet appearing to more or less touch the ground.

Shit, maybe he could smell the mix of herbs burning in the spare bedroom. I hadn't even realized he could change his clothes, for Christ's sake. Who was I to say he couldn't detect the smoke?

Gideon didn't stop or fixate on the spare-bedroom door as he continued his slow turn and examination of my apartment.

I crossed my arms and hid my hands to keep from fidgeting as his gaze passed over the contents of my small kitchen and living room.

"Please make yourself at home," I said dryly.

Gideon ignored me.

"How are things? They could be better. I've got a paranormal murder in the city to sort out, but otherwise—"

Gideon turned to face me. "Are you well?" he asked.

The attention surprised me. "I suppose," I said. "With the exception of a dead body, that is."

"Hunh." I caught a flicker of interest.

"Let me guess. The possibility of a paranormal murder interests you?"

He arched an eyebrow at me before turning his gaze back to my place. "No— I mean, it does interest me. There aren't many entities besides myself and a few poltergeists who can muster up enough energy or the concentration required to kill a human, so by its nature a paranormal murder of the living is an event that interests me. I inquired about your well-being because I was curious if I would actually care about your response. It's been a while since I've spent much time with the living." He turned his eyes back on me, but this time they were once again the ghost blue-grey. "I don't. Care, that is. I find it rather surprising and unsettling, to be honest."

The homicidal ghost found it unsettling that he didn't care whether I was at death's door, being chased by a poltergeist or doing just swell. Fantastic. "Yeah, sorry, I got nothing," I said. I noticed I was fidgeting again, so I shoved my hands into my sweater pockets.

Gideon glided around the living room, touching the furniture and walls as if memorizing their location.

"While it's true ghosts are non-corporeal and can pass through objects on this side of the barrier with ease, I prefer to know where things are."

I sucked in my breath as he traced his hand over my bedroom door and then the spare-bedroom door.

My eyes zeroed in on the outside bolts I'd locked out of habit. If Gideon noticed them and opened the door . . . But he only ran his hand along the wood and seams of the doorway, as if it were something foreign. If he noticed anything beyond, he didn't mention it. He stepped away from the spare-bedroom door and I did my best not to appear relieved as I let out my breath. He came back to the centre of the room and looked at me. "Besides, my more intricate bindings are more stable when I take into account the objects on this side. It's a bit like being blind," he added. "I can see the furniture and walls, but I can't feel them unless I concentrate. You'll find out that's a theme with Otherside that's touched with sorcery. The normal rules begin to change."

"I've come to think of the effect more as warping, not changing," I said, and mentally kicked myself for not self-filtering.

But Gideon only inclined his chin. "It fits, though I'm not fond of the negative connotation that word brings, however accurate." I checked the corners of my living space and kitchen for any stray appliances.

"What are you doing?" he asked, frowning at me.

"Checking for stray electrical cords. Never know when they're going to take on a life of their own."

Gideon's lip twitched. I noted he looked more corporeal than he had a minute ago as he headed over to my desk and bookshelf. "You think I'm going to kill you," he said as he began to peruse the books piled on my desk, the voodoo practitioner texts still destined for eBay.

I didn't answer.

"I'm not," he said, glancing back at me as he picked up a book. "Going to kill you. Not today, at least." He opened the book and flipped through the pages before exchanging it for another. "If you don't believe the sincerity of the sentiment, believe that you're more useful to me alive than dead. I have enough ghosts to do my bidding. I need a working practitioner. A medium would have sufficed, but he's dead and no longer available. What I have is you." He looked up at me over the pages and I wondered if he blamed me for Max's death as well. God knows I blamed myself, at least partially.

"Where is your ghost?" he asked as he set the book down.

Nerves, don't fail me now . . . I clenched my fists under my arms. "I sent him away for the lesson," I said. Not a lie. I wasn't willing to risk lying to Gideon. If he had a ghost lie radar anything like Nate's . . .

Gideon only frowned. "Shame, we could have begun with ghost binding."

"Yeah, no," I said, leaving no room for interpretation in my tone. Ghost binding was a hard limit. It is a despicable exercise at best, even when used to rein in a poltergeist. A soothsayer's collection of undead, vapid slaves was most definitely not my thing.

I kept my breath even as Gideon watched me, his brow furrowing. "Learning about something distasteful is not the same thing as doing it. Rather the same as learning about one of your serial killers, I imagine."

If he said I had to call Nate . . .

But for whatever reason, Gideon decided that ghost binding was not the hill to wage his war on. Today, at least.

He turned his attention to the books still left on my shelf, sparse though they were. He selected one of my binders, which held a collection of research articles I'd assembled over the last few years on the known effects modern diseases have on zombieism.

"I wanted to go through your reference materials before we begin," Gideon offered as he opened the binder and began flipping through the pages.

"What do my voodoo and practitioning textbooks have to do with learning sorcery?"

"Surprisingly much. The basics of sorcery are built on practitioning."

Now *that* I hadn't known . . .

"I will give you that your practitioning basics are sound, I imagine courtesy of Max—though lacking a few notable texts," he continued, cutting his eyes at me. "How familiar are you with this one?" he asked, picking up a text from my eBay pile and handing it to me.

I took the book. *Ghost Binding*. Great. "Not very," I said as I flipped it open. I realized he was waiting for me to elaborate, so I added, "Max lent this to me a few years back for the first chapter. The basic bindings work particularly well for banishing poltergeists and nuisance ghosts that possess things like pay phones. *Not* for binding them." I slammed it shut and carefully placed it back on the desk.

Gideon either didn't care or took no notice. "And how often do you use this one?" he asked, holding up a book with a dark-red cover.

Another one I wasn't very familiar with, a collection of old European bindings. I probably hadn't opened that textbook in two years—one of the reasons it was on my eBay listings. I shrugged. "As far as calling spirits and zombies goes, there are more efficient ways of doing it, so . . . not much," I said when Gideon gestured for me to answer.

He seemed to consider my response. "For raising zombies and calling and banishing the dead, you are correct. However, the bindings in here are familiar to you and form the basis for many sorcery bindings." He put it on the table. "We'll be using this textbook."

"Wait a minute—" It was already listed on eBay, and I had buyers lined up for it.

But Gideon cut me off. "You can start by setting the mirror with the first set in Chapter 3."

I was about to counter, but the look Gideon gave me . . . Ten minutes and there hadn't been any threats of murder and mayhem. I was setting a record. "Isn't there another textbook I could use?"

"No. You need a basis in sorcery, and of the texts I see here, that's the closest."

"Gideon—" I started, then stopped as his ghost-grey eyes started to turn black again, glittering with Otherside.

I'd assumed Gideon's eyes turned black like that when he was losing his temper—and they did—but I was beginning to realize it signalled something else as well: an effort to rein in his temper.

I carefully phrased what I wanted to say next. "I don't know the first thing about sorcery. There must be a beginner's text somewhere I can get my hands on."

His eyes faded back to grey-blue and he started perusing the binder again. "Your self-esteem issues are not my problem. Open the book and start the set while I finish going through what meagre references you have."

Just when I was inspired to show a modicum of empathy for the sorcerer's ghost . . . I grabbed a mirror out of my desk and managed to keep my distance from Gideon, which was a significant feat considering that the desk and shelf were pressed against one another.

I took the mirror over to the kitchen table, where Gideon had left my book, and took a seat. The set he wanted me to use was a basic one for calling a ghost—any ghost, provided they were willing and you had a name. It was an interesting way to do it; once the mirror was set, you could write the name of the ghost you wanted to talk to in the centre, call them, then erase it without disturbing the rest of the bindings and call a different ghost. All without running the risk of getting your wires crossed. It had been popular with gypsies and fortune tellers throughout Europe during the Middle Ages.

Useful if you had a string of people outside your caravan wanting to talk to their dead relatives. Problem is, I rarely called dead who wanted to be called and often had to contend with the bigger issue of their uncooperativeness . . . as Mr. Graeme had been two nights before. When the deceased has buried their life savings in a tin can in the backyard or stashed it in a secret bank account, usually the last thing they want to do is hand it over to their good-for-nothing relatives. Their words, not mine.

"Your handwriting is atrocious," Gideon said.

I glanced up from the text. He was flipping through my note-book—technical notes and observations and papers I'd collected. "That's because they're my personal notes—meant for me, not you."

"It's a shame. Otherwise, these are well organized."

It occurred to me Gideon might not have access to or knowledge of a computer. The papers would be difficult to find without the use of a search engine. They were eclectic enough in their sources and it was difficult to sieve the authoritative researchers from the evangelical and straight-out charlatans. I shook my head and went back to the mirror. Well, at least Gideon hadn't tried to enter my spare bedroom. I'd take my small victories. . . .

I tried to focus on the instructions. There was a complicated loop of Otherside connecting all the symbols together at once rather than anchoring them to the mirror individually. I traced the design on the pages, trying to figure out the best place to start. I'd have to wait to anchor the symbols on the glass as I laid the Otherside lines . . . then hold the whole thing open and unstable using my globe as the anchor until I was ready to make the last connection.

I let out a breath. It was beginner's practitioner stuff, *but* I hadn't bothered setting a mirror like this in ages. In many ways the advanced stuff was easier and more economical when it came to Otherside. Or maybe I was just used to doing things my way? Why learn to walk if you can already fly?

"I'm surprised Maximillian let you get away with such a sparse collection," Gideon said.

His voice was mild and conversational, but I bristled at the casual mention of Max. I hadn't had to ask Aaron not to bring Max or Randall up. Even Nate and Lee had enough humanity left to figure it out on their own.

"He didn't," I said, hoping to head off that avenue of conversation. Ah, that was how I rejoined the two ends and set the mirror.

I gauged whether I'd need a china marker, but it was a simple-enough pattern I figured I could freestyle without much trouble. Would save me time and cleaning the mirror after.

I pulled a globe and placed a finger on the glass, letting the Otherside trickle down as I traced the first symbol. Not so much a symbol as a word—*Phasma*—which in Latin translates to "ghost." The Latin anchors and set patterns tend to be easier for beginners to write since they use the same alphabet. I finished writing *Phasma* and trailed a line with the appropriate loops and numbers spaced to where I figured the next symbol would best balance out the set. This time I wrote *Umbra*, which means "shade, or bad ghost." I continued on through the rest of the anchors: *Larva*, their word for "poltergeist"; *Effigia*, more an empty shell, or a copy, probably referring to a bound ghost; and finally *Idolum*, which I guessed was an older ghost close to the end of its afterlife line.

Clever, isn't it? A mirror anchored with a bunch of different words in Latin that all mean "ghost." I was holding all five anchoring symbols with my globe, keeping it stable before I could set the mirror. That was the tricky part: holding the entire pattern—numbers, symbols, anchors and lines included—before you could finish it.

I checked the image in the book again and compared it with mine. All the pieces were present except for two. I looped to the bottom of the mirror where I'd started and wrote the last anchor right beside the first, almost touching.

Speculum. "Mirror." Ghost mirror—or mirror for many types of ghosts. Why be sneaky when you could be obvious. Besides, it wasn't likely you would be caught as a practitioner in the Middle Ages. Do you have any idea how many people couldn't write or read? And I doubted very much there were priests out there who used Otherside.

I tied the end of *Speculum* to the first anchoring symbol, *Phasma*, and checked for stability. The lines and numbers all held, and I couldn't feel any Otherside slipping away.

Good enough.

The mirror was stable—time to set and prime it.

I pooled more Otherside into my head and let it run into the design now hovering over the mirror. In response, the Latin words flared and the lines stopped wavering and stabilized. I felt a bead of sweat run down my nose. I'd forgotten how hard it was to keep one of these stable before I could set it on the mirror. . . .

I sent another wave of Otherside at the mirror, this time angling it down. The diagram, which up until now had been touching the mirror but not attached to it, settled in. When I was certain the image was embedded in the glass, I finally let go. It stayed where it was, as if it had always been there. I looked at my reflection, since that was the true test of a set mirror. My pale skin and dark hair stared back at me with the telltale ghost-grey cast.

Far be it from me to pat myself on the back but a freestyle set using a method I hadn't used in years? I was good.

"You're not done until it's workable," Gideon said.

I stifled the first unsavoury response that came to mind and instead wiped the sweat from my face before glancing back down at the book. Now, what symbols did it want me to use to open the damn thing? This time, instead of Latin, a Greek word stared back at me.

Ανοίγω. That one I recognized, but only because it was basic and popped up in practitioning. Hunh, the open symbol for the mirror was the Greek verb for "open"? Seemed like an awful lot of trouble. It meant I'd have to go back and add in all the specifications and restrictions later. . . .

"Would have been easier to mix in Nordic or Egyptian symbols to restrict the mirror," I said to Gideon. Nordic runes and Egyptian cartouches work on the basis that the mirror set is restricted until the practitioner says otherwise, not the other way around, which is how Latin works.

"Except that's not what I asked you to do. At all," Gideon said. He didn't even bother looking up from my notebook this time.

I shook my head. "Just saying." Now . . . the diagram wanted me to centre it. Well, as good a place as any now that the mirror was set.

"It'd also be a lot easier to put the open command in the corner," I said. "Leaves room to add the other commands in later." The one benefit to the Latin mirror is that although it is essentially open, it doesn't act like a beacon. Not until you call a specific ghost; hence its use as a beginner's mirror. If something goes horribly wrong, you can't do much damage. I pooled more Otherside and touched my finger to the centre. "Not that I want an argument," I said as I traced the Greek letters. "I'm just naturally opposed to doing things because that's the way they're done."

"And I sympathize. There's a reason to do it this way."

I waited for Gideon to explain. Big surprise it didn't come. I went back to the Greek letters until they were etched into the glass. Now that the mirror was set and stable, adding more symbols was simpler but required more Otherside. I felt the sweat continue to trickle down my forehead as I pulled more Otherside into my globe.

"Tell me, why is your collection so pathetic?" Gideon said. He had resumed perusing the books and binders.

I kept my focus on the mirror. "Because I've been selling them on eBay."

I caught the movement in my periphery as Gideon looked up, characteristic frown on his face. "Why on earth would you do that?" he asked.

"Because I've already read them and I can get money? Bills don't pay themselves on time, and since raising zombies is one legal bitch at the moment . . ." I let the thought trail off as I etched the final letter. I checked them over and gave the mirror a final pulse of Otherside. I watched the shift in the glass—a quick shimmer of grey—as it activated.

Done. I let out the breath I'd been holding. The whole process had been harder than I'd remembered, or expected. I hated to admit it, but Gideon might have a point about refreshing the basics. Not that I was about to tell him that, but it was food for thought—for later. Once I had every other disaster on my plate thinned out.

I sat back from my work and looked up. Gideon had abandoned the binder on the desk and was watching me.

He shook his head. "What if you need them in the future? For reference, or to look up something you've forgotten?"

It took me a second to realize he meant the books I'd been selling. Now that I was actually trying to set a mirror the Latin way, I was wondering the same thing myself, though I wouldn't be caught dead admitting it to him. "That's what notebooks are for, and research articles, and the Internet."

His expression told me he knew as well as I did that that was a lousy excuse, but to his credit he didn't argue.

I gestured at the mirror. "Besides, this is an inefficient way to set a mirror. Once you know the basics, it makes more sense to mix and match."

I felt the air chill as Gideon drifted over to me. I tensed, thinking maybe he'd given in to his temper. But his eyes were still ghost grey and all he did was lean over the mirror, checking my work. I got a better look at the bindings that covered him, very few of which I recognized. Definitely not enough to determine their purpose.

"Not every practitioner has a knack for patching together bindings the way you do," he said.

Maybe it was the stress of the last twenty minutes under Gideon's scrutiny, or the fact that I can only hold back my snark for so long . . . even in the presence of a murderous ghost. "My god. Was that a compliment?"

Gideon braced himself against the wall, a strange affectation considering he was translucent. "While you're learning sorcery, I expect no shortcuts."

"I already got the message."

"Considering your track record following directions, it bears repeating."

I didn't have a response for that.

His gaze returned to the mirror. "Most practitioners use a substance such as wax to help the Otherside adhere to the glass before the bindings are set," he said, and I caught him glancing at the china marker off to the side.

"Only when I need to. It's a bitch to wipe off later."

He nodded to himself, as if I'd confirmed something he'd already suspected. "You don't need to draw the symbols out to etch them into a mirror. Yet another skill you failed to mention." He studied me, his eyes darkening. "Now, was that on purpose, or did you simply not think it was worth noting? To be quite honest, I can't tell. Yet."

I swallowed. "I use a china marker. And I need it for anything complicated, but not a beginner's set like this."

Gideon gave me a dark look, but he didn't press it, and his eyes stayed ghost grey, though darker than I would have liked.

"It's good work," he finally said after checking my mirror again. "Now do it again. Faster this time."

"Why?"

"Just do it," he said, cutting me off and going back to my desk.

I bit my tongue, reached out and pulled the original circle of Otherside and Latin I'd etched in and began all over again. Luckily, I'd had the forethought not to drop my globe. . . .

Out of the corner of my eye, I noticed Gideon had abandoned my binder on diseases and zombieism and moved on to a second one—the one I did use, and often: my collection of zombie raisings. I hadn't been able to find any texts that listed all the different methods for raising a zombie from various practitioning backgrounds, and there were a lot, I'd learned—as many as there were cultures and practitioning traditions. Ghouls, African vodun zombies, voodoo zombies, Nordic versions, the variations from the Far East. Some of them began the process with the living. A Buddhist method preserved the body with a steady diet of pine needles, the resin acting as disinfectant and natural embalming fluid as it seeped into tissue, carried by blood, until the subject died from voluntary starvation and the toxic resin building up in their organs—the ultimate religious sacrifice. The Russian version entailed trapping a living victim in a pit for days without water to dehydrate the body before raising them as a ghoul. Each method was unique, with its own twist and emphasis. I'd started recording my findings years ago to keep them all in one place, and added my own notes on the variations along the way. I'd even begun adding notes on Jinn, though they were nowhere near finished. I couldn't bring myself to do that yet.

I forced myself to concentrate on the task of resetting the mirror. I wasn't sure how I felt about Gideon going through my personal findings. Unlike the other binders, this one was important to me. I'd worked hard to put it together. It was one of the few projects that Max hadn't complained about, only sniffed and handed back, mentioning that I was missing a subset of bindings for a particular category.

I pushed away that train of thought as I set my finger to etching the first Latin word for "ghost" onto the glass again. But as I moved on to *Umbra* and the others, a thought, or a question, occurred to me. Runes, Greek letters, numbers, Latin words—though no one was quite sure why, they all held power on the Otherside. They directed the intention of the bindings. I held the half set in my head as it hovered over the glass, then asked Gideon, "So why did they go out of their way to specify ghost?"

Gideon didn't bother glancing up from my binder. "I'm fairly certain I said 'faster,' not 'let's have a discussion about it.'"

Gideon and Max must have gone to the same teaching school. At least I was on familiar ground. "It's a valid question about the bindings you're asking me to use."

"Then ask while you set the mirror. Faster."

A curse almost escaped under my breath. Don't antagonize the homicidal ghost, Kincaid. I traced my finger across the mirror and let the Otherside trail down and into the glass.

"I mentioned that sorcery has its basis in practitioning, yes?"

I nodded but didn't look up from the bindings.

"Though often I've thought it's rather the other way around, and practitioning was adapted from basic sorcery principles," he continued.

"I'd say voodoo argues against that." Voodoo has its own history of manipulating Otherside beyond basic practitioning, but it stops well short of warping it. More like ask it to do what you'd like and cross your fingers that it complies.

"Vodun. And though I will concede its origins are unique, that is only one example of convergent practitioning." He looked up at me. "The reason that mirror specifies ghosts is that there are other things that can be drawn across the barrier."

That made me pause. It was the first time Gideon had ever mentioned other entities besides ghosts going across the barrier. I glanced up from my bindings. I couldn't resist. "What lives across the barrier besides ghosts and poltergeists?"

"Nothing lives across the barrier," Gideon said, giving me a pointed stare from over my binder. "They're all dead. Your bindings?" Gideon said, nodding at the mirror. He'd moved on to my collection of newspaper clippings, mostly about murders and deaths that involved practitioners or poltergeists, along with the changing legalities of practitioning.

"That's not what I meant."

"There are no other entities that reside across the barrier beyond the ghosts you are already familiar with."

There was something about the way he said it. I frowned as I went back to the binding.

Gideon had either seen my expression or had more to say on the matter. "By other things, I wasn't referring to calling another sentient entity," he said. "I meant calling Otherside for a purpose, to bend it to your will across the mirror."

The air around me cooled—more so than the Otherside I was using to set the mirror would have accounted for. I looked up to find Gideon watching me again, his eyes not black yet, but a much darker grey-blue.

"Sorcery," he said, showing his teeth as he pronounced the word.

The air chilled even more and I detected a slight breeze. All the windows were closed. I shivered, but it wasn't from the cold. I focused on my mirror and, for the first time since our lesson had started, hoped Gideon went back to my binders.

I finished the mirror for a second time and checked it for stability. I looked at the Latin inscriptions that formed the base of the set in an entirely different light. Calling Otherside to do something before it had even reached the mirror . . .

"You call it to freeze things. Why?"

Gideon frowned at me.

"Not that I'm a professional on sorcery, but there have to be other things it can do." Fireballs and lightning came to mind, from Nate's various video games and stories about sorcerers I'd found online, but I didn't suggest these. Didn't want to give Gideon any ideas. "What's with the ice?"

He gave me a hard look, and I kept my face as blank as possible.

"Cold is easier than other manipulations," he said. "One of the easiest, in fact, as Otherside already has an affinity for the cold. I, like you, see no reason to be wasteful with time or energy when simple works just as well, if not better."

I didn't remind him that he'd disdained my own preference for simple and efficient. I was still working through the first part of what he'd said. "You mean Otherside *is* cold."

"*That* is a practitioner's assumption. Otherside isn't anything. It's Otherside, not part of this world, and as such can be nothing—neither cold nor hot."

Something clicked. "It reacts with air and makes *it* turn cold."

Gideon nodded but didn't look up. "And water, and skin. Anything of this world."

If I remembered my high school chemistry, that meant Otherside had to slow molecules down . . . like when water freezes. I shelved that as something to investigate later. The physicists studying Otherside had to be looking into it. . . .

I felt the brush of ice again and glanced up.

Gideon had left his post by my shelf and was leaning over the kitchen table. "Why do you ask?" he said with a predatory look.

For a brief moment I thought about saying it was none of his business—but that was a gut reaction. Warped Otherside was involved in Jacob's death, if not the cause of it. That meant sorcery, and Gideon was the only sorcerer I knew, let alone knew of. . . .

This is the part where I discovered Gideon had decided to freeze Jacob to death out of misplaced spite. . . .

"I was brought in to see a body this morning," I said carefully as I finished the mirror binding and tied off the set. "It was found frozen on the floor of a bar basement, covered in what I've been calling Otherside dust. Except it doesn't behave like Otherside anymore. Doesn't react, doesn't filter back—it just sits there. And freezes things." I glanced up at him. "The body was still frozen hours later, after we took it to the morgue, and I'm pretty damn sure it's the Otherside powder that's doing it." I wetted my lips against the feverish sweat from holding my globe as I decided whether to continue. I'd come this far, what the hell. "I think it was a wraith."

I expected him to make another snide comment about not working on the mirror. But he didn't. Instead, he listened with interest. "Were there any bindings? Any at all in the area, on the body?"

I shook my head. "No, those were the first things I looked for. There was nothing hidden either—as far as I could tell."

"And there was no reaction to Otherside?"

Again I shook my head. "No, I used two waves of Otherside and it didn't react, and I wasn't stingy on the amount. Touching the body did more to the dust."

Gideon went silent and seemed to stare through me. "It's not exclusively sorcery," he finally said. "Otherwise there would have been bindings somewhere—a directed spell, perhaps. But there are no sorcerers nearby who could accomplish that."

"There is no way in hell it was normal Otherside."

"I didn't say it was, nor that it didn't have its origins in sorcery. A wraith, as you suggested, is one such possibility."

Goddamnit, I couldn't help myself. "I thought you said there weren't other things across the barrier besides ghosts."

Gideon's eyes burrowed into me. I swallowed hard. Maybe I really did have a death wish.

"There *aren't*," he said with emphasis. "A wraith is an undead caught between two worlds. It's neither here nor in the Otherside, therefore it can't be called across. The Otherside that animates a wraith is warped by sorcery, and *ergo* its effect." He narrowed his eyes at me. "A wraith loose in a city is a very dangerous thing. I'm surprised there's only one body. Then again, maybe it's conserving its energy—or more likely killing the disenfranchised undesirables who live on the edges of your society, though I would have thought someone would have noticed the ice. Contrary to popular belief, wraiths are sentient undead, but, unlike zombies and ghouls, they're consumed with an insatiable hunger for Otherside, one that drives them mad and typically leads to violence and chaos."

Fantastic, though Lee's story about the wraith girl who had ravaged her village had suggested as much. The wraith girl had been less a tool of the witch, more a chaotic force targeting those who had wronged her in her own life. Zombies that have gone feral are one thing; they're a mess, but they aren't bright about it. A sentient crazy monster . . .

As if sensing my train of thought, Gideon added, "If a sorcerer wants revenge, a wraith is not the way to do it. Unless your intention is to wipe out the odd town or city."

On the one hand, I was happy he was telling me all this. On the other hand, it was terrifying to think there was more violence to come. . . .

"I could tell you more if I could see it," he added.

I blinked, more than a little surprised Gideon had made the offer.

"There are other possible explanations. Other undead. Any of the possibilities are—undesirable. Even for me, as they draw attention to the community."

Right. There had to be a selfish reason for his interest. . . .

"I might be able to go back tomorrow," I said.

Gideon nodded. "Contact me through a mirror when you are there. I'm curious. I haven't seen a wraith in . . ." His eyes turned a darker blue-grey for a moment before he said, "A very long time." He turned his head to the side. "You seem to attract death."

"Wow. Thanks."

There was the sneer again. "I didn't mean it as an insult. It's a statement of fact."

"Still, it isn't a nice thing to say to the living—especially the ones who are trying to stay that way."

"I won't bring it up again."

"Thank you." I wasn't sure how to take the almost-apology. Without thinking, I added, "And this time it has less to do with me attracting attention and more with my friend in the Seattle PD knowing when to bring in a practitioner."

"Still, others will make the association."

I don't know why, but his words hit a nerve. A small one, but it resonated nonetheless. "Something paranormal happens and they call me, not the other way around."

"From my experience the difference in order is subjective when you're relying on human memory of events." He gave me an unfriendly smile. "Most people tend towards convenient inversion."

Okay, that one definitely hit a little too close to home. "Aaron isn't like that."

"No, he strikes me more as a survivor." Before I could reply, Gideon said, "Rather than argue with me, why not ask yourself a simple question: what does involving yourself in their affairs do for you?"

"They'll give me my old job back," I said, my throat tightening.

One of Gideon's grey-blond eyebrows arched. "Really? You have someone's word on that? Have it in writing, I suppose? Well, then, I stand corrected. You've struck a very good deal with them."

He came around the side of the table to examine the mirror. I stood there despite the drop in temperature at his proximity, an acrid taste in my mouth. Goddamnit . . . Gideon had an uncanny way of bringing to light uncomfortable truths I'd rather ignore.

And coming from him, it bothered me that much more.

His ghost-grey eyes bored into me. "Ahhh—I see. You have no commitment. Just the possibility." He shrugged and made as if he was leaning against the table. "I admit I would have struck a better deal, considering the risk to yourself."

"Risk?"

"Personal association with the things that go bump in the night. Would you like to know one of the secrets to making deals?" he asked, holding up the set mirror.

I swallowed, though my mouth was dry, and it wasn't entirely from the Otherside I was still holding.

"Finding out what someone wants more than anything else is the first part," he said, "but the second is arguably more important: making sure you know their price." He turned the mirror around so I could see my own grey-tinged reflection behind the bindings. "My advice is that you take a very good look at yourself, Kincaid, because your Seattle PD friend knows your price better than you do."

I knew better than to get angry at Gideon, but I did snatch the mirror back from his translucent hand.

It didn't faze him. "Unless something comes up, we'll meet again tomorrow at this time." He picked up the textbook and, after flipping through a few pages, handed it to me open. I peered at a series of sets—voodoo exercises.

"I want the exercises on those two pages finished by the time we meet next. No wax markers."

I scanned the sets. "There are seven in here," I said.

"And I want them on separate mirrors."

I put the book down. "I don't have seven mirrors lying around!"

"Then break one. From what I understand, the modern ones shatter quite easily."

"Oh, for . . ." I would have continued, but Gideon's eyes glittered at me.

Don't push him, Kincaid . . . Besides, I had compacts lying around and I could grab cheap mirrors at the pharmacy. They'd be tiny mirrors, but he hadn't specified size.

"Call me when you're at the murder scene again. I'll be waiting," Gideon said. And with the slightest of nods, he dissolved into Otherside smoke, filtering back across the barrier.

I dropped my globe and let out a breath as the cold Otherside left me. I wrapped my arms around my shoulders to stifle the shudder from the deep chill in my bones. Well, that hadn't been half as painful as I'd expected.

Tea—a hot pot of tea was what I needed. With another shiver, I headed into my kitchen.

I stopped at the muffled knock from the spare-bedroom door.

Nate. I unlocked the latches and let him out.

Nate was waiting in the doorway, smoke from the burning sage and various herbs billowing around him. His brow was knit—as much as it could be, considering the nerve and muscle deterioration. "Seriously, K. You forgot I was in here, didn't you?"

I wiped my forehead, trying to get rid of the clammy sensation that the Otherside had left. "I was a little preoccupied."

Nate peered down at me. "Shit, K. You don't look so hot."

I wiped my forehead again. "I'm fine. He just had me doing a set. I didn't overuse. I'll recover by the morning." A hot shower and tea was what I needed—that and a good night's sleep.

Nate looked as if he was going to argue, but thought better of it.

"Look, I'm being careful. If I can't handle the amount of Otherside he wants me to use . . ." I trailed off. Gideon didn't exactly have my best interests at heart, but he also was the one who'd come up with the Otherside sight to circumvent my need to pull a globe. I doubted he would push me past my limit. "He won't burn me out," I said, and was surprised how confident I was in that statement.

"I just really hope you know what you're doing, K," Nate said as he pushed past me.

Yeah, so did I. I wiped my damp palms on my jeans.

"I've got the books from Mork. We can start going through them tonight, after I do one more thing." The set mirror had given me an idea.

"And what exactly would that be, K? You're tapped out."

I shook my head. It wouldn't take much Otherside—if any. Not with a mirror already set and primed. All I had to do was write the name and it would do the work for me.

Nate was watching me with concern. I pulled the T-shirt Mindy had given me out of my backpack and held it up. The scent of cigarettes was still on it. "Time to call Damien and see if he's home."

CHAPTER 10

CADMIUM COFFEE

I refilled my mug of tea and held it with both hands. They'd almost warmed up to normal—enough so I thought I could tap the barrier again if necessary. I'd also slipped a sweater over my flannel. I wanted to be prepared for the second ghost encounter of the day. . . .

"Are you sure this is the smartest place to try this?" Nate said.

I shrugged and sat cross-legged on my living room floor in the middle of the sage pentagram I'd set out in fresh bowls. "Might as well get it out of the way now, Nate. Gideon won't come back tonight, and I've already got a mirror to use."

Max had always made me use wax candles for European-style set mirrors; according to textbooks and many a practitioner, smoke from beeswax candles conducts Otherside. But I'd never seen any evidence of it and I wasn't sure whether wax would come out of the wood floor. I still entertained dreams of getting my deposit back one day. Instead, I'd gone with bowls of burning sage minus the candles. Again, the sage wasn't necessary for calling a ghost through a mirror—but it helped, and it'd be easier to channel Damien's

T-shirt through the barrier using the sage smoke as a conduit. I've said it before and I'll say again: the first thing the dead try to do is take their shit with them. Waving Damien's unwashed, sage-laced T-shirt in front of the mirror would be well-nigh irresistible.

"If I'm lucky, I won't even have to pull a globe to get Damien's attention." Or that was the plan: write the ghost's name in the centre of the mirror and go, no globe required . . .

Provided he wanted to talk. If he didn't, things got tricky, all bets were off, and I'd move on to plan B. . . . Not an ideal scenario, but as far as contacting Damien went, this was my best chance. If he got spooked and went to ground, well, things got a lot harder.

I had a suspicion Nate was worried about me not getting back to Mork's books. For all his bravado and laissez-faire attitude about being stuck in Cameron's body, the formaldehyde smell was intensifying and his fingers weren't nearly as nimble as they had been even a day ago. He was seriously wanting out. I wanted to help, but the sooner I could get Damien's testimony, the sooner Nate would be out of Aaron's sights. The last thing we needed was Aaron demanding I march Nate in for a statement. That would not go well, considering my lousy poker face and Aaron's bullshit radar.

"I'll get back to Mork's books as soon as I talk to Damien," I said, and added, "Nate, the books are a long shot. If they're useful—and that's a *big* if—they'll only give me an idea of what might have happened. I'll still need to—"

He held up his hands. "No, seriously, this has nothing to do with me. Two weeks ago you were a wreck, K."

I flinched. "And I'm not a wreck now. I'm being very careful with how much Otherside I'm using. Remember? I don't have to pull a globe to see Otherside anymore."

"But you've already been using Otherside with Gideon, and I'm guessing that's what Aaron had you doing at the crime scene. Don't you think this would be better left until tomorrow?"

Yeah, I'd considered that. "I'll have to pull another globe tomorrow, probably two. If I have to access more Otherside tonight, at least I'll have the chance to sleep it off."

Nate ran his hand through the greasy mess that was Cameron's hair. It still hadn't started to fall out. The shower had only done so much. I'd have to see about getting him dry shampoo. . . .

"Okay, I realize this is fucking comical coming from me, but isn't that how you got into this whole mess in the first place? Not knowing you were using too much Otherside?"

Nate had a point. I clenched my teeth and willed myself to be patient. "You're just going to have to trust me on this one."

He shook his head but plunked down beside me. "Why do I think this is going to be a fucking disaster?"

"Because unlike me, you have a pathological impulse control problem."

Nate snorted loudly, and mumbled something about a black kettle. I ignored him and rechecked the bowls of sage. They were all smouldering, so I picked up the mirror, careful not to look at my reflection in it, and made sure Damien's concert T was still beside me.

Nate shuffled closer to me as I picked up the china marker and touched it to the glass. I began to etch Damien's name and cut my eyes at him. "And you're the last person who should be criticizing me for overindulging."

"No, I'm exactly the person." He held out his arms, now a nauseating shade of formaldehyde yellow. "Look at me. I'm the poster boy warning against indulgence. I've died, what, twice now?" He frowned.

I glared at him. "It's just a quick summoning, Nate. What's ever gone wrong at a quick summoning?"

Nate sighed but didn't leave. "When the fuck did I become the voice of reason?"

I closed my eyes and focused. Not essential for calling ghosts, but as a matter of practice I like to make sure I set out my own intentions before they show up. To a ghost, time really isn't worth much—well, your time, at least. As such, they tend to digress. Keeping them on topic is like herding cats. I find it helps to have a list of pertinent questions front of mind.

I inhaled the sage smoke and went over the questions that would direct the conversation. *Do you know your name?* Always a good place to start; you never know with ghosts. *Do you know how long you've been dead?* Again, following the passage of time is not a strong suit for ghosts. It was irrelevant to me, but if Damien said he thought it had only been five years, it'd influence exactly how many details I let slide. The game was keeping the ghost oriented—not trying to figure out what the hell an MP3 player is. . . .

Once I had an idea just how aware Damien was of his predicament, then I'd ask about his death. *Do you remember anything?* And regardless of his answer, did he know who might have wanted him dead?

I shot Nate a quick glance. I just hoped that if Mindy came up in the conversation, he would keep his cool. "Nate?" I said.

He'd been off in his own world. "What?" he said, frowning.

"Ghost?" I nodded at the sage and pentagram. "You're a zombie?"

"Oh, come on. I haven't seen Damien in years. He was kind of a friend."

"He stole your girlfriend."

He shrugged. "Happens. In the sixties and seventies people experimented with sex and drugs, in the nineties we experimented with relationship dynamics . . . and drugs and sex."

I closed my eyes for a moment. "I want to keep him on track. You'll distract him."

"I want to hear what he has to say. I was alive then, remember? I can help."

I recognized his nervous energy as he shifted his weight on the floor. Nate wasn't going to budge on this one.

"Fine. But stay out of sight. I want to spend the next twenty minutes explaining what you are about as much as I want to explain Bluetooth and smartphones."

Nate made a derisive noise but moved so he was sitting behind the mirror, opposite me. Damien would see him if he decided to take a look around, but he wouldn't be in his direct line of sight.

"Out of sight out of mind enough for you?"

I narrowed my eyes at him. "No jumping into the conversation, either."

Nate glared but kept his mouth shut. Good enough. I drew in a deep breath, filling my lungs and letting the scent of burnt sage clear my head.

Here went everything . . . I let out my breath and tapped the barrier.

I won't lie—it stung. The nausea hit me more strongly than it had even an hour ago.

Focus, Kincaid.

I clenched my teeth and pushed through the discomfort as I touched the mirror, letting the Otherside fill it and not me. A benefit of using the Latin-style mirror was that I didn't have to hold the Otherside, only act as a brief conduit. Still unpleasant, but nowhere near as bad as it could have been. Maybe that was why a seemingly difficult set of bindings and inscriptions were used as a basic teaching tool. Difficult to make but very easy to use.

Apparently, Gideon's preferred method was to throw his practitioning students into the deep end headfirst to teach them how to swim. Not a comforting thought. I let the Otherside flood through my hand as I started to trace the wax. The mirror's inscriptions pulsed.

Time to call Damien. "Damien Fell?" I said, and felt the echo of my words carry through the mirror and across the barrier. I repeated his name. Otherside surged through the mirror. I watched the sage smoke lick the glass before being drawn in.

I held my breath and waited.

It wasn't long, maybe fifteen seconds or so, before the mirror pinged back. I flinched at the Otherside echo.

"There you are," I whispered. The electric-like pulse of Otherside was more chilling than I remembered with this type of mirror. Maybe it was the Latin bindings, but it felt stronger, and more targeted than my usual sets.

This technique might come in handy for such specific callings. It wasn't like I had to undo the mirror after this. . . .

Another ping. It had found something.

"Come on, Damien," I coaxed as I felt the tug along the line of Otherside that stretched across the barrier.

I waited for him to start coalescing—but he didn't.

I frowned and reached out, mentally checking and probing the bindings. He wasn't resisting, like a ghost who didn't want to talk. It was more sluggish than that.

I felt around for the Otherside line and pulled. Not hard, but enough that he'd get the picture.

Still no response. The sensation reminded me of a fishing line caught on dead wood. If I had to hazard a guess, I'd say he was sleeping, but that was impossible. Ghosts don't sleep. Then again, I'd never tried calling a Mormon ghost before—not that I was aware of, anyway. If Damien hadn't ended up wherever Mormons figured they should . . . well, maybe he'd lightened up on the "no booze and drugs." I mean, he was dead, after all. If there was ever a time to experiment . . .

But I'd never heard of a ghost picking up a *new* bad habit. Expanding on their old ones, sure.

I felt the first drop of sweat collect on my upper lip.

I swore and wiped it off. Great. Fantastic.

"K?" Nate asked. I caught the worry in his voice.

I gave my head a quick shake. I was overthinking it and using up my window of safe Otherside. I'd seen ghosts figure out stranger things than how to pick up new vices after they were dead. . . .

Strengthen the beacon, Kincaid.

I let more Otherside into my head and flooded the bindings with it.

The line pulled again but still felt as if it was attached to a leaden weight. It moved, but not much.

Well, this was exactly what I'd brought the T-shirt along for. Keeping my focus on the mirror, I felt beside me until my fingers closed around the soft cotton. I ignored the fact that it was much warmer than it should be in my hand.

I waved it in front of the sage smoke, watching as the smoke and Otherside twined around it.

"Come on, Damien," I whispered. "Even you can't resist something that was yours." I'd yet to meet a ghost who could.

It gave only a fraction, but I felt the line stretch. "Come *on*," I whispered at the mirror, and pulled harder.

"K," Nate said, warning in his voice. "Not that you don't know what you're doing, but there's an awful lot of Otherside wrapped up in that mirror."

There—it gave again, sharply this time. "Just a second, Nate. I've almost got him." I narrowed my eyes. Nate was right, there was an awful lot of Otherside building up around the mirror. I focused on keeping the bindings stable. The last thing I wanted was to shear through whatever tentative line of Otherside was holding on to Damien.

"Hey!" Nate had reached over the mirror and grabbed my shoulders; his hands were warm even through the bulk of my sweater. "K, if he was going to come through, he'd have shown up by now," Nate said, then winced as the mirror sent out another pulse of Otherside. "Damn, I barely knew the guy and I can feel the mirror calling. And I'm a zombie, not a ghost."

I was channelling the Otherside, not collecting it, but I could still feel the cold seeping through my skin. I was almost out of my window. "Give me a second more," I said through clenched teeth. If I held on just a little longer, either Damien would have to come through or the tether holding him to the mirror would snap.

The line shifted again, loosening whatever he was stuck on—or under.

I felt a drop of sweat fall on my hand and glanced down. It wasn't sweat. It was blood.

Well, shit.

"K—it's too much!"

I wiped the blood off on my jeans. "He's not resisting, Nate, he's stuck," I whispered. I couldn't drop the connection now; we were too close. It'd be a waste of an Otherside hangover if I gave up now.

"I mean it, you need to stop!"

"If I did that every time things get hard, Nate— Shit!"

Whatever Damien had been stuck on gave and I recoiled at the rush of Otherside back into my skull as the tension snapped. I fought a wave of nausea and bit my tongue—hard—as I tried to get the teeth chattering under control. I held my barrier in place with all I had, fearing the raw burn of unadulterated Otherside on my senses. It took me a few seconds to clear my eyes.

I stared at the Otherside fog that began to coalesce on our side of the mirror. It didn't look like Damien, or any ghost, and it should have taken shape by now.

"K? Remember what I said about a really fucking bad idea?" Nate said as the smoke and Otherside continued to undulate, not forming any real shape but not dispersing either.

I watched the smoke. Maybe it was residual Otherside? Like the cloud of fishing line that snaps back in a feathery mess when a fish breaks loose . . .

"K, I mean it—you need to shut it down!"

It wasn't my imagination. Nate was jumpy.

Maybe he was right. The smoke had begun expanding, and it definitely shouldn't be doing that.

I chided myself. It'd be a cold day in hell before I gave a ghost the satisfaction of scaring me. *Me.*

"When in doubt, stoke the fire," I said. I reached for the remaining sage and tossed it on the nearest bowl, then held up the T-shirt. "Damien?" I said, projecting my voice into the mirror.

The smoke immediately turned a darker shade of grey and appeared to have . . . substance. I caught a glimpse of gold Otherside threads weaving their way through it.

I frowned. They weren't normal Otherside threads; these ones were winding and disorganized.

"Damien?" I tried again. "How about you come out of there and play nice?"

But Damien didn't answer. If anything, my voice sent the cloud and threads churning violently.

They sure as hell weren't my bindings . . . or the mirror's. In fact, as far as I could tell, there wasn't any pattern to them at all.

"Nate, please tell me you're the one behind that cloud?" I said. "You know—one of your really badly calculated pranks."

"K, can I just say I told you so?"

"I'll take that as a no," I said. My face was covered with sweat now, and not entirely from the Otherside.

"For the record, I totally fucking told you so— *Shit!*"

The cloud had turned nearly black and expanded in Nate's direction, the Otherside threads churning rapidly as they sought out the source of the new voice. Nate stumbled as he threw himself out of the way.

"Nate! Are you— Damn it!" I scrambled out of the way as a lazy tendril lapped at me. I noticed a red dot on the surface of the mirror. It had crystallized . . . a drop of my own blood.

It was frozen.

I glanced back up at the expanding cloud of Otherside and smoke.

Otherside is cold, but it doesn't freeze.

"Nate!" I started, but my warning came too late.

An icy gust hit me, knocking me over and burning my lungs. The back of my head bounced off the hardwood floor. Dazed, I pushed myself up and felt my hair. It was wet with blood.

I coughed, lungs still burning, as I peered at the thing hovering over the mirror. My eyes were blurry from the icy blast of Otherside, so I blinked to clear them. Thick coils of dark smoke wound through the cloud alongside threads of gold Otherside . . . but the threads weren't arranged like bindings, more like chaotic debris in a storm.

Whatever it was, it wasn't orchestrated the way Gideon's attacks had been. It was more primal—visceral.

Nate was on his knees outside the pentagram. I swore as he lifted his head and looked at me, his eyes widening. There was a nasty gash on his face. It'd need stitches for sure.

I turned my attention back to the mirror as the thing let out a low, rumbling growl that reminded me of thunder. Whatever it was, it wasn't friendly. I needed to get rid of it. *Now.*

I racked my brain for anything about exorcising boiling black clouds of Otherside and smoke. Use a funnel? I couldn't safely collect enough Otherside to do that. Hit it with a big pulse of Otherside and hope the mirror pulled it back through? Less reliable, but I wasn't exactly loaded with appealing options.

So much for being conservative with Otherside . . . I dropped my mental barriers to collect a lot of Otherside, and fast—and grimaced as the nauseating flood rushed my senses, frying a few of them. When I had enough, I shoved it at the mirror.

The cloud of Otherside smoke stirred as the mirror flared. It had worked—the mirror was siphoning it back through.

I smelled something mixing with the burning sage . . . a spice, warmer and sweeter than most. Not altogether unpleasant.

Wait a minute—I recognized that smell. It followed Gideon everywhere.

Oh hell no . . . "Nate, watch out! Sorcery!"

"Shit, shit, shit," I heard him chant from where he was recovering on all fours just outside the pentagram. He ducked out of the way just in time as "it" reached out towards him with a thick arm of smoke. I squinted at it; I could have sworn it had substance.

I expected Nate to run or hide, but all he did was stare at the entity, a haunted look in his eyes.

Fine, the elemental blob of smoke and Otherside wanted to play dirty? Time for the practitioner's version of an ice ball . . .

"Nate—get me sage, now!"

My tone must have jolted him out of his shock, because he lurched to his feet and stumbled for the kitchen.

The sentient cloud, or whatever it was, ignored him. Instead, the winding, broken threads drifted towards me. It was getting ready to do something and I was pretty sure I wasn't going to like it. . . . I pulled in more Otherside.

"Where's your sage?" Nate yelled from the kitchen.

"Cutlery drawer!" The threads were twining faster, more violently than they had a moment before.

"It's not here!" I heard him yell amidst the clattering of metal.

"Not that one, the other one!"

I heard swearing and kitchen utensils crashing to the ground as Nate emptied the drawers.

I so did not like how fast those threads of Otherside were twining. I gauged how much Otherside I had stored. Well, now was as good a time as any. . . . I threw what I had at it, letting the energy out in a fast wave. It struck the black cloud, which condensed into a smaller black ball. The lights in my apartment flickered three times, then the living room went dark.

"K!"

I could make out Nate's outline in the kitchen doorway holding the bag of sage.

"Stop throwing Otherside at it!"

I frowned. Why? It was working. Nate swore and pointed.

Son of a bitch . . . it was multiplying in size. Damn it.

This time I managed to cover my head and face before the second icy blast hit. How the hell was it doing that?

"K, stop pissing it off!" Nate shouted. He'd taken refuge under the kitchen table. The entire apartment was freezing now.

That's when I noticed the gold Otherside dust falling around me. The exact same substance that had covered the murder scene.

No way this was from a summoning gone wrong. It was the wraith, or whatever had killed Jacob, and maybe Damien too, if Aaron was right about him being frozen. . . .

Shit.

"It's back," Nate said. "I don't know how it found me, but it did, K. It must have been waiting for me across the barrier."

Many thoughts ran through my head. What the hell Nate was talking about was at the top of the list, but I shelved that one for later. For the immediate situation, one word rang out in my mind: *mirror.*

The thing was drawing Otherside through the mirror to fuel its attack from across the barrier. If I took the mirror off-line, I'd be taking away its power source.

I spooled more Otherside into what remained of my globe and braced myself for the surge of cold as I reached out for the strands that ran between the Latin words. When I got a hold of one, I pulled and the bindings that held the mirror together started to give. It wasn't pretty; pulling apart a mirror during a seance falls into the stupid-idea pile. The bindings weakened, though, and the Otherside, having no place to go, settled.

I let go of the mirror and sucked in air, trying to warm my lungs. But the coalescing thing wasn't ready to give up.

So much for an unthinking blob of smoke . . .

The threads shifted their focus away from me and back onto Nate.

"Toss me the sage," I croaked, my throat still raw.

He did as I asked from behind the kitchen table, which he'd turned on its side like a barricade.

The Otherside threads flashed and sparked before the coils of smoke lashed out towards the table.

My bowls of smouldering sage, which had burnt out when the room went dark, burst back into flames, reviving my pentagram. The bag of sage hit an invisible wall and fell to the floor just outside the pentagram.

"Oh, you got to be kidding me."

Nate, peering around the table, saw the sage and abandoned his barricade to run towards me. Now was not the time for heroics. . . .

"Nate—no!"

He either didn't hear me or didn't care. He swore as his fists came up against the invisible sage-smoke pentagram wall. "What the hell?"

A black coil of Otherside-laced smoke snaked towards his hand and Nate yelled and jerked it away. Through the thickening smoke, I could see the gold glow of Otherside dust settling on his hand and sleeve. Fuck me, the thing was freezing him.

"K, shut the mirror down!"

"What do you think I'm trying to do?"

At the sound of my voice, the black cloud—wraith? ghost? monster?—swivelled its attention back on me, the smoke swelling and the gold threads flashing and rippling.

I sneered at it and pulled more Otherside into my globe until my nerves were so numb I couldn't feel anything, the nausea totally absent. I wasn't sure if that was a good thing or a bad—odds were bad. I was done playing it safe.

"I don't know if you can hear me, whatever the hell you are, but I'm about done with this, so . . ."

Nate yelled something, but I couldn't make out the words as I unleashed the Otherside at the thing. Like before, it fell in on itself, compressing or regrouping.

I went for the mirror again and pulled at the bindings as fast as I could. I didn't stop until I was certain I felt them come untethered, destabilize, then begin to unravel.

The mirror started to draw in the thing as it tried to close itself. I watched, mesmerized, as the angry ball of smoke and Otherside churned violently, desperately trying to keep the mirror open.

Something had to give. . . .

Illuminated by the gold dust, I saw Nate scramble to his feet and run for the kitchen. What the hell was he doing now?

Before I could yell, the thing expanded again, and black, smoky tendrils shot out, wrapping around my throat in freezing coils.

My apartment faded. Fractured images floated to the front of my mind like a poorly curated photo album with random sound bites: my parents screaming at each other, my own violent outbursts at school and at home with my mother, being fired by the Seattle PD, Max dying, Randall trying to kill me . . . It was like rewatching the worst moments of my life in slow motion. And it made me angry—so angry.

I felt the anger siphon away, leaving me empty. The thing was feeding on it.

Like it was stripping off the dark part of my soul, one painful memory at a time.

I could feel it searching my mind, probing . . . but for what else, I didn't know.

"K!"

Nate's voice pierced through the cold fog.

And that interested the thing—it began to pull up images and snippets of my memories of Nate. And then Cameron. Instead of finding what it wanted, though, it seemed to be getting pissed off.

Why the hell did it want to know about Nate and Cameron?

I shrieked as frustrated tendrils dug further into my memories, as if more pain would somehow make me show it what it wanted.

More of the Otherside powder fell around me, chilling me to the very marrow of my bones. It probed more recent memories of Nate: Lee calling in his tab, the YouTube concert. This must have been how it killed Jacob: freezing him to death while consuming his memories. . . .

"Hey—over here!" Nate yelled. The thing let out a growl, and switched focus.

It loosened its grip but didn't let go. Out of the corner of my eye, I caught Nate sliding back out of the kitchen, hitting his shoulder against the doorway.

"Hey, I'm talking to you!"

The coils loosened their grip on my throat as the thing turned its attention back on Nate.

I tried to warn him, but my throat was too cold and a rasping noise was the only sound that came out. My lips had cracked and I could taste blood dripping from my nose. Still, I drew in the Otherside, as much of it as I could. . . .

The thing grumbled and gold Otherside dust kicked up as it wavered, deciding whom to torture next. In the flicker of Otherside, I could just make out Nate's silhouette. He had something in his hand—a box, one I didn't recognize.

Somewhere, past the cold, I felt a substance like sand sprinkle on my skin. The chill lessened.

Then the low, rumbling growls twisted into shrieks—agonized, furious shrieks.

The tendrils released me and I slid to the floor, knocking over a bowl of sage. The lights in the kitchen flickered back on.

I managed to lift my head to see Nate wielding an old, dusty box of kitchen salt—one I didn't even know I'd had. He flung a handful of it towards the thing, and it screamed again.

Salt. Plain old table salt hurt it. Each time it was struck, the thing howled and shrank—but it didn't disappear.

It dove for Nate with a baleful shriek and he stumbled back into the table, almost falling over.

He threw another handful of salt at it, sending it writhing, and tossed the box at me. "Mirror," he said.

I shook my head to clear it and pushed myself up onto all fours. I crawled to where the box had landed, grabbed it and went for the mirror.

The mirror bindings were gone, but it was still open. *How?* One of the tendrils writhed as if in pain, lashing out blindly. The thing was keeping the portal open, like a foot caught in a closing door.

In no reputable practitioning book had I ever heard of salt stopping anything. But then again, the entity didn't resemble anything I'd ever read about in a textbook . . .

I dumped the contents onto the mirror and watched the grains spread over the smooth glass. The Otherside ignored it, but the dust covering the mirror and on the floor around me? It sparked and crackled as the salt hit it.

And then the mirror started to do what it should have done as soon as I unravelled the set: it began to siphon the thing back.

The thing turned on me, tendrils lashing, but it couldn't resist the pull.

The mirror sucked it and every last bit of shadow back into its reflective surface as it closed. With one last growl and a flare of smoke and Otherside, the thing was gone. My apartment went silent for a brief, sweet moment. And then the rest of the lights flickered back on.

I slumped back onto the floor and closed my eyes.

I felt grains falling on me, and opened my eyes to find Nate standing over me, emptying the remaining contents of the salt box over my head.

He stared at me. "K?"

I nodded. Against the odds, I was alive and conscious. I rolled over—god, that hurt—and grabbed a handful of the salt now covering my living room floor and rubbed it on my skin to get rid of the remaining Otherside dust. Like on the mirror, it flickered and disappeared as if it had never existed.

With my arms, I swept the salt around the floor. I thought about moving to the couch, but it was awfully far. I lay back down on the floor on my back. It didn't help much. I stared up at the ceiling while Nate took over, spreading the salt around with his feet.

I closed my eyes. I felt fucking terrible. "Water," I said after maybe five seconds of doing sweet nothing except concentrating on the pounding headache that was taking over.

I was rewarded by the sound of the running faucet.

I didn't sit up when he brought the glass over because my head was spinning. Instead, I rolled over and propped myself up on my elbow to take it. I shivered, remembering the bone-chilling cold. Should have asked for tea. "Is it totally gone?" I croaked.

Nate looked around before nodding. "Yeah. If it wasn't, I think we'd know by now."

I nodded and wiped my face. Blood and sweat dampened my sleeve.

Great, just fucking fantastic. Another complete fail at not overusing Otherside. Otherside one, Kincaid Strange minus four . . .

There was one bowl of sage nearby that hadn't been upended. I knocked it over for good measure and forced myself to crawl over and check the mirror.

It was covered in black soot that clung to my fingers. The black ink underneath had been burned away. I shook my head. Yet another first in the world of Otherside shit . . .

What the fuck had happened to getting back to normal? Why, O universe, do you hate me this much?

Nate was still standing over me, watching and waiting. I gazed at the ugly gash on his face.

"Nate, what the fuck was that? And how the hell did you know to use salt?"

He didn't answer, just sat down outside what was left of my pentagram, five scorch marks singed into the floorboards where the bowls had burned too hot.

There went my fucking deposit. . . .

"*Nate?*" I said. I waited for him to meet my eyes with Cameron's faded green ones. The haunted look was back on his face, made worse by the formaldehyde yellow of his skin. And the gash. "You know what that was, don't you?"

"It wasn't supposed to be able to find me, K. I swear, if I had known . . . I'm so sorry, K." Nate shook his head. "I really fucked up this time." He went back to staring at his slippered feet.

I was going to get some fucking answers. Now. "*Nate*," I said, and waited for him to refocus on me. "*What did you do?* And I swear to god, if you lie to me one more time—"

Nate blinked once and swallowed—twice. "I sold my soul to a demon, K. And he's trying to cash in."

CHAPTER 11

PERSONAL DEMONS

"You did *what?*"

I didn't know whether to punch Nate or—oh, hell—punch him.

I needed to get off the floor. I reached behind me for a chair only to find it wasn't there. Oh yeah, Nate had knocked over the kitchen table to use as a barricade. I grabbed a handful of loose salt and threw it in that general direction. Sparks flared wherever the salt connected with the Otherside dust.

The lights were still flickering intermittently. Hopefully, it was only my apartment. Between the knocked-over chairs and table and my books and papers strewn everywhere . . . it was a fucking disaster area.

I tried to stand up again and this time succeeded with Nate's help. He brought me over to the couch—which was still standing—before I could fall over.

Despite the fact that my place was now covered in salt, everywhere I looked there seemed to be a thin coating of the Otherside dust that drifted in amongst the grains. When the two collided, there was a spark and flash of Otherside as the dust disappeared . . . or exploded.

Well, at least I didn't live in a place where people cared about noise. Maybe I'd get lucky and the neighbours would assume it was an art project. There was plenty of abysmal art in my building, no reason why I couldn't join in the fun. . . .

I sat down on the couch and Nate sat across from me on the coffee table. He tried to cover his hands, which had begun shaking in frenzied spurts—fear or nerve deterioration, take your pick.

I glared at Nate and shook my head. We'd get back to his new drama in a second; but before I forgot, I needed to get in touch with Aaron. I pulled out my phone and dialled.

Straight to voice mail. Of course, the one time I needed to talk to him and not the other way around . . . "Aaron, call me back. It's about Jacob. I have a hunch—tell Dr. Blanc to toss salt over him. Good old-fashioned table salt. And don't ask where the idea came from." I hung up and texted Aaron to check his voice mail before calling me back. Then I glanced back up at Nate. My head was pounding and, though I was groggy from the Otherside, I'd started putting two and two together.

Nate had known what we were getting ourselves into with this summoning. Or at the very least, he'd suspected. And he hadn't told me.

I don't know how I did it—maybe it was the Otherside hangover settling in and the numbness from the cold and having been attacked by that thing—but I kept my temper under control.

"A *demon*?" I said. I didn't bother hiding my incredulity. I raised zombies and ghosts for a living, and even I found demons hard to swallow.

"I swear to god, Kincaid, I didn't know it was going to come through the mirror. I thought it might show up, but . . ."

I closed my eyes. Well, now I knew why Nate had been so insistent about sticking around. . . . I suppressed the anger boiling up inside me.

"Nate—stop. Breathe."

"I don't need to."

I shook my head at him. "Just do it," I said, and waited for him to draw in breath and let it out. The motions have a calming effect, even for the dead.

When his hands were under control, I said, "Now, start from the beginning."

"Okay, it all goes back to Dead Men in '95. We hit rock bottom. Nowhere near where we wanted to be." Nate gave a depressed laugh. "I mean, we'd play regular gigs, get a bit of coverage, but grunge bands were a dime a dozen. The scene was oversaturated. Nothing we did got us any traction. No radio play, none of the record producers were interested in us . . ." He glanced down at his hands and shook his head. "We'd been at it for four years, prostrate at the foot of the grunge shrine, for all the good it was doing us. Everyone was at the end of their rope and we were one fight away from being finished. We were imploding, we all knew it." He tore his eyes off his hands. "Mindy had left, Cole kept threatening to leave. It all would have been for nothing. I couldn't let it happen, K. I was desperate."

Yeah. Desperation was something I could sympathize with all too well. . . . I could see where this was going. "So how did you find the demon?"

"That's just it. I didn't go looking for it. It found me."

I frowned—more to myself than to Nate, who was looking down at his fingers, playing with salt. Ghosts don't find people. Not without help.

I didn't have to ask how, though, as Nate kept going. . . .

"I was drunk. Very drunk. Mindy and I had broken up a couple weeks earlier and Cole let it slip that she had started seeing Damien. I did what most idiot twentysomethings do, I showed up at the bar where Cadmium Coffee was playing and made an ass out of myself. I was in the bathroom puking after Cole stopped me from turning idiocy into assault."

"You were going to punch someone?"

"No, I wasn't the violent type. I was just going to break Damien's guitar, mess up his show."

I stopped myself from pointing out that assault on a guitar was still violent. It would just get Nate off track, and I didn't want to appeal to his undead penchant for tangents. . . .

"Where did the demon find you?"

"It was waiting for me in the bathroom mirror."

"You saw it?" Even through the grogginess, the wheels in my head were churning. You can only see ghosts once they have crossed over the barrier or someone has pulled them through a mirror. Either the mirror had been set, which is unlikely in a bar, or we were in poltergeist territory at the very least. Or possibly a sorcerer— or maybe even a wraith . . .

But Nate was shaking his head as he wrung his hands on the coffee table across from me. "Naw. I never saw it. Ever. It wrote to me, though. Not with Otherside, like I used to do, but with a black soot that came from inside the mirror. I tried wiping it off—that was the very first thing I did. I yelled and started wiping it away with my sleeve."

"What did it say?"

Nate drew in another breath. "It said it could make me famous."

I sat back and placed my hand against my forehead. I didn't know if I should be happy or a little concerned that my freezing hand felt good on my sweaty, overheated face. . . .

Fuck, this wasn't supposed to happen. I'd practically sold my soul—or three years of it—to Gideon to *not* end up with a string of Otherside hangovers. Two goddamned days later and I was already pushing myself over the edge. Pretty coat of lipstick, anyone?

Goddamnit.

I shook my head. "Okay, first—the demon didn't make you famous. This was '95, right?" I waited for Nate to nod. "I can understand things were bad, and the booze couldn't have been helping your mental state, but a run-in with a demon in the bathroom mirror of a bar didn't make you famous. Your songs did." Along with some spectacular and well-publicized antics, but I left that out. I racked my memory. "'Nicotine'—that was your first radio play song, right?"

Nate nodded. "That's what I mean. We got 'Nicotine' right after I met the demon."

I was starting to suspect Nate had been conned by either an industrious ghost or a poltergeist. The secret to being a good con man is being a good liar. But a fantastic con man? They know how to make it look as though they've delivered. "Not buying it, Nate. Even if whatever you saw in the mirror said you'd get famous the next week, it was a coincidence that you came out with 'Nicotine'— not divine intervention."

But Nate was shaking his head again. "No, K—that's just it." He looked up at me, his eyes bleak. "The demon wrote 'Nicotine.' That's what it gave me on the bathroom wall."

Impossible. The dead can't create things. . . . Unless the message sender wasn't dead. I stopped my brain right there. No way in hell was I entertaining the idea that this might *actually* be a demon.

"Are you telling me you got all your songs from a mirror? Music, lyrics—you didn't write any of them?" Part of me still wasn't buying it. I mean, alive or dead, Nate had always been proud of his music.

It was his turn to shake his head. "No—not entirely—but it helped me write and finish them. 'Nicotine' had been something I was working on, but no one in the band was happy with it. I'd scrapped it. I don't know how it got the song, but it did, and the version it put up on the mirror was better. It took me a while to get over seeing it there. I figured I must have hallucinated it—but it was in my head the next day and I wrote it down and showed it to the band. We recorded it and the next thing I knew we had our first radio play. More gigs started coming in. *Hardwire* magazine did its first piece on us.

"'Nicotine' wasn't a huge hit, but it got us noticed. The guys were excited. We even had a producer give us his card. Granted, we'd been trying to get a record deal for years and had had every sleazy producer in Seattle try to screw us over at least once. I was half-convinced I'd imagined the whole mirror thing, but a week after 'Nicotine' came out, the demon contacted me again. This time it wanted to deal."

My throat was dry. "Where did it contact you this time?"

Nate looked sheepish. "The second time, I . . . found it. At first I wanted to know if it had all been a hallucination—and then . . ."

He trailed off. I had a good idea of what had happened. He'd had a taste of success and wanted to know if the source could deliver again.

"That's how it made me famous. It didn't write the songs, but it fixed the ones I had. Years ahead of what I would have been able to do, K."

I wanted to be mad. I *was* mad . . . but I also understood what it was like to have something you really wanted dangled in front of you.

Nate was not holding up well. Even though booze is bad for zombies, I decided the pros outweighed the cons under the current circumstances, and all the formaldehyde Mork had pumped into him would mitigate the damage. I also needed to deal with the gash on the side of his face sooner rather than later, and bourbon was as good a distraction as any.

I stood up shakily and stepped into the kitchen to retrieve my bourbon from behind the radio. Kept there for special occasions only . . . I grabbed a suture kit from a lower drawer, the one where I kept the less palatable tools of my trade, including a Civil War amputation kit and a somewhat more modern surgery kit. I found the older, heavier needles were better for sewing through zombie hides, since formaldehyde stops fluids from seeping.

I sat back down on the couch across from Nate and passed him a glass and the whisky bottle. He eyed me warily, well aware of my zombie booze policy.

I put the suture kit on the coffee table beside him.

"Aw—seriously?"

"Yeah, seriously, Nate." I picked out one of the thinner needles so the sutures would be smaller and threaded it with one of the heavier threads that I found worked better with zombie flesh.

Nate downed half a glass, poured another, swore and turned his face to the side. The gash was far enough away from his mouth the motion wouldn't bother the stitches.

"So, I take it the demon was there and waiting?"

"With bells on. It was as if it had been expecting me. I went in the middle of the day when the bar was empty. There was a message waiting for me on the mirror, same black soot writing. He said he could make me famous."

"And you took the bait?"

Nate gave me a wry smile. "You'd think that, wouldn't you." His face twisted in pain. "Ow! Will you watch it?"

"Sorry."

"Wow, how many fucks do you not give? And I told it to fuck off. I didn't give a shit about getting famous. Never did."

"Then what did it offer you?"

"It said it could fix my songs."

I let out a short breath. "It knew exactly what to offer you."

"Yup," Nate said.

A silence fell between us as I finished the stitches and tied off the wound.

"It never spoke, only ever wrote. Said its name was Eloch. I brought it my songs, wrote them on the mirror of the bathroom, and it fixed them. Lyrics, music, whatever the song needed, it knew."

"What was the next song?"

Nate stared back down at his glass. "'Manhunt.' The song was 'Manhunt.'"

Jesus. Nate's first big hit. Not the most famous, but the first one to top the charts.

"You wrote the songs, Nate."

He shook his head and finished off his second bourbon. "Only half of them."

A silence stretched out. "You still haven't told me the price."

Nate shook his head and poured another glass. I didn't stop him—his hands had finally stopped shaking. "That's where things get weird. At first it didn't want anything. It said I could have the songs so long as I performed them. I thought maybe it was some ghost having fun, or some dead musician having another shot—a weird second shot, calling itself a demon, but hey, who was I to judge? It was fixing all my songs."

"Then?"

"Then we got the gig at the Cage. And I found out Damien had died." He inclined his head. "I was telling the truth when I said I felt bad, but at first I thought it was just shitty luck. That is until Mindy showed up at my door in a panic saying something had killed Damien. I started to wonder if the demon had done it. I was pissed. I hadn't wanted anyone to die. My god, I didn't want the songs that badly. I told it that—or yelled that at it."

So Damien hadn't died accidentally of an overdose. He'd probably been killed by Eloch, maybe with Mindy's help—or complicity. I was willing to bet the bank Nate's demon had killed Jacob as well. Except Eloch wasn't a demon. Eloch was my wraith. Was it covering its tracks from twenty years ago . . . and if so, why?

Nate looked up at me, his face empty. "It said I didn't have a choice. Then it hit me with one of those icy blasts. I thought I was going to die, but all that happened was I woke up freezing cold with a bad headache."

"What did you do?"

"I tried cancelling the concert. Cole and the rest of the band freaked out—and that's when the demon struck its bargain with me."

"What was it Eloch wanted?"

Nate smiled grimly. "Either I played along and kept giving it songs or it killed everyone I cared about and made sure Mindy was thrown in jail for Damien's death. That, and it wanted my soul. And Damien was just proof it could commit murder."

I'd been partly mad at Nate for not telling me about this before the seance, but the other half had been furious he'd done something so selfish as to make a deal that put everyone he ever knew in danger.

He hadn't. He'd been reckless, but he'd made the deal to save everyone.

I felt like a heel. I should have known Nate wouldn't have sold his soul for a couple of songs, fame and fortune.

My rage shifted to a new target: this Eloch, demon, wraith . . . I didn't care. It had manipulated Nate. It knew how to bait him, it knew what to threaten, and it knew exactly what price Nate was willing to pay.

A good con artist tries to be your friend. A great one doesn't bother: they use the ones you already have.

Mindy popped into my mind, but I'd have to revisit that thought later.

For the immediate moment I needed to know what Eloch, or the thing, was. It clearly had a malevolent disposition, but demon was still not cutting it for me. It had needed Nate's proximity, which was why it had used the songs as bait. But why? I held up my wrist. "How was the deal set? Was it with Otherside, like this?"

"Naw—it was with blood. I saw its eyes once. In the mirror," he added. "When I signed the deal with blood. I swear, K, it was evil."

Yeah, I didn't doubt it. Well, a poltergeist would like nothing more than to get someone's blood on a mirror—but there was no way it would have been able to resist fucking up Nate's life permanently when the opportunity presented itself. And I didn't have any confidence in a poltergeist's ability to concentrate long enough to write a song, let alone execute an elaborate plan. So cross that off the list.

If sorcerers were anything like practitioners, they could use blood to catalyze their bindings. Gideon had proven his love of deals. Could it be another sorcerer? That would explain the ice and strange Otherside dust.

There was another option I wasn't crazy about: the zebra in Central Park . . . or a wraith in Seattle. I didn't want to write it off after Lee's story, but I also didn't want to start chasing one without ruling out the others first. The thing that had come out of the mirror hadn't resembled the wraith Lee had described. . . .

The sooner I showed Gideon the basement of the Rex, the better.

"You don't believe me, do you?" Nate's voice jarred me out of my thoughts. "That it was a demon—do you?" he asked.

I drew in my own breath while I thought of what to say. Clearly, this thing wasn't simply a ghost—but a demon? I raise ghosts and zombies for a living, and even I found that hard to swallow.

When the dead start to pass themselves off as Biblical, I get real skeptical. In my experience they're either nuts or trying to sell you something—maybe a little bit of both.

My gut told me this was a con . . . a paranormal con, but a con nonetheless.

"Nate, I believe you made a deal with something very dangerous," I said carefully. "But there's got to be another explanation for my charred and seared mirror besides a demon."

"In other words, you don't believe me."

"Just because this Eloch calls itself a demon doesn't mean it is. It wouldn't be the first undead to lie about being a religious coming." Something else niggled at me. "Why is it coming after you now? I mean, it's been twenty years. And if it really was a demon, how did you get out of it taking your soul?"

"Ah, yeah. I might have screwed it over—accidentally, I might add."

"How?"

"Easy. We agreed on ten songs. I died before I could finish number ten."

Otherside is funny when it comes to using it to bind deals—at least in the voodoo world. It sometimes has a mind of its own and interprets language differently than you intend.

Especially if you are an amateur.

If Eloch had set up the pact to make it look as though Nate was getting something in exchange for his soul, then the Otherside and bindings involved—because there would have to have been bindings involved—may have interpreted the pact as having been broken when he died.

Meaning whatever hold Eloch had had on Nate would have been severed, or partially severed. I still wasn't sure how broken deals with sorcery worked. And would a sorcerer bother seeking revenge years later? Gideon was ultimately a ghost, but he struck me as spontaneous with his rage.

Though stranger things had happened. Especially when it came to using Otherside to seal an agreement.

"The blood did something," Nate said. "I mean, I think it did. It tried pulling me when I died. And then it stopped. I felt it looking for me early on, but whenever I crossed over the barrier to the Otherside, it lost my trail. It hadn't tried in years. Not until the concert."

Shit.

"This round, though, it was stronger, more serious. I could feel it reaching for me every time I went through the barrier."

"And the last time?"

Nate laughed. "Ah, the last time. You're going to love this, K. I was trying to find you in Randall's cellar. I got worried when you didn't come out and it was going up in flames. You weren't there—and there was Cameron on the floor." Nate shook his head. "I tried to get him up, and he wouldn't move. And then I felt a pull like I never had before, like I was being summoned . . . It was weird and scared the shit out of me."

"And then?"

"And then I woke up and I was in Cameron's body. I got out of the basement as fast as I could—and hid."

That was almost two weeks ago. Then Jacob was murdered and the wraith started raising frozen hell. . . .

"Oh, fuck," I said as I realized the implications. "Nate, it wasn't trying to *summon* you. It was trying to *bind* you."

The demon, or whatever the hell Eloch was, had tried to bind Nate—that was what the blood and the proximity had been for. It made no difference whether you knew a ghost or a person when they'd been alive if you were summoning them, but binding was a different matter.

That was what it needed the contract for. And when Eloch ran into Nate and what was left of Cameron's bindings . . .

Cameron's odd bindings had been designed by a sorcerer—namely, Gideon—to enable his body to be inhabited by a ghost, and Gideon had intended to inhabit Cameron himself. With Nate in close proximity to the vacated corpse, and the binding contract with Eloch never fulfilled, or at best in limbo . . .

It had been a complete accident—a comedy of disasters.

"Are you telling me if it hadn't been for Cameron's zombie body two weeks ago I would have been bound?" he asked.

I nodded. Nate wouldn't have known the difference. It was all the same to ghosts; they can't tell the difference between a summoning and a binding, because all they feel is the Otherside. A bound Nathan Cade. Nate's worst nightmare.

"Gideon is going to kill us, Nate. I know you didn't do it on purpose, but let's just say he's not exactly . . . open-minded."

"K, you can't get me out of here, not before I figure out how to get this thing off my tail. I couldn't resist it last time. I'd rather die in here than end up bound."

He had a point.

"Why didn't you tell me all this a week ago?"

"Did you not hear the part about Damien dying and it threatening to kill everyone? You saw it tonight, it almost killed you."

If it hadn't been for the salt, it would have. . . .

He shook his head. "I know you, K. You would have poked around until it got wind."

"How did you know about the salt?"

"That was kind of a fluke. About a year after I died, I was doing tequila shots off this really hot zombie chick who used to be a fan and—"

I cringed. "Spare me the details."

"No, I know—no gratuitous dead sex stories." I cringed again at the involuntary mental images. It was a rule we had: I didn't want to know what Nate got up to. . . . "But it's totally relevant to the salt thing. So, I was about six tequila shots in at this bar in the Portland underground city, and I felt the pull, as if I were about to bug off back to the Otherside—but then nothing happened. It fizzled out. It took me a while, but I figured out it was the salt since that was the only real variable."

Which explained Nate's penchant for tequila . . . Of course, it would be Nate who figured out salt hurt whatever this undead monster was while getting drunk and making out with a zombie chick. Jesus Christ.

I turned my thoughts back to the problem at hand. I knew the how and why of Nate's predicament, and I knew why it had killed Damien—or at least some of the motive . . .

"We're missing something about Jacob. It's looking for you and it can't find you in that body; we can assume that's why it started killing people again. So why go after Jacob? Why not Mindy, Cole or me? If it only wanted to get to you, we're much better targets, Nate."

"Ah, remember that big black cold blob that just attacked us? Yeah . . ."

"But it wasn't trying to get to me at all, Nate—it was trying to stop me from getting to Damien. That's why it showed up. And on the subject of Damien's death, why bother with the planted heroin?"

"To cover its tracks. So that no one would call Damien's death a murder. What's more terrifying—having everyone think you were murdered, or that you just offed yourself one day?"

I mulled that over. The other result, besides terrifying Nate, was that no one would be looking for a killer. Eloch had been staying under the radar, probably scared of practitioners like Max . . . only now it wasn't. Desperation? Overconfidence? What had changed? It clearly had weaknesses.

Shit . . . "Nate, it specifically doesn't want anyone talking to its victims. Why?"

Nate shook his head. "I've got no idea, K. I mean, I remember Jacob. But there was nothing about him that stood out. He just wanted to be friends with everyone."

Yeah, call me jaded, but those kinds of people tend to be the ones who get dragged in way over their heads. Excessive niceness and people pleasing will do that to you.

I needed to find out what Aaron had discovered about Jacob, and fast. Now that I was on Eloch's tail, I expected he was going to go full force covering its tracks.

I checked my phone. Still nothing from Aaron, so I messaged him.

"You should have told me, Nate."

"I didn't think, K, okay?"

"You didn't *think*? Nate, a murder investigation gets reopened concerning your and Damien's deaths because Aaron suspects supernatural causes, an old roadie winds up dead due to what sounds an awful lot like a wraith, and you didn't think we were on a need-to-know basis about some mysterious undead chasing you?"

"I didn't want it to hurt you, all right?" Nate said, raising his voice.

My phone buzzed in my pocket before I could respond.

Nate grabbed the suture kit and bourbon—managing to pile it all in his arms on the third try—and headed into the kitchen.

I swore under my breath and answered the phone. "Hey, Aaron, how come when you try to call me, if I don't answer immediately, it's the end of the world and an onslaught of messages, but when I try to call you, it takes a message and three texts—"

"I called as soon as I could, I was on the phone with the captain. He found out I was looking into a paranormal murder and wanted to yell at me for fifteen minutes."

That gave me pause. "I thought they reinstated you as head of the paranormal department."

"Yeah, a promotion was not the intent. In the eyes of Marks, it's a demotion." After a moment he added, "Your name came up, but I didn't mention your recent involvement."

Gideon's comment about cause and effect came back to me. . . . I shook it off but said, "I thought my co-operation was part of getting a new contract?"

There was silence on the other end of the line.

Great. I did not need the captain blaming a murder on me because I was one of the only people who could see how it happened . . . and who, since the latest encounter, now knew how to neutralize the effects. Dr. Blanc could claim he came up with the idea to use salt from an old wives' tale or something. I'd be happy to let him take the credit.

"Aaron?" I prompted. "Did you try the salt?"

"Yeah, it worked. I think you need to get to the morgue. Now."

Oh, hell. I'd assumed the salt would have the same effect . . . "What happened?"

"This time, Kincaid, I don't think you'd believe me if I told you. You need to see it for yourself."

I ran my hand through my hair. Yeah, there was no way I was getting any sleep tonight. . . . "All right, I'll meet you there in fifteen." I hung up and headed into the bathroom to wash the blood off my face and hair, then tied my hair back. It would have to do.

There was still coffee in the kitchen, so I poured a mug and downed it.

Warm and caffeinated. I gave myself ten seconds to close my eyes and plan out what the hell I was going to do next.

First things first. I grabbed every bit of salt I could find, which consisted of two full salt shakers. I'm not much for cooking.

"Nate, sweep up as much salt as you can from the floor and funnel it back into a bowl. I'll pick more up on the way home."

"Where are you going?"

I shoved the salt shakers into my bag. "Something went wrong at the morgue. Aaron asked me to come check it out."

"K—"

I held up my hand. "I'm going in with a plan. They've got salt there. I think we hurt Eloch enough it won't be coming back tonight."

"What if it does?"

"We'll call Lee."

"And if she tells us to fuck off?"

I didn't think she would. Regardless of whether or not she was pissed at me, a paranormal killing machine was bad for her. If she did, though . . . "Then I'll call Gideon."

"Oh, fuck me."

"But I'm pretty sure it won't come to that."

Nate had a tetchy look on his face and shoved his hands in his pockets. The last thing I wanted to do was leave him ruminating. I spotted Mork's books on the floor, picked them up and shoved them at Nate.

"Stay here and deal with these. Put a sticker on any pages that mention an aversion to salt or a penchant for freezing things."

He took the books from me. There—idle hands gone.

"If I'm not going to be back in a couple of hours, I'll call you. Promise." I grabbed my jacket and tossed my backpack on. I really hoped Aaron didn't notice the Otherside hangover. This headache was going to kill me. . . .

"K?"

I turned back to face him before putting on my helmet.

"I won't let you down, K."

I nodded and grabbed my bike.

Was I still a little mad at Nate? Sure. Making a deal like that with a ghost—demon, or whatever the hell it wanted to call itself—had been stupid. But I kept my mouth shut. I was the last person to judge an act of desperation.

Hit songs, seeing Otherside . . . I wasn't stupid or arrogant enough to start splitting hairs.

I thought about the so-called demon on the elevator ride down. Did it have some tricks up its sleeve? Sure, but where there are tricks, there are usually weaknesses. Take poltergeists, for example. Most of the time all you have to do is get them to lose their temper and anything remotely resembling a plan falls apart.

Whether it was a demon or not didn't matter. I needed to get it off Nate's tail—and figuring out how to get it to stop killing people would be a fantastic start.

I could see the drizzle falling on the sidewalk, so I pulled my collar up before pushing my bike out the lobby door.

When it rains, it pours. . . .

CHAPTER 12

GHOST OF A REASON

I pulled up outside the morgue and checked the time: 9 p.m. The lights were all still on, but the traffic in and out was slow, even considering the time of night.

And there I was being paranoid. I pushed my bike around back, keeping my eye on the shadows. I know, ghosts and monsters don't actually come out of the shadows, but considering what I'd already seen tonight . . .

The gate to the back parking lot was still open, despite the late hour, and as I pushed my bike through it, the floodlights turned on.

I put the kickstand down and took my helmet off, then took a good look around. I spotted Aaron's sedan in the back of the lot, but that was it. I jumped and swore a blue streak as a hand clamped down on my shoulder.

"Jesus Christ, Aaron. Don't ever do that." I shuddered. "I know it's a Saturday night, but isn't this place usually a little livelier?"

He shook his head. "Dr. Blanc sent the staff home. He bluffed something about a potential leak and health risk. Not too far off the truth, and we figured it'd be easier to keep our emergency under wraps if fewer eyes and ears were here."

I narrowed my eyes. Aaron was tense. "You still haven't told me what this emergency is."

"I couldn't risk it. I don't even want the service staff to know what's going on, let alone anyone else at the police station." He glanced around nervously. "Dr. Blanc and I have no idea what the hell is going on with Jacob."

"I figured that much—unless any more paranormal murders happened in the last twenty-four hours? No? Good." I shook my head. "The salt didn't work, did it?" I should have known better. Just because it worked on the residual Otherside dust at my apartment didn't mean it would do the same thing here. . . .

He inclined his head. "I'll let you be the judge of that, Kincaid." And with that, he gently grabbed my elbow and led me in through the back delivery door of the morgue. I suppressed my own heebie-jeebies. Even practitioners have their limits; we eventually get creeped out like anybody else.

The single person at the front counter barely looked up at me as we entered. That suited me just fine. I kept my head low to encourage her indifference.

The coffee machine was on and Aaron was kind enough to pour me a mug. As I sipped the hot coffee, I once again regretted the fact that I hadn't taken a hot shower before I left. The warmup would have done me good, and somehow I doubted that an extra fifteen minutes would have matter— Oh, man.

We had turned the hall corner to the observation window where Dr. Blanc was waiting for us, and my thoughts were derailed by the scene inside.

It was Jacob's body, but the position had changed. No longer were his arms rigid and frozen in sharp angles but resting by his side. His clothing had been removed, though Dr. Blanc or an assistant had covered his lower half with a sheet.

His unfrozen state should have made him seem more peaceful,

as the dead usually look, but all it did was exaggerate his grotesque appearance.

His face was still twisted in terror, his eyes stretched wide open.

I shuddered. Even I am not immune to the grotesque. "Okay—creepy and disconcerting expression, but I'm still not sure exactly what the emergency is."

"Initially, that was my response as well," Dr. Blanc said.

I shook my head and took another look through the glass, almost pressing my face up against it. There was nothing that stood out—besides his expression—that raised any alarm bells. Grey-blue flesh, faded colour from his lips and fingers . . . All disturbing, but essentially normal.

Panic ran through me at something I'd discounted as only a remote possibility. "The dust is carcinogenic?"

Dr. Blanc *tsk*ed and shook his head. "No, I've tested 'the dust,' as you've called it at length, and I am confident it has no effects beyond the cold."

My relief was momentary. Both Aaron and Dr. Blanc still looked tense, and neither of them were amateurs.

"Okay, guys. What am I not seeing from out here?"

I caught Aaron glancing at Dr. Blanc, who nodded and headed inside after pulling up his mask.

Aaron handed me a lab coat, mask and goggles.

"Doctor's orders," he said when I held them up and gave him a questioning look. I usually don't wear protective clothing at the morgue. But Aaron didn't offer an explanation. "Come on," he said, and walked inside.

I slipped the coat on and wound my hair back until it fit under the cap—whether to protect the body from my hair or me from the body was yet to be seen.

I followed him in, feeling the air leave the negative-pressure room, carrying with it the sterile scent of disinfectants and bleach.

Dr. Blanc and Aaron were standing at the side of the room, within observing distance but out of my way. Taking a deep breath, I approached the body.

The trick to bringing in an expert for an opinion is to keep them unbiased—so they aren't making the same assumptions you are when they see the data. I prefer it that way. It's how I pick out the details others might miss.

It also meant I was looking at the body before asking questions.

I noticed that the camera light above the observation table was off. I nodded and arched my eyebrow at Aaron. It wasn't like him to turn the camera off during an autopsy—especially a paranormal autopsy.

He just shrugged. "Like I said, the fewer people who see this, the better."

I went back to examining the body. Jacob looked thawed—completely. Though the dotted lines had been drawn on his chest, no cuts had been made, meaning Dr. Blanc hadn't got to the internal examination part of the autopsy.

Dr. Blanc didn't strike me as the type to shirk duty or leave an autopsy halfway through. So something must have stopped him from making the first cut . . . Let's try to see what that was, shall we?

I glanced over at Dr. Blanc. Both he and Aaron were still watching me, silent. "Gloves?" I asked. He handed me a pair, and once I'd pulled them on I picked up Jacob's hand. It was chilled but not frozen to the touch, and the skin gave way under my fingers as I pressed.

I turned the hand over. Oddly, the fingers didn't show any damage from being frozen. Not that I had a lot of experience with frozen bodies, but I knew from dealing with zombies that skin, blood and bones are fragile. Surely freezing should leave more of a mark than this?

Though, I had to admit, I didn't know what the signs of frostbite after death are. Blackened, parsed or split skin is what I'd expected.

"Dr. Blanc, shouldn't there be damage from being frozen solid like that?" I held up the hand I'd been examining.

Dr. Blanc looked to Aaron this time, who nodded. Interesting. Aaron was really set on me finding whatever had set them into a panic on my own. . . .

"Yes. There should be more damage to the body visible with the bare eye. When water freezes, it expands and bursts the cells. The hide is still there, but once thawed—well, it should have begun to break down. That was one of the first things that struck me as peculiar," he added.

Right, body not damaged from being frozen . . . Now, was that a side effect of the Otherside dust? Something else occurred to me, and I ran the bottom of my boot around the floor. It was smooth and polished clean.

"What happened to the salt?" I asked. Neither of them answered. "Aaron, I need to know."

Dr. Blanc cleared his throat. "My assistant and I cleaned it up with a laboratory vacuum. After the body thawed."

"How long did that take? And how much salt did you use?" I said as I moved around the table, checking Jacob's arms and legs. All mobile . . .

"The thaw was instantaneous. And about three kitchen boxes— it was all my assistant could carry from the corner store. I'll be making an official order for future circumstances. Might I ask—"

"Just keep my name out of it, Dr. Blanc," I said. The room went silent as I finished checking Jacob's body for marks and anything unusual. Silence in the morgue . . . There was a bad pun to be made there.

I could barely bring myself to say it out loud.

"Was there any visible reaction when you tossed the salt on him? Besides the fact that he thawed out instantaneously?"

"No. None. It was like he'd been holding the pose and decided to relax."

Well, that confirmed my other suspicion—that whatever reaction the salt catalyzed, it wasn't visible to a normal eye. Only in the spectrum of Otherside . . . I glanced at Aaron and Dr. Blanc but neither of them gave any indication of what I should be looking for.

I finished checking Jacob's feet, even giving the toes a cursory look. There was no more putting it off; I'd run out of things to look at besides his face.

I moved to the top of the table and stared at his terrified expression and wide-open eyes.

I frowned as I examined his petrified features. There was something strange, and it wasn't just the expression.

I glanced back at his eyes. I could have sworn I caught a muscle twitch . . . or maybe it had been a trick of the fluorescent lights. No, there it was again—not so much a twitch as a shudder.

"Could the ice have done something—odd to the body, Dr. Blanc?"

"Such as?"

There it was again—in the corner of the right eye. A tiny movement, and definitely not a figment of my imagination. Well, now I knew what had frightened Aaron and Dr. Blanc so. It wasn't every day a body began to spasm on the dissecting table.

"Micro muscle spasms as it defrosts?" That was the only thing I could come up with to explain what I was seeing. "Do you have a penlight?" I asked.

Dr. Blanc fumbled me a flashlight from his lab coat pocket. I nodded thanks and turned it on.

Here goes . . .

I aimed the flashlight at Jacob's terrorized face and held my breath.

"Son of a bitch!" I dropped the flashlight and recoiled as Jacob's eyes shuddered under the fluorescent lights and focused on me.

I raise bodies for a living; I don't react to much anymore. Then again, I'm the one usually getting the bodies to open their eyes and look at me—not standing around waiting for them to do it on their own.

It couldn't be. Seriously, there was no way . . .

"Kincaid, what?" Aaron sounded concerned. Considering how I'd recoiled, I didn't blame him.

Get a grip, Kincaid.

I picked up the flashlight from where it had rolled to a stop on the concrete floor. "I'm—fine. Something startled me is all."

"What?"

"That's what I'm going to find out." I held the flashlight over Jacob's face, moving it back and forth. The eyes didn't follow—they were open and still, as the eyes of the dead usually are—but layered over his real eyes were a ghostly grey pair. While the corpse's eyeballs stayed perfectly still, the ghostly pair flickered back and forth, tracking the penlight. They sped up, as if in a panic or trying to get my attention. Possibly both.

In my head I started going through examples I'd read of ghosts being stuck in their own bodies, not in the traditional zombie way but in the nasty bound-in-servitude or torture way courtesy of a voodoo curse or ghost binding.

Now that I knew what to look for, I detected a ghost-grey sheen layered over Jacob's entire body, like an immobile veil—except for the roaming eyes.

A curse would make sense. What worse fate than to be bound to your own body? Unable to talk but still able to watch and hear the world go by.

I had to be certain, though, before I said anything to Aaron or Dr. Blanc. It isn't every day you hear of a ghost being tied to its own corpse.

It sure put a morbid spin on the phrase "you can't take it with you," though apparently Jacob was trying, however involuntarily that might be. I closed my eyes and pulled up my Otherside sight. When I was ready, I opened them and looked at Jacob.

Sure enough, the bindings were visible. And as opposed to an animation, this was most definitely a ghost binding.

Binding a ghost is a very different process from animating a zombie. Typically, animation is a fluid process, integrating the ghost into the body so you can't see a demarcation between the two. For all intents and purposes, in a zombie the body and ghost are one— totally blended. But a bound ghost? That's a different ball game entirely. Rather than fluid, the bindings and anchors are restrictive, meant to trap and keep a ghost in one place, not integrate them into the whole. Probably one of the reasons they burn through their Otherside so fast. Being bound isn't a good way to go out.

Here was the interesting thing, though. I recognized some of the bindings—not all, but most. They were a modern mix of symbols and anchors, borrowed from a few different practices. If this was the work of Nate's Biblical demon, Eloch, it was awfully up on its modern practitioning and voodoo. Either this demon spent a lot of time studying or I'd just peeled the first layer off whatever con it was running. Meaning I had my first clue to its real identity.

"Kincaid?"

I glanced at Aaron over my shoulder. I had to blink a few times before I realized that he looked muted and grey because of the veil of Otherside I was looking through. Odd, that had never once bothered me before.

"What do you see?" he asked.

Right. Jacob. "Remember I said there weren't any bindings? There are now."

Aaron frowned. "No one's been in here, have they, Dr. Blanc?"

He shook his head. "Myself and one of my assistants. No one besides you, Ms. Strange, with a practitioning background."

Again, that warning Gideon had given me flared up. Goddamnit, he was getting under my skin. It was like having a worm burrowing through my brain. . . .

Well, now I had that pleasant analogy in my head too. Fucking fantastic.

"Well, it might have been hiding under the Otherside dust—or . . ." I stopped, not sure how much to say.

"Or?" Aaron prompted.

Oh, what the hell. I knew it was possible. "Or it was set to go off in case someone managed to get rid of the Otherside dust. Like a fail-safe."

"Why would anyone want to do that?"

Again, I wondered how much to tell Aaron. . . . I had no intention of letting on how involved Nate was in this, or what I'd learned about Eloch. But at this point I needed Aaron's help too much to be hiding important details. "Because I think whatever caused this is hell-bent on making sure we can't talk to Jacob—or Damien."

Briefly, I related my experience trying to contact Damien: the dust, the ice, the thing in my mirror—my now-scorched mirror. I omitted that Nate had been the one to tell me about the salt, instead telling them I had stumbled across it in a book. Anything to steer the conversation away from Nate . . .

Actually, the more I thought about it, the more sense it made. If this thing could freeze living creatures, maybe it had another specialty: ghost binding. If it had tried to bind Nate, managed to kill and bind Jacob . . .

"Shit." When Aaron and Dr. Blanc looked at me, I added, "That was why I couldn't reach Damien. If we assume it killed Jacob the same way—"

"Then it stands to reason Damien was also bound to his body," Dr. Blanc finished.

I nodded. Still creepy, but right.

It also explained why calling Damien had felt like reeling in dead weight. I'd never tried calling a bound ghost before. Well, learn something new every day—one to add to the notebooks.

"We need to find the rest of the band," I said.

Aaron nodded and turned his gaze back to the body. "I'm on it. Cole is the only one in town. Nicklas and Shaun are both in Europe, have been for over a year. I checked when I took on Damien's cold case."

"Get in touch with Cole. And you might want to put a guard on Mindy." And speak to her again . . . though I hadn't decided if I should try to handle that myself first. "If Jacob and Damien were linked . . ." I left the thought open.

"Then there's a good chance whatever killed them is keeping an eye on her as well," Aaron said, finishing the thought for me.

"And we need to find out what it was Jacob knew that got him killed."

"I'll get the search warrant," Aaron said, finally tearing his gaze off the body and turning it on me. "We've got the personal effects he was found with here. Until then, we can start with those."

I shook my head. "Go ahead, but if it went to this much trouble to make sure we'd never be able to talk to him, I seriously doubt it was careless at the crime scene."

"You never know. Everyone screws up somewhere. Murderers always do, because deep down they want someone to discover their cunning genius."

The warrant would have to wait until the morning. Well, it was a start.

"Regardless, Aaron, I need supplies. Something to amplify the Otherside." For me that meant sacrificing a sea urchin, and the fish market was most definitely closed by now.

Dr. Blanc cleared his throat. Aaron and I both looked at him. "I have an admission to make. You see, I have been looking at how practitioners generate Otherside—sacrificial Otherside."

I lowered my head. Please, oh please, don't let Dr. Blanc have a collection of kittens, mice and rats to use for sacrifice. Just when I was starting to get semi-comfortable with him . . .

"But when I heard that you preferred sea urchins, I did some searching and found out that a number of modern practitioners along the west coast and in Japan were also using a variety of echinoderms, and, well, I couldn't resist. I was curious what properties gave them predilection to Otherside."

"Unilateral symmetry," I offered. It didn't matter which way you cut an echinoderm, you always got a matching half. Rats, mice, lizards, et cetera, are all bilaterally symmetrical. There's something about symmetry that Otherside likes.

We followed him to his office. There was an aquarium in the corner with a handful of sea urchins and sea cucumbers roaming the bottom.

"Would one of these do?" he asked.

I stared at the tank. There were even little decorations inside: a pirate ship, a couple of skeletons . . . "You want me to sacrifice one of your pets to free Jacob's ghost?"

"Well, though I'll admit I've grown attached to them, it's for the greater good of one of my patients. They also aren't sentient, whereas Jacob most certainly still is."

And the good morgue doctor managed to hit an entirely new level of creepiness in the eyes of the woman who raised corpses and talked to ghosts. Still, I couldn't argue with his logic. And it'd save me a trip back.

"Okay, the doctor's pet sea urchins it is."

✳

I got the sea urchin ready, balancing it on Jacob's chest. "I feel weird doing this with an audience," I said.

"You volunteered. And he's the one who donated a pet."

"A sea urchin. Also known as sushi."

Aaron shrugged. "One person's pet, another person's dinner."

I elbowed him. "Enough," I whispered. "My stomach is taking enough of a hit as it is, remember? And stand back, will you?"

He backed away. I reflected that I should probably wait until tomorrow to tap the barrier again. But my conscience wouldn't be okay leaving Jacob tied up in there for another twelve hours. Not when it would only take a quick tap.

I took a few minutes to examine the bindings. They were complicated but familiar. Like I said, Nate's demon was awfully up on modern trends in practitioning. I decided it was a voodoo curse that had been modified. The modifications were likely what had made it activate after the salt.

I won't lie—the whole thing worried me. I don't like pulling out bindings I don't fully understand. But if I did what I'd done with Max and bypassed the unfamiliar bindings, leaving them untouched while I unhooked the anchors binding the ghost to itself, I should be okay.

I did my best to block out the fact that Max had ended up bursting into flames. . . . Besides, Jacob's fate couldn't get much worse than being trapped inside his own corpse.

I lined up the scalpel I'd borrowed from Dr. Blanc with the sea urchin and got ready to tap the barrier.

I leaned over until Jacob could see me. "All right, Jacob. My name is Kincaid Strange. I'm the practitioner they've brought in to try and fix things." Always good to start with the basics when dealing with the newly dead. "Look down twice if you understand and can hear me."

His ghost's eyes flickered down twice in rapid succession.

Well, small miracles—whoever bound him had left his ears intact too. I'd figured as much since that was the way these curses usually went.

"Okay, Jacob, you're dead and there's nothing I can do about that. I'm sorry, but that's the way things go sometimes."

Aaron jabbed me in the shoulder. When I looked away from Jacob, he was glaring at me.

"What?" I whispered at Aaron.

"A little compassion?"

This is why I don't like audiences when I'm having a serious conversation with a ghost. "Who's the practitioner here, Aaron, you or me?"

Aaron rolled his eyes. "You are."

"Then stop interrupting and let me do my job." I shooed Aaron back a few more steps before turning back to the corpse.

"All right, Jacob. So there's some good news and some bad news—on top of the bad news that you're dead," I added, just to be clear. "Swipe up for good news, down for bad news first."

There was a pause and Jacob's eyes swiped down. Good choice.

"The bad news is the person who killed you bound your ghost to your body. That's why you can't move. Sweep up if you understand."

His eyes swept up.

"The good news is I think I can get you out. But we'd like to ask you a few questions first. Sweep down if you can answer questions." I always alternate to make sure the person is still competent. You never know with bound ghosts . . . they tend to go loopy fast. Seeing Jacob's state, it was no wonder why.

His eyes swept up.

I frowned. "No? You don't *want* to answer questions? Sweep down if you don't want to answer questions, sweep up if you do."

He swept up.

Okay, so it wasn't that he didn't want to answer my questions. . . . "You *can't* answer my questions? Sweep down for yes, up for no."

His eyes swept down.

Shit. Well, there went Plan A. I turned to Aaron. "It's a no go, Aaron. He can't answer." I'd known that was a possibility and had prepped accordingly.

Aaron ran his hand through his short hair. "Okay, Kincaid. Go ahead."

Plan B: I would free him from the bindings and try to hold him here long enough to answer a few questions. The problem was, Jacob's ghost would be weak, drained; at most, he'd be able to shake or nod his head. If he didn't disappear entirely.

"If I can hold him, what do you want me to ask first? It's got to be yes or no."

"If he knows his name and if he knew his killer. It'll show he's competent and narrow down the suspects." We'd decided on that route since we didn't have a decent list of suspects to rhyme off and it'd take too long. "Then we can go with your questions. If he's still around."

My questions—less pertinent to the investigation, but still useful.

All right. Time to sever the bindings. I tapped the barrier and waited until I had enough Otherside in my globe. I took another good look at the bindings holding Jacob down and picked the anchor I thought was weakest—I'd start there.

I cut the sea urchin in half and watched as the Otherside flowed out of it, over Jacob's body. The bindings reacted, flaring with the influx and proximity.

"Here goes, Jacob," I murmured. I reached for the anchor and pulled. It held for a moment, then unravelled. Jacob's fingers—or the translucent ghost ones—twitched.

I pulled the next anchor out, then the next. By the third, I'd destabilized the bindings enough that they started to unravel themselves, until they'd dissolved in one last shudder of Otherside.

Now was the tricky part. As Jacob's depleted ghost started to rise up and follow the Otherside back across the barrier where he belonged, I reached out with the Otherside I had left and stopped him.

I winced at the effort to hold him in place. He looked startled and not a little worried. He started shaking his translucent head and the rest of him flickered.

Damn it, he wasn't going to last long. I raised my hand. "Just a couple questions, promise. Nod yes or shake no. Is your name Jacob?"

He nodded.

"Do you know what killed you?" If he did know, then we needed to search his place for practitioning equipment, because there was no way in hell a non-practitioner would know what it was.

Another nod.

"Is it sorcery?" I was pretty sure, but confirmation was always welcome.

A shake and a nod this time. Yes and no. That was something to ponder later; Jacob had started to glimmer and I could feel my hold slipping.

I looked to Aaron. "That's it," I said. Time for my last question.

I opened my mouth to ask if Mindy was involved, but Aaron spoke first.

"Was Nathan Cade involved in the murder of Damien Fell?" he shouted.

Jacob almost smiled—then shook his head.

Then, after flickering like a dying light bulb, he went out—the remnant of his ghost disappearing, finally heading off to the Otherside.

I turned on Aaron, fists clenched. "Was Nate involved?" I repeated.

"We said we'd ad lib," Aaron said, his tone reasonable.

My nails dug into my slick, sweating palms. "You were *waiting* to do that. Aaron, what the hell, we agreed to ask about Mindy."

Aaron's brow furrowed. "I just cleared your best friend of murder."

"Which we knew he didn't commit!"

But Aaron didn't answer. He just inclined his head.

He hadn't cleared Nate; he'd just been pretending to. "Un-fucking believable," I muttered. I let the globe go before the Otherside could tease at my temper any more than Aaron already had. My head pounded with the absence of Otherside. I knew I should cool it but couldn't rein in my anger. "What happened to working together? I'm not your subordinate—you can't do that to me."

Dr. Blanc cleared his throat. He was standing a few feet away, his eyes wide.

"Give us a minute," I said, though even to my ear it sounded more like a snarl.

I pressed my hands against my eyes and noticed that the usual Otherside sweat wasn't just on my palms and face . . . my shirt was wet, as well as my hair.

Shit, I'd overextended myself.

I turned back to yell some more at Aaron, but my head was swimming and the floor had started to move in waves. . . .

I didn't have a chance to let loose at him before the room faded to dark.

CHAPTER 13

FAMILIAR HAUNTS

I was groggy, and my head hurt, and I was thirsty, really thirsty. I could smell bacon—and coffee. . . .

Which should have made me feel better, not worse.

I pushed myself up. I was in a bed—Aaron's bed.

What was the last thing that had happened? Nate, crazy demon story, morgue, ghost trapped in unfrozen body—Aaron.

Shit . . .

The curtains were closed and I had no idea what time it was. It took me a few seconds to find the bedside light, partially on account of there being not one but three blankets loaded on top of the comforter. I'd complained about his thin, synthetic blankets not being warm enough many a time before.

Guess he'd finally listened. Shame he couldn't have been bothered to do that three months ago. No, it was after we broke up he decided to pay attention to my concerns about his freezing apartment and complete lack of decent coffee.

Speaking of which . . . I pushed the comforter and blankets

off and swung my legs over the side of the bed. I was still dressed, though my jacket and boots were gone.

I shook my head, trying to clear the grogginess, and tested my feet on the floor, though I was in no rush to stand. I liked Aaron's new bed; the mattress was firmer and didn't cave in at the centre. The frame was also close to the floor, meaning that if I rolled off I had a short drop. It had been known to happen.

Okay, not the time to reminisce about our relationship.

Back to the central question: what was I doing here, in his room?

I glanced over at the alarm clock—exactly where it had always been. It was nine in the morning. It was Sunday. Damn . . . I checked for my phone in my jean pockets and on the night table, but it wasn't there. Probably left it in my jacket pocket or my bag.

I grabbed one of Aaron's sweatshirts from where it was folded on the chair with the rest of his clean laundry. I didn't know how he managed to keep the place so much tidier and brighter-looking than my place. Maybe it was an effect of living in my old, decrepit warehouse of a building, where everything, including my furniture and walls, was tinged with grey.

Or maybe I was just imagining things again. Fifty-fifty.

I threw on the red sweatshirt and opened the door.

The rest of the apartment was pretty much the way I remembered it from a few weeks back. The kitchen table had been tucked farther into the living room, probably so that Aaron could better use it as a desk, since his computer and notebooks were set up there. He rarely ate meals there anyway, preferring the couch and coffee table like everyone else. But the rest of the living room looked familiar and very clean. Smaller than mine, square footage–wise, but he managed to make better use of the space.

It had to be my building. I alone couldn't catalyze that much of a mess.

Aaron looked up from his computer screen where he'd been hunched over. "Kincaid."

We stared at each other for a moment.

He broke the silence first. "How are you feeling?"

There wasn't a hint of accusation in his voice. Not yet. That would be coming, I'd wager. Still, I decided to give him the benefit of the doubt and play along.

"A little groggy but otherwise fine."

He watched me for a moment, waiting for me to offer more.

"Aaron, if you want to ask me something, then ask. Don't wait for me to guess."

Another pause. "There's coffee in the kitchen," he said. "I only had a few slices of bacon left, so I put tomatoes and bagels out as well. There might be cream cheese in the fridge."

I went in and helped myself to food and coffee. I didn't look over at Aaron, but I could feel his eyes watching me.

He waited until I returned to the living room and placed my plate and mug on the opposite side of the table from him.

"That's it? No explanation?"

I took a bite of my sandwich and mentally pushed down the reflexive shame—at collapsing, at using too much Otherside, at feeling stupid.

I had made a mistake. I was learning from my mistakes—or trying to. Carrying guilt around and letting Aaron dictate how I should feel—I was done with that.

"I don't owe you an explanation, Aaron. What do you want to know?" I said calmly, gripping my warm mug.

He looked up, frowning at me. This wasn't the way these conversations used to go.

"I thought you had the Otherside under control," he finally said.

"Most of the time I do," I said. It was true—I was more in control of it than I had been in months.

"Then what happened?" he said, with real concern in his face. And something else—accusation, or anger. Or maybe guilt. I realized that was one thing Aaron never talked about with me: his own mistakes.

"You called me to use Otherside, Aaron. Twice. Using the barrier that much . . ." I shrugged. "There's a risk. I decided it was more important to try and get whatever we could out of Jacob now rather than wait. If I'd waited until tomorrow, he might not have been able to answer any questions." Aaron didn't say anything, so I added, "I channelled too much Otherside. I admit it. Sometimes it's hard to tell. This was one of those times." I took a bite out of my sandwich.

"It's become normal."

I chewed my food and swallowed. "There's nothing wrong with me," I said, enunciating each word carefully. "I'm not an Otherside junkie."

"I know, and I'm starting to think this is worse. You didn't *stop*," he said. This time the accusation was clear.

The last person I needed a lecture from on Otherside use was Aaron. "I made a *choice*."

"What happens if you really use too much?"

I didn't answer him; he knew the answer already. I crossed my arms. I might not know what I felt for Aaron anymore, but that didn't mean he couldn't hurt me.

He nodded and stood up, the chair scraping behind him. "That's what I thought. You die. Fucking fantastic, Kincaid."

"Aaron—"

Aaron headed into his bedroom. A moment later I heard his ensuite shower start.

I stayed at the kitchen table, staring at the back of his laptop, wondering if I was making things worse or better. I've always had a hard time figuring that out when it comes to people I have feelings for—or used to have feelings for.

A buzzing sound jarred me out of my reverie. I searched for the source until I found the neat pile consisting of my jacket, backpack and helmet by the door.

Shit, Nate. I scrambled to find my phone and answer it before it went to voice mail.

"Nate, I'm sorry."

"It's okay, K. Aaron texted me back last night. I told him to keep you there."

Considering Nate's current state . . . "It was the smart thing to do. I'm fine. How did the books go?"

"Oh, you're going to love this, K. First off, these books are nuts. I mean, I knew Mork was into some messed-up shit, but this stuff—"

"*Nate.*" Aaron wouldn't shower forever.

"Okay, so I marked down all the pages you asked about, that mention an affinity for ice and an aversion to salt."

"Please tell me that list was short."

"Yes and no." There was a pause. "Did Lee mention that there are many kinds of wraiths?"

"No, she only mentioned the one." There were different types? Fuck me, that was not what I wanted to hear. I needed to figure out what weaknesses this one might have. That would be a lot harder if there were all sorts of different types.

"Most of them are really unpredictable. I mean, they're about on line with a poltergeist in the brains department. They eat Otherside—but it's got to be on this side of the barrier, which is why they do the whole killing thing."

So they feed off the Otherside generated at the moment of death. "That explains why it's killing people but not binding ghosts to this side."

"K, these things eat *a lot* of Otherside, like piles of bodies' worth."

"It could be killing people, or house pets, and hiding them."

"Not as many as they're supposed to need. And I don't think they bother hiding them. At no point do any of the occult crazy people who wrote these books describe wraiths as ghosts with a plan beyond their own warped idea of vengeance. And dinner." After a moment he added, "K, I don't think Eloch is one of these."

I frowned. He was still fixated on the demon idea. "What about demons? Any mention of those?"

There was a pause. "No. But I'm not done looking yet."

"I want you to keep your eye out for something else too: ghost binding." I filled Nate in on Jacob.

"Son of a bitch. Is that what happened to Damien?"

"I don't know. Maybe." I didn't want to jump to any conclusions—or elicit any more panic in Nate than was absolutely necessary. "Damien wasn't frozen like Jacob, so I doubt it. Just keep reading. There has to be something in there that fits Eloch's description and isn't a demon." Something else occurred to me. "I need you to look another thing up for me—online."

"Shoot."

"I need you to see if there were any links between Jacob and Damien—or Cadmium Coffee. And add in Mindy, Cole and the rest of your band—hobbies, clubs, schools. Anything and everything, no matter how minor." We had to look beyond the obvious connections between Cadmium Coffee, Dead Men and Jacob. It might be a twenty-year-old needle in the haystack, but Jacob's death was too much of a coincidence and I wanted to find out who else might be in danger. Something out there really didn't want Damien or Jacob to talk to anyone. Desperate measures only ever led to more desperate measures.

I jostled Aaron's laptop by accident on my way to the kitchen to refill my coffee. The screen unfroze and out of the corner of my eye I caught a glimpse of the web browser. I tried not to look but could have sworn I'd seen the PubDead icon on one of the tabs.

"Anything specific?"

I continued on to the kitchen and filled my mug. "You won't know until you see it. Just hold out a couple more hours. I need to swing by the library." I was hoping to find something—anything—that would help me get Nate out of Cameron's body. I won't lie, I also wanted to avoid my lesson with Gideon. I figured collapsing from using too much Otherside meant I could call in sick. . . .

"How are you holding up, Nate?"

"I look fucking terrible."

"I thought I told you not to look in any mirrors? Even if Eloch doesn't show up, Gideon might. And you won't get any better-looking."

"I don't know, K. It's like a highway pile-up. Cameron was a good-looking guy. I keep staring at my—his face trying to figure out where everything went wrong. . . ."

I rolled my eyes. A botched binding and a couple of days' worth of formaldehyde soaks will do that. . . . "Call if you have a real problem—or if you find something useful."

I heard the shower in Aaron's bedroom stop.

"Look, Nate, I have to go. Just get back to the books, will you? I'll let you know what I find at the library," I said, and hung up.

I wandered back to the living room and my gaze returned to Aaron's computer. I hadn't meant to unfreeze it, but now that its LEDs were just staring at me . . .

What is it they say about curiosity killing the cat?

The open page on the web browser was from the NCBI website, talking about the known effects of Otherside on human health.

I sighed. Aaron was seriously worried.

I clicked on the second and third tabs. A research article on practitioners and Otherside, and, as I suspected, a page from AnimateMed, the paranormal version of PubMed, or PubDead as some liked to call it, a source for scientific research on all things undead—not the snake oil stuff, but actual research.

All three pages were about the effects of Otherside. One of the papers stood out: "Signs of Otherside Overuse/Abuse."

Breathe, Kincaid. Aaron thinking you have a problem isn't news.

The anger coursed through me anyway. Aaron had always looked down on my Otherside use, and he still couldn't leave it the hell alone, three months after we'd broken up.

I grabbed the laptop and headed for Aaron's room. I knocked and then barged in before he could answer.

His jeans were already on, but he was bare chested. I glared at him and held up the computer. "Since when do you consult Dr. Internet on Otherside instead of me?"

"What are you doing on my laptop?"

"I knocked it by accident and saw the screen. And you didn't answer my question."

"Because you were passed out for twelve hours!" He grabbed a grey T-shirt and pulled it over his head.

I bit my lip as my anger fizzled. "I'm sorry I passed out on you. I wasn't expecting that to happen," I said.

He took the laptop from my hands and closed it before tucking it under his arm. I expected him to storm out of the bedroom, but he didn't. He stayed right where he was and caressed my face before cupping my chin gently. "I don't like seeing you like this, Kincaid."

It was enough to kick-start whatever inside me had taken an extended vacation. . . .

"You can't always have it your way, Aaron." I felt raw, my nerves already bracing, anticipating Aaron's rejection of me that inevitably followed these protestations. There was still something there between us—a pull beyond just the physical attraction. I knew I shouldn't give in to it. Aaron had hurt me more than once. I was better off where I was, keeping him at arm's length.

I closed the distance anyway. I wrapped my arms around Aaron and placed my head on his chest, feeling his warmth.

It took Aaron a moment, but he eventually wrapped his arms around me, tentatively, as if he couldn't decide what to do next. "I wish you didn't need to reach a breaking point before you want me," he muttered. After a moment he added, "I feel like I barely know you anymore."

And there was the kick my heart had braced for. Just when I was starting to really try to open up to him. "I needed to hear that months ago."

"I know." He drew me in again and pressed his lips against my forehead. "I always felt that you were half-present—but the other half? It's like you—"

"Prefer the dead?" It wasn't exactly a new conversation between us.

He looked me in the eyes. "That you're already living with them." Aaron shook his head. "I'm more worried now than I was three months ago. You used to talk to me about your practitioning work. Christ, I used to be the first person you'd tell about the raising you did a few days ago."

"I told you about that—"

"After I'd already heard about it from the lawyer."

"Cody can blow me." I would have added more, but Aaron wasn't receptive to me brushing off legal trouble. I sighed and looked at him. "It's better this way." Aaron knowing about my Otherside sight and Gideon would not exactly ease his mind. . . . "I'm not going to change, Aaron. Not for you."

"I know. And that's my problem, Kincaid. Not yours."

And as quickly as the familiar excitement of being near Aaron had returned, it vanished. Part of me wasn't willing to admit defeat, that it was too late for us. One thing the dead always agree on is that regrets suck. I didn't want to let Aaron walk away without absolute certainty that my feelings had changed. But these days I wasn't certain about anything anymore . . . I also didn't want to give everything a coat of lipstick and pretend it was all okay.

Neither of us was going to change. We both knew it, so how had we started beating this dead horse?

I knew the answer to that as well. This, with Aaron, was familiar. The devil you know . . .

I grabbed my coat and picked up my bag. "Where's my bike?" I asked.

"I didn't mean to—" Aaron closed his eyes and stopped. "What do you need from me?" he finally said.

"I need space—professional and personal." I decided to share something with him. Give and take, right? "I've also got someone who's teaching me more about Otherside."

"Who?"

I frowned. "Professional space, Aaron."

"Fine—I trust you. If you need my help, you'll ask?" There was a pleading there I couldn't say no to. I nodded.

That seemed to mollify him. He followed me out to the front door, where I slid on my jacket and picked up my backpack and helmet. I almost didn't want to know whether Aaron had picked up my bike after the fact or managed to drive me to his place unconscious on it.

"I also need access to the crime scene again. I . . ." How to describe Gideon to Aaron without triggering alarm bells. "There's a ghost I want to call—one that was an expert on the occult. He might be willing to help." For a price . . . Definitely wasn't adding that part. "I'm hoping he knows more about what killed Jacob."

Aaron watched me for a moment. He nodded. "I can buy you some time around 2 p.m.—will that work?"

"I'll make it work."

He didn't say anything else as he slid on his own jacket. I followed him down the hall and we rode the elevator to the garage in silence.

"Kincaid?" Aaron said as I was getting on my bike.

I glanced over at him.

"I meant it when I said be careful. And call me if you need anything—I meant that too."

I forced a smile. I was never very good at faking them, much to my mother's disappointment. I put my helmet on. "Do me a favour and look quietly into Mindy, Cole and the rest of Nate's band while you're checking up on Jacob."

He frowned. "What for?"

It was less of a what, more of an I'll-know-it-when-I-see-it.

"Feuds, infighting, hidden bags of money . . ."

"Anything that could count as motive."

I nodded and gunned my Hawk as Aaron opened the parking garage gate. On my way to the library, I couldn't shake the feeling that I should hurt more than this.

CHAPTER 14

THE DEVIL YOU KNOW

I propped my bike against the brick wall of the university library and messaged Lee about the paranormal murder. I asked if she'd be oh so kind as to look into my suspected wraith problem a little more. She had more resources than me, and it was in her best interest to help. The City of Seattle was paranoid enough about the hidden underground zombie community. A homicidal wraith would attract more scrutiny to the paranormally inclined, which Lee wouldn't appreciate.

By the time I reached the elevator, she had messaged me back to call her. She even answered on the first ring.

"Lee, please tell me you have something useful for me," I said quietly.

"Over the past day I've gone through Lou's texts and asked a few ghosts and occult experts in the city on your behalf, but I have yet to find anything useful. Suffice to say there are not many survivors to tell the tale when it comes to wraiths—living or dead."

Considering the fact that the thing seemed to eat Otherside, I wasn't exactly surprised. "Thanks for trying, Lee."

But she wasn't done. "You have been reluctant to follow my advice, but I pray you do it this time. Tell the sorcerer's ghost what has transpired."

"I remember you distinctly telling me *not* to call the sorcerer—"

"Unfortunately, your situation now calls for it. The tools you have at your disposal are dangerous, but that does not mean you should not use them."

"I have no idea what he'll do to Nate." Hell, for that matter I had no idea what he'd do to me.

"That is Nate's concern, not yours," Lee said, her voice even colder than usual.

"Oh, come on— Lee?" I stared at the phone. She'd hung up. "You got to be kidding me . . ."

I shoved it back into my pocket and jabbed the elevator call button.

Sometimes I really wished Lee hadn't died at the turn of the last century. None of the ancient zombies had a sympathetic bone in their bodies. . . . Then again, she probably wouldn't be running the underground city if she did.

I rode the elevator up to the paranormal floor at the top of the library. The ghost librarian wasn't waiting at her usual spot at the special collections desk when I exited. I squeezed my arm under the plastic guard and helped myself to a pass from a neat stack, along with a computer password on a slip of paper, and let myself in.

The paranormal floor was deserted, so I retrieved an armload of books and deposited them loudly on a table, letting them spread out. I was especially hopeful that the ghoul and ghost binding texts might shed light on the problems I was having with Nate's bindings. The ghost binding was obvious, but ghouls are an interesting mix of practitioning schools. The ghost is incorporated back into the body, as with a zombie, but there are some subtle differences that skirt the line where ghost bindings and possession meet reanimation. And Nate seemed to be a messed-up cross between the two.

I made some notes and sketched some bindings that sounded similar to Nate's, but I'll admit I was grasping at straws.

I checked my phone and realized an hour and a half had gone by. I should be getting back, but there were no messages from Nate or Aaron with an emergency. Oh, what the hell—it wasn't like I was needed anywhere else.

I left my reference books on the table and headed over to the computer. I searched for every book I could find that mentioned the paranormal beyond zombies, ghosts and ghouls—anything to do with entities that might hint at what could be terrorizing Nate. As I've said before, everything has a reasonable explanation. Including Eloch. And discovering what he was and wanted might just buy me more time to get Nate out.

An uncomfortable thought occurred to me. What if Eloch was another sorcerer's ghost having some fun at Nate's expense? I shivered involuntarily at the idea of something as powerful as Gideon with a bone to pick with Nate. . . .

There was one term I hadn't searched for. That I'd avoided searching for. I let my fingers hover over the computer keys before typing in "demon."

Biblical references, a few myths—lo and behold, there was Dungeons and Dragons again . . . Just as I'd thought, nothing reliable or beyond the usual brimstone-and-fire bullshit. Mythology, monsters, videogame bosses . . .

I sat back in the chair and sighed. I don't know what I'd been expecting. I raise the dead for a living; I can suspend disbelief, but demons were pushing it. As far as I knew, vampires, demons and angels didn't exist outside mythology. But a couple of weeks ago I would have said there was no such thing as a sorcerer's ghost. I was open to grains of truth—evidence of something real enough to inspire belief but rare enough to evade discovery.

Everything had an explanation. I'd talked to countless ghosts who lived on the Otherside, and none of them ever mentioned encounters with angels, demons, vampires or other monsters from myths—except for Nate, and he wasn't reliable on account of being terrified. There was no good side versus bad as far as the undead were concerned, only the Otherside. An inspiration for purgatory?

Sure, I'd buy that, but there weren't any battles going on for anyone's immortal soul. A battle to get them to pay outstanding bar tabs at Lee's, maybe.

But if there wasn't any mention of demons in reputable texts, and no practitioner I knew of had ever thought to report one, and even Mork's obscure occult texts didn't mention them.

The undead feed off fear, and what better way to generate it than to convince people they were dealing with a real demon. I was convinced poltergeists couldn't pull it off, but a sorcerer's ghost or ghoul? Where there was one, there had to be more. Probably all just as arrogant as Gideon . . .

I cleared the search for "demon" and typed in "Eloch." Specific names generally don't have a great track record at returning useful references—not unless it was someone famous. I was banking on Eloch having other victims and an ego. People with an ego, alive or dead, always want the credit.

Nothing came up.

What the hell. I tried "Eloch" and "sorcerer" next, and frowned at the results.

There was still no reference to an Eloch, but there was a short list of books—only ten or so—that held references to sorcerers. It included a collection of diaries from Christian monks from northern Europe dating back to the 1600s. I looked closely at the description: accounts of supernatural happenings, lists of names, crimes, victims . . .

A chill settled over me. Witch trials. I was looking at the accounts of medieval witch trials. There was also a handful of journals of the accused, supposed witches and sorcerers who'd been burned at the stake.

Nothing about making deals for people's souls, but still . . .

I jotted down the reference numbers and headed into the archive shelves, a section I wasn't familiar with and had never really perused, as it dealt more with the history of practitioning as opposed to its uses.

You'd be surprised what people used to write down in journals before the advent of TV . . . or electricity. It wasn't as if they had much besides time to kill—metaphorically speaking. If I was lucky, I might find accounts of demons or wraiths. Or if I was very lucky, mention of a paranormal entity that called itself Eloch.

The accounts of the accused were all over the place—witch trials, encounters with dangerous practitioners and even a few self-proclaimed magicians—though they all struck me more as fantasy than reality on account of the complete lack of references to bindings or symbols. Those I discarded as useless. I was getting the impression that real sorcerers weren't the type who left their notebooks around for people to stumble across. Otherwise, they'd be more well-known in the practitioning community. . . .

But the eyewitness accounts of witch trials by the monks who had persecuted them . . . Leave it to the people who hate you the most to leave a decent record of your demise.

I began reading about a witch trial that had occurred in Denmark during the late Dark Ages, early Middle Ages. Well before the Salem witch trials and Inquisition, by almost five hundred years. At this time most trials targeted a particular witch or sorcerer, more often than not a woman and often for something slight, like unleashing a poltergeist or ghost on the town. The religious authorities got that part wrong more frequently than I cared to imagine. Ghosts are like cats—you can barely get them to stay on talking points let alone direct them to haunt someone. And most of the people they'd managed to target were village healers or minor practitioners. Why is it that the mob with pitchforks always attacks the harmless?

The monk or priest who had recorded the account had veered from the typical practice of focusing on one person or haunting, deciding instead to rout out every practitioner—or witch, or sorcerer—he could find. He'd made a list of names and included underneath the evidence for their connection to the paranormal.

Some of it was the typical BS—likely some rich patron in the middle of a land grab—but there were definitely some real practitioners, with evidence of symbols and seances and binding spells. Not proof on its own, but an indication that at least some of the names had been involved in the paranormal. There was even a mention of the walking dead, "abominations," et cetera. Probably a zombie or ghoul.

Not exactly useful in determining what Eloch might be, though it painted an interesting picture of how people in the Middle Ages viewed us. It wasn't all that far off from the present, though without the stakes and pitchfork-wielding mobs. . . .

I froze as a name jumped out at me, halfway down the list of suspects.

Gideon Lawrence.

That couldn't be right. . . . This had happened a thousand years ago. There was no way.

Just how long did a sorcerer's ghost survive? I knew Gideon had to be old . . .

Maybe he'd taken the name of another sorcerer?

I skimmed the account. It was unusual in its own right, as men were rarely prosecuted for sorcery and witchcraft. It said he'd been burned at the stake for dereliction of duty and treason as the court sorcerer. At least in this case they'd persecuted an actual sorcerer. There was even a list of his properties and goods.

I frowned at the passage, wondering if the translation was right. Gideon hadn't mentioned treason or being a court-appointed sorcerer. Though he had mentioned being a scapegoat. The monk was thorough with most individuals, detailing treason, witchcraft, consorting with devils . . . except when it came to Gideon Lawrence. There, he only hinted at the charges. Gideon had displeased the king by refusing to use his evil powers for the Crown's good, but there was no mention of what he'd refused to do. Strange—what kind of deed would earn itself an omission, when so many other details had been laid bare?

The trials had happened over the course of a month or so— twenty people, including Gideon, accused of witchcraft and sorcery. Clearly, not all of them were guilty, and the property transfers indicated as much.

I glanced at my phone; I had run out of time. I had to get back to Nate.

I grabbed the book and headed to the photocopier and began scanning the pages related to Gideon.

What was it Gideon had said? People like to find someone to blame. . . .

I wondered how many of the real witches or sorcerers who'd been burned at the stake had returned the next day to wreak vengeance. I knew how I reacted when push came to shove. . . .

I finished the photocopies and tucked them into my backpack. I retrieved my water bottle and headed into the bathroom to fill it up and run cold water over my face. The discovery had shaken me, and not with the usual fear that Gideon inspired. It piqued my curiosity. I shelved my own jumble of thoughts to look at later as something cold prickled along the back of my neck, raising the hairs.

I straightened with a start and searched the bathroom. I looked in the mirror. My normal, pale reflection and red-rimmed eyes stared back at me. No grey cast—the mirror wasn't set.

Still, the cold prickling didn't pass.

I pulled my Otherside sight. The bindings that rimmed my eyes flared gold in the mirror, and I looked down to see the binding on my wrist flare too, but otherwise there was nothing—no bindings, no trace of Otherside.

"Gideon?" I whispered. My breath fogged in front of me.

But there was no answer. The cold faded, as did my condensed breath. I searched the mirror one last time but saw only myself. No grey cast, no writing in charred black, not even the red demon eyes Nate had described.

I turned the faucet on and threw more cold water on my face— this time to calm my nerves. I didn't take my eyes off the mirror.

But there was nothing.

It had to be my imagination. Too much Otherside and my nerves on edge. My hand shook slightly as I filled the water bottle.

I jumped as something buzzed loudly, echoing off the porcelain tiles of the washroom walls. I swore and pulled my phone out. It was Nate. I left the bathroom before answering.

"Tell me you found something, K," he said.

I reached my desk and slumped back into my seat. "Well, that depends. I found some interesting ghoul bindings to look through when I get home." I decided to omit that I'd searched for Eloch amongst the collection. "Oh, and I've got some fascinating information on a sorcerer's ghost we both know and fear."

I didn't mention that I'd also done an online search of old entertainment and music magazines that had featured Mindy, Nate and Cole. I needed more info on the dynamics that Nate wasn't willing or able to describe. Mindy had witnessed something at Damien's death and had already lied. My gut said she was hiding something; the question was what. And I doubted more and more that she was as oblivious as Nate insisted with regard to his notebook full of unrecorded songs. When people start off with outright obfuscation, it's impossible to divine the big lies from the small ones.

Maybe Aaron had had better luck. "Nothing useful, Nate," I repeated.

"Considering my fucking abysmal luck, I half-expected that."

"Your turn," I said.

I heard the rustling of paper on the other end. "Well, almost everything dead likes the fucking cold."

I closed my eyes and massaged my forehead. "What about stuff on wraiths?"

I heard him sigh. "They like the cold, eat copious amounts of Otherside, are prone to fits of rage, match the description of a bunch of my exes . . . Nothing about salt anywhere."

That just meant no one had figured it out in time to live to write about it.

"A few things on salt water, though. Witches, sorcerers and practitioners aren't supposed to like them."

Hunh. It seemed awful simple—throw salt on a sorcerer or witch? Maybe not the best topic to broach with Gideon. There had to be something more to it, like combining it with specific kinds of spells or bindings? Or a particular warping of Otherside . . .

"Keep in mind I'm pretty sure the guy who wrote that book was dabbling in altered states of reality."

"Why?"

"Because he thought vampires might exist, but there's not a goddamn fucking word on demons."

I sighed and pinched my nose. "Nate—"

"I mean, come on, K—this Russian spent an entire chapter on the origin of vampire myths, but does he mention demons once?"

"*Nate.*"

"*Fine.*"

I let out a breath. "How are you holding up?"

"Well, K, besides the fact that my hair is falling out, my skin is yellow, that scar you sewed hasn't done a damn thing as far as healing up, and—just let me check here—yup, my eyes are definitely a new shade I've dubbed puke green, I'm just spunky." There was another sigh. "I mean, I feel like I've desecrated the temple of Cameron or something. I know it's just his body, but still."

"Nate, not what I meant."

"I don't want to talk about it and I don't feel like putting the energy into lying well, so I'm lying badly. See, solves multiple problems."

"It *really* doesn't."

"Perspective, K."

My eyes drifted back to the accounts of the witch trials open on my desk. I knew I should be concentrating on getting Nate out—or at the very least the wraith—but my curiosity about the sorcerer's ghost got the better of me.

It couldn't be possible, could it? I mean, that would make Gideon over a thousand years old.

"Got to go, Nate. Keep looking and call if there are any emergencies."

"Or if I find something?"

"That too." I hung up.

There was still no message from Aaron to say if he'd gotten me my window at the crime scene. I should try and swing home to check on Nate in person and at the very least shower, but couldn't resist going back to the computer, where I typed "Gideon Lawrence" in the search engine.

Five entries came up, but the one that caught my eye wasn't from a library book; it was from a British archive, a London diary entry written in 1753. I clicked on it and waited as it downloaded. It was a practitioner's account of a powerful ghost who went by the name of Gideon Lawrence and matched Gideon's description. I sent it to the printer before I finished reading. I clicked on the second entry, this one from 1493, Paris. Another account, this time from a French medium, on his business dealings with a ghost who claimed to be a sorcerer and went by the name of Gideon. Again, the description was uncanny in its similarities to the Gideon I knew, right down to his glittering eyes. The next entries were from early 1800s Berlin—brief mentions of sorcerer's spells credited to a ghost named Gideon Lawrence in two different practitioners' accounts. Interesting. I printed them off as well.

The oldest and last entry was the one that really got me.

Denmark, 1052. I had to squint to read the scanned originals, for all the good it did me with the Old Danish. But the translation and drawing beside the text . . .

It was Gideon described to a T. Arrogant, aggressive, cold. The drawing even resembled him, though he appeared to be wearing different clothing than I'd originally seen him in.

I swallowed. My god, Gideon had been a ghost for almost a thousand years. . . .

It was another account of the witch trial as documented by the local clergy.

The translation wasn't easy to comb through, but it had to be him. Executed by the same court where he'd been retained as a sorcerer. Where the other account had omitted details of Gideon's crimes, this one elaborated. He'd been sentenced to death for his "vindictiveness and cruelty in refusing to perform a miracle and bring one of the king's subjects back from the dead."

Why? And whom had he refused to raise?

My mind reeled. A thousand years. Gideon had been a ghost for almost a thousand years in part because he'd refused to raise the dead. There was irony there. . . .

I mean, I knew poltergeists could last a few hundred, but eventually ghosts either go on to something else or just disappear. . . . How long could a ghost keep sane on the Otherside? From what Nate had said, after fifty years or so people tend to go a bit batty. . . .

Was there anything beyond the barrier for sorcerers, or was that the only afterlife they got? Did the fact they'd manipulated Otherside so much preclude them from going where all the other ghosts eventually went? Where the dead who didn't become ghosts went? I was starting to understand his obsession with getting a body. . . .

I scanned through the material, trying to find out why it was they'd turned on him.

I felt a chill run down my arm, followed by a prickling at my wrist—not unpleasant, but definitely there. I watched as the bindings on my wrist flared. The air beside me chilled and I picked up the scent of burnt firewood.

Shit. Gideon.

I sent the last account to the printer before closing the browser window and shoving my photocopies into my bag.

A moment later, none other than Gideon Lawrence, in all his violent translucent glory, appeared at the desk beside me. Still dressed in modern clothes. The leather jacket was the same, but the rest had changed.

"I got your message," he said, appearing to glance at his fingernails, a very human gesture for a ghost.

I tensed. "What message?"

He glared at me, his eyes flashing black with annoyance. "You said my name a few minutes ago, near a mirror. Unless things have changed drastically, this is neither the basement of a bar nor a crime scene, and our lesson isn't for another few hours, so—" He arched an eyebrow. "Let me guess. You've finished selling off all your own reference material and are reduced to using this library?"

I chided myself. Of course, all Gideon needed was a reflection to cross over. "Two reasons," I said. "First, I can't do the lesson."

His lip twitched and his eyes glittered.

I ploughed forward before the snide comment came. "I used too much Otherside yesterday, accidentally calling something that thinks it's a demon and wants my roommate's soul—apparently. Oh yeah, and then I unbound a ghost from that corpse, you know, the one that was frozen with Otherside dust at the crime scene you want to see."

Gideon closed his eyes. "Dear god, I think you're serious." He made a noise reminiscent of a sigh—though it wasn't like he had to breathe. "Why didn't you call me sooner?"

"On account of the fact that I passed out?"

Gideon shot me a glare. "I need details. You'd best start at the beginning."

I gave Gideon the precise if not short version of events, starting with my botched attempt at a seance with Damien.

"Where did you find out about the salt?"

Shit—I'd hoped to skim over that. "What do you mean?"

"Don't play stupid. Where did you find out that salt would disrupt the Otherside dust?" he said, his lip curling up, exposing a translucent incisor.

"It was more accident than anything else." When Gideon frowned, I added, "My roommate saw something about it in a textbook." The accident part was true, if not the textbook.

Gideon evaluated me for a moment before nodding. "I concede you have a reasonable excuse to cancel our lesson."

Just fantastic. I was so grateful he agreed that my almost getting killed using Otherside was a reasonable excuse to skip class—real generous of him . . .

"And I agree with your assessment."

That distracted me from my mental list of witty insults. "That it's a wraith?" I asked.

He shrugged. "Or something else like it."

"Such as?" I said when he didn't offer any further explanation.

This time he gave me a slight smile, and as usual it didn't get anywhere close to reaching his eyes. "Show me where the most recent murder took place and I'll tell you. Use one of your compact mirrors. I'll be waiting, so don't take too long—my patience is neither infinite nor generous." And with that, he dissolved into Otherside smoke, leaving a faint scent of burnt firewood in his wake.

I shook my head. "Thanks a bunch," I said to myself, then glanced around, hoping he hadn't heard.

If I didn't need his damn opinion so badly . . .

I collected my things in my bag and returned the books to the trolley. Might as well give the ghost librarian something to do.

The last book on my desk contained the list of sorcerers where I'd first seen Gideon's name—the original account of his trial. I hesitated before putting it on the trolley. Instead, I stuck it behind the books on a shelf I knew, from the covering of dust, was rarely referenced. I made a mental note of the spot before throwing on my jacket and grabbing my backpack and helmet. The last thing I did before heading downstairs was to message Aaron that I needed a window at the crime scene—*now*, instead of going home.

I had a sinking suspicion I wasn't done with the book yet. What's that old saying—keep your friends close and your enemies closer? I don't know if Gideon counted as an enemy, but the homicidal ghost was definitely not my friend.

CHAPTER 15

DEAD AND FROZEN

I parked my bike a block away from the Rex, in a back alley behind one of the Dumpsters. I pulled out my phone; Aaron had told me to call him as soon as I arrived.

He answered on the first ring.

"Tell me you got me my window," I said.

I heard the tension in Aaron's breathing. "Yes. You've got inside an hour." There was a pause on his end. "I'd feel a hell of a lot better about this if you told me who your contact is."

Yeah, in his case I probably would too. "It's a ghost—one you wouldn't like. I don't like him, but he knows his stuff. He's about the only person—living or dead—who can explain this case. I'd be lying if I said this ghost was safe. Suffice to say the less you know about them the better."

There was another deep breath on Aaron's end. "All right, just let me know as soon as you're done. And tell me what you find this time."

I let the jibe go. I'd tell Aaron what I could, as always. "I'm hoping I won't need the whole hour."

"It would be best if you didn't."

Aaron hung up.

It sounded an awful lot like he was trying to tell me something without telling me something. . . .

I hated it when he did that. I shoved my phone back in my pocket and headed off at a fast walk for the hotel's back entrance.

Whereas the front and interior of the Rex Hotel had had a substantial facelift, the back had pretty well been left in its original state. The brick and mortar was exposed and faded to a dull grey. They hadn't bothered to mend the chips or the cracks in the cement from decades of sink.

The parts of buildings the public isn't supposed to see always tell you the most about them. I guess most things are that way.

At least the old wooden cellar-style doors that led into the basement had been replaced. Someone had had the sense to install metal ones and a decent set of locks.

Luckily for me (or thanks to Aaron) one of the cellar doors was propped open with a rock. I checked around the alley to make sure no one was skulking or watching me from the windows above before sliding inside. I closed the door gently behind me. I headed down the steps, careful to keep my boots light so the old wood didn't creak. The smell of stale beer mixed with bleach hit my nose, just like the last time I'd been here—along with something else. The cold. I surveyed what was left of the yellow-taped crime scene.

"Hello?" I said, loudly enough for someone in the near vicinity to hear me but not enough for it to carry far. Aaron might have been able to thin the herd of cops but not to clear the place out. There was no way he had that much power—or that many favours. Sarah maybe, but I was hoping to leave her out of the paranormal fray.

I held perfectly still and listened carefully to the distant footsteps above. The pub was closed, so it must be the officers left on scene or maybe the owners moving chairs upstairs. Nothing to be alarmed about, I decided.

I shook my head. I couldn't get rid of the feeling that someone was watching me.

Okay, Kincaid, stop being scared of the shadows and get back to work.

As I reached the last step, I pulled up my Otherside sight and took a look around the basement.

The scene itself hadn't changed, except that where Jacob's body used to be there was now an outline, not drawn in chalk but left by frost. My guess was no one had been willing to cross the police tape to mark it out. The ring of yellow police tape around the still-frosted area supported my suspicion.

A quick look with my Otherside sight showed that the Otherside dust was still there. I'd have to push Aaron to bring a bag of rock salt down.

Time to bring in the expert.

I pulled out a set compact mirror from my backpack. *Gideon?*, I wrote with a china marker, and waited.

The air around me chilled and I watched the fog coalesce in front of me as Gideon's translucent form took shape.

"You're late," he said.

Yeah, that was often a sticking point with me. . . . I nodded towards the tape. "That's it, the crime scene. Knock yourself out— all I could afford was an hour."

To his credit, he immediately turned his attention towards the crime scene.

"Whoa, are you sure you want to step there? Never mind . . ."

I crossed my arms and fell silent as Gideon approached the tape, strode through it, and crouched down in the middle of the frost and Otherside dust. His eyes stayed a ghost grey and his features took on a concentrated look as he reached out and ran his fingers along the frosted floor.

I couldn't help myself. I cringed as the Otherside dust swirled up into the air around him, shimmering through his translucent form.

"This is quite the show," he said, more to himself than to me. Somehow he managed to pick the dust up on his non-corporeal fingers, and rubbed it between them. "This Otherside has definitely been warped to freeze things on contact, so much so it no longer shows any affinity at all for the barrier. It's completely cut off—most likely the work of sorcery."

"Fantastic. So it's powerful." That was not the conclusion I'd hoped for.

Gideon glanced up at me and arched a ghost-grey eyebrow. "It certainly wants us to believe it's very powerful—anyone who knows to look for Otherside, that is." He went back to considering the Otherside powder on his hand. "Which is why I'm suspicious."

I frowned. "It froze a man in no time flat and managed to bind his ghost to his corpse. Based on the fact that my seance went to hell as soon as I really pushed to get to Damien's ghost, I figure Damien's stuck in the same state. And that happened almost twenty years ago." I pointed at the scene. "If that takes power to generate and the wraith needs to kill people to recharge, shouldn't it be leaving a trail of corpsicles?"

"You explained the circumstances to me already, and yes, there should be a trail of frozen corpses." He glanced around the basement. "If this ghost is so powerful, don't you think it odd how easily you were able to unbind its most recent victim?"

I paused. I hadn't thought about that at all, to be honest.

"If I bound a victim's ghost to a body," Gideon continued, "you can be certain you wouldn't have been able to undo it with a sea urchin. I suggest that you've concerned yourself so much with the *what* in this case that you've ignored the *how* and *why*."

"That's completely not true. I've been racking my brain trying to figure out why it killed Jacob."

Gideon made a *tsk*ing noise and gestured with the hand that was covered in Otherside dust. He spoke in Latin, his voice deep enough it carried through the room, reverberating through my bones.

The dust burst into shards of light, just as it had when Nate had thrown salt on it back at the apartment.

"I would also be asking yourself why the show if the ghost of the spirit you tried to call was truly bound. If it wanted to hurt you, it could simply have continued draining you during the seance. No, it wanted to frighten you." He stood up, and the Otherside dust swirled and settled around him, returning to its inert state.

"How did you do that?" I asked.

He inclined his head to the side, as if caught up in his own thoughts. "Much more easily than I should have been able to," he said.

Before I could ask him to elaborate, he turned his ghostly grey-blue eyes on me and said, "Instead of a lesson today, you can think on this: yes, wraiths exist, but they are undead monsters stuck between this world and the next and because of that are starved for Otherside."

He walked towards me, and didn't stop until I could feel the cold coming off his face, only a few inches away from mine.

"Imagine being dead and tied to your corpse, but unlike a zombie or a ghoul, your spirit isn't bound—not entirely—and because of that you have a greater affinity for the Otherside, and an ability to use it, more so than the most talented undead and strongest poltergeists. Dead, but still able to use the abilities others lose when they die."

What I would have given to step back—but I didn't. I wasn't going to give Gideon the satisfaction. I wetted my lips. "There's always a price," I said.

Gideon almost smiled. "The price? Your very essence is constantly called towards the Otherside, an unyielding pull that reaches into the very core of your being. You crave Otherside like nothing ever before—you *feed* on it—but the source is the one thing in the world you can't reach. Not from here, not ever, not even after you're finally separated from your corpse." He leaned in, his eyes glittering.

I held my breath and clenched my fists. I would not let him see me scared. . . .

"So strong is the desperation that it drives you mad, and you turn to the only source of Otherside you can find this side: *death*."

I shuddered but still didn't step back or look away.

"So desperate does the craving for Otherside make you that eventually it eats away at your self-control until all you can do is drain the life out of everything around you." Gideon took a step back and the air warmed up.

"How many do they kill?" I asked.

"Entire villages and towns in a matter of days without a sorcerer or a very adept practitioner to deal with them. Luckily, it takes a sorcerer to make a proper wraith, and as a practice we frown on it, unless a sorcerer is good enough they can maintain control."

"Could you?" I said before my verbal filter could kick into gear.

Gideon just looked at me, his face unreadable. I was starting to think that was the more dangerous expression. . . .

"Yes," he finally said, spitting the word at me. "With enough preparation." He glanced back at the crime scene and when he looked at me again, his eyes were black flecked with gold. "But I'm not convinced this is a wraith, not even one controlled by a practitioner. Twenty years? No one could control a wraith that long. No, I believe this is something else. But I'm not ready to speculate. Not until I know more."

"So what now? We leave it to kill people until it screws up enough that you figure out what the hell it is?"

Gideon regarded me blankly again.

Shut your mouth, Kincaid.

But his eyes were their normal ghost grey. I took in a breath and turned back to the police tape, where the Otherside dust had been swirling moments before.

"Kincaid, do you know what a con artist's greatest tool is?"

Hunh? "Ah—manipulation. They figure out what your weaknesses are, try to make friends with you, work their way into your life . . ."

"Misdirection," Gideon said. His eyes narrowed. "Now, where have you been misled, Kincaid?" Before I could answer, he lifted his head. "Someone's coming. Deal with them. I've given you enough to work with for now. Don't get yourself killed."

"Oh, come on—"

But Gideon had already dissolved. I shook my head.

I heard the cellar door creak open upstairs. Probably one of the policemen guarding the scene . . .

Except I heard the distinct click of heels descending the stairs. Definitely not a police officer. I swivelled, re-examining the room. Hiding spot, hiding spot, where are you? Crates? No, too obvious. Storage room? Too many horror films.

The footsteps were getting closer. I ducked behind the stairs. Not a hiding spot exactly, but the stairs offered some shadows and a good vantage point through the steps.

A woman in white heels came into view. As she descended, she carefully placed her feet so that the heels wouldn't get caught between the cracks in the wooden boards. She wore an elegant white peacoat and white jeans. A bold choice considering the morning's rain.

She alighted off the last step and I got a good look at her face. Mindy.

I moved into the light. "Mindy—what are you doing here?"

It took her a second to register me and when she did, she smiled. But like a certain ghost, it didn't reach her eyes.

"Cole wasn't very happy after you left. Doesn't think I should have let you in." She trailed her fingers along the wood beam. Despite the elegant clothes, she looked the worse for wear since our last encounter. "Think this is original?" she asked.

"Tell Cole I apologized," I started.

"You didn't answer my question." She continued staring at the greyed wood beam, caressing it as if it were artwork.

I shrugged. "I guess. Why put in a new beam when the customers don't come down here?"

"Because this is Seattle and things rot. The rot gets into the wood and years later you find out that it hasn't been supporting weight for half a decade." She looked away from the wall, fixing her eyes on me. "What do you think they do when that happens?"

Oh yeah, Mindy was definitely giving off the unhinged vibe. "Try to replace it?"

"Sometimes. And other times, if the wood isn't completely rotted through, they'll try to treat it with chemicals until it's barely a wooden beam anymore. But it'll hold the weight, whatever it is. For a while."

She traced her fingernails in a pattern along the edge of the wood, and her eyes glazed over. I pulled up my Otherside sight just in case, but there was nothing there, no bindings, no Otherside dust. Only Mindy, with the normal ghost-grey cast.

Her eyes cleared. "I made a phone call after you came over. You don't really work for the SPD."

"I contract. Case by case."

She let out a wry laugh. "You're as good at bending the truth as Nathan was. Did you learn it from him?" She took a few more steps into the basement, towards me. I stayed where I was. She wasn't using Otherside—I didn't think she could—but given the unstable vibe, I was on my guard. There were a lot of ways this could go.

"What are you doing here?" I asked.

She shrugged and pulled out a cigarette. She took her time lighting it and taking the first drag. "Curious. And I wanted to talk to you. Off the record, away from Cole. Private, like."

Up close I could see her eyes were red and puffy. Had she been crying? Or, true to her grunge radio persona, maybe she'd forgone removing last night's makeup. "About what?"

Mindy laughed. "Girl talk."

I waited.

"You really friends with Nate?"

I drew in a breath. "When he pays rent on time."

Mindy choked on the cigarette smoke as she laughed. The cigarette shook between her fingers. "Fuck you, Kincaid Strange, and I mean that." She covered her mouth to cough, but I caught the bitterness in her eyes.

"Yes, we're friends."

"The shows—like the one on YouTube. Is that him or you?"

Him—especially that last one, the impromptu grunge concert bowl disaster at the university. "It's always his call. He never has to do the gigs if he doesn't want to."

"He's not bound or something else bad, is he?" she asked.

I took a gamble. "You can ask him yourself." Once I got him out of Cameron's body, that is . . .

Mindy gave me a hard look before dropping her cigarette and crushing it under the toe of her white shoe.

"Cole looked into you too. And Nate," she added after a moment.

I took a step back. "Yeah, and what did he find?"

She smiled and the corners of her eyes crinkled. The first real smile I think I'd seen out of her. "That the SPD would be mighty unimpressed that you were hanging out here right now."

I flinched. She was right about that. "Nathan's notebook, the one I asked you about. Did you find it?" I asked.

Her smile widened. "You mean his unrecorded songs?" She laughed. "Yeah, I know what's in there. Figured I'd sold them? No, don't answer that. Do you think I'd be here if I planned on doing that?"

I changed course. "What happened to Damien?"

She wasn't stupid. "Tell me, you think Nate's the only one who ever made a deal with the devil?"

I knew better than to ask outright if she'd made a deal. "What would your price be—back then?"

The smile faded. "Easy. Make me famous—a fucking famous groupie. I was a fucking idiot of a girl. Can you think of a better way to waste my youth?" She laughed again and this time it didn't sound altogether sane. "Can you imagine that? Not pretty or tall enough to be a model, not talented enough to act, but interesting enough so that guys who wrote songs about being depressed fawned over me. Twenty years later it's made me the reigning radio queen of all things grunge nostalgia."

"From where I'm standing, you're doing a hell of a lot better than Damien."

Her mouth twisted and she bared her teeth. "Now *that* you're right about." As an afterthought she added, "And I already told you, if anyone stood to gain off Damien's death, it was Nate and the rest of his band."

From Nate's account, Eloch had orchestrated if not caused Damien's death. He saw Mindy as an innocent witness of the murder and unknowing caretaker of his unrecorded songs—and now she was doubling down on Nate as the cause of Damien's death. What if her link was more sinister, and more participatory? It wasn't every day a demon came threatening at your door.

She turned to leave, but paused before ascending the stairs. "And tell your cop friend to stay out of my affairs—and Cole's." The way she separated their names gave me pause.

"What does Cole have to hide?"

"And I don't need to talk to Nate. He doesn't need to see me like this. I'd rather he remember—" She shook her head and laughed. "You know, it doesn't matter what I'd like him to remember." Her face hardened. "What you can tell him is, if he doesn't want things to get worse, he should pay his debts. That's what's got us all here, isn't it? Even you."

I went cold. "Mindy, what do you know about Eloch?"

Another strange twist to her lips. "I know the last thing Nate should be worrying about is that damned notebook full of old songs. They aren't what the demon wants."

She knew about Eloch. The question was, how much?

She turned her back to me.

"Hey, Mindy?"

She glanced over her shoulder.

"How the hell did you find me?"

There was that smile I didn't like. "Easy. I followed you. And if I can find you—"

I heard a commotion upstairs—feet scuffling over the floors followed by raised voices. The muffled sound of a radio call alerting a potential break-in.

"Cops? Seriously?"

She shrugged. "Wasn't me."

Right.

"Better run, Kincaid Strange." And with that, she disappeared up the stairs. I heard the cellar door clang shut as she left.

I swore. I had to get out of the cops' range before they closed the perimeter. It was a high-traffic area and my bike was a block away.

And the fact that I had done this enough times to know the drill should probably be worrying me more than it was . . .

Voices filtered down. The cops were increasing in numbers. Time to go.

I shoved my mirror in my backpack. Life lesson: don't try to run from cops and security guards with glass in your hand, it doesn't end well. I threw my pack over my shoulder and grabbed my helmet before bolting up the stairs to the cellar doors.

Or that was the plan, anyway.

The sole hanging light flickered as I reached the doors. They wouldn't budge—and they were ice-cold to the touch.

Oh, damn . . . "Gideon?" I said, actually hopeful.

The air around me chilled, more so than I'd ever felt from Gideon's appearances.

Smoke seeped upwards from the shadows of the basement and crawled across the floor until it had wedged between me and the doors. Frost crept up the stairs towards me. A tendril of smoke licked at my feet as if tasting, searching. Otherside dust began to fall on the steps around me.

Of all the lousy times for Nate's demon to track me down . . .

A black entity—not Otherside and not entirely smoke, but smelling of wet ash—coalesced in front of the door. I took another step backwards and reached around into my backpack as the thing gave a low growl. If I didn't know better, I'd have said it was laughing. More smoky tendrils laced with Otherside threads crept up the stairs towards me, leaving a trail of thin ice in their wake.

"Yeah, keep laughing," I muttered, as I palmed what I was looking for. Rule number one when dealing with the dead? Don't fall for the same trick twice. Beat one trick and it takes them a while to come up with a new one . . .

I took another step away from the doors as I screwed the lid off the salt shaker. When I heard the lid click to the floor, I threw the shaker's entire contents at the tendrils and frost collecting around me.

It shrieked loud enough that the wood floor shook. I heard a bang. If the cops hadn't been trying to get down here before, they really were now.

But the salt had the desired effect. The thing's tendrils retreated back into the shadows of the room. Then I heard the commotion behind the mud room door that led to the bar. The cops were mounting their assault.

Exit stage right. I slammed into the double doors before the thing could come back, and for good measure kicked some salt over the threshold. Unlikely it had to use doors, but you never know and the idea of it burning its feet gave me the warm fuzzies.

The mud room door behind me creaked open. I bolted out into the rain . . .

And into the bulk of a cop who was more than happy to catch me. I didn't recognize him; either he was new or Aaron had steered me clear of him. Considering his burly frame, my bet was on the latter. In my experience, the type of cop hired for brawn, not brains, is usually the kind looking for an excuse to be offended.

I kept my mouth shut as the door of the police car that was parked at the end of the alley opened and none other than Captain Marks stepped out.

Every bone in my body tensed. Not only hadn't I expected Marks, but we had about as abysmal a history as it gets. He made his opinion about practitioners very public. *Snake oil salesmen* and *con artists* were terms he favoured, and those were the polite ones. He'd tried to arrest me the first chance he'd got, then threw my history with my father and my mother's supposedly accidental death in my face. He'd got just the kind of reaction he'd hoped for.

The only reason I'd escaped assault charges was he'd gone well beyond reasonable interrogation methods. He'd let me go, but I had no illusions; he was an asshole and biding his time. I was already a criminal in his books, and guilty as hell.

"Why, Ms. Kincaid Strange." He made a show of looking around. "What a surprise seeing someone of your spotless reputation trespassing on a crime scene."

For once I was smart and didn't respond.

He looked way too chipper for my peace of mind. He nodded to the cop gripping both my arms from behind and wrenching my shoulders—probably an illegal move, but hey, when there aren't any witnesses . . .

He opened the car's back door. "Hop in. You're coming with us."

"Why?" I winced.

Mouth shut, Kincaid.

But Captain Marks just smiled. "For questioning on paranormal activity. Since you are a practitioner and this is a paranormal crime scene."

I decided arguing was only going to get me beaten up—which, interestingly enough, doesn't help you, and makes you look more guilty. So I did about the only thing I could.

I shook off Burly, walked over to where Marks held the door ajar and climbed into the back seat. The door slammed behind me.

I was going to have a fantastic time explaining this to Aaron—and come to think of it, he had some explaining to do as well.

CHAPTER 16

JAIL . . . AGAIN

Why, whenever I tried to help Aaron out, did I somehow manage to end up in jail? This was the second time in three weeks. It was a new dynamic in our relationship we'd have to work on. But first I had to deal with my best friend in law enforcement, Captain Marks.

At least this time I wasn't in a jail cell. I was in an interview room . . . or interrogation room, if I let my inner pessimist do the talking.

Stupid on Marks's part. He wasn't ready to arrest me yet, which meant he didn't have anything concrete. That, and he'd got in enough trouble from the higher-ups about our last encounter that he had to be more careful.

No sign of Aaron yet . . .

I'd see if I could keep it that way and handle this myself.

"So tell me, Kincaid. To what do we owe your trespassing escapades today?" Captain Marks asked.

I wrapped my ankles around the chair legs and leaned across the table. They hadn't put me in handcuffs—yet. "Clearly you already have a theory. Why don't we cut to the chase and you tell me?"

He folded his hands and sat back in his chair. "I think I'd rather hear it from you."

There were a few ways I could handle this. Lie through my teeth—never a good idea unless you are a spectacular liar, because you'll only trip yourself up. Or tell the entire truth: that Aaron asked me to peruse the crime scene because I'm the only person in town who knows what the hell they're doing with Otherside. But that would probably get both of us thrown in jail. Or I could go with my old, reliable fallback and tell half the truth. Now *that* I was great at.

I shrugged. "Curiosity. I heard something paranormal happened."

"So you just—what? Decided to let yourself in?"

I shrugged again. "Door was ajar. I popped my head in and called out." Again, completely true. I just hadn't wanted anyone to hear me.

"Then why were you running from a cordoned-off crime scene? One with a potential paranormal biohazard."

Of all the damnable things for Aaron to keep the captain abreast of . . . I raised both my eyebrows. "Scared of the dark."

Sticking my head into a place of business to see if someone was there wasn't a crime. Especially if the cops who'd been tasked with guarding the place had stepped out for a moment . . . He could try to charge me with trespassing, but it wouldn't stick.

The captain's nostrils flared. "You know what I think?" he said. "I think you're involved."

I kept my face impassive. "Why? How?"

"I think paranormal frauds like you feed off the attention your lies get you. I think you're craving it, and I think you're the kind of person who would stoop to murder to get it."

That took me aback. "How— Why on earth would I want to kill someone?"

"A few people die by alleged paranormal means, and once again the Seattle PD is in need of a paranormal investigator. How did you do it? Freeze the body like that?"

If he hadn't sounded so serious, I might have dropped my poker face and laughed out loud. How the hell had this man kept his job as captain of the Seattle PD? Nepotism only went so far. . . . "You think I'm behind a murder and orchestrated an elaborate hoax about cause of death because I can't stand losing my job?"

He smiled at me. It wasn't friendly. "People have killed for less."

That was true. But I hadn't. "You're right, Captain. Charlatans feed off the challenge of lying to people. So do con artists. But you're forgetting one very important thing."

"What's that?"

"I'm the real deal."

I watched his face turn an odd shade of red, which amplified the layers of his double chin. He stood up, and the chair made an ugly scraping noise against the concrete floor.

"How about I just lock you up and throw away the key?"

"Pretty sure you can't."

He gave a noncommittal shrug. "A couple of days if I have reason to think you're implicated in a paranormal crime."

I wondered what had happened to innocent before proven guilty. Guess Captain Marks figured it was easier to throw potential criminals in jail. Just to be on the safe side. "You won't."

He smiled. "What do you think you can do to stop me?"

I shrugged, keeping my body language as non-threatening as possible—a feat for me, all things considered. "Nothing. But I'm pretty sure my lawyer will take it upon herself to sue the pants off you. And win." I looked around and added, "You guys aren't making so much money that you can afford to bring lawsuits down on yourself, unless I'm—"

I stopped speaking as the captain's fist slammed down on the metal table. As fantastic as it felt making him angry, I was pretty sure I'd only dug myself in deeper.

"I'll throw you in holding," Marks hissed.

I snorted. "For what?"

"Twelve hours."

As long as they legally could without charging me under the Paranormal Act, but that applied to holding someone suspected of a crime using paranormal elements until an expert could be brought in; it wasn't for tossing practitioners in jail at random.

It took everything I had to keep my mouth shut. No way in hell was I leaving Nate alone for twelve hours on his own, not in his deteriorating state. If the lines destabilized, he could end up paralyzed and stranded on the spare bedroom floor—or, worse, he could go feral.

"Fine—you win. What is it you want to know?"

"I want to know how you killed that guy," the captain said.

I stared at him. "Why would I kill him? For what?"

But the captain just leaned against the table and crossed his arms. "Maybe by the letter of the law you're not guilty. I don't really care. Any excuse to keep someone as dangerous as you off the street for twelve hours is a win in my mind. I'm doing my job."

I knew the captain hated practitioners and the paranormal, but this was—well . . . "Do you have any idea how illegal that is?"

He looked me up and down. "Who do you think people are going to believe, Strange, you or me?"

He slammed his fist against the table three times. The door opened and Burly appeared. I didn't say a word as he grasped my arm and led me out, my head spinning. This wasn't just the captain's grudge against practitioners, this was personal, and it was crazy. It wasn't an honest attempt to keep a criminal off the streets; it was outright prejudice.

I waited until we were halfway down the hall and hopefully out of Marks's hearing range.

"You know you have to give me a phone call?" I said in a low voice.

"No phone calls!" I heard Marks shout after us.

That made Burly nervous. I felt his grip tighten on my arm and saw his jaw clench. I kept going. "Look, your captain can make your life a living hell, I get it. You might even get a real kick out of doing what he wants, or you might hate practitioners as much as he does. You haven't bent the rules too badly yet. But do you really want to find out what happens to cops who deny people their rights?"

He didn't say anything, but there was a new hesitation in his walk. I licked my lips and gave it one last try.

"Notice the captain isn't around for this. Wonder why? Probably because he doesn't want to be implicated in any wrongdoing, and from what I hear, the captain tends not to interfere when you lower-downs get disciplined. Not much of a helping hand, him—"

Burly spun on me. "All right, you can have your phone call. Just stop talking at me."

He changed directions and deposited me in front of a phone before retreating. Not out of sight, but far enough to give me a modicum of privacy.

I hesitated over the keys. One phone call. Who could I get to check on Nate? Not Aaron, Mork or Sarah, and I wasn't about to pull out a mirror and ask Gideon . . .

Lee. It would have to be Lee. And if I was really lucky, I could hit two birds with one stone.

I dialled and waited three rings. Pick up, Lee . . .

"Hello."

I breathed out with relief. "Lee, thank god you picked up. Listen, before you start yelling at me for calling, you're still my lawyer, right?"

I counted three full seconds before Lee responded. "Yes."

Less than enthused, but I'd take it.

"Thank god. Look, I can't give you any details over the phone, but I need you to get me out of jail and check up on Nate—preferably in that order, but I'll take what I can get at this point."

"Time's up," Burly said.

I covered the receiver and frowned at him. "That was barely a minute," I said.

"What has happened?" Lee said. Bless my heart, she actually sounded concerned.

"Detention without cause under the Paranormal Act. Apparently they can hold me for twelve hours."

There was a hiss on the other end. Lee was not a fan of the Paranormal Act or any laws that she felt overreached the intent of

law. Like the Chinese head tax that had been little more than a
cash grab, the Paranormal Act was much too easily abused.

"I will deal with this myself," Lee said. "I need to make a few
phone calls. I will also look in on Nate. You can expect to be released
within the next two hours."

I didn't know who was about to be on the listening end of Lee's
shouting, but I was very glad it wasn't me.

"Time's up," Burly said again, glancing over his shoulder.

"Fine, almost done," I said to him, then whispered into the
receiver, "Lee, thank you!"

I didn't catch her response as Burly grabbed the receiver,
slammed it down and helped me away from the phone.

He escorted me down the long, silent hall to a cell at the end—
one I'd been in before, without any reflective surfaces. I held my
breath while the cop locked me inside. Funny, when you're being
locked up and you know there's a reason, that's one thing—that I
can take. It's an entirely different matter when they're sticking you
in jail because they can. Especially when they know you haven't
done a damn thing.

Burly gave me a once-over, as if assessing whether I might pose
a threat or required more intimidation. Then he turned around
and left.

I sat on the bench and shivered, rubbing my arms, as a chill ran
through me. Unfortunately, this time I was pretty sure it was only
my imagination and the cold bench that conjured the dropping
temperature. I didn't know quite how to feel about the fact that the
dead were the ones my subconscious counted on to come to my
aid when the chips were down. And here I thought I already had
enough to worry about.

✳

It took him half an hour. I felt the familiar chill in the air before
the Otherside fog began to coalesce.

For once, I preferred Gideon's brand of verbal assholery, at least to the assholes on the other side of the bars.

"Here you are. In jail. Again." He crossed his legs and leaned back against the brick wall, feigning closed eyes. Ghosts don't see with their eyes. The organs are long gone, so they get an impression of the real world through memory and Otherside. Closing their eyes is just an affectation, like breathing, or yawning. Either out of habit or to lull you into a false sense of familiarity. In Gideon's case, I was going with the latter. . . .

"Why do I get the distinct impression that you could have helped me back there—or at least warned me the police were on their way?"

"Because I consider independence a virtue. I don't like to step in until it's necessary."

He had a point. What did I say to that?

"They only have you on trespassing," Gideon continued. "And the zombie Lee Ling will likely get you out."

I didn't want to know how he'd familiarized himself with the details of my unjust incarceration. "*Likely?*" I asked.

Gideon opened his eyes and looked at me. "Well, we wouldn't have any fun if outcomes were always a certainty. Life wouldn't be nearly so interesting if you couldn't end up dead."

"It's not exactly a mystery. Last time I checked, death was the final destination."

"The *when*, dear, is where the fun is. The devil is in the details."

I dropped my head back against the brick.

"What have we learned this time?" Gideon said, raising his voice.

After half an hour in the jail cell, my filter had deactivated. "You're an asshole who's enjoying watching me rot in jail?"

"We already knew I find your missteps mildly entertaining. Try again."

I let out a long breath. "That I stepped on someone's toes. That's the only reason I'm in here."

He nodded. "Good. Whose?"

"Mindy's. She was the one who showed up and probably called the cops."

Gideon inclined his head. "Possible. A little unhinged to be orchestrating all this, though."

I half-mounted an argument in my head but let it go. He had a point. "The captain."

"He certainly has it in for you. If the wraith was going to do us any favours on its killing spree, it could start by killing him."

"Watch it."

"What? I'm only being practical. Final destination, remember?"

"It's the *when*."

Gideon smiled. It might have been the first real smile I'd ever seen on him. "The captain certainly has a bone to pick with you, but he's more concerned about dead bodies turning up in your city. He knows it's not you, though he'd like you to take the fall. Who else?"

"Cole."

"Now, he strikes me as interesting. Quiet, out of the way, satisfied to ride her coattails." He switched focus. "Why did she follow you there, of all places?"

"I have no idea. She said she wanted 'girl talk.' Whatever the hell that's supposed to be. And she delivered a message for Nate to pay his debts, but I can't be sure she wasn't just playing yet another game."

"That she wanted to speak with you is the one thing you can take at face value. But you're missing something."

For the moment I wasn't concerned with the fact Gideon had obviously listened in. "What?"

"What kind of teacher would I be if I told you?"

"One with a living student. I don't know if you realize this, but I'm in a jail cell and this wraith is killing people."

"I have faith you'll figure it out. If not, well, I'll have to decide if I can use an assistant who doesn't live up to expectations or . . ."

He stopped and tilted his head to the side as we both heard footsteps in the hall. Gideon vanished just before Aaron came into view in front of the cell bars.

"Well, fancy running into you here. I'd offer you a seat and drink, but as you can see . . ." I said.

He didn't look happy as he checked behind him and leaned into the bars. "I told you to be careful."

"And you said I had an hour."

Aaron closed his eyes. "What happened?"

Briefly, I told him about Mindy's surprise appearance and the wraith's attack, but not her message to Nate.

That seemed to mollify him. Incompetence was one thing; a potential suspect slinking around the crime scene and calling the cops on me . . . well, that was something else entirely.

"What did she want?"

I wasn't clear on that but didn't have to tell Aaron that now. "Get me out first and I'll tell you."

"It doesn't work like that."

"Fine, then you get to share first."

Aaron frowned, but he acquiesced. "Something that points towards Mindy. Files from about ten years back. I'm not sharing more until I have a chance to confirm. It might be nothing." He glanced around at my cell. "I can't promise anything, Kincaid, but I'll try my best to get you out before the twelve hours are up."

Getting me my job back, getting me out of jail for helping him—Aaron was doing an awful lot of trying without many results. From where I was standing, I knew better than to say that. "Aaron, I can't do anything from in here. No contacting the Otherside, no investigating the deaths. While I'm in here, you're on your own," I said.

Aaron didn't dignify that with an answer. He turned and left. I felt bad for a moment, before the anger won out again.

Once again the air beside me chilled.

"Now that is the mark of a complication," Gideon said as he re-formed beside me.

"The fact that I'm in jail is the complication I'm concerned about."

Gideon continued as if I hadn't said anything. "I know the type. Caught in between doing the right thing and following orders."

He looked at me. "I'll give you some insight. In the end, they convince themselves their orders *are* the right thing."

The accounts of Gideon's trial came to mind before I pushed them back down. "Aaron isn't going to send me up the river."

"And the fact that you're in love with him is already causing problems."

I didn't say anything.

Gideon watched me before raising his ghostly grey eyebrows. "Ah, my mistake. The fact that you are *not* in love with him anymore is the source of discord between you."

Of all the times for Gideon to pay attention to what I did and didn't say . . .

"You crossed a boundary, ghost."

"Not if this little issue might get you killed."

"Look, Aaron isn't going to kill me. For the most part he's been trying to keep me out of the captain's sights, not in them. He's my friend."

Whatever had been the inspiration for Gideon's jovial mood, it was gone now. His lip curled. "You'd be surprised how quickly things like that change." For a moment I thought he was going to add something, but he only shrugged. "Keep the man, leave the man, just make up your mind before you tangle the web between you even more. Those relationships always end messily."

An uncomfortable silence stretched between us. Gideon broke it. "I've decided this is as good as any exercise in sorcery I could have devised. Figure out what's going on with the so-called wraith and stop it."

"Gideon—"

"And don't fail. I'll bail you out only so many times, assistant, before I decide it isn't worth the effort. Remember that."

I watched as he dissolved into Otherside fog and disappeared.

I shook my head. Why did he always have to end on a sociopathic, homicidal note?

But he did have a point: someone had aimed Mindy in my direction. Who, how and why?

An awkward throat-clearing sound jerked me out of my own thoughts.

I glanced up. It was Burly again, standing on the other side of the bars, tense and avoiding eye contact even more than last time.

He cleared his throat again. "Sorry for rushing your phone call, Ms. Strange. That was, ah, very unbecoming of me," he said.

Oh, I could smell Lee in that syntax from a mile away. I'd hate to know who she'd lambasted for it to have reached all the way to Burly. . . . The one thing that works on bullies to make them behave? Another bully.

He opened the cell door for me and stepped back a respectable distance. I nodded at him politely. Antagonizing a bully while he's down is also not a wise course of action.

I collected my things from the front desk and took a quick look around the station. There was no sign of Aaron or Captain Marks. Perfect.

I headed outside as fast as I could. It was late afternoon now. My phone had died, but I could tell it was coming on evening—5 p.m., maybe 6 . . .

Pulled up at the curb was an old antique Ford from the 1940s. Beautifully restored and maintained, with tinted windows. If that didn't scream zombie . . . I shook my head and slid inside. Lee herself was waiting in the back.

"Let me guess. You had a lovely discussion with the captain," I said.

She arched one of her perfectly drawn black eyebrows at me. "No. The mayor."

Apparently Lee's talons were deeply sunk into modern-day Seattle. . . . The captain was the mayor's brother-in-law, and had been hired by him personally. Oh, if only they knew that the lawyer who had bullied them with legalese into letting me go *twice* now was the infamous zombie queen of Underground Seattle . . .

"How much of this is going to blow back on me?" I asked.

Lee bowed her head. "A substantial amount. I imagine the captain will not appreciate the attention he has drawn to himself today.

I suppose he will try in the very near future to take it out of you."

"Out *on* me."

"No, I believe he will try to take it out of you. In strips of flesh."

Great. Fucking fantastic. At least I wasn't in a cell anymore. . . .

I glanced over at Lee again, who was dressed in an expensive, well-tailored suit. Her scars were expertly concealed behind a thick layer of cosmetics—hard to see even up close, unless you knew to look for them. "Don't take this the wrong way, Lee, but I was not expecting to see you here."

She pursed her red-lacquered lips as she examined me. Lee wasn't the sympathetic type, but she was always thorough with her work as my lawyer. She was making sure I hadn't been roughed up.

After a moment she tapped on the back of the front seat. The car started. "You need to see something," Lee said.

"Fine, but I need to see Nate first."

She turned her borrowed green eyes on me and fixed me with a piercing gaze. "In this case they are one and the same."

I sat back. The words were congenial enough, but the steel running underneath was disconcerting. I sighed. "Fine, just swing by the Rex first so I can grab my bike, okay?" I said, and crossed my fingers that my sole mode of transportation would still be waiting for me where I'd hidden it.

Lee inclined her head, the only signal that she acquiesced, leaving me to my own thoughts. Her ominous statement regarding Nate overshadowed the questionable state of my bike. When the queen of the zombies says you need to do something, it's usually serious.

CHAPTER 17

DEAD AND BURIED

I crossed my arms and did my best
to pretend I wasn't upset. I didn't think it was working. I'm a practitioner, I practise voodoo, so a little déjà vu is par for the course,
but this was too much even for me.

Well, on the bright side, my bike had been where I'd left it. . . .
Silver linings?

"How long?" I asked.

Mork and Lee both looked at me.

"How long does Nate have?" I repeated, and gestured at Nate,
who was sitting on my kitchen table. His shirt was off, exposing the
festering gash on Cameron's torso—my handiwork from two weeks
ago, courtesy of my Civil War–era amputation blade.

The wound was black. Which meant that, despite the formaldehyde, it was rotting and taking the surrounding tissue with it.

I'd watched Mork treat it with another formaldehyde bath and
now he was covering it with a bandage.

"I'm trying a different mix of embalming fluid over this," Mork
said. "But I don't know if it'll halt the rot. I mean, once those

flesh-eating bacteria get in, nothing kills them. It's like they're the universe's answer to zombie overpopulation. . . ."

Lee hissed.

Mork shook his head as he held the bandage in place. Despite me not being here when he'd arrived he'd still had the decency to take his cowboy hat off inside my apartment. He'd be almost non-descript if not for the clothes and messy brown hair.

"I wouldn't give him more than a week," he said. "Two if the embalming fluid kicks in and beats the rot back, but it's extremely unlikely. I'd recommend burning."

I made a face. "I'm not burning Nate."

Mork shrugged. "You asked for my professional opinion and I'm answering."

"Hey, both of you—I'm right here," Nate started. "Ow! Hey, grunge star cowboy, that hurts!"

Mork glanced up at him as he began stitching the bandage onto the un-rotted flesh. "You're dead. You have been for twenty years. Suck it up."

I ran my hand through my hair. Lee was being awful silent through all this. "Well, what happens after a week—or two weeks if we're being optimistic?"

Mork shook his head. "No way, this is as far as I get dragged into your shit show, Strange."

Lee barked something at him in Chinese.

Mork just shook his head. "Your problem, Lee." He finished the last stitch and began packing up his leather bag.

Lee pursed her lips and gestured towards my bedroom with her chin.

Nate must have caught sight of it. "K?"

"Just stay there." I held the door open for Lee then closed it behind me. "All right, what's so bad about what happens next that you don't want to talk about it in front of Nate?"

"Get the sorcerer involved now," Lee said.

I crossed my arms. "What happens?"

Lee tensed and I glimpsed the shadow of a scar underneath the makeup. "If it was up to me and there were not extenuating circumstances, I would have Nathan Cade in his current state put down."

I froze. Dangerous zombies are typically banished to the third levels. Only in extreme circumstances are they ordered by Lee put down. It took me a moment to recover. "He's not dangerous," I said, carefully.

Lee gave a slight nod. "No, but for how much longer will that be the case? He is not a true zombie and he is not a bound ghost. It is a tentative state with no balance of Otherside. It makes me nervous."

My first inclination is usually to push and argue. But Lee wasn't mincing words with me. Her recommendation was going against her rules that both protected zombies and contained them. Yes, Nate was stable at the moment, but if he went feral and was discovered? It put everyone at risk.

"Give me another couple days, Lee."

Her nostrils flared.

"Lee, I can't get Nate out until I take care of whatever is after him. You heard him. The only reason he didn't end up bound was luck."

"One day, Kincaid. After that, get the sorcerer involved or I will. You will not like my methods."

Lee opened the door to my bedroom and let herself out. She barked a command to Mork and the two of them left. I stepped outside my front door to watch them head to the elevator. One of my floormates—no idea what his name was and didn't care—was getting out of the elevator as Lee was getting in. He did a double take and choked on his coffee.

We didn't live in an environment where you saw women dressed like Lee . . . let alone hanging out with, well, Mork.

"Yeah, I so wish I was a ghost so I could still hear the laundry room convos. That run-in is going to be a doozy. They're definitely going to think you're a hooker now, or maybe a dominatrix," Nate murmured.

I turned to find him looking over my shoulder into the hall as the elevator closed, my neighbour still staring.

I shoved him back inside before the gawker turned his attention our way.

"I'm guessing the conversation did not go well," Nate said.

"Sit," I said, and waited for Nate to take the chair across from me at the table. I started to fill him in on what had happened, including the parts about Mindy.

"It's not her, K," Nate said, shaking his head. "Mindy is a lot of things, but she wouldn't set you up to get arrested."

"She practically admitted to it. Nate, you don't know her anymore."

"I do, I see her—"

"No. You occasionally watch her. It's not the same thing. All you've been doing is fuelling your own fantasies. It's what ghosts do." I decided to broach a topic I'd been avoiding. "Why do you think she never reached out to you?"

Nate glanced up from his hands and frowned at me. "What do you mean? I'm dead. I've been dead twenty years."

I stood up and went to fill the kettle. "And you've been working with me for over a year now."

"Still not seeing the point here."

"My point is, why hasn't Mindy ever called, or at least e-mailed?"

"Maybe she's asking the same thing about me."

Why hasn't he/she called me? Maybe they're waiting to see if I'll call first? Maybe they're just shy? It was the script of every high school romance ever, and it was being played out in my kitchen. . . .

"I mean, maybe, just possibly, she isn't the same person you remember from twenty years ago. You haven't changed, but that doesn't mean she falls into that same equation." There. That was about as nicely as I could put it.

"She's got all my stuff," Nate said.

I nodded. "Yup." It wasn't exactly Nate's fault. He was a ghost, and ghosts obsess about their old lives. What is it I always say about ghosts? The first thing they try to do is take all their stuff with them . . . or in Nate's case, never stop trying to take it back.

The kettle finished boiling, so I made my tea and took it back to the table. Where Nate was now glaring at me.

"Look, when I was at her apartment, I asked her if she wanted to talk to you. She threw a tumbler full of vodka at me. Good vodka, too, from the look of it. The glass wasn't cheap either. That was about when Cole walked in."

Nate stared at me. "You're lying."

I shook my head. "No, Nate. You'd know if I was lying. Even trapped in a zombie body, you'd still know."

Nate slammed his fists on the table. "K, for once you just don't understand."

I sipped my tea and waited patiently. How many times had I had this same kind of conversation with my mother? Maybe that was why I was so calm about it. Acknowledge their belief—however deluded it might be—and then, while they present their reasoning and logic, confront them with the realities they can't deny. Like, in Mom's case, the fact that she was sporting a black eye on her way home from the hospital with a compound fracture.

"I understand more than you think, Nate. She's built her entire life, her entire reputation on being your girlfriend, and yet she wants nothing to do with you."

I let that one sit, and calmly waited as Nate stewed in front of me.

"It sucks," I continued. "And to me, at least, it raises a lot of questions as to what kind of person she's become." I didn't say "is" because that would take Nate to a place I didn't want him—where he'd feel honour bound to defend Mindy. "She might play the grieving girlfriend, but she's not. Not anymore, at least." Again, I needed to keep it current, not in the past. That always gets you into trouble. The past brings up memories of romantic dates, and thoughtful birthday presents, and late night conversations. . . . The thing is, abusive husbands and sociopathic girlfriends usually don't start out that way.

Like most ghosts, Nate didn't have a lot of friends. I don't think he had many while he was alive. He put on a lot of bravado, but when he let you in, he was vulnerable.

"You don't know her like I do."

I put my cup down and met his eyes. "No. I know her better than you. I'm the only one out of the two of us who has spoken to her in the last twenty years. She's not the same person you knew. No one you knew is the same. Except for you."

Nate looked as if I'd struck him, and I felt like a heel.

"Nate, look, I'm . . ." But any apology I could muster would ring hollow. I couldn't be sorry. Ghosts don't learn, they can't create. For the most part, they're destined to live out their afterlife as the exact same person they were when they died, making the same mistakes over and over again.

That's why I gave Nate such a long lead to hang himself with, that's why I put up with his outbursts and irresponsibility. Nate couldn't help repeating his mistakes. And I hated watching him go through it, every time. Yet I did.

He stood up, violently shoving the chair back. I didn't flinch. I'd seen worse from my mother over the years. Usually those conversations had ended up with something being thrown.

"Why are you being such an asshole about this, K?"

I didn't take the bait. To Nate, the reality was I was being an asshole. "Because I don't know who or what is behind the wraith yet. All I have are a handful of suspects, a twenty-year-old murder paired with a brand new one, and the only ghost I still have access to is you. What I do know is that someone sent Mindy to find me at the Rex, and I need to find out who that is."

He lowered his head as he trailed off. "She wouldn't be involved. Not if she didn't have to be."

I thought back to my conversation with her at the Rex. I wasn't so sure about that.

Where to start, though?

"We need to find out who this Eloch really is and why it's taken him twenty years to reappear. I need you to bring me back to the original mirror, where you contacted the ghost." Bindings, like the ones used to set a mirror, are personal; every practitioner develops their own style and patterns. Paranormal or not, Eloch would have his own style and patterns. If we could find the original mirror maybe I could learn something.

"The Cage? It's a rundown building. It might not even be there anymore."

"No harm in finding out," I said. Find the patterns. As Gideon had said, Eloch wanted us to think he was powerful—but at the end of the day, it had been easy for him to get rid of the Otherside dust.

The mirror was where it had all started. And it was likely that's where Eloch made his first mistakes . . .

I threw Nate a hoodie, one I'd had the foresight to douse with an incredibly strong teen fragrance in a can, then grabbed my own jacket, a bag of sage from the kitchen and a box of salt. "At this point, we don't have anything to lose. Unless you want to talk to Gideon?"

Nate pulled the bright red sweatshirt over his head. The red made what was still showing of his skin look less yellow . . . or that was my hope.

"For the record, I think this is a really bad idea."

I checked the time on my charged phone before shoving Nate out the front door and down the hall: 8 p.m. "Yeah, well, we're out of the good ones." And we were running out of time.

Here's the thing about cultural cornerstones such as bars or restaurants in a city like Seattle: either they change with the times, as the Rex had, or they start to rot. The Cage, Nate's old hangout from the mid-nineties, fit the latter description. Between the gentrification and rent hikes that drove the students and dive-bar regulars out of the area, and a fire that gutted the place in the late 2000s, the Cage had worn out its welcome. Insurance claims battles and loss of a liquor licence had been the final nails in the coffin. Now the bar was a condemned money pit, boarded up and visited by the odd security guard to chase out squatters.

Luckily for us, judging by the stained and bedbug-ridden mattresses and sleeping bags we saw stacked outside when we drove by the bar, the security guards had given the place a pass in the last few days. I parked my bike a couple of blocks away along a busier street, where it was less likely to be stolen or raise suspicion, and the two of us backtracked on foot. I quickly scanned the back of the building for cameras and any lingering security. Nothing. Apparently it was an important-enough piece of property to chase out the odd squatters but not enough to warrant a security system.

"It's boarded up."

"I can read, Nate," I said. I pulled out my flashlight and checked the padlock on the door before shining it through the pieces of wood that had been nailed across a broken window. "Well, the good news is there isn't a poltergeist in there."

"How do you know?"

"Squatters never would have lasted long enough to get their mattresses through the window, let alone store a sleeping bag." Poltergeists love these kinds of haunts.

I didn't see anything moving inside, and my flashlight didn't trigger a commotion. That was all the invitation I needed. I tested one of the wood boards across the window. It had been shoddily set and gave with my first tug.

"Have I mentioned this is a stupid idea?"

"And I told you I need to see Eloch's mirror." The second board gave way. I checked for broken glass, but it had long since been cleared away. Still no sign of activity.

"Look, the coast is clear." Carefully, I lowered myself down into the basement of the Cage, checking the ground again for glass. Not for me; I didn't want to risk Nate cutting himself. "I'll take a quick look at the mirror and we'll get out."

Nate backed in after me, hitting his head more than once on the top of the window. Cramming a large body into a small space after spending twenty years as a ghost will do that to you. . . . "Promise?" he said as he dropped to the ground.

"Just keep the salt ready." I'd divided up our supplies between the two of us when I'd parked my bike. "I don't think whatever Eloch is can bypass a set mirror, but I don't want to take any chances."

Now that we were both through, I turned the flashlight on the basement of what had once been one of Seattle's finest dive-bar establishments. The infrastructure had been left intact, but the smoke and fire had left their mark. All that remained was broken furniture and the odd pile of clothes that gave off what I always think of as the stink of people.

"Mirror wasn't in here," Nate said. "It was in back—through that archway—though I remember there being a door here."

"Probably was. Anything useful not ruined by the fire would have been stripped years ago." Of course, the mirror would have to be in back. . . . Well, here goes.

"K?"

"Just keep the salt ready. If there was a poltergeist, it would have started throwing things by now."

We made our way into the backstage area.

"Over here," Nate said, and headed to an alcove I would have missed. There was a table built into the wall and above it was a mirror—charred from the fire and dusty from years of neglect.

I shone my flashlight on it and pulled up my Otherside sight, but the dust was so thick I couldn't even see my own face, let alone if the mirror was set.

I handed the flashlight to Nate as I stepped closer.

"Should you be getting that close, K?" Nate said.

He was starting to make me nervous. I took a breath to calm myself and, using my sleeve, started wiping the dust off. "Just keep it aimed on me and the mirror so I can see what I'm doing, all right?"

Slowly, the years of dust gave way to my leather jacket and my own ghost-grey reflection.

"Not bad. Twenty years and still standing. Let's see what you're made of, shall we?" I said.

"There is no reason to talk to it!" Nate whispered.

"It's not activated."

"Just keep it that way," Nate said, and shone the light around the backstage area.

"Light on me, Nate."

It took me a sec, but I picked up the main lines of Otherside. They were faded—common with older mirrors, especially if they haven't been used in a few decades. But also the sign of an amateur, or of someone very talented who wanted to hide under the guise of mediocrity.

I frowned as I traced the lines to the anchor symbols. It was an advanced set mirror. The lines were good and the anchors still stable, but they were all symbols I recognized. Whoever had set this was adept, but nowhere close to what a sorcerer like Gideon was capable of.

Meaning someone living had probably set the mirror.

I zeroed in on the name that the mirror was attuned to at its centre, layered underneath the bindings . . .

Eloc.

Wasn't even spelled right—but close enough.

I turned to face Nate. "It's not complicated. I mean, it's a set mirror," I clarified, "but there's nothing special about it."

Nate wasn't paying attention to me, though. He was shining the flashlight at the mirror behind me. "K, I thought we agreed no turning the damn mirror on."

"I didn't turn it on."

"Then how do you explain that?"

I turned back to the mirror. Sure enough, where it had been silent a moment ago, now the bindings were activated, simmering with Otherside.

I shook my head. "It wasn't me."

"Are you sure? Maybe you just let some Otherside slide off?" Nate started to back up.

"Yeah, doesn't work that way." I joined Nate in backing up.

"Maybe he can feel me—you know, like a disturbance in the force?"

I shot Nate a look.

"Okay, it sounded better in my head. . . ."

The mirror shimmered; something was coming through from the Otherside. . . . I shoved Nate between a pair of burned-out rafters. "Stay there," I said.

"What the hell are you planning on doing?"

"Just stay in the corner."

"K, watch it!"

I should have responded but couldn't tear my eyes away from the mirror, which had started to leak Otherside. The bindings hadn't stood the test of time and the set was giving way . . .

And then the Otherside shifted to dust. Fantastic.

What was it Max used to say? When the dead try to give you lemons, keep them talking. . . .

"Who are you? What do you want?" I said loudly, taking another step back from the bone-chilling Otherside dust that was creeping towards me.

Slowly, black lettering like what Nate had described started to etch itself in the mirror.

Nathan Cade.

I shook my head. "I'll need more to go on than that. What about Nathan Cade? Are you after his songs? We know where they are— we'll give them to you if you stop killing people."

"K!"

I shushed Nate and focused on the mirror.

The black letters vanished and were replaced by new ones.

It's too late for that. Where is he?

"Where is he?" I echoed. He was around the corner. Even if it couldn't see him, it should be able to feel the Otherside bindings on him. . . .

I have no interest in you or your zombie, Kincaid Strange. Where are you hiding him?

I licked my lips. I had a theory. . . . I glanced over at Nate and mouthed, "Follow my lead."

"Do you know where the ghost Nathan Cade is?" I said to Nate, and prayed to hell he caught on.

"Ah—the *ghost* of Nathan Cade? Naw, haven't a clue," Nate said. Not exactly a lie. At the moment there was no ghost of Nathan Cade, only a zombie. Devil's in the details when talking to ghosts.

This is your last warning.

Give me Nathan Cade.

Jesus. Now that Nate was in Cameron's body, Eloch couldn't find him—that's why he'd gone ballistic. . . . He had tried binding him and then he'd disappeared. I glanced back at Nate and nodded. He swore but reached into his pockets.

"What if we don't want to deal?" I said to the mirror.

There was a pause before more black ink scrawled across.

Then we're going to have a problem.

"Yeah, get in line— Now!" I yelled, and ducked.

Nate hurled a handful of salt, which rained down in front of me. Sparks of Otherside flared wherever it struck the dust, but when it hit the mirror, there was a hissing sound and streams of smoke spiralled up.

I took that as my cue. I quickly tapped the barrier and reached out for the mirror, then grabbed hold of the bindings and pulled, teasing them away from the glass in strips. They gave, and the mirror's bindings started to unravel.

I felt more salt rain down on me. Well, better too much than not enough. Instead of retaliating the way it had at my apartment or outright fleeing as it had at the Rex, this time the wraith screamed louder, and more Otherside dust spilled out of the mirror around my feet.

What the hell was going on? "You're not a demon, Eloch," I shouted, hoping to anger and distract him from whatever he was playing at. "You're a fraud, like every other ghost with delusions of grandeur."

If there's one thing the undead hate, it's being called an ordinary ghost. Black tendrils of Otherside began a slow crawl across the floor, like the tentacles of a sea creature. I smelled burnt Otherside mixed with plastic as the mirror started to melt. My flashlight flickered and went out.

What it couldn't do with mirrors, it made up for in fancy parlour tricks.

"Any salt left?" I asked Nate.

"Not much," he said, backing even farther away from the mirror and the creeping Otherside dust.

Well . . . when in doubt . . . "Run. Run now," I said. The two of us turned and bolted for the open window.

I shoved Nate through and scrambled after him before dropping to my knees outside. "I've decided I hate close calls."

"Ahh—K?" Nate said, pointing a shaking hand behind me. . . .

I stared inside at black tendrils of Otherside creeping along the floor, following our path. I threw my own handful of salt at it. Though it shrieked back at the touch, I could see it mapping a course, a way around it. To us.

Nate tried to push the plywood back on top of the window.

"Not helping," I said.

"Well, at least I'm trying!"

I took what remained of the salt and sprinkled it outside the window and around the alley. Hopefully, it would slow Eloch down, since I knew from my apartment that throwing Otherside at it didn't do a damn thing. I grabbed Nate and started to run. "Please tell me you learned something useful about wraiths from those texts?"

"Salt was it. And I'm out."

Where the hell was I going to find salt back here? Wait a minute—what was I talking about? There was an entire body of salt all around us. . . .

I glanced behind us in time to see smoky tendrils slither out of the boarded-up window. I ducked into a side alley, dragging Nate with me.

"Nate, you knew this area. Think fast. Where can we find salt water?"

"What?"

I shoved him and checked over my shoulder. "Less talk, more think."

Eloch's tendrils were jolting at the salt, but they were still coming for us, licking at the shadows.

"Ahhh—sewers and storm ditches?"

"Those are for taking rainwater out!"

"Not during high tide they're not."

He was right. During high tide the salt water filled the sewer pipes back up. Was it high tide, though? I yelped and looked down as something bit my heel. Eloch's tendrils had caught up—and one of them had tagged me. The back of my leg was stained with blood.

Oh, hell.

"Run, nearest sewer drain," I said.

We took off down the alley, but in his deteriorating state Nate began to stumble. I ducked under his arm to shoulder some of his weight.

"Ahh—right up here—no, left! See? Up there is the culvert."

I knew there was a decent-sized storm drain that let out a few blocks away. Nate was steering us straight for one of the ditches. *Come on* . . . Relief hit me as I saw the ditch was brimming with a good three feet of running water. Here's hoping it was sea water . . .

"On three," I said to Nate, gasping for breath. "One, two—jump!"

I hit the gravel on the other side of the water-filled ditch followed by a less graceful Nate, who collapsed in a swearing heap. I spun around and waited as Eloch reached the water—and recoiled. The tendrils snaked to the left and right, but stopped short of crossing.

"We did good—right?" Nate said, doubled over with cramps and looking the worse for wear.

I wiped my hair out of my face as I caught my breath, watching the tendrils test the edge of the ditch. "I'll tell you when we get home." But my mind had already turned back to the set mirror. If I was trying to pass myself off as a powerful demon, I'd want to get rid of any evidence to the contrary. . . .

I pulled out my cellphone and messaged Aaron.

I think whatever killed Jacob had to have had a human accomplice at some point. I'm starting to think it might have been Jacob. It was up to Aaron to find the evidence.

"K?" Nate said.

I glanced at the other side of the storm drain. Eloch's black tendrils were lashing at the edges now, testing every few feet along for a break in the salt.

"Come on. Let's get the hell out of here before it figures out a way across."

＊

I got my door open on the second jiggle this time. The lock was losing its touch.

I shoved Nate in first and locked it behind us. What a day. The Rex, jail, Lee, the Cage . . . What I wanted to do was collapse into bed and not wake up for a week. Not happening.

"Nate, get the salt, will you?"

"Right." He dragged himself into the kitchen.

I dropped my jacket and headed to my room to get the remaining sage and ash mix that Lee had sold me. I figured if it could keep out Gideon, it could keep out Eloch the wraith.

"K, we don't have much left."

"I thought I told you to sweep it up into the dustpan."

"Yeah, and do you have any idea how many cracks there are in the floor?"

I brushed hair out of my face that had escaped its tie once again. I was too exhausted to argue anymore. Fortify the apartment, lock Nate in the spare and collapse into bed. "Just bring what you have."

I could lace the doorway with salt, put buckets of salt water under the windows . . .

I heard the metal dustpan hit the floor.

"Ah, K—you should maybe come out here—"

Shit, what now? I stepped out of my bedroom to see Nate standing in the kitchen doorway. His face had gone cold and blank. "Nate, what's . . ." I trailed off as I saw what he was staring at. "Shit."

Gideon. Standing in my kitchen, looking angrier and more corporeal by the second.

"What the hell is this?" he said, his voice low and menacing.

Okay, this might be worse than the wraith. "Gideon, whatever you think this is right now, it's not."

Gideon turned his attention from Nate to me, his eyes darkening as the seconds passed. "One of you had better tell me what the hell is going on. Before you *both* end up as ghosts."

CHAPTER 18

CRASH AND BURN

"And this is the thanks I get for saving your life? *Hiding* things from me?" Gideon shouted.

Yeah, Gideon had reacted to Nate's occupation of Cameron's body and my shorthand retelling of the last week's events about as well as I'd expected, but whether it was due to the bizarre nature of our story or the sheer shock of seeing Cameron's deteriorating body in all its Nathan Cade–filled glory, he'd decided not to kill either of us.

Yet.

Every time his attention drifted from me to Nate, the air temperature dropped a few more degrees. . . . Pretty sure that was frost creeping up the inside of my windows.

Nate remained silent—or paralyzed with fear. I needed him out of Gideon's crosshairs.

I grabbed Nate by the shoulders and steered him towards the spare bedroom. "Come on, twinkletoes," I said as I shunted him through the doorway.

"Good thinking. The window's there, I can get out on the fire escape."

"You're not going anywhere." I motioned at him for his hat and sweatshirt.

Nate swore but took them off and forked them over. I gestured for the shoes.

"Seriously?"

"You're desperate. And desperate Nate is not someone I trust as far as I can throw him."

He sat on the bed and undid his red Converses. "Fine—staying. Happy?"

"Very."

"What do you plan to do, K?"

Good question . . . "Try to convince Gideon not to kill us?"

I closed and locked the door before turning my attention to the other, much more dangerous undead in the apartment.

Gideon had watched me lock Nate in the spare bedroom without comment, his eyes a dangerous, glittering black. I was hoping the adage "out of sight, out of mind" held true for ghosts too.

"There's no such thing as a demon," Gideon said, his voice tense. The first thing he hadn't shouted at me, in fact, since we'd related our tale of Nate's accidental possession and Eloch the Demon. "And your ghost is an idiot for believing such nonsense."

Carefully, I sat back down at the kitchen table. At least Gideon wasn't calling Nate a liar. My teacup was empty and I was cold enough that all I wanted to do was fill it, but I didn't dare take my eyes off him. "It claims it's a demon. I never said it was. Whatever Eloch is, he killed a man, and I think it was to cover up the deal he struck with my ghost twenty years ago. It's probably behind a cold-case murder I'm looking into," I said.

"Wraiths don't make deals," he said, his lip curling into a sneer.

"Well, apparently this one does—or whoever was controlling it." I elaborated on what I'd found out about the set mirror at the Cage.

When I finished, Gideon closed his eyes as though he was willing himself to be patient. "I already explained to you that a wraith is an entity driven by its insatiable hunger for Otherside. It can control its hunger about as well as a poltergeist can carry on a civil conversation. I've yet to see it happen."

"But what about someone controlling the wraith to exact revenge? Like the practitioner who raised it?"

Gideon's eyes flickered. "A remote possibility. Wraiths are unlike zombies and ghosts—they encompass a limbo state, so the same rules do not apply. Their hunger and drive for vengeance is all-encompassing, and they quickly break whatever leashes their raiser concocts. Only a very experienced and powerful practitioner, more likely a sorcerer, could hold one. *You* couldn't. And neither could the dead man, or he would never have ended up bound to his own body."

I rolled my eyes at the jibe. "Then we're looking for another party. I bet that's why Jacob was silenced—he must have known who the controller was." And my guess was that Mindy also knew. I'd heard back from Aaron, and he was serving her a search warrant. He knew what to look for: any and all practitioner paraphernalia, unexplained frost . . . Something in her collection would point us in the right direction. With luck, Aaron might even uncover Nate's notebook of songs—which as far as I could tell only Nate was after, but still . . .

"Contact with a wraith would leave an unmistakable mark of Otherside," Gideon said.

Which I hadn't seen at Mindy's apartment. Not one trace . . .

"And no sorcerer or sorcerer's ghost with the ability to raise a wraith properly would do so for such a frivolous task, the Otherside imbalance alone makes it prohibitive." Gideon made an irritated *tsk*ing sound.

"What do you mean imbalance?"

"Like everything on your side of the barrier, Otherside also leans towards entropy. The more you attempt to warp and bend Otherside to your will in a spell casting, the more it fights to achieve entropy and the more power is needed to contain it through to the completion of a spell. The nature of a wraith, trapped between this world and the next, goes against that entropy. The resulting imbalance of

Otherside is so great both the wraith and the sorcerer take on the natural imbalance." He arched a ghost-grey eyebrow. "Do you have any idea what happens when there is an imbalance?"

"Sacrifice," I said, my voice a whisper. That was something that didn't change between sorcery and voodoo. Bending Otherside, even within its natural bounds, requires sacrifice.

"No sorcerer in their right mind would take on that kind of imbalance willingly; the body count alone would be astronomical. No, there is another explanation." He looked at me. "Vengeance was the reason the witch set the wraith on the town in the zombie queen's story, but she had no illusions about what it would take. She was willing to sacrifice the entire village to restore the balance of Otherside."

And there weren't that many dead bodies. Not yet, at any rate. "Maybe we aren't looking for someone who knows what they're doing? This is the age of information. What's to say this isn't the work of an amateur?"

I knew I had a point from the way Gideon glowered at me. "It's possible," he said. "But unlikely. In my experience, it's another sorcerer behind these kinds of machinations." He sighed. "Though I'll admit the chain of events seems too blundering for one of my own ilk. Wraith or not, it makes no difference and is inconsequential to the problem at hand."

"Really? Undead monster freezing people to death strikes me as a pretty substantial problem."

Gideon wasn't impressed. "Your idiot friend made an idiotic deal with an entity that claimed to be a demon, then stole my body."

I took in a big breath. "That's what I'm trying to explain—he didn't steal it. The wraith tried to bind Nate and in the process he got stuck in Cameron's body." In a colossal example of wrong place, wrong time.

His lip curled into a familiar snarl. "The proximity of your ghost to my body is exactly why your wraith failed to bind him. Otherside always tries to go where it's easiest, and an empty body conditioned to be a vessel would have caused an irresistible pull. It's a damnable comedy of errors, is what it is. All of which I would have told you days ago if you'd bothered to share any of those incredibly important details." His voice was back to yelling volume.

"I didn't tell you because I figured you'd blame me!"

Gideon snorted. "Of course you didn't do *that*," he said, pointing at the spare bedroom. "And neither did your idiot ghost. It's the work of a practitioner or undead who has an aptitude for binding ghosts but no discipline or proper education. It's sloppy work, and as much as it pains me to admit this right now, you are not sloppy in your bindings."

That made me feel slightly guilty.

Gideon's expression shifted from anger to exasperation. "I've given my word I won't kill you. I've been more than fair."

"Intimidation and thinly veiled threats isn't fair. It's coercion!"

Gideon glowered. "Oh, you haven't seen intimidating yet," he said, as the bindings on my wrist flared. "The terms of our agreement prevent me from killing you, though if I'd known you'd let your ghost steal my body . . ."

"Accidentally possess it." Not a small distinction.

Gideon fell silent for a count of three. "I told you, I always keep my word." He ran his hand through his hair. "I need to get away from here so I can think clearly. Don't do anything stupid before I get back."

"What about Nate?"

Gideon's eyes stopped glittering and the shadow of an unfriendly smile touched his mouth. "If the bindings give out before it can be undone, he'll be gone. Forever. It strikes me as a fair consequence, all things considered."

Oh, for . . . If I could throttle the sorcerer's ghost . . . "I'm serious."

Gideon gave me a bored look.

"I don't know how to get him out!"

"Well, then, I suggest your ghost adapt to the idea that he is about to live out the rest of his very short existence as a gutter-trash zombie. Even I can smell the decay coming off him."

I took a deep breath. Yelling at Gideon would get me nowhere. "I need your help."

Gideon went silent. I watched my breath condense in front of me.

"You expect *me* to help *you*?" There was a threatening tone in his voice that made my stomach drop. "You went out of your way to hide the fact that your reject of a ghost stole my body. One I went to great lengths to secure. You single-handedly scuttled the arrangement because of your pathetically misplaced conscience and desire to make up for your own shortcomings. And you want my help?"

It hadn't been my misplaced conscience, it had been the right thing to do. I'd do it again, too, though I wasn't about to share that gem with him right now. . . .

Still, he picked it up from my face. "You have no concept of what you cost me. And you have the audacity to ask me for favours?"

"I'm sorry," I said, surprising myself that I actually meant it. "But I need—"

"You realize I'm stuck like this forever?" he said.

That halted my train of thought. "Ghosts don't last forever, Max always said—"

"And yet again you demonstrate a total lack of comprehension about how much you do not know." I could have sworn he took a deep breath and closed his eyes. Or the ghost equivalent.

God help me, I was actually seeing Gideon in a different, almost sympathetic light. Trapped on the Otherside forever . . . it would be enough to drive anyone mad.

I counted to three in my mind. "I don't expect your help. In fact, I completely understand if you tell me to fuck off. But I'm still asking."

Gideon leaned in until I could feel an icy burning on my skin. "Tell me the truth and I'll consider helping you, but only if you tell me the truth. And trust me, I'll know."

I held my breath and waited.

"Were you planning on telling me about the zombie even if you could have figured out on your own how to reverse it?"

I took my time answering. "Only if I had to," I admitted.

Gideon shot me a predatory look. "After a few hundred years or so, you forget the effects of violence except its ability to elicit information from people who try to cheat you. It becomes nothing more than another tool to coerce the living into paying what they owe." His eyes glittered. "You're not the only one in this arrangement who has been used. I'd hazard I've been on the short end of it more than you, particularly recently."

It went against every particle of my being to agree, but he had a point. How many people did I know who tried to use the dead? If I was being honest, it was more than half my clientele. . . .

"Ghouls," Gideon finally spat out. "Maximillian was very negligent in your study of ghouls. Start with those bindings," he said.

He then added something under his breath, too soft for me to catch. From the tone, it had to be a curse.

"I don't have any patience left for you today. Add what's sitting in that room to your substantial homework," he said, gesturing at the spare.

Gideon was halfway faded when he paused. "There is one thing you do need to consider, Kincaid."

"Which is?"

"That the easiest way out of this is to give this Eloch what it believes it was cheated out of. One Nathan Cade."

And with that, Gideon vanished.

I shivered. Ghouls. He was right, I hadn't studied them with Max. He'd always brushed them off as being a simple take on an eastern European zombie. It was the first real breakthrough I'd had in understanding Nate's bindings since he'd knocked on my door a week ago.

I rubbed my arms and paced the living room a few times to calm my nerves. I spotted a package on my desk, sitting on top of my laptop. It had been carefully wrapped with brown paper and secured with string instead of tape, and was addressed to me in elegant script, the old-fashioned way—something I could imagine Lee doing. . . .

I opened it warily. It was a pile of books.

I frowned as I picked up the first ones: A *Comparative Guide to Voodoo and Vaduan Techniques, Voodoo of North America . . .* There were five texts in total, and they were all books I'd sold on eBay over the last few months—some of them in better condition than the ones I'd sold. One of them was a first edition with an appendix my copy hadn't had, which included lists of basic bindings that could be adapted for sorcery.

I flipped open the final book in the pile and went cold: *Curses of Louisiana*—and not just any copy. It was the same one I'd sold only a few days ago. I recognized the faint soup stains I'd tried so hard to remove from the cover. There was a card enclosed with the same tight script. *I thought you might have use for these.* It was signed, *Gideon.*

Son of a bitch.

I slammed the book shut. Goddamnit, Gideon had bought the book I'd been selling and returned it to me.

I would not sympathize with the homicidal sorcerer's ghost. Not for getting me books I needed to be his assistant and not for refraining from *killing* me . . . I'd had enough emotionally abusive relationships to last me a lifetime; I knew what the start of one looked like.

Don't let him fool you, Kincaid. Underneath he's as evil as any poltergeist. Just remember what he'd had planned for Cameron . . . And he's not trying to be your friend, he's holding a debt over your head.

It was a logical argument.

Then why did I feel like such an asshole?

I knocked on the spare-bedroom door. Sleep would have to wait a little longer. "Nate?"

He opened the door and stuck his head out. "Okay, I only heard half of that. Is he killing us or . . . ?"

I waved him out of the room. "Optimistically, I'd put it at fifty-fifty. Come on, the coast is clear." After a moment I added, "Gideon suggested we look into ghoul bindings."

"K, I'm up for anything at this point. I mean, I didn't want to tell you, but my right hand has been tingly since this morning, like permanent pins and needles."

"That's the nerves dying. Or the formaldehyde preserving them." Or a combination of both.

"And did I mention I don't smell bad anymore? Look at me—the fact that I don't smell bad to myself anymore is a huge fucking problem."

"Point made."

"So . . . we're giving ghoul bindings a try?"

"Yeah, but not on you first," I said, and headed into my bedroom, where I kept the burner phones—the ones I stored in my dresser drawer for just these purposes. Luckily, I knew where I could find an abundance of feral ghouls running around. . . .

I didn't have much faith Lee would return my call, so I called the only other person in the underground city who might possibly be willing and able to help me track down a couple of deranged ghouls.

I typed Mork's number from memory into my burner as I turned on the kettle for tea and my hot water bottle. He called me back before the water had come to a boil.

"Kincaid."

"Hey, Mork," I said, while I poured the steaming water over a tea bag. "Listen, how would I go about getting a feral ghoul? You know, one of the ones who wander around in the third level." Where Lee sent all the feral and dangerous ghouls and zombies to spend the remainder of their mindless afterlife.

There was a pause. "And just why would you want one of those?"

"Preferably one with two or three different types of bindings."

"You still haven't answered my question."

"Because I want to dismantle it."

There was another pause. "You know what, it's worth it to see this for myself. Meet me by the bottom of the stairs to the underground at 4 p.m. tomorrow. And don't be late."

"Wouldn't dream of it . . ." I hung up and checked the time: 1 a.m. The adrenalin rush from seeing Gideon had disappeared and exhaustion was back in full swing. I needed sleep, and now.

I took a sip of my tea and poured the remainder of the hot water into my hot water bottle. Then I grabbed the Thermos of fixative mix Mork had left for Nate and a Baggie of brains from the freezer. After setting the brains to defrost in the microwave, I finished checking the apartment, setting salt and sage to ward off Eloch. It would have to suffice until the morning.

I brought the soggy, warmish Baggie and Thermos to Nate. "Here, nighttime snack. You can wash it down with Mork's formaldehyde mix."

"Ew," he said, but took them. He held the brains out at arm's length.

"No argument. I need to sleep or I'm going to end up dead too." I ushered him into the spare room, making sure the sage was burning and the sill was lined with an ample supply of salt before locking him in.

Skipping the shower, I grabbed my tea and hot water bottle and barely got my shoes and pants off before crawling under the duvet. I set my alarm for noon and sipped at the blissfully warm liquid to settle my mind before sleep overcame me.

Despite my exhaustion and everything that had gone on in the last two days, I found my thoughts drifting towards the one place I didn't want them to go: Gideon. Had he started off evil or had something made him that way?

I pushed those thoughts aside and my mind towards sleep. I'd only have four hours to prep for our meeting with Mork tomorrow. Here's hoping I figured out what it was about the ghoul bindings that would help get Nate out.

Because, evil or not, Gideon wasn't going to be any more help.

CHAPTER 19

GHOULS

"Have you ever thought, for one single moment, that the reason everything goes to shit is that you don't know what the hell you're doing?" Mork said.

I glanced away from the pen we'd constructed with discarded chicken wire and four-by-fours to corral the ghouls Mork had found. Their growling had shifted from a low roar when we'd arrived to a dull murmur, but if anything, the smell of formaldehyde-cured hides had got stronger.

"What choice do I have?" If I couldn't unravel Nate's zombie bindings, maybe I could unravel the parts that mimicked the ghoul possession. . . . It was worth a try. "I notice you were more than happy to take us right to them," I added. Mork had met us at the stairs and led us to a series of tunnels out of the way of the main underground promenade. The nine ghouls had been waiting there for us in a makeshift coral. All they needed were morbid black bows.

Mork shrugged. "What can I say? My curiosity outweighs my sense of propriety."

"That I believe." And truth be told, my curiosity was also starting to get the better of me. Don't get many chances to see a feral ghoul up close.

"Have I mentioned yet this is a really stupid idea?" Nate called out. He was stationed a ways back—ever since one of the ghouls had fallen over the fence and made a run for him.

"Yes," Mork and I said in stereo. Okay, maybe I should be worried if Mork and I were in sync. . . .

"Where did you say you found them?" I asked, tuning out Nate.

Mork shrugged. "Various spots. Some of them escaped the third level and were caught roaming these outer tunnels, but we pick up most of them when they crawl through the stairwell. Ghouls like to squeeze through those cracks. My theory? Has to do with the rats that die behind the wood panels."

"Surprised they fit," I said. "The ghouls, not the rats."

He shook his head. "They don't. Almost always lose something on the way through—" He looked away from the makeshift enclosure of ghouls and frowned at me. "Is it me or is this really uncomfortable?"

"Oh, it's really weird. We've never shared more than a few civil words."

Mork nodded. "Glad it's not just me."

I could see why Gideon had pointed me in this direction. Ghouls are a far cry from zombies. Instead of just bindings to animate the body, ghouls have a heavy dose of possession thrown in. A lot more like Nate's state, stuck in some strange stasis.

"Incoming," Mork said, and nodded at them.

Sure enough, a ghoul had got our scent and was breaking away from the pack of six left over from the nine Mork had assembled. The first three were in a heap by the pen, where we'd stacked their corpses after I'd managed to disassemble their bindings. Not my most elegant work, mind you, but I was hoping my technique would improve with practice. Mork and I waited at the end of a run they could fit down one by one.

"How exactly did you lure them in here again?"

"Oh, you know. They're feral, so finding ones with their limbs intact is the tricky part. . . . After that? Pole with a loop at the end." Mork glanced back at Nate. "You might want to stand farther back." Sure enough, the ghouls were all looking in Nate's direction again.

Nate swore. He was already up against a rock wall. "Seriously, you two, I'm feeling a little violated right now."

I rolled my eyes and glanced at Mork. "Not that I'm complaining—it's a good selection of bindings." I'd already observed a variety of Polish bindings, a few Croatian bindings with a Mediterranean influence, and everything in between.

I frowned as I caught sight of the bindings on the incoming ghoul—a series of anchor symbols I recognized from the southern Slavic countries, but with some slight modifications. . . .

"Is that a Serbian ghoul?"

"I didn't categorize them as I was picking them out."

"I know, just, there probably hasn't been a new Serbian ghoul made since the early nineties." A side effect of the Bosnian war was that a lot of practitioners had been wiped out.

Mork frowned and shook his head at me. "So?"

"So, I feel like I should be taking notes or something, you know?"

It was picking up speed as it moved towards us. Unlike feral zombies, who tend to slow down as they lose parts, ghouls maintain their mobility.

Mork gave me an exasperated look and shoved me towards the chute. "Sure, whatever works. Will you dismantle the ghoul already? Before it tries to take a bite out of us?"

The ghoul stopped mid-run and turned its nose up, having caught the scent of rotting flesh from the zombie torso we'd suspended from a rafter with a heavy rope. The ghoul version of a donkey carrot.

"Hey you, over here," I shouted, and waved a stick with Nate's red sweatshirt tied to the end of it. The ghoul fixed what was left of its eyes on me. We'd initially tried waving a red handkerchief Mork had brought to get their attention, but when the first one had made a dash for Nate, we'd realized the zombie scent mixed with his red sweatshirt worked much better.

The feral Serbian ghoul growled and came at me once again, hands outstretched. "This one's fast," I muttered, backing away.

"Yeah. They do that sometimes."

I felt a little guilty this time as I tapped my globe and readied to untie the ghoul's bindings as it careened down the run towards me. Granted, it probably hadn't had an independent thought in the past couple of decades beyond "mmm, rotting flesh" and "dinner"—but still, it felt as though I was somehow desecrating history.

As the ghoul got closer, I could see his bindings more clearly, both the larger, concentrated anchoring points and the thinner, marionette-like lines that animated its limbs. I aimed for the thinner ones. After dismantling the first three ghouls, I more or less had the hang of it. The trick wasn't to aim for the big anchor points, which bound the soul or ghost to the body rather than integrating it; every time I'd tried teasing them apart, they'd snapped right back into place. But the thinner lines weren't nearly as stable, and once a few were severed . . . I'd taken to calling them marionette strings because cutting them dropped a ghoul mid-run.

I discovered this strategy on the ghoul who'd jumped the chicken wire and tried to eat Nate. Cutting the thin lines destabilized everything else, and as an added bonus, once the ghoul couldn't move, I'd had plenty of time to play around with the anchors.

I pulled the first line of Otherside, which was powering one of the ghoul's legs. It stumbled but continued to hop towards us.

"You know, you should probably be more concerned about that—the speed thing," I said to Mork. "If a fast one ever crawls back up to the second or first level . . ."

"Lee's problem, not mine. She's the one in charge. See if you can drop it on top of the other three."

Waving Nate's shirt on a stick, I backed up, leading the hopping ghoul to where we'd piled the others. I got a good look at its Serbian anchors while I was at it.

"You really aren't much of an academic on these things, are you?" I said to Mork.

Mork glared at me. "Do you have any idea how much bacteria is in their mouths?"

Point taken. The Serbian ghoul lunged at me, but the other dead—or deader—ghouls were in his way and he tripped, falling on top of them. That made things easier. I grabbed hold of the other leg line and pulled, then the arms. The ghoul shuddered once, twice, then came to a stop. I went to work on the anchors, and in a few seconds had them unravelled.

"No offence, Strange, but if these weren't feral, I'd consider this a little macabre."

"You don't have to watch, Mork."

"I didn't say it wasn't fun."

"Okay, does this not seem wrong to either of you?" Nate said.

I glanced over at him.

"I mean, how do you think that feels, your getting them to pile themselves up for you!"

I looked back at the pile. "I'm pretty sure these ghouls don't have any feeling beyond 'Mmmm, flesh.' I'm doing them a favour."

Nate shook his head and turned his back on us. "Man, K, sometimes you just have no sympathy for the dead. And—maybe enough practice?" Nate said, and nodded at me.

I ran my hand over my face. Sure enough, I was covered in a thin layer of sweat. I'd been so caught up in figuring out the ghoul bindings that I hadn't noticed.

What I'd discovered over the past hour was that Nate was no more a ghoul than he was a typical zombie. But the way the ghouls' souls were bound to their bodies was similar to the way Nate was tangled up in Cameron's. Gideon had been right to send me this way. Added to the books he'd gifted me, it made me feel even more guilty.

I used the sleeve of my shirt to wipe my forehead. Well, now or never. I waved Nate over. "I think I've got the hang of it," I said.

Nate slowly approached and then paused, staring at the pile of ghouls on the tunnel floor. "Actually, maybe I was hasty. You could, I don't know, practise on a few more?"

Mork and I looked at the four ghouls I'd dismantled, then back at him.

The deep, jaundiced yellow Nate's skin had darkened to was also kind of fitting with his new-found ghoul kinship.

"Batter up, Cade," Mork said. "Time to take one for the team in the name of experimental practitioning."

Nate backed away from Mork. "Can you say anything without making it sound creepy?" He tripped over the pile of ghouls, landing on top of them ass first. He scrambled back up, and it was hard to tell who or what he was more terrified of—the deader ghouls or Mork.

"Enough, both of you. Look, it's a basic possession that's been tied into animation, like a jerry rig. The zombie animation bindings are supporting the ghoul possession like anchors, and vice versa. Yours are a lot messier, Nate, but if it's running on the same principle—which I'm convinced it is—all I need to do is pull the animation strands first. It should destabilize the possession anchors like it did to the ghouls and I should be able to pull you out."

"That's an awful lot of 'should,' K." He was on the other side of the corpse pile now, still backing away.

"Will you stand still?"

"Fuck no!"

I took a deep breath and once again focused on his tangled bindings. All right, simple, Kincaid—just go for the animating strands and leave the anchors alone for now . . . Nate stood still and I took the opportunity to grab one of the thinner animation lines in his leg, and tugged.

Nate winced and stumbled. "K, are you sure that's the right one?"

"Quiet, Nate. And stop moving."

"Ouch!" Nate jerked violently to the side.

"Whoops, my bad," I said, and wiped sweat off my forehead before regrouping. . . . I'd tried snaring the other leg line, but everything was so tangled he lurched backwards, his back bending on an unnatural curve.

"*Whoops, my bad?*" Nate tried to face me, his spine still arched.

I'd have to do all four at once. I managed to tease them out. Like trying to unravel a ball of string that a couple of cats high on catnip have had their way with . . .

"I've got it this time . . ." I said through clenched teeth as I tugged all four lines. For the first time in two weeks I got a good look at Nate's ghost as it separated from the mess of anchors and hovered over Cameron's body.

"Son of a bitch, you got it, Strange," Mork whispered, with just a little awe in his voice. "I just lost two bar shifts to Lee."

I frowned at him. "You bet against me? Seriously?"

He shrugged. "Nothing personal—but I mean, what were the odds?"

At least Lee had had faith. . . .

"Hey, K, I don't feel so good."

"I'll have you out in a sec, Nate." Next up: dismantle the anchors.

"It's not that. I can feel something pulling. Eloch—he's trying to bind me again."

I frowned and peered into his mess of Otherside lines and anchors. Sure enough, now that Nate's ghost was separated from the body, there were faint black tendrils of Otherside smoke grasping on to him, crawling out of his bindings. As if they'd been lying in wait all this time.

Shit.

I gently tugged the anchors, but every time I tried to separate Nate from the body, the tendrils tightened their grip, sucking the Otherside out of him.

I swore and let go.

Like elastic bands, the bindings snapped back into place, trapping Nate once more in Cameron's body. Back to square one. But Eloch's black tendrils were gone. I was stuck. As soon as I tried to unbind Nate, Eloch would try to bind him.

"Nate, I'm sorry, but Eloch must have gotten a foothold when he tried the first binding." I gestured at the body. "I can get you out, but I can't hold you here."

Mork, who'd been watching with mild interest, looked from Nate, now crumpled on the ground, to me. "You're fucked, Strange."

"Thank you for that insight." I turned back to Nate. There had to be a way to unhook Eloch's tendrils. . . .

My pocket started to buzz and I fumbled out my phone. It was Aaron.

"I need to get this," I said, moving out of the ghouls' growling range. "Hey, Aaron."

"I'm finished the first pass of Jacob's apartment. I found something. We're not finished going through his stuff. There are boxes and boxes of paper clippings. But we found a message on Jacob's phone from Cole, asking Jacob to fill in for the night. Apparently Cole was picking up extra work and shifts at the Rex."

Guess selling the odd Dead Men candid interview and mooching off Mindy didn't pay as well as one might assume . . . "You're certain Cole was the one who was supposed to be at the bar?" It raised two distinct possibilities: had Cole been the intended victim, or had he lured Jacob in? Either way made Cole an intriguing lead. "What did Cole say?"

"That's just it. He's supposed to be at the Rex working the bar shift right now, but he's not answering his phone and the bar isn't picking up either."

It was early evening; if a band was playing, that wasn't surprising. "Should you be sharing this information with me?"

"No, but I figure if an undead bent on freezing people is on the hunt for Cole, it might be really useful if the one practitioner in the city who stands a chance of dealing with it is there too."

"All right, I'll look into it, Aaron."

I was about to hang up when Aaron stopped me. "Kincaid? Be careful. And don't hurt yourself."

I sucked in my breath before I spoke. Despite his sincerity, Aaron was shifting the responsibility onto me. It was a failing of *my* character if I went too far. After everything, he still didn't get it. What he was asking me to do was hurt myself; there was no separating the two.

"Yeah, sure thing, Aaron," I said, not mustering the energy to make it sound sincere. I hung up and turned to Nate. "Good news. This will have to wait. We have a bigger problem."

CHAPTER 20

DRUMMER'S TAILS AND DEAD ENDS

I tightened my hood around my face and shot another glance over at Nate. "I can't believe I let you talk me into bringing you," I said. Every now and then the street lights would hit his face, highlighting just how yellow he'd become. At least there weren't many people around, despite our proximity to the Rex Hotel, it being 7 p.m. on a Monday night.

I stalled, unable to shake the feeling that, despite the emptiness of the street, someone was watching us. Nate gave me a gentle push to keep me moving forward. My head pounded from using Otherside and I was chilled to the bone . . . but we needed to get to Cole.

"Who out of the two of us actually knows Cole?" Nate said.

And that was the crux of it. Nate had known the guy since high school. Me? The meeting at Mindy's was our first encounter and I hadn't made a fantastic impression. Granted, neither would a zombie . . .

"I'll stay out of sight, K. Promise. You brought salt, right?"

I stopped where I was. Okay, stopping felt just as bad as walking . . . I held up my backpack. "Yes, in here."

Nate stopped me and turned me around. He looked at me—really looked at me—with Cameron's watery green eyes. Then he swore and pulled me into an alley beside the Rex. "Shit, K, are you stoned?"

"No." When he glared at me, I added, "I'll be fine provided I don't have to use any Otherside, which is what this is for," I said, and shook my backpack again.

Nate glanced towards the street and back at me, as if he was making a decision.

"Nate, which of the two of us is in charge?"

"You, when you're not stoned on Otherside."

"That's not a thing."

A heavy door slammed shut in back of the Rex and Nate dragged me farther into the alley.

"They're in between sets now," he said. "That's good. Cole always used to hang out on his own between sets."

"I'll be fast."

"I'm not worried about speed, I'm worried about them letting you in. Couldn't you get Aaron to do this?"

Maybe I should have. The problem was, I was the practitioner. I was the only one who would see Eloch coming.

And the longer a killer was left on the loose . . .

I did my best to clear my head and push aside the jitters, and looked at Nate. "I can handle this. I just need to ask him a few questions and I need you in earshot to tell me if he's lying. It won't matter how well I hold up my side of the conversation."

Nate nodded. "Okay, then, no sneaking in around back. We'll go in the front."

"Not with you looking like that."

Nate smiled and shook his head before pulling his hat down and his collar up. "Trust me, K. I fit in with the hipsters. Besides, people see what they want, and this is a bar specializing in nineties nostalgia. Now, a five-star restaurant or the opera . . . I'd be worried too."

Nate stepped around me out of the alley and into the Rex. I didn't have much of a choice. I followed him inside. Thank god the music had stopped and the lights were dim.

I needed a drink. I headed to the bar, hood hiding my tangled black hair. "Whisky sour," I said, placing a ten on the bar.

The bartender barely glanced up as he put the drink in front of me and grabbed the money. I took a sip then stuck my hands back into my jacket pockets to warm them.

Nate sat down beside me. God help me, the bartender didn't look twice at him either. Nate was right: it might have had an expensive makeover, but at its heart it was still a nineties dive bar.

"Told you."

The bartender returned with my change and I shook my head. At least, with the overwhelming smell of stale beer in here, no one would notice the formaldehyde. . . .

I swore under my breath. "Where the hell is Cole?"

"There, K—end of the bar."

I glanced over. Sure enough, there was Cole, nursing a beer, hunched over the glass in a jacket that was easily a size too large, making him look smaller than he was.

Funny, even a day ago I'd had Cole on my list of suspects for who might have killed Damien—especially after talking to Mindy. Now, seeing the kind of place where he played, a pale reflection of its former self, and the meagre crowd the former Dead Man pulled in . . . Working bar shifts for stage time to boot. His caustic, bitter nature I didn't doubt, but he struck me as sad, not Machiavellian.

"If he got a damn thing out of you or Damien dying, I'm not seeing it now," I muttered. Or the windfall had been very short-lived.

Or he'd been cheated . . .

Nate frowned at me.

"Never mind," I said. "Just thinking out loud."

I took another sip of my whisky sour. Not as good as Lee's, but unlike hers I think it was clearing my head.

Cole didn't appear threatening, but I also didn't see any indication that he was in danger. There was a small crowd in here, and one thing our killer undead hadn't done so far was murder with an audience.

"He looks fine, Nate. I don't think we need to be here." Time to leave well enough alone, call Aaron and let him interview Cole. That was his job, after all.

"K, I can't believe I'm the one saying this, but looks can be deceiving. Especially with Cole. You're here, so we might as well make sure."

Well, what was the worst thing that could happen? He'd tell me off again?

Or a wraith came out of nowhere and murdered everyone . . .

I downed my drink, letting the alcohol drown out that particular thought. My worst-case scenarios had a bad habit of coming to fruition.

"Wait until after I'm talking to him before you come over," I said, and with that, I stood up and strode over to Cole.

He didn't seem to notice me as I sat down on the stool beside him. I cleared my throat.

He glanced at me over his shoulder.

"You again," he said, and turned back to his beer. When I didn't respond, he added, "I'm pretty sure I didn't ask you to sit down."

"No, but that went so much better than expected, I figured I'd press my luck while the going was good."

Cole let out a cross between a snort and a laugh. He took another sip of his beer. "Mindy says you two are friends. To be honest, I didn't believe her. I figured you were just another kind of leech who figured out a way to use Nate."

"Sounds like you've changed your mind."

"You have the same sense of humour as Nate." He took a bigger swig of his beer before meeting my eyes again. "I already told you everything I know. I don't want to be involved."

I nodded. "Yeah. And that was before Jacob died."

Cole didn't say anything, but his knuckles went white as he gripped the glass. It wasn't "fuck off," so I pressed on.

"Look, I know you were supposed to be here Friday night, when he was killed."

Cole put the glass down and looked at me coldly. I kept my expression as neutral as I could. "So what is it you want to know,

Kincaid Strange?" he said, pronouncing my last name with added emphasis.

Here's the thing. The more predictable the questions I asked, the more screwed I was. People can figure out a million ways to lie or evade the truth. I did it all the time. How to throw them off balance and get an honest answer? Ask them what they're not expecting. Boil it all down to one single question.

"Only one thing, Cole."

He picked up the glass again and gestured for me to continue.

"Was Jacob killed instead of you or because of you?"

For the life of me, I couldn't read him.

The corner of his eye crinkled. "Tell you what, Kincaid Strange. I'll answer if you answer one of mine."

I nodded.

"Do you really believe Nathan Cade wouldn't have killed to become famous?"

"Yes. The Nate I know is a narcissistic bastard, but he'd never kill anyone."

Cole nodded. "I respect that. But what about for Mindy? Can you honestly tell me he'd never do it?"

I looked at him steadily. There was no point in lying. Nate had walked over and was eavesdropping behind me, and he'd know. "No." I prayed Nate would stay silent.

"Brave thing to admit."

"Your turn."

"Both. Jacob died because I was stupid enough to think if I wasn't at the Rex, it wouldn't kill anyone. "

He'd spoken to Eloch. I shoved my surprise down. "It gave you a warning? What did it want?"

Cole shook his head and stood up. "One question, Strange."

I grabbed his arm. He didn't look happy and neither did the bartender, so I let go. "I can get you help. Aaron Baal—"

Cole laughed at me. "Seriously? A detective—sorry, the paranormal detective?" He shook his head. "He can't do anything, Strange."

"That's not true."

"You know, a lot of people seem to be dying around you lately."

That caught me off guard. I started to shake my head. "I was involved in a paranormal murder investigation. That's what I used to do for the police."

"Used to?" There was an air of incredulity about Cole now. "Seems the murders only stepped up once they fired you."

"A bit trigger-happy for a witch hunt, aren't you?" I shot back, but my voice sounded weaker, less confident than I was used to.

Cole leaned forward slightly, his eyes narrowing. "Come to think of it, I do have another question for you. Do you tell yourself you're actually trying to help people?"

"Of course I am."

He leaned in close enough I could smell beer on his stale breath. "The only thing you're doing is protecting Nathan Cade." He took a step back. "And I thought he was self-serving. You're just interested in protecting your cash cow and your own claim to fame." He shook his head. "You've got a lot of nerve coming and talking to me. Stick with the dead, Kincaid Strange. I plan on staying a member of the living."

Cole started to walk away but turned before he disappeared through the doorway to the basement.

"You want to do everyone a favour, Strange? Give it Nathan Cade—that's what it's wanted all along. Start batting for the living instead of the dead for once."

That stung. I watched him leave, and turned to face Nate.

"Was he lying?" I asked.

"No. He was telling the truth. About everything." He looked distracted as he stared after Cole.

"I need some fresh air." I made a beeline for the exit.

Nate followed close behind. "What about Cole?"

I shook my head. "He's in a bar full of people. Besides, he said he didn't want my help."

"K, he sounded scared. Look, Cole doesn't know what he wants—especially if Eloch's been getting to him."

"I can't make him do anything, Nate."

Nate grabbed my arm and stopped me just outside the door. "Yes, you can. What is wrong with you, K? You never take no—"

"I'm a horrible person. Are you happy?" I pulled away from him. "I'm sick and tired of being blamed every time something goes wrong."

"He's scared—"

"No, Nate, he's right." Cole and Gideon were both right: the more I helped, the more people figured out a way to blame me for their paranormal problems.

"K, you're not thinking straight. You're upset."

I ignored him and kept walking. We were half a block away from the Rex when we heard a man scream. Blood-curdling and filled with fear.

More screams, and people began to pour out of the bar.

Shit.

Eloch had arrived. I pivoted and ran towards the hysteria. I could feel sorry for myself later. Nate tried to follow, but I shoved him into an alley. "Stay here. It's looking for you, remember?" I hissed, not waiting for an answer. My bet was Eloch still didn't know what had happened to Nate, but it was the only card I had to play. I wasn't about to fold.

It wasn't hard to figure out where the screams were coming from. The black tendrils and ice were creeping from the basement windows. . . .

I ignored the cold and ran through the back doors, left wedged open by the staff, bolted down the steps that led into the cellar—and stopped.

Lying motionless in the centre of a ring of ice was Cole. Eyes open, arms extended, looking utterly terrified and frozen solid. Just like Jacob.

The wraith had found and killed him. He was dead.

It was my fault. If I hadn't taken off, if I hadn't let Cole get to me . . .

I accessed my Otherside sight and saw the letters start to scrawl their way across the floor in the Otherside dust.

Bring me Nathan Cade.

I ran back upstairs and outside. I eventually found the bartender amongst the customers who had fled, and grabbed him. "Don't let anyone back inside, and call for detectives Baal and McColl at the Seattle PD. Only talk to one of them, got it?"

He nodded, staring fearfully at the ice now creeping out the front doors. Hopefully, with my mass of black hair tucked under my hood, he wouldn't be able to place me. . . .

Who was I kidding? Who else in Seattle would know to ask for them directly? I'd worry about Aaron and Sarah later. I moved towards the alley and Nate pulled me in.

"K, where's Cole?" Panic in his voice.

I only shook my head.

He let go of my shoulders and slumped to the ground, head in his hands.

I was numb. I'd been so close to stopping it, to saving him. . . . Sirens screamed in the distance. I leaned against the brick wall and pulled out my phone.

"What are you doing?" Nate asked.

"I'm calling Aaron." I couldn't help but remember Gideon's and Cole's words as the phone rang.

Eventually they start explaining the coincidence as causation.

Funny thing was, I'd have a hard time arguing with that right now.

CHAPTER 21

HEROIN AND MURDER

"Ah, I was just talking to him. About five minutes before it happened. I was trying to get him to call you," I added, rubbing my arms to ward off the chill while Aaron stood a respectable distance from me on the sidewalk. Sarah was interviewing a witness. A large crowd was still milling around. I'd sent Nate home before the police had arrived, with an order to keep to the alleys when possible.

"How was he behaving? Did he seem worried?" Aaron asked, jotting down notes.

"Angry, a little depressed, fed up. He, ah, indicated the wraith had threatened him, but he wouldn't tell me how exactly, and then . . ." I took a breath. "Then the conversation turned to how I was the one really responsible for the murders, for not giving the wraith Nathan Cade."

Aaron looked up from his notepad. "You realize it's not actually your fault?"

I glared at him. The last thing I wanted to talk about was my feelings.

"It's a hostage tactic, Kincaid. You know that. Start blaming the authorities for not giving in to your demands. If only they'd delivered the helicopter in time, no one would have died. . . ."

I made a face. "I know that. It doesn't mean I don't get to feel like shit." We were away from the crowd and out of earshot. The police had cordoned off the Rex—again—and Sarah was wrangling statements from the other witnesses, but Aaron had managed to get me out of the fray.

"Was there anything else?"

I shook my head, trying to clear away the fog and recall anything, no matter how insignificant, that might be useful. . . . I'm familiar with death, it's part of my job, but it's not every day you're talking to someone and then a minute later standing over their dead body. "He was scared but resigned. He refused to call you or take my help."

I noticed Sarah had finished talking with the witnesses and was watching us. Aaron must have seen me glancing at her, because he added, "You aren't a suspect. For one, I know you didn't do it, and second, if the department asks, you've got an airtight alibi."

I frowned. "How do you know that for sure?"

"You were outside talking to someone. We have you on camera when the screams sounded."

Shit, when I was outside talking to Nate, I hadn't even thought to look for cameras.

"It looked heated," Aaron asked.

"An—ah—a Dead Men fan. Had some questions about Nate." Thank god it was dark and Nate was wearing a hood. If Aaron had recognized Cameron . . .

"What were you talking to Cole about? Before he got upset?"

Oh, you know, whether Nate was capable of murder . . .

"About Jacob." When Aaron frowned, I added, "Nothing serious. Just why he'd switched shifts with Jacob."

Another police car came around the corner, siren blaring, and pulled in beside Aaron and Sarah's sedan and two other marked police cars. Aaron swore as Sarah strode over.

"It's the captain. Get her out of here, now," Sarah hissed when she reached us.

Aaron nodded and took my arm. "Come on, I'm taking you home. Sarah can handle things." He started to steer me towards his car, using his taller frame to block me from view.

"I thought I wasn't a suspect."

"You're not the murderer any more than I am, but that won't stop the captain from trying to throw you in jail, which won't help anyone, especially me." He opened the passenger door and let me in. "Where the hell is Nate in all this?" he asked, once we were both inside.

I shook my head. "You wouldn't believe me if I told you. . . ." I trailed off as I saw the stretcher carrying Cole's frozen body emerge from the back of the Rex—his arms still rigid, trying to fend off his attackers. It would be a long time before I got his terrified face out of my mind.

I shivered. One other corollary of Cole's death: we were running out of suspects.

"He couldn't have been behind the murders," I said.

"I'm starting to like this idea of a wraith more and more."

"My source says if it is a wraith, it can't be working alone. There'd be a higher body count."

"Was that supposed to put me at ease?"

"No, it's meant to light a fire. Did you get anything useful from Mindy?" When Aaron didn't answer, I added, "I need to find out who else is working with this wraith before it finds Nate or the rest of his band."

"Or her," Aaron said.

I sighed. "At least talk to her. Someone has to tell her about Cole. I'm guessing, since this is paranormal, that's going to be you?"

Aaron pursed his lips. "Kincaid, it's not that simple. . . ." Aaron started the car and pulled away from the Rex, navigating the still-milling crowd.

"What's not simple? If this was any other murder, you'd have dragged her in for an interrogation by now."

"I have to be careful, otherwise some uncomfortable questions could arise."

A chill ran through me. "What kind of questions?"

"Kincaid, Nate isn't alive anymore. . . ."

"So?"

He inclined his head. "So . . . the laws aren't clear on what to do when a killer effectively holds the threat of murder as a bargaining chip in exchange for a dead hostage."

I sat back in the sedan. "I can't believe you're suggesting—"

"I'm not," Aaron rushed to say. "I'm saying if I'm not careful, someone else might ask." We hit a red light and Aaron glanced over at me. "I shouldn't be telling you this, but there's another reason you're not a suspect—not just to me but to anyone. The person who killed Jacob struck him on the back of the head with a very heavy object before he was frozen. We think a stage stand was the murder weapon, though the killer knew to dispose of it." The light changed and Aaron's eyes were back on the road as he pulled forward.

"Wait—he was murdered before he was frozen?"

Aaron nodded.

I sat back in the seat. A wraith wouldn't need to kill someone first—they'd just freeze them, that's what Mork's books said, and what Gideon and Lee had both echoed. Premeditated murder with an instrument is a human behaviour. . . .

"Even if I *wanted* to detain you for questioning—which the captain might, at least for twelve hours—the angle and height are all wrong. You didn't do it because you physically couldn't do it."

"You looked?"

"We ran some simulations. Best defence is removing the possibility."

I knew Aaron had been trying to look out for me, but I still felt betrayed that he'd gone out of his way to prove I hadn't committed a crime.

"Wait—blunt force trauma? That makes no sense."

"Your wraith has proven it has no trouble exerting its will on this world. That was one of the rules you taught me about determining if an undead could be the culprit. It can't kill someone unless it can exert its will on the real world in a meaningful way."

"Yeah, in theory—but this isn't a zombie or ghoul. Wraiths feed off Otherside, and they don't have nearly as much control. They aren't as bad as a poltergeist, they're more purposeful, but . . ." I trailed off. "It might hit something after draining it of its life energy, but not before."

"You kill things all the time to release Otherside."

"Yeah, but I'm channelling it into a binding. Kill something outright and some Otherside will always be wasted. A wraith is like an addict—it wants every last drop."

"Maybe he didn't mean to kill him?" Aaron offered.

Or maybe it was simpler. Why would something that feeds off Otherside kill someone first? Because they weren't strong enough to pull the Otherside out on their own. The wraith hadn't been able to bind Nate, or to kill Jacob or me on sight. Its victims needed to be dying first. The way Damien had been after his overdose . . . except Damien hadn't been flash-frozen, he'd been found in a puddle of water.

"Son of a bitch," I swore, making Aaron take his eyes off the road. I ignored the dirty look he shot me as I asked, "Aaron, did anyone notice salt around Damien's body? What about the coroner's report? Was there any tissue damage consistent with flash freezing?"

He started to shake his head, his eyes back on the road, then they widened. "You think the killer got rid of the ice with salt water? There was no autopsy, not after the overdose was confirmed with a blood test. The medical examiners were overextended at the time, and with the rash of overdoses, they forwent autopsies on most of the routine cases."

"How much do you want to bet Damien suffered blunt force trauma?" I asked.

Aaron didn't answer as he pulled up outside my apartment.

Despite the paranormal chill factor, Eloch was looking less like a wraith and more like a run-of-the-mill clever killer. A wraith is a rare undead construct. What's one of the biggest challenges with rare bindings? Getting them right . . .

I opened the door and started to get out of the car.

"Kincaid, there's something else," he said.

I didn't like the set of his mouth. "If it's about the Otherside use—"

He looked at the steering wheel to avoid looking at me. "It's not that. I mean, yes, I'm still concerned, but it's not that."

I sat back down and closed the door of the idling car.

Aaron licked his lips as if trying to decide how to broach whatever it was he wanted to say. "It has to do with internal politics."

"I should have known—you couldn't get me my job back. Not even a contract."

He didn't agree, but he didn't argue either. "The mayor's trying to keep the captain quiet."

That wasn't what I'd expected. "That's good, isn't it?"

Aaron glanced back up and met my eyes. "At least until he can figure out a way to shift public opinion in the captain's favour over the new stance on paranormal policies."

I tried to stuff the black, broiling pit that had become my stomach back down. . . .

"That's— There is no way, this is Seattle. Everyone knows there's ghosts. All you need to do is walk down the pier on a rainy day—"

"I'm not saying it will be easy, but that doesn't mean they're not trying. The mayor's office has hired PR experts to design a campaign to shift public opinion in line with the captain's belief."

That the paranormal doesn't exist? That we are all a bunch of hucksters shilling snake oil? Then it hit me. As one of the few voodoo practitioners left in Seattle, and the only one with something resembling a public profile and a record of working with the police, I would be their target.

I closed my eyes and laid my head against the headrest. On top of the wraith, this was too much. I did my best to hold back tears. That was something else I had years of experience with. . . .

"Look, Aaron, I cannot handle this right now."

"Things could get worse fast. You need to be aware." After a moment of silence he added, "I'm working on something. I can't tell you what, but it will get you out of the crosshairs."

I looked at him. There wasn't any guile written in his features—only the same worry I'd seen yesterday morning.

Before I could say anything, Aaron leaned over and kissed me. It was quick and light, and I didn't have time to react.

"Be careful. Of Marks and the wraith," he said.

I forced a smile and nodded before getting out of the car. My emotions were so raw that I just felt numb. I processed what he'd told me all the way up to my apartment. Hiring Marks hadn't been a mistake; it was what the mayor had wanted all along. If there was ever a time to leave Seattle . . .

I reached my door and put the key in the lock, ready to wrestle with it, but the handle clicked open.

A chill fell over me. I never leave the door unlocked. I eased the door open and reached for the baseball bat I kept behind the coat stand.

The wraith had to have an accomplice. . . .

I heard sounds coming from the spare bedroom—drawers opening and closing, someone rifling through them. I readied the bat over my shoulder and eased the door open with my foot.

"Ah— Hey!" Nate spun around, a new sweatshirt in his hands. He stared at the bat. "Jesus, K, you scared the shit out of me."

I put the bat down. "I thought we agreed to wait until the coast was clear. And what are you doing leaving the door unlocked? "

"You realize every alley for four blocks was crawling with cops? Figured it was worth the risk trying to get home than hiding in a Dumpster." He held up his hands. "And I didn't lock the door because no fucking dexterity. I was looking for something to help."

I let out a breath. "Sorry, Nate." I related what Aaron had told me. "What's more, I'm running out of suspects. First Jacob, now Cole."

I left it unsaid that Mindy was the only one left. . . . I went into the kitchen to set the kettle to boil and waited with my back to the living room.

"K?" Nate called.

I watched the kettle simmer. I needed a minute before getting into Mindy again with him.

"K, seriously, your phone is ringing."

Shit. I ran back into the living room, where Nate was holding the phone. It was an unfamiliar number, but I answered anyway.

"Hello?"

"Kincaid?" I caught a sob in her voice.

"Mindy?" I shot Nate a panicked look. What if she didn't know about Cole yet?

But she answered that. "Kincaid, it got Cole." She let out another sob.

Her emotion took me aback. It's funny, but working with the dead, I often forget that the living are left grieving the loss of their loved ones—until I have it thrown in my face, like now. "Mindy, I'm so sorry. Where are you?"

"I'm at the docks." She choked back another sob. "Kincaid, I tried to forget about Damien. After fifteen years I started to think what I saw was the heroin talking. It wasn't."

Damn it, where was a recorder when I needed one. I put the phone on speaker, delicately placed it on my desk and started fumbling around the drawer. There. I flicked on a small recorder and put it beside the phone.

"Mindy." Repeating their names often works on zombies; I hoped it worked on grieving girlfriends. "I need you to tell me exactly where you are."

"I'm at the marina. Nate knows which one."

I glanced up at Nate. There were an awful lot of marinas in Seattle. Nate nodded.

"I thought it wasn't real—I figured it had to be some kind of hoax, my fucking memory. Then Cole wanted me to find you at the Rex and tell you to give it Nate, and now he's dead."

She was losing it. "Mindy." It came out sharper than I would have liked, but I needed her lucid, not crying in a heap.

"It says you need to come down alone, except for Nate—no cops or it'll kill them too."

Now that I doubted very much. It didn't want the cops there because it couldn't kill all of them first. . . . On the other hand, if I did show up with Aaron and Sarah, I might not get another chance at the wraith before Nate ran out of time—and there was no telling what it would do to Mindy.

"That's all it wants. And if you don't . . ." She trailed off into another round of sobs.

"Mindy, who—who is with you?"

She hung up.

I checked the number. Public, from one of the yacht marinas.

I looked at Nate. He was already sliding his sweatshirt back on and had grabbed the helmets plus the extra salt.

"Something's wrong. None of this fits. . . ."

"No offence, K, but unless you have any better ideas . . ." He tossed me my helmet.

I shook my head but took the helmet and grabbed my jacket. The last thing I needed was more bodies on my hands—Mindy's or otherwise. Not after what Aaron had told me about the mayor and Captain Marks.

"Unfortunately, Nate, I'm still out of good ones. Time to start using the bad."

CHAPTER 22

THE WRAITH OF MINDY PINE

We didn't have far to go to reach the Fisherman's Terminal, though the October rain had picked up from its usual drizzle to pouring en route, so we were both soaked by the time we arrived.

On the bright side, the lights at the marina were still on, but at this late hour the docks were empty.

"I thought this was a commercial fishing dock?" I said as I followed Nate down one of the thinner docks that branched out into the harbour, lined with boats that moored year-round or hadn't been dry-docked yet. We seemed to be veering more and more into the smaller pleasure vessels, not the ones outfitted for fishing.

"It was—it's changed. I haven't been down here since . . ." Nate let the thought trail off.

"Are we even going the right way?"

Nate nodded. "Mindy's dad used to be a fisherman and we'd hang out here sometimes. It's up here," he said, and turned down another stretch of dock towards a set of slightly larger pleasure boats.

I pulled my wet leather jacket tighter and followed Nate. The fact that we were about as far away as we could get from the marina proper bothered the hell out of me. Add to that the fact that the dock lights out here were sporadic and I could barely hear my own thoughts over the rain hitting the water . . .

"Here," Nate said as we reached the end of the dock. There were a couple of boats on either side but no sign of Mindy.

"Are you sure this is the right spot?"

"Yes," Nate said as he pivoted, looking frantic. "This is it exactly, but the boats are different."

We both heard it over the rain, what sounded like a sob.

Nate started to move towards the noise, but I stopped him. "Look at all the water—it could be a ghost." One of the reasons Seattle was such a magnet for the paranormal was all the water. Ghosts had a much easier time crossing over in the harbour. That and the rain.

He shook my hand off. "It's not a ghost."

I was about to argue—this entire set-up was unsettling me—but we heard it again.

"Nate?" I spotted someone huddled on the small, unlit yacht on our left, just inside the cabin. "Mindy?" I said, and took a cautious step forward.

Nate ran past me and stepped onto the boat.

I swore. If I'd been freaked out before, this sealed it.

"Nate, I have a bad feeling about this." I shook my head as he crouched down beside her.

"Mindy?"

"Who are you?" Her voice was hesitant. "It wants Nathan Cade."

I stayed put and accessed my Otherside sight. As far as finding hostages went, this was way too easy.

Translation: we were walking into a trap.

She didn't look like a wraith—not huddled in a white leather jacket and heeled boots, her polished bleached bob crimped and frizzy from the sea air and breeze. Was she Eloch's accomplice?

Not likely, unless she'd wanted to off Cole. Was it possible she was the wraith and didn't know? It wouldn't be the first time the dead were caught clueless. . . .

"Nate, will you get her and get off the damn boat?" I hissed.

I surveyed the harbour around us but couldn't see Otherside.

The temperature dropped, a subtle chill, easily written off as just the October night air. But the ice crystals that crept along the boat rail and the sudden fog of my breath said otherwise.

"Nate, now is not— Shit!" Tendrils of black smoke lashed out of the water and scurried across the dock towards me. I dodged one that struck at my feet. We were going to be boxed in.

"I need help—she's out of it." Nate was trying to lift Mindy with one arm.

I swore and hopped onto the boat, and reached under Mindy's other arm, helping Nate hoist her up. "Come on, if we don't get off this thing fast, the wraith is going to corner us."

I stepped onto the dock first and bit back a yelp as cold laced through my leg all the way up to my spine, coating my boot in crystals. Still holding Mindy upright between us, we scrambled back onto the boat, away from the tendrils, now lapping at the fibreglass sides, leaving an icy trail in their wake. We deposited Mindy back on the bench where Nate had found her.

"K, it's coming over the side."

Sure enough, Eloch's tendrils had a grip on the boat, straddling the gap and stretching over the water. It couldn't cross salt water—once we were cast off. . . .

"Nate, do you know how to drive one of these?"

"Yeah. You drop the moorings. I'll get the engine."

Time to add grand theft to my rap sheet; somehow I didn't think the captain would accept the fleeing-a-wraith excuse.

I darted to the back, sliding on my icy boots, and worked at the thick knot until it came loose and the boat began to drift.

Why wasn't the engine on? I found Nate in the cabin. "We're unhooked from the dock."

He was standing in front of the controls, staring.

Not the best time for a bright-light zombie trance moment . . . "Nate?"

"K, I recognize this." He turned to me with wide-eyed horror and held up a key chain with a dyed green rabbit's foot. "Do you know what this is? It's my old yacht," he said.

A new coat of paint and some modernization, but yes, it looked familiar from Nate's photos. The undead and their obsessions . . .

"Just get it moving? Once we're over salt water, remember?"

Understanding dawned on Nate's face and he started the engines. The lights blinked on and I stuck my head out the cabin door to check the wraith's progress, but the smoky tendrils on the dock and deck had disappeared.

I turned to find Mindy awake and staring at me with a defeated expression.

Alarm bells sounded in my head. We were sitting ducks on the boat, so where had Eloch gone? Nate revved the engine.

"What's going on?" I asked Mindy.

Her eyes were glassy. "You shouldn't have come," she said.

Sympathy's never been my strong suit. I grabbed her by the collar of her expensive white leather jacket. "Mindy, what happened?"

She started to laugh. I dropped her back onto the bench as Nate steered the boat away from the docks. We were free and clear of Eloch. We should be safe.

Then why the hell didn't I feel safe?

Because there was no way Eloch was giving up this easily. As the lights of the docks receded, I noticed that the air had cooled even more and my breath was fogging. I switched to Otherside again and saw the dust collecting on the deck.

Shit. I turned to Mindy. She hadn't moved from her spot, and she was still staring at me, her arms wrapped around her knees as she shivered.

The wraith couldn't get us on salt water—unless it was already on the boat. I took a step back.

"Mindy, what are you doing?" I said, keeping my voice even.

She shook her head and began to mumble, "It's not my fault," though it took a few repetitions for me to catch it.

"Nate!" I yelled into the steering cabin, all the while backing away from Mindy as the ice and Otherside dust continued to creep along the open deck towards me.

My phone buzzed in my pocket. I ignored it, but once the ringing stopped, it started all over again. Careful not to take my eyes off Mindy, I answered.

"Yeah?"

"Kincaid?" Aaron sounded panicky.

"Yeah, Aaron, this is bad timing—"

"Where are you?"

"I'm at the Fisherman's Marina. Look, I'm in the middle of something—"

"Cole's body is gone."

Oh, hell, no . . . A sick feeling settled in my stomach. "Let me guess—no blunt force trauma?"

"Never got the chance to look. Dr. Blanc just called me. He went in to start on the body and it was gone. There's more. Remember you asked me to take a look into Mindy and Cole? Mindy took out a restraining order against Cole fifteen years ago, then revoked it one year ago for no apparent reason. Not many couples go from restraining order to engaged and married."

Cole had been frozen solid. There was no question he'd had no vital signs. The question was had he fooled us all into believing he was dead or that he was still alive? In my experience there's only one reason why a body gets up and leaves . . . I hate it when the pieces fall into place a minute too late.

"Aaron, I'm hanging up. You might want to— Shit!" Before I could finish, ice gripped my hands. My phone clattered to the deck, the screen shattering.

Nate rushed out from inside the cabin. "K?" He stopped short at the sight of the ice and swirling Otherside dust.

I held my hand up to stop him as I searched the boat for Eloch, the recessed lights on the boat's deck still bathing us in a flickering flood of LEDs. I followed the thin tendrils inching their way towards us, like a net closing in, to a dark outline at the bow of the boat—the source of the Otherside smoke. It was slowly moving in our direction.

"I've got good news and bad news, Nate."

"Good news, please god, give me the good news," he said as he moved to stand beside me.

"The wraith isn't Mindy."

"Bad news?"

"It's Cole."

Cole stepped into the deck light as the boat continued to run slowly out into the harbour. I'd had a preconceived notion of what a wraith should look like, and the figure at the centre of the smoke wasn't it. I'd thought it would be more ghost than undead, dressed in white, tattered clothes, maybe a dress. I guess after Lee's story I'd assumed a wraith would be female, which was just, well, sexist when it came right down to it.

Besides the Otherside shimmer flickering over him, Cole looked as he always had. He was wearing a pair of jeans and a black Gore-Tex rain jacket, the hood dropped back and hands in his pockets. Normal.

"Nathan Cade." He smiled and stepped into the lights. "You always did have a problem paying up."

The lights flickered again as if Cole were sucking the very life out of his surroundings.

"The whole zombie thing, now that was clever. I don't know how you pulled it off. Wasn't until I saw you in the Rex earlier tonight, trying to figure out what Kincaid was doing with a zombie as messed up as you in broad daylight, that I put two and two together."

The chill in the air picked up. I could see threads of grey Otherside smoke curling around Cole as if searching for something.

"Got to hand it to you though, Nate, when you try something out, you can't fucking help but screw it all to hell. I mean, look at you!" Cole crinkled his nose. "Are you rotting?"

Nate bunched his fists up as he stepped closer to me. "You know,

I'd forgotten the relentless criticism. You never fucking shut up—I mean, my clothes, how I stored my guitar, put the toilet seat down, take out the garbage . . . Jesus, talk about a control freak."

"You know, from where I'm standing, that doesn't seem so bad."

"Eloch?" I said. My mind was reeling. Cole had to be the wraith . . . but he was alive . . . ish. And he was in control. I'd say it wasn't possible, but I'd been wrong enough lately to know that was a futile observation.

Cole smiled. "Nate never could spell."

I closed my eyes. Cole, Eloc—Eloch. Really fucking hilarious.

To Nate's credit, he recovered faster than I did. "You want the songs, Cole? If Mindy doesn't have them, I don't know where they fucking went!"

Cole shrugged and pulled out a red notebook from inside his jacket pocket—one that had seen better days. "You mean these, Nate?"

Nate's face fell. "Where did you—"

He waved the book. "I've had these for years. Actually, I did you a favour. Mindy was going to auction them off about—oh, a year after you died. I stopped her. You're welcome." He looked at the notebook again. "You have no idea how pissed I was about fifteen years back. I had the songs, I had a line on your ghost, but for the life of me, no matter how hard I tried, I could never tag your ghost long enough to bind you."

Just when I thought Nate had lost his cool. "You were trying to *bind* me—to, what, record some fucking songs? Are you out of your fucking mind?"

"The rest of us had lives and careers to think about, Nate. The songs, the tour, our manager—not that you ever cared. It was me and Jacob who came up with that stupid demon in the mirror so you'd fucking edit your damn songs."

Nate took a step towards Cole, but he stopped as a tendril of smoky Otherside lashed out, chasing him back. "There is no fucking way, Cole. No fucking way this is about a bunch of songs and a tour I vetoed. I wasn't the only one who thought it was a stupid idea."

"You were the only one! No one ever told you to fuck off because you ended up the poster boy for the band. Without you we were nothing, and you were so goddamned arrogant, any time there was a decision to be made, you'd trot that gem out. You never let us forget it."

"I did *not* hold it over your head."

"You might as well have." Cole curled his lip. "Your crap self-esteem was your undoing—there was no point encouraging you. You hated yourself and took it out on us. It took a fictional demon to turn you into a songwriter. The worst part is, you would have been *nothing* without me and you didn't even know it!"

I frowned as I turned my Otherside sight on Cole. He was covered in Otherside dust—not controlled and organized, but swirling and chaotic. I squinted. There was something else, underneath . . . but it was obscured by all the dust.

"I had big plans to have you finish these, release them, auction them off—oh, *fifteen years ago*."

"You want me to finish and record them?" Nate shouted back at Cole. "*Fine*. Let everyone else go if that is seriously what this is about."

Practitioners sometimes use Otherside to distort images. Cole's shimmering exterior reminded me of a basic illusion. Only it shouldn't be this strong. With Gideon's Otherside sight I should be able to see beyond it. . . .

"Look at me!" Cole screamed, and the illusion wavered under the flickering boat lights. "No, Nate. It's too late to record the songs. It's too late for me."

Cole smiled wide and the Otherside illusion dropped. I bit back a scream. In front of me was Cole—I was sure of it—but he didn't look human. His skin was pale grey with residual Otherside and he was skeletal, his arms and legs reduced to bone under his loose clothing. But his face . . . His cheeks were sunken and the skin drawn tight over his skull, lips dry and stretched thin. His eyes were dry grey orbs set into hollowed sockets. He looked mummified. Only the barest remnants of bindings flickered alongside the illusion.

He should be dead—his vitals had read as dead little more than an hour before and he'd been reduced to a walking corpse.

But somehow he was still alive. Barely, from the looks of it, but still counted amongst the living. That was how he was staying sane and able to control the wraith hunger . . . but at what cost?

The life source that pours out of anything at death is finite, but so is the life force of anything living. Whatever Otherside works had been done to Cole were leaching his life force away, bit by bit, leaving him not really alive—which was how he'd fooled everyone at the Rex—but also not dead. It had taken almost twenty years, but if I was any expert—and I was—the flickering meant Cole had finally burned to the last of his life energy. He needed a fix. And if he'd already burned through what Otherside he'd drained off Jacob . . . Cole wasn't kidding: his time was up. And he knew it. And here we were, out in the middle of the harbour.

Cole turned his attention to me. He smiled—hollow, empty and *hungry*.

"Now you're sporting some fancy work," Cole said to me. "If Jacob had known half the stuff you did, this wouldn't have happened." He gestured to his eyes. "These dried out five years ago. They work, but nowhere near as good as the real thing."

"Wha—what did you do to yourself?" I said.

"Is it possible the great Kincaid Strange, practitioner extraordinaire, hasn't figured that part out yet?" He made a *tsk*ing noise. "You were on Mindy so fast, and hiding Nate to boot, so I thought you had it figured out." Otherside dust swirled around him. "I'm the wraith, Kincaid Strange."

I caught movement of something white out of the corner of my eye. Mindy had crawled over to the railing, huddled into her coat. Her makeup was ruined. She watched us with dry, calculating eyes. She'd known. She'd known all along.

I inclined my head. "That part I figured out."

"You know, it occurred to me to kill your detective off at the beginning. But Jacob disagreed, said it'd just piss you off, and he was scared of you. He'd been disagreeing a lot lately. Me? I don't see what the fuss is about.

"Do you know how you become a wraith, Nate? What about you, Kincaid? You're the paranormal expert."

Neither of us answered as he advanced. So Jacob had been a practitioner—a talented hobbyist, but a hobbyist, with no formal training. That was why Cole's bindings were such a mishmash. I was willing to bet they'd eventually find the binding texts hidden away in Jacob's pack rat collection.

"It was Jacob's idea. Said we could bind Damien and drain the talent out of him. Or that's what we thought it meant: *talent*."

I flinched. . . . Depending on what part of the world the practitioning texts came from, *talent* was sometimes used to describe Otherside.

"You were trying to give yourself the power to drain the talent out of people."

What was it Gideon had said? That when practitioners stumbled into sorcery, it was often by accident and out of desperation? People trying to bend the will of Otherside and force it to do what they wanted . . . We were witnessing the horrible results.

One of the first rules Max had taught me: make sure they're dead first. Now I knew what happened when you tried old, powerful binding spells on someone who was still alive.

"Hindsight is twenty-twenty," Cole said with another corpse's grin.

I needed to derail Cole's script—and now. "Pretty stupid, killing off the one person who was helping you."

Cole's shrivelled smile faltered. "Jacob stopped being able to help me."

Think, Kincaid. He's not a real wraith—he's not even dead, he's a bungled version.

I'm all for lying to killers and crazy undead when the occasion calls for it, but this? There was no way in a million years I could even *begin* to fix this. I shook my head. "Maybe with a few months and Jacob's notes I could start to fix this."

"I wouldn't trust you anywhere near me with Otherside. Get Cade out of that zombie."

"I can't."

Cole isn't dead yet, please let him not see that I'm lying . . .

Cole only smiled. "You just need the right motivation. So let's raise the stakes, shall we?"

He walked over to where Mindy was cowering by the railing and dragged her up by the collar of her leather jacket, now slick with sea spray.

"Cole—no!" she screamed, her lips tinged blue from the cold.

Cole ignored her. "Stand up," he snapped. When she didn't, he dropped the illusion completely. "I said stand up!"

She broke into another round of sobs and obliged. He reached into his jacket pocket, pulled out a gun and pointed it at her.

Considering the previous murder weapons had been heroin and a stage stand I'd been hoping Cole would stick with non-firearm options.

"Cole!" Nate screamed.

Oh, this was not good. . . . "Cole, if you shoot her, you have no leverage."

The smile Cole gave me made my stomach lurch once more. He didn't shoot Mindy; he turned the gun around and handed it to her. Still shaking violently, but eyes dry once more, she took it.

And pointed it at me.

"Hands up, Strange," Cole said.

I raised my hands.

"My first choice wouldn't be to have Mindy here shoot you somewhere vital, but she's pretty shaky right now, so . . . Here's the deal, you two fuck-ups. Kincaid, Jacob thought you were good enough to fix me, but I don't trust you as far as I can throw you, so that's out. He also figured if I drained Nate here, it might be enough to last me another few years."

I rolled that one over. Considering that Cole had been linked through Otherside to Nate for almost twenty years, albeit periph-erally, there was something to that. Otherside doesn't conserve itself the way matter does. . . . Still, considering how far gone Cole was . . .

"So, I'll make it real simple. Get Nate out of there so I can drain him dry of Otherside or Mindy shoots you and I drain you. Then I kill Mindy and drain her, and after all that I figure out how to take Nate's rotting zombie hidey-hole here apart piece by piece until I get him too."

"Come on, Cole. Don't make Mindy do it," Nate begged.

He laughed. "Oh, Mindy's done this before."

Mindy went white. "You promised, Cole."

"I don't know about you, Nate, but I've had to put up with her shit for a year now while I've been trying to track you down. How the hell did we do it back in the nineties? I mean, she was never that hot, was she?"

Nate shot him a despairing look.

"Oh, don't look at me like that. I'm not going to kill her. Not like I had her kill Damien, way back when."

"You promised!" Mindy screamed this time.

Nate lunged at Cole but was stopped by an Otherside tendril that lashed out. "What did you make her do?"

Cole smiled. "That was the best part. I didn't *make* her do anything, Nate—to kill you or Damien. As soon as Jacob and I told her we had bindings that would steal Damien's talent, she was totally on board. You always were a desperate, talentless hack, weren't you, Mindy?"

She'd been the one to kill Damien. Another sickening chip clicked into place. "You thought it worked. And you needed more," I muttered. It wasn't obvious for the first few years that anything had gone horribly wrong—the wraith's strange hunger taking over his living body. Dead Men got famous, after all. "You had Mindy give Nate the same lethal dose of heroin that killed Damien so you could drain him of talent too," I said.

He smiled. "Didn't have to. All she had to do was push him off the side of the boat when he passed out drunk." He shrugged. "Worst-case scenario, she'd be more famous as a dead rocker's grieving girlfriend than the eventual washed-up groupie she was destined to become." To Nate he said, "I mean, you were going to be big—you were already big. It was only a matter of time before you got tired of her and moved on."

"That's not true," Nate started.

"And you weren't the one I had to convince. You didn't drown by accident, Nate. You were murdered by the love of your life for a chance at fame. How does it feel?"

Nate turned to Mindy. She didn't say anything, she didn't even look at him. She kept the gun pointed at me.

The salt water . . . shit. That was why he'd never been able to get a real bind on Nate the way he had on Damien. Cole had planned to dispose of the paranormal evidence just like he had with Damien, but Nate drowning in it must have interfered more than Cole had anticipated. Which raised the question, why were we on a boat now? What did Cole know that we didn't?

That we'd die from hypothermia before any of us could swim to land, except for Nate, and I was dubious he could swim at all.

Nate looked shell-shocked. "Why?" he asked.

"That's between Mindy and me," he said, and brushed her hair out of her face.

I remembered something Gideon had told me. Everyone has their price, you just need to find it.

I knew somewhere deep inside I should feel sorry for her, standing there in tears and cringing from Cole . . .

But I didn't. I felt numb, and for once it wasn't from the Otherside. It was anger. If it wasn't for the gun, I'd have knocked her off the boat myself.

"Well, what about it, Kincaid?"

I shook my head.

"Mindy, kill Kincaid."

Her eyes took on that emptiness again—the same kind I'd seen when I'd first asked about Nate, though this time the carefully crafted veneer was absent.

"Mindy, no—don't do it!" Nate yelled. Whether it was the fact that it was Cameron's voice, not Nate's, or the fact that Mindy just couldn't muster enough energy to care anymore, I didn't know.

She lifted her other hand to steady the gun.

Nate wouldn't let up. "Mindy, he tricked you—you can still fix this." When she didn't lower the gun, he turned on Cole. "You did this to her."

"No, Nate. She did this to herself, with a little help from you and every other guy who ever treated her like a cheap piece of groupie tail."

I felt the ice creeping up my boots as Cole turned his attention back to me. "Time's running out, Kincaid. What'll it be?"

I snorted. "There is no choice. I get Nate out, you shoot me anyways and probably Mindy. If I have to die, I'm better off watching you get screwed."

"Think of it this way, Kincaid." He took Mindy's arm and pointed the gun towards my face. "If you do what I want, there's a *chance* I'll let you two go. There isn't one if you're dead."

If he had any idea how many deranged poltergeists had used that line on me . . .

Cole stroked Mindy's face and her tears froze wherever his fingers touched. She cringed, but his fingers gripped her chin.

"Mindy?"

A bit of her returned—not much, but there was a glimmer in her eyes, which she fixed on me. "You said I wouldn't have to kill any more people."

"What do I always say, Mindy?"

"Keep to the plan," she said, her voice thin and frail, nothing like the woman who hosted *Glitter Hole*.

"And?"

She bit her lip, holding in a sob. "And everything will turn out fine," she whispered.

Nate was clenching his fists. "Cole, I'll do whatever you want—just let her and Kincaid go."

I took another quick peek at the bindings while Nate pleaded with him. Cole was right about one thing: he was fading, fast. Damn it.

The question was, would he turn into a real wraith or just die?

"All right." I said.

Cole and Nate both turned to me. "K," Nate started.

But I shook my head. "He said it, it's the only chance Mindy and I have to get off the boat alive."

I locked eyes with Nate and hoped he got the message.

Cole seemed appeased. He made Mindy lower the gun.

First goal down; there wasn't a gun pointed at me anymore.

Slowly, I made my way across the deck to where Nate stood. We were well out of the harbour now. No chance anyone would hear me if I screamed, not with the engine running.

"And don't let me find you checking out my bindings, Strange. If I think, for one second . . ."

I turned around so I was facing Nate and my back was to Cole. I only had a few moments . . .

"K, I sure hope you know what you're doing," Nate whispered.

I shrugged. No time for explanations. "I need you to be my eyes," I whispered back. "How does Cole look?"

"Really fucking lousy."

"The *Otherside*."

Nate shook his head and whispered, "Ah, flickering, and his bindings are all over."

Okay, that was good. They weren't nearly as stable as Cole seemed to think. I pulled a globe.

"K, what are you doing?"

"What I said, getting you out." If Cole's bindings were all flickering, then it stood to reason his hold on Nate was flickering too. Which meant this time I stood a chance of severing them. "I think I can unlink you two first."

"Then he'll just drain you dry—that's not beating him."

"I have a theory. Trust me."

He nodded. "Okay, K."

Here went everything . . .

I reached out for the lines of Otherside animating Nate's limbs, just as I'd done in the underground city, and gently teased them out. Once again the tendrils attaching Nate's ghost to Cole floated to the surface. The difference was, this time I knew what they were.

And as I'd suspected, they were flickering, just like Cole's. I was tempted to yank Nate out first then sever the ties to Cole, but it was too risky. Once I got Cole's claws out of Nate, Cole's payoff would be gone. And if I was lucky, he would lose what little grip on reality he had left.

I felt for where the tendrils had latched on and, with a push of Otherside, severed them.

"K, you did it—I don't feel him anymore."

Now to finish the job . . . "Stay still— Ow!" The icy blast hit me in the back, chilling me to the bone and knocking me to my knees.

"What did I say about not trying to screw me over, Strange? What did you do?"

I turned around and looked at Cole. His face was contorted with rage, and underneath he was terrified.

It's amazing what fear does to people who've abused power.

"Oops," I said.

I screamed as Cole kicked me in the stomach. It hurt, but the worst part was the icy feeling that shot through my gut, squeezing the breath out of me.

"Fine, I'll do it myself." Cole started for Nate—but he stumbled, his bindings flickering wildly. He was weakening.

Nate tried to tackle him, but Cole still had enough power to stop him with a blast of icy air.

The Otherside was really flickering now; there was no way those bindings would hold when he died. Cole just didn't know it yet.

He held up his hands. "I need Otherside, so it might as well be you."

I glanced at Nate and edged backwards until I felt the railing behind me. His eyes went wide.

"You want to drain me of Otherside?" I asked.

Cole smiled and the dust crept towards me.

God, I hoped to hell all the freezing from pulling globes over the years had prepared me for what was coming next. . . .

I pushed myself backwards, over the edge.

"K!"

For a second I didn't feel anything except the full-body shock of cold water. Then the ice bit through my skin. I swam for the surface, my boots and wet clothes dragging me down.

My teeth were already chattering uncontrollably. I heard Cole scream as I treaded water. I might not be dead yet, but I sure knew someone who was about to be.

Nate threw me a life preserver and helped me clamber back onto the boat. "K—of all the stupid things."

I slumped to the deck, leaning against the railing. Through my chattering I said, "It's why he couldn't bind you—when Mindy pushed you over the side. They knew the salt water got rid of the dust, but they never figured on it blocking the bindings."

Mindy gave us a glazed look. She was sitting back on the deck, the gun in her lap.

Cole was fracturing. The bindings were sputtering and he was barely more than a husk of a person, but still he didn't give up.

"Say goodbye, Kincaid."

I felt it—the pull—as Cole's tendrils reached out and tried to suck the life out of me.

And then it stopped, causing no more than a mild static shock.

Cole caught on. "Mindy, shoot her!"

Mindy looked at me and raised the gun again. Then her eyes drifted to Cole. I remembered the restraining order she'd taken out on him years ago. "You want to escape Cole even more than we do," I said.

Another lesson I learned from Aaron: shooting someone is hard. Commitment, action, living with the consequences of your choice.

But doing nothing? That's easy.

Mindy didn't pull the trigger. She watched Cole as the Otherside dust around him started to do something it hadn't before: burn up.

But I could still feel the ice gather around him as the Otherside dust swirled.

I peered at his bindings. The burning dust was taking Cole's bindings with it. It wouldn't be long now, but since I was already here . . .

I reached out with Otherside and started to pull the threads, anchors, symbols, whatever seemed the most fragile. The gold threads snapped and faded until all that was left was the burning gold dust, whirling around him like snow caught in a street light.

His bindings weren't the product of sorcery—but they were close. Warped into unnatural shapes. Jacob had almost managed to create a wraith. But almost only counts in horseshoes and hand grenades, never with Otherside.

Cole screamed again, a high-pitched wail that carried across the boat, despite the rain and motor. I covered my ears and a flash of light forced me to shut my eyes. When I opened them, all that was left of Cole was a pile of ash and bone.

People might always have their price, but so does power.

"K, speak to me. You okay?" Nate was leaning over me, shaking my shoulders. I clenched and unclenched my hands. They were numb, but everything was still working.

I nodded. "I'll live." I started looking for my phone. I needed to call Aaron before someone reported the light show to the coast guard . . . or decided to investigate.

I stopped when I heard the gun cock.

I raised my hands and turned to face her. "Mindy, it's over," I said. "You're not the victim anymore, Cole's gone. He can't hurt you."

She was shaking her head. "No—it's not over. You know what I did."

I went through my options: I could charge her, maybe knock her down before she shot me . . .

There was a light touch at my shoulder. "K—you've got to trust me," Nate whispered in my ear. "Please," he said, desperation in his eyes.

I let out my breath and nodded.

He turned to Mindy and placed himself between us. Then he started to walk towards her. "Mindy, I love you," he said.

Her eyes watered as she looked at him, and for a moment I thought she might put down the gun.

Instead, she said, "I stopped loving anything twenty years ago."

I knew Mindy was dead inside—that there wasn't much left beyond the damage that she'd done to herself and that Cole and Jacob had done to her.

Still, it broke my heart to watch my best friend's breaking.

In a burst of movement, he went for the gun. Mindy screamed and a gunshot rang out across the water. By the time I registered that Mindy had fired, Nate was leaning against the rails with a gaping wound in his chest and Mindy had collapsed.

He tipped backwards. "Nate!" I tried to grab him, but I wasn't fast enough.

He went over the rail.

Lying on my stomach, hand under the railing, I got hold of the back of his jacket before he began to disappear under the cold Seattle harbour waters.

"Nate—of all the stupid . . ."

Despite the dazed look of him, he managed to wink up at me. "On the deck, should be right near your hands."

There was his bag. It only had salt in it, but it was enough to pack a punch.

Nate's eyes were glazing over. He wouldn't last in the water.

"I'm getting you out now."

I ignored the nausea and pulled more Otherside into my globe—no time to filter it, so I just pulled raw. I went for the lines.

"It's okay, K—you did your best. Get off the boat," he said.

Nate began to slip out of my grip. The lines were done, but now there was the tangled mess of anchors to deal with. . . . I untied them as fast as I could, but his jacket came off in my hand.

"No, no, no—" I kept pulling as he sank, disappearing from sight. Maybe I'd got them in time. "Nate?" I called out. "Nate?"

No answer.

I grabbed the backpack and turned my sights on Mindy. She still had the gun pointed at me, but she looked stunned. Like I said, shooting people is hard. . . .

"I'm sorry," she said. "It's not personal, but I'm not going to jail. With you and Nate both gone, and Cole and whatever the fuck he was gone, I can finally forget."

I felt the weight of the bag of salt in my hand. "You really can't forget, Mindy."

She bit her lip and steadied the gun. "Says you."

Another thing Aaron had drilled into me about handguns: they're a bitch to keep trained and shoot at the same time.

I threw the backpack at her as hard as I could. It hit her square in the chest as I dropped to the deck and the gun went off. It's also hard to shoot at a moving target.

I don't know what was more surprising to her, that she'd shot or that she'd missed.

I lunged forward and slammed into her torso. We hit the deck and the gun went sliding into the cabin.

Mindy was taller than me, but she was exhausted and emotionally broken—not a great combination in a fight. I straddled her before she could get up and punched her, then again, and her lip split.

"*You shot Nate,*" I heard myself shout.

"I didn't want to—" she cried out, but I hit her again.

"You are the lowest piece of self-victimized trash I've ever met." I hit her again, and again. God help me, it felt good. . . . "You deserve whatever personal hell you've been wallowing in these last twenty years, and do you know why?" I was really yelling now. She whimpered, but I ignored her. "Because you killed my best friend! If I have anything to say about it, you will be rotting inside a jail cell for the rest of your life."

She tried to say something, but for the life of me I couldn't stop pummelling her.

Not until she stopped struggling. It was then I let go. There was blood on my hands. I crawled back to the other side of the boat, as far away from her as I could get.

For a second I'd been so tempted . . . But no coat of lipstick was ever going to cover up what she'd done. Not to her, not to anyone.

She was still breathing. She was alive—knocked out, but alive.

I couldn't believe what I'd almost done. . . .

It took me a second to notice the sirens in the distance. I scrounged on the deck for a phone—any phone that wasn't soaked through with rain. I found Mindy's in her front pocket.

I called Aaron. On the bright side, I was not calling him to a basement full of dead people. Not this time. This time it was a live person on a boat. And a pile of ash that he wouldn't be able to explain without career suicide. . . .

Still, that had to be better than a cellar full of dead people.

"Hello?"

"It's Kincaid." I thought about how to phrase it. "You really won't believe what happened. Just—get to the docks before the coast guard brings me in."

I tied Mindy up—unconscious or not, I wasn't stupid enough to leave her unrestrained—and then sat shivering in the corner while I waited for the coast guard to find us. Between the gunshot and the flickering boat lights, they'd be well on their way. . . .

For a moment I thought I felt the touch of cold Otherside.

"Nate? Nate?" I called out. But there wasn't any answer.

I closed my eyes.

CHAPTER 23

NO GOOD DEED

I had on a dry track suit, courtesy of Aaron, and a blanket wrapped around me as I stood back on dry land a short distance away from the docks. I was still freezing, but the coffee was helping.

Aaron ran his hand through his hair. Sarah was keeping a close eye on Mindy, stashed in the back of their cruiser.

I'd waited for Sarah and Aaron to show up before I said a word to anyone, including the coast guard, who'd searched the boat, scratched their heads, then pulled us in. I'd briefly considered tossing Mindy off the side of the boat a few times, but knew it sure as hell wouldn't change one damn thing.

Someone needed to take the fall for all this.

I was leaving it up to Aaron and Sarah to decide what exactly to put on the record—and how Sarah might "suggest" Mindy phrase her confession. A little dirty, but the lines get blurry in police work when the main perpetrator isn't a member of the living. There's a certain amount of creative licence expected . . . and the world keeps turning.

"So let me get this straight," Aaron said. "A wraith, a previously undocumented ghost—"

I shook my head. "Just call it a rare poltergeist." That wasn't accurate either since Cole hadn't really been dead, but it was easier for Aaron to understand.

"—has been manipulating Mindy Pine, ex-girlfriend of Nathan Cade, for almost two decades."

I closed my eyes and sipped my coffee. I'd been over this already, in painstaking detail. "To kill Damien Fell, Nathan Cade and most recently Jacob Buchanan in a paranormal ritual they hoped would give them the ability to drain people's talent and make themselves rich and famous. They didn't read the fine print. It also didn't work."

It was the short version, but it was accurate.

Aaron swore. I'd told him he could decide what details to fudge. All I wanted to do at this point was get home so I could drink about a gallon of hot tea, take a shower and crawl into bed.

"One thing bothers me."

I glanced up at him.

"Why now? Why not fifteen or twenty years ago?"

I'd been waiting for that one. And it was a question I was still trying to figure out myself . . . "Cole had the songs but could never get a hold on Nate." I nodded at the harbour. "The salt water messed up the original ritual. Nathan was never really bound. Cole only got a lock on him a few weeks back. Fuelled by desperation and a sense that he was nearing the end of his life force, Cole was motivated to give wrangling Nate one last shot."

"Those videos," Aaron said.

"You were right—it was stupid."

Aaron looked back at Nathan's boat. "On one hand I should be thanking you for not tampering with the scene, but on the other hand—how the hell am I going to explain a wraith?"

I shrugged. Aaron could take the headache for once. I started for the docks, where fewer people were milling. I couldn't leave yet, but I could get away from the commotion to think. "Above my pay grade."

"Kincaid."

I stopped.

"She says Nate was there and she shot him."

I shook my head. I'd been trying to decide how to handle that for the past hour. "Nate was there, but she didn't shoot him. He's a ghost. Like I said, Cole had her pretty riled up by the time I got there. She was . . ." I thought about it before settling on, "Broken. Very broken."

Aaron nodded. "Because of Cole. We're going with drugs."

I threw back my head and laughed, which earned me a dirty look from Aaron.

"Do you have a better idea?"

"Oh, no. I just find it hilarious you're the one suggesting it for once."

"It isn't, it was Sarah's suggestion. We'll say they took you since you were one of the few people who knew Cole faked a paranormal monster to cover up a pair of twenty-year-old murders committed by him and Nathan Cade's girlfriend at the time, Mindy Pine. I still have no idea how we're going to write up the motivation."

"Wait until she wakes up and see what she offers. My guess? She'll say Cole coerced her and blame everything on him. If she's smart and lawyers up, it'll be some kind of abuse syndrome."

"Stockholm syndrome. Sarah already said that."

A woman after my own heart. As jaded as me.

"Though from what you've told me, there is likely truth in there," Aaron said.

There probably was. It raised the question, though, at what point do we lose our agency and devolve into a cipher for someone else's machinations?

I shook my head. "This time round? Maybe. Twenty years ago? Cole and maybe Jacob offered her a deal she couldn't refuse. Simple as that. The details don't matter."

Aaron held something out to me. "I figured you might want this."

It was Nate's red notebook of unpublished songs—the ones he never wanted to see the light of day. I'd wondered where they'd got to. I took it, looking skeptically at Aaron.

"I know—evidence. But even I don't trust it in evidence. Word will get out and then I'll never have any peace. Besides, I figured Nate might want them."

I tucked it in my bag.

"What are you going to do with it?"

"Honestly? Right now, burning it strikes me as the smartest option."

He nodded, but there was a troubled look on his face. He stepped in close. "You would tell me if there was something serious going on in the paranormal community?" he said.

I froze. That I hadn't been expecting. . . .

"Two rare paranormal monsters, a Jinn and a wraith, two weeks apart."

With everything that had happened—Max, Randall, Gideon, Nathan—the coincidence hadn't occurred to me. Maybe it was just bad luck.

"You've never been one to believe in coincidences," Aaron said, as if reading my thoughts.

Sarah called him over before I could offer anything useful. "You'll be all right?" he asked.

I nodded and waved at Sarah as he headed back to the rest of the police.

I wished I knew what I felt, buried underneath all the anger.

Maybe I was becoming like Mindy, too numb to feel anything anymore. . . .

What I really needed was bed. But first, there was something I had to find out. Better to rip off the Band-Aid than let it fester. A little gem my mother used to say but never bothered to practise.

I moved a little farther away from the police and coast guard and sat down on the dock. Not too far out of the light or into the shadows.

I dangled my legs over the side and took a mirror out of my pocket—one I'd removed from my bag before the coast guard showed up. It was tuned for Nate. Before I lost my nerve, I traced a message into the glass.

Nate, you still there?

I counted three long breaths while I waited, and pushed down the tears. Nate was already dead, I shouldn't be this upset. . . .

I held my breath as the mirror fogged over.

ALIVE AND KICKING

I exhaled. Where I'd failed Max, failed Randall—I hadn't failed Nate. A weight lifted off my shoulders.

GIMME A PUSH?

I gave the mirror a kick of Otherside so he could pass through. Nathan Cade, the one I recognized, coalesced beside me down to his bright red Converse sneakers and flannel shirt.

He held his translucent hands out in front of him. "You know, I never thought I'd say this, but it's good to be dead again." He said it in his usual laissez-faire manner, but there was something darker, sadder under the surface.

We sat there for a moment in silence until Nate started to flicker. He saw me watching and shook his head. "I'm fine, K, I just need to go back to my side of the barrier and lick my wounds in a dark corner of Otherside—just a couple days, promise."

"Aaron gave me your old notebook."

Nate just shook his head. "Just hold on to it somewhere safe until I decide what to do with it."

"How's it feel to give up that shiny new body?"

Nate shot me a sideways glance. "I still owe you an apology for not telling you everything, don't I?"

"And so many, many more things."

"Honestly? I'm not alive anymore, K. I didn't think I'd ever be okay with being a ghost, but I am. Besides, what would you do without me? Now I can go back to ignoring you behind a mirror . . . unless you've got a certain new release waiting for me . . ."

"I'm not buying you Battlemage."

"Way to cheapen a moment, K," Nate said.

"Right back at you." I took another sip of my coffee.

"Aaron and Sarah at four o'clock. I'm out. He'll want to ask me about my murder and I'll tell him to fuck off and then things will get uncomfortable." He narrowed his eyes at me. "We're still lying about the whole zombie thing, right?"

"Oh dear god, yes."

"Good. Let's face it, Aaron would have been a total dick about me being a zombie."

I spit out my coffee.

"Seriously. He'd have gone ballistic. Can't blame him. He'd be pissed we left Cameron's zombie body in the water and call it a mess." He paused. "I heard what you said. To Mindy."

"Nate, I'm sorry—"

He shook his head. "She stole my life from me, K. I can't unknow that. I can't forgive her. And I don't ever want to talk about this, ever again. Maybe if I drink enough, I'll forget."

"Maybe," I said, though we both knew damn well he never would.

Nate jabbed me in the shoulder. Not a real jab—the chilled ghost version. "See you back at the apartment," he said, and vanished, back to the Otherside. Where he belonged.

I started to get up but felt the cold brush against my shoulder. I sighed and waited for Gideon to materialize. "Not you too," I said.

"Considering everything, that went well."

"Let me guess, you saw most of it?"

"Enough. I'm impressed. I barely had to step in."

I snorted. "Barely? Try not at all."

He inclined his head but didn't agree or disagree. It struck me. The bindings. I knew I hadn't got them off Nate in time.

"Why? Why did you save him? And don't try to deny it, I know you did."

"Your ghost was already dead."

"Not my point."

"Maybe you got him out in time. It was fast work."

I glared.

Gideon pursed his lips in a very human expression. "The point was for you to determine how to remove the bindings. You did—a wraith got in your way. I decided that the point of the lesson had been served." I picked up the shadow of a smile. "Or maybe I just decided I could use a favour?"

Now that I could believe. Altruistic to the end . . .

"I'm surprised you let her live, though. That I didn't expect," he added.

I shook my head. "You would have let her die, wouldn't you?"

Gideon went silent and watched me again, his face rippling as the rain fell through him. When he spoke, it was in clipped, crisp words. "There was no saving her, so, yes, you're right. I don't think she deserved to be saved—for both her stupidity and her cruelty." He tilted his head. "Is it because you truly value other lives above yours? Commendable. Or is it simply that you put so little value on our own? I think you hide your intentions well, even from yourself."

I didn't have an answer to that. A moment later, he vanished.

I was still unsettled. But somehow, with Nate on the Otherside, it felt as if life was back to something resembling normal. Maybe that was the best I could hope for.

I got up and headed for my bike. I had days' worth of sleep to catch up on, and a lot to think about.

SHANGHAIED

Forensics twenty years after the fact are a fascinating thing . . . especially when you know where and what to look for.

Mindy's fingerprints had been all over the syringe that had killed Damien; Aaron figured she'd administered the heroin while he was asleep. Her fingerprints had also been found on the syringe amongst Nate's things, though she'd never used it. Opportunity had knocked for a better and much less suspicious method.

All because Aaron had listened to Damien's still-grieving parents and reopened the case . . .

Mindy had confessed everything eventually. Nate figured the guilt had been eating away at her for years. Maybe. I'm more of a cynic. Mindy regretted being caught—or agreeing to help Cole in the first place. But Mindy had been a willing participant all those years ago, even if Cole had been running the show.

Though maybe Nate was on to something with the guilt. Mindy hadn't killed Jacob; she'd watched Cole do it, but she hadn't acted. And she'd confirmed that Jacob had been the one helping Cole with the Otherside; he'd devised the idea to trick Nate into letting Cole edit his songs fifteen years ago. Though Jacob had never wanted anyone to die. He'd written as much down in the diaries Aaron and Sarah found amongst his piles of things. Maybe the hoarding had been his way of hiding his own evidence from Cole, in case the unforeseeable happened.

Killing the person who knows what they're doing. That hadn't been the start of Cole's downfall, but it had certainly ushered in the end, after almost twenty years of greed, jealousy and a lust for vengeance. . . .

Cole might be dead, but Mindy was going to jail for a long, long time.

She'd killed my best friend. That was why she'd never wanted to see Nate: the guilt. And maybe she was a little worried he knew.

Nate and I had an ironclad agreement never to talk about Mindy again. Another name on a growing list of no-go subjects. It was a relief having someone I could count on to not bring up my own troubling past, while I did my best to keep Nate off his. Anti-catharsis therapy. Difficult to stay away from the past with a ghost, but what is life without a few challenges?

The media, however, was having a field day dredging up the past. Once again I lay low and let Aaron deal with the paranormal fallout. He and Sarah both claimed they'd had help from a paranormal consultant, but they were kind enough to keep my name out of it.

Didn't stop people from speculating it had been me. When Cody volunteered his opinion about my lack of professionalism and poor character on camera was when I turned the TV off.

Fucking lawyers . . .

Three days after the yacht incident I finally felt normal enough to do something I'd thought about since discovering what had happened to Damien.

Nate, you OK? I wrote in the bathroom mirror.

R&R. FOR THE RECORD I NEVER WANT TO BE A ZOMBIE EVER AGAIN.

After a moment, as if reading my mind, Nate added, *DON'T DO ANYTHING TOO STUPID, OK, K?*

"No more than usual," I muttered. *Just lay low for the next half-hour,* I wrote.

I sat down in the middle of a pentagram I'd laid out on my living room floor, my furniture pushed to the side. I placed a new mirror on my lap, but with the same Latin symbols I'd first used to call Damien.

I took a deep breath. Here went nothing.

I pulled my globe and funnelled it into the mirror. Without Cole there to bind his ghost, it took me no time to find Damien. His Otherside bindings gave with little more than a tug.

Damien didn't say anything. Didn't even really look at me as he came through the mirror.

"Hello, Damien. Your mother misses you. It took her twenty years but she finally convinced a detective to chase Cole and Mindy down. She never once believed you overdosed. I'm sorry to say you'll be seeing her soon." I'd decided to tell Damien that much, in case he chose to wait a little longer on the Otherside to see her one last time. For her more than him. "We didn't tell her what you've been through, only that Mindy is finally being held accountable for your murder. And Cole—well, we decided she didn't need to know that much." He looked relieved. Then he blinked out of existence. Either to the Otherside or wherever it is ghosts go afterwards.

I let out the breath I was holding and dropped my globe. Now it was over.

I wrote a message for Nate on the bathroom mirror telling him it was safe to come out.

PlayStation is on and your controller is out. I even left beer in the fridge. I'll be at the library.

I didn't wait for Nate's foggy-script reply. I grabbed my helmet and backpack off the coat stand. Time to finish some research. On one Gideon Lawrence . . .

∗

This time when I exited the elevator to the archives, Carol was there. She smiled and cheerfully held out a pass.

The glass screen hid it well, but now that I was looking for it, I had no trouble picking out the ghost-grey sheen.

I stuffed my own ethics and the urge to tell her the jig was up.

Another problem for another day, Kincaid . . .

I paused, my hand on the archives door.

Damn it . . .

I turned back to face her. "You know, you're going to burn out doing this," I said.

She gave me a blank stare.

"This?" I said, waving at the archives. "Keeping corporeal enough to hold passes and restock books?" I'd overheard a few people below whispering about mysterious overtime going unclocked. I tapped a bit of the Otherside just to get my point across. She jumped back a step as the Otherside flooded into me, and frowned, pushing her glasses up onto her nose.

"I'm not hurting anyone," she said, with an indignant expression.

"I know you aren't. You died six months ago. Car crash. I looked it up." I softened my voice. "Look, far be it from me to tell you how to spend your afterlife, but if you keep doing this, you'll be gone within a half century. Pretending you aren't dead won't change things."

Her face lost the indignant expression and saddened. "I know I died. They had a meeting the morning after—I always liked showing up fifteen minutes early. I was still hoping." She shook her head. "I liked my job. I always wanted to be a librarian. I was happy here."

I'd been expecting denial, anger—those are normal emotions for new ghosts. Wish to hell I knew how Max would handle a despondent ghost like this one.

I gave it my best shot. "Look, I get you wanted to be a librarian, I just don't see why this place has to be the end-all be-all. Aren't there other libraries on the planet you've always wanted to see—or work in?"

She stared at me for a moment then nodded, slowly. "I always wanted to see Europe."

"There! Now, I'm not an expert on libraries, but there must be a way in." I was losing her at the uncertainty, so I added, "I mean, you can always come back here, but it couldn't hurt to try. What's the point of having an afterlife if you don't use it?"

I noticed she made an effort not to glance at the sign that said Closed Until Further Notice. Eventually they would find a replacement for Carol, and despite my complete lack of responsibility in the matter, it bothered me that she might be left floundering here once there was a living replacement. . . . It's harder for ghosts haunting a place to hold on after the space is filled.

Carol's face began to brighten. "You know what? You're right. There are all sorts of libraries in Europe I used to read about. What's to stop me from going?"

She was staring at me again and it took me a second to realize she was looking for an answer. "Nothing," I offered.

"I could see the world, places I've only read about in books. There are even libraries on the bottom of the ocean." Her expression wavered.

"You'll never know if you don't try," I said.

Carol became more translucent and after a moment she began to dissolve into Otherside smoke. Then she was gone.

I headed into the archives and found the book on the witch trials exactly where I'd hidden it. Thank god Carol hadn't seen fit to re-shelve it.

No sooner did I sit down at my desk and open the book than I felt the telltale chill on my left.

Shit. I shoved the book under my backpack.

"Congratulations, you may just have succeeded in sending that harmless librarian off on the path to becoming a full-fledged poltergeist," Gideon said as he materialized beside me.

"She wasn't angry. She was sad."

"She was distraught, and now you've given her an obsession with a purpose. Do you think all poltergeists start off as evil personalities set on mayhem and revenge?"

"Yes. So sue me for not wanting to leave a ghost wasting away, trapped in the routine of a job so ingrained she's kept it up after death."

"You can't save every single ghost you come across. That's one of the lessons Max was trying to teach you. Otherwise you'll go mad, like every other mediocre practitioner out there."

"I'm not mediocre. And so I gave her a modicum of hope that there might be something more for her." I held my arms out, showcasing a room filled with old books and dusty computers. "You know, you almost had me convinced you might have actually been a person at some point in time, and then you go say something completely dickish."

"I'm here on business."

That sent a chill down my spine and I hazarded a second glance to make sure the book was still covered.

"You're not dead and you have your ghost back," Gideon continued. "And your detective is none the wiser to your zombie." He arched a ghostly grey eyebrow. "No one was tied up and burned at the stake."

"We don't do that anymore."

"Proverbially speaking. The point stands. It's high time you got back to my tasks."

I shivered—and not from the chill. "I'm not finding you another body," I said.

There was a faint smile on his face. "That's not what I want. I've decided I'm not as angry about you destroying Cameron's body as I initially thought. In fact, I rather think it worked out for the best," he said.

I held my breath; this was better than I could have hoped for. He'd given up trying to find a body and turn himself into a zombie. "I'm glad you came to your senses?"

He shrugged. "Attractive-enough man, but wrong height, wrong body type—not me at all. I likely wouldn't have done any better wearing him than your bumbling ghost."

"Wow. Stealing a body to make the right fashion statement." I was choking inside. I didn't care what kind of deal I'd struck, Gideon wasn't turning me into a grave robber. . . .

"Oh, I don't plan on stealing a body," he said. "It's occurred to me there is a much more innovative solution." When I didn't answer, his eyes shifted from grey-blue to the glittering black as he started to fade. "I plan on making one. And you're going to help me."

Then he disappeared.

With that choice declaration to consider, I re-shelved the book and left the library. I didn't think things could possibly get worse.

I had stopped at the market for an afternoon coffee when the dark sedan pulled up. The back door opened and a plainclothes police officer got out—one I recognized as friendly. Which is why I didn't panic when he gestured for me to get in.

I slid into the back seat to find Aaron already there—not surprising—but the person in the driver's seat was unexpected.

Captain Marks.

The car started to move, the plainclothes officer stationed outside where I'd left my bike.

"Aaron," I said, and nodded. "Is this your idea of a job interview or a bad joke?"

"Detective Baal was under my orders, Ms. Strange. I asked him to sit back there with you, since we don't exactly have a good track record in that department." Marks watched me in the rear-view, his face puffy and his eyes crinkled in amusement.

The fact that he was enjoying himself really pissed me off.

"You know who the White Picket Fence Killer is, Ms. Strange?" Marks said.

I pulled up short on the barrage of outrage at having been dragged into an unmarked car in broad daylight—at the market, no less. I'd be outraged later. I nodded. "Martin Dane, the serial killer who was killed outside a gas station two weeks ago. Liam Sinclair raised him in that TV fiasco. Dane targeted families along the west coast who lived behind a white picket fence." The quintessential American dream . . . pretty sure it hadn't involved serial murder. "They were looking for his last victim—a young girl. A young family member was always abducted, to be left at the subsequent victims' home like a misplaced doll," I added, as if I was answering one of Max's quizzes.

Jesus, it'd only been a week since the idiot practitioner had raised Dane, nearly dying in the process . . . and failing to get the location of the girl.

I could see Captain Marks nodding at me in the mirror as the car came to a red light. "That's right, Strange."

I glared at Aaron. A warning would have been nice. He didn't meet my eyes this time. "What does that have to do with me? Unless you seriously think I managed to be involved from *Seattle*."

"There's been another victim. Portland, Oregon. Seventeen-year-old Katy Price, disappeared from her high school in the middle of the day on her way to the washroom. The police found her family murdered, Katy gone and his last abductee left in her place, dressed in a 1950s poodle skirt costume." He opened a folder with a flourish, and even I almost cringed at the crime scene photo.

Jesus Christ, poor girl. A bit off his MO taking a family member in broad daylight. But he was supposed to be dead—as in good old-fashioned buried six feet under not getting back up . . .

I ran through the possibilities in my mind. Serial killers can be a pain in the ass when they're dead—the hunger to kill people never dies. "It could be anything from his violent poltergeist to a copycat fan. . . ." I said. You'd be surprised how great serial killer ghosts are at finding the one person on the other side of the mirror who's a fan and itching to dabble in a little mayhem and terror. I mean, statistically, you should have a better chance of winning a jackpot lottery. Like, how many budding serial killers could possibly be out there playing with mirrors? The ghosts have got to have a sixth sense.

But Marks just shook his head. "The experts have ruled those possibilities out already. It's not a ghost and it's not a copycat. It's a completely new murder, same chemical traces, same MO." Marks looked at me. "They want you to find out how he's still killing and kidnapping from six feet under, and I plan on giving you to them. Consider yourself shanghaied."

ACKNOWLEDGEMENTS

Thank you Steve, Cindy, Wally and Whisky Jack for all the support (and or patience) while I edited this. Also thank you to my friends Leanne Tremblay and Mary Gilbert, who read each and every early draft chapter. I don't know if I would have finished this book, or any book, without all of your feedback and encouragement.

I also want to thank my agent, Carolyn Forde, who picked my first manuscript out of the slush pile and perked up when I described this new project. Also Anne Collins, publisher at Random House Canada. I will never forget the day Anne reluctantly admitted she "liked" my novel, with its voodoo and zombies. And a huge thank you to Amanda Betts for editing this manuscript and helping tease out story nuances. *Lipstick Voodoo* wouldn't be in nearly as good shape without her.

There are many other people who have mentored and encouraged me in my writing career over the past few years—thanks to all of you!

VOODOO
SHANGHAI

THE THIRD AND FINAL INSTALLMENT IN THE KINCAID STRANGE SERIES
ARRIVING JANUARY 2020 FROM VINTAGE CANADA

Just when Kincaid Strange thinks her life is back on track and she has finally put her time with the Seattle PD to rest, Aaron shows up with yet another strange and ominous case she can't refuse.

Martin Dane, the White Picket Fence Serial Killer who terrorized West Coast families living the suburban American dream, appears to be back at it with a fresh murder in Portland.

There's only one problem: Martin Dane has been dead for three weeks.

Kincaid can't resist a paranormal mystery, so she agrees to examine the Portland crime scene. What she discovers is a place of supernatural power unlike anywhere she's ever been—and the reason Aaron had been so tight-lipped. There's already a voodoo practitioner on the case: Liam Sinclair, a TV celebrity of dubious talent and even more dubious intent.

Kincaid wants nothing more than to wrap things up and retreat to Seattle, as does Gideon, the powerful sorcerer's ghost who is Kincaid's new mentor and teacher. But the deeper she looks, the less the murder adds up. When she uncovers a much more sinister mystery—missing ghosts, scores of them, whom no one is looking for—there's no turning back.

And then there's a second murder . . .

KRISTI CHARISH spent her formative high school years listening to a lot of grunge music. She has a PhD in zoology from the University of British Columbia. She has worked as a scientific advisor on projects such as fantasy and science fiction writer Diana Rowland's series, White Trash Zombie, and is the author of *The Voodoo Killings* and the four books in the Owl series: *Owl and the Tiger Thieves, Owl and the Electric Samurai, Owl and the Japanese Circus* and *Owl and the City of Angels*. She lives in Vancouver. www.kristicharish.com